Time to Wed

Book Five of the Viper Clan

A Series from Beyond the Veil

Clare SM Keating

This book may not be reproduced or used in any manner without the express written permission of the copyright holder.

This story contains explicit content that is intended for adult audiences only. All characters involved in sexual situations are 18 years of age or older.

This story is a work of fiction. Names, characters, places and events are all products of the author's imagination and are meant to be fictitious. Any resemblance to persons, living or dead, actual events, locales or organisations is entirely coincidental.

This book is dedicated to my parents, whom I love and thank for everything they've taught me over the years.

I would also like to dedicate this book to Kirsty Mott as always and my Patreon supporters –

Lucia

Casey

John

And Badger

Thanks for supporting me this far!

Stories Currently Available on Amazon

Available in the Viper Clan Series

Foundations of Blood *(Clare SM Keating)*

Viper in the Shadows *(Clare SM Keating)*

Ancient Venom *(Clare SM Keating)*

The Bat and the Snake *(Clare SM Keating)*

Beyond the Veil Series

My Dearest Loathe (*Beyond the Veil Story – Clare SM Keating)*

Changeling Heart (*Beyond the Veil Story – Clare SM Keating*)

Other Series/ Titles

The Dragon's Art (*Draco Imperium Series – Clare SM Keating)*

Between Brothers *(Sons of the Order Series – Clare Keating)*

Sons of the Order (*Sons of the Order Series – Clare SM Keating)*

Traitor to the King (*Tale of the Benaga Sisters Series – Clare SM Keating)*

Falling at His Feet (*Clare S M Keating)*

Lord of the Lakes (*Clare Keating)*

Last of the Sabre-Fangs *(Guardians of Yedidya Series – Clare Keating)*

The Wolf and the Tiger (*Day Clan Series – C.S.M Keating)*

Moon Guardian (*Day Clan Series – C.S.M Keating*)

The Swallowed Moon (*Day Clan Series – C.S.M Keating)*

The Breath Taker (*C.S.M Keating)*

Prologue: The Chosen Bride

Salle des Morts, Rennes, Brittany, France January 1926

Thibaut Viper turned down the lane towards the household of the Vulturie's Count, his manner relaxed and his looks as regal as they ever were within the dark hours of the night. He looked as if he were going to another business meeting, his manner always charming and confident as he greeted the security guard at the gate, but in truth he was hardly confident. His body was trembling with excitement and horror all at once, the fate of the entire family in France resting on his shoulders, resting on this one decision. He could trust that Phillippe Vulturie would make a good decision for him, would choose with the best interest for his daughter and the future in mind, but Thibaut was anxious. After everything that had happened, everything that had occurred in the household with his sisters and indeed the shame Dio still held the family in, everything was on him and Thibaut froze by the garden maze. He grasped the firm square hedge to steady himself, feeling the uncomfortable and horrible agonies within his body as if he were being riddled with holes and he clenched his teeth firmly to stop himself hollering out, the stress too much. At least, it would have been too much, if someone had not stepped out of the maze in time to grasp his hand, giving him reassurance as the wave of pain passed by.

"Monsieur Viper, you're in agony, are you quite well? Have you had enough blood or are you in need? Are you alright?" The soft words from the trembling figure reached Thibaut's ears and he breathed a sigh of complete relief and tightened his own grasp around the hand in thanks. It was always reassuring when the one to find him weak was someone he knew he could overpower, someone that was too simpering to use such a thing against him, too gentile and compassionate to ever be a threat. But more than that, to know that it was Jacinthe holding his hand, somehow it made his heart ease and his anxieties fade when he opened his eyes and he saw her soft little hazel-coloured eyes with that lovely auburn hair… he gave a soft mention of how pretty her hair looked today and her face went bright red. "Well… well, mon Père asked us to be at our most beautiful today. I knew it was because you were visiting but… but… uh, thank you."

"Dear Jacinthe, you should know, it is not for my usual business today… do you know that today your father has summoned me, because he has made his decision. From today, I will know where I will stand in your future and it… it quite upsets me." Thibaut grimaced in frustration as he straightened up and to his surprise Jacinthe led him into the hedges where there was a small enclave with a little ornament of a nymph with a satyr chasing it near a little fountain where a smaller faun was spewing water from some panpipes into a frog pond. Here there was a stone bench to sit upon as the frogs croaked and skipped upon their lily pads in blissful ignorance to the predators in their midst, here Jacinthe urged Thibaut to sit but he grimaced at the thought of the hard stone to his wounded posterior and was unsure how to say anything about it. But Jacinthe had been noticing those few little weaknesses that Thibaut showed the world, things that embarrassed him terribly and though she could not comprehend them, she swiftly scooped up her large red velvet skirt into a ball and sat it upon the bench beside her, showing off her little brown shoes and her neat little nylon stockings without shame as she patted it for him to sit on the fabric. Thibaut just blushed as he sat beside her, comfortable and yet so very depressed. "Jacinthe… do you have any thought on what your father has planned?"

"My father would like to think it is a surprise to us all, but my sisters and I have never been so utterly foolish we didn't have a thought. I am aware that today he will make his decision on which of us you will marry. Well, I include myself in that… but I know the decision is between my more beautiful of sisters." Jacinthe stated, forlornly though she tried to hide it with a sweet smile and to her own upset she gripped at Thibaut's hand tenderly as he leant against his cane with his head lowered and looking to the ground. He looked ill and she knew it was from the stress this choice had brought down upon him. Jacinthe understood that there was not a romantic bone in Thibaut Viper's body, that he did not see the need to marry but for the sake of his bloodline and for the fact his family needed him to make the decisions for their future on firm grounding. The Viper Clan looked due to marry off all its eldest children within the course of the year if rumour were true and with Theodosius already having a son to beat any of Thibaut's in a quarrel for first place in inheritance… everything was important for Thibaut to get right. But Jacinthe could see the sorrow in his expression as he held her hand again and she gave a soft sigh, trying to hold back her upset. "Whatever the decision though, it will not affect our friendship. I know you are not the emotional type, Thibaut, you are the rock for your family since your father's death… but though some may say you have singled me out to supress all these years we've known one another, I know you have only been looking out for my welfare."

"Your knowledge of my intentions is rare, Jacinthe… not many people take the time to understand that I do what I must for the sake of the family and for the sake of others. I have never meant insult in my words to you, though I am aware I have been rather unkind and selective in my treatment… but I do see you as my friend, but to let anyone come as close to me as you holds a dangerous price. Forgive my calumny… it muses me that your name is Jacinthe… for I had thought that presenting a purple hyacinth to you today would have been appropriate no matter the outcome… but alas, I was in a panic and could only offer this to you…" Thibaut sighed, sagging at the shoulders as he shifted his black jacket aside and tenderly removed something wrapped up in purple tissue paper. Jacinthe was confused, she knew that there was an old fashion for the meanings behind flowers and though she had been named for these flowers purely for the sound of her name than the meaning, she was impressed with Thibaut. She was even more impressed when he uncurled the paper and the single stem of a hyacinth with many white star-like flowers sat there and Jacinthe could have cried as he lay it upon her skirt and breathed a sigh of frustration. "I don't need to say anymore, but no matter what occurs today, know that of all your sisters, I still believe you are the perfect one."

Jacinthe looked to the flower as Thibaut stood up and seemed to regain his composure as he walked towards the main house; it would be inappropriate to arrive with Jacinthe and inappropriate to have given her the flower in view of her sisters or her father. But Jacinthe looked to the flower on her skirt with a few thin tears dribbling from her eyes, each hyacinth flower's colour held with it a unique scent and the white flower held the sweetest and most alluring of the scents, but it had such a strong meaning that Jacinthe gripped it tightly to her, taking a soft sniff and noting the unique cologne that Thibaut always wore mixing with the flower's scent.

The purple hyacinth was to be offered as a gift of apology for thoughtless actions but the white… oh the white was for purity, for untainted loveliness… a gift for someone you care about to say, 'I'll be praying for you' and oft times the only flower needed for a bride's bouquet. His statement was clear and Jacinthe could not have been happier and more tragically upset then at any other time in her life… Thibaut wanted her to be chosen for him, yet she knew her sisters were the ones to stand out and the ones suited to grace vampire society. She was meek, she was silent and gracious but she could not stand out in a crowd and she would never be chosen for Thibaut's wife when the position on offer was one that could hurl the French Nobles into the most dynamic relationship they had known since befriending the Italians!

How cruel Thibaut was to her... how truly cruel he was to confess now when she knew he was so completely out of reach....

Thibaut gifted the servants of the Vulturie Household his cane, coat and hat before they led him to an area to clean his boots and then permitted him to accompany them up the stairs. Thibaut looked as calm and arrogant as ever, knowing to give these lesser beings the harsh glower of a Vampire Count, for he was Count Viper after-all, but his heart was already broken now that he had finally made his point to Jacinthe, whether she might understand it or not. Indeed, though for all the years he had known her, others had believed him to bully her and, though Gaston had been the closest to clocking on that he might have feelings for her, Thibaut's insecurities had meant he could say no truth but stated he'd been grooming her to be a simpering wife. It was true perhaps, he had been hopeful that the wife he took on would be weak, simpering, would be the kind he could control through words and not need to fear ever expecting anything of him but complete loyalty and love. He would give loyalty and love, but Thibaut was not an affectionate person, he did not show his feelings as zealously as his father did... he was reserved and calm like his mother and his injuries in life had meant there was a stone shield over his heart... but such places were the home of wallflowers like Jacinthe.

As he was led up to the main living room and meeting hall of the household, Thibaut could feel the grinding return to his stomach but he could not stop or faint now... they had made the decision on his future and he must expect it.

Thibaut was able to come into the room in time to see that Phillippe was talking to his wife, a woman that Thibaut was often told to only refer to as 'Madame Vulturie', a lady that apparently might have a bit of a well-known name if the rumours were true and she was the replacement for the mother of Phillippe's children. Madame Vulturie was not in the same loving relationship with her husband as the previous, but she had formed an instant attachment to all the girls, save Jacinthe whom she seemed to enjoy belittling, making her almost to be the Cinderella of the three possible brides to be chosen from. But she was worried about handing any child over to Thibaut as he had made it quite clear during the issue with the Elders and the Serpents that he took no prisoners and quite delighted in torturing. He could already hear her whispering that Thibaut was probably a 'Caligula' type of vampire and it made a crooked smirk fall upon Thibaut's face as he stepped into the room and gently bowed in front of the Count, his soft dirty blonde locks slipping forward slightly as he then straightened and brushed the wavy lengths back behind his ears. At his greeting, Phillippe sat his wife aside and beckoned Thibaut to sit in the chair nearest his own large one before he gave a clap of his hands and the side door was opened for the three women to step in.

As always Thibaut kept a straight and composed figure, a charismatic smile upon his face as he turned towards the two busty blondes strolling in wearing their Robe de style, trying not to giggle with excitement although Phillippe looked to the twin pair of airheads with a visible grimace. Thibaut turned to greet them properly with the usual grace and charm he greeted Marie and Michelle with, swallowing back his desire to just turn away and leave them to rot in his shadow as they brought their hands forward with firm blushes at his compliments. He took each hand, kissed each and informed Marie that she was looking quite fashionable with her bobbed haircut and the black and white dress, as if she were about to go out and stun the world before telling Michelle she looked elegant in light blue and it showed off her exquisite face. But the truth was, all Thibaut wanted to do was tell Marie that she was the most aggravating chatterbox he'd ever known and for having commented on Elaine's choice to aid Theodosius's partner gain a child he should slap her and Michelle... well, there were rumours she'd taken after the Madame with a fancy for men of a lower rank. But just as they went to settle down, Jacinthe stepped out from the shadow of her sisters and grimaced slightly as she brought her hand to Thibaut to kiss and though he said 'hello Jacinthe', there was no compliment given but a gentle stroke of his thumb over her gloved hand that he'd not given her sisters, something no one else noticed.

"So then dear friend, I'm sorry I ended up delayed in my decision... but to decide between three daughters is problematic. I have to consider all their best points, worst points and of course your own. But do not get me wrong and please, sit down Thibaut." Phillippe stated with a soft expression upon his face as he turned to point a hand to the spare chair and Thibaut went to sit at it. The chair had a harder bottom, though fabric, than Thibaut could quite endure and no cushion and it made him grip his hands into his knuckles, wringing them as he settled into the chair.

He held off the grimace as he settled down, felt the pinch against the tender flesh stab up to exposed nerves that began a hammering of many tiny needles into his spine and Thibaut did not think he could quite cope until he managed to shift slightly to the side. Phillippe looked at him, a little confused for a moment and Thibaut was able to make a brief note of a sudden little spot of nerves at this moment. It soothed the fellow Count and Thibaut knew he could not reveal weakness and he could not seem to be rude to his host at this moment as Phillippe sat down and decided first to list the good points and bad points of Thibaut.

"With regards to you, Thibaut, your clan is lesser but at the highest position and your association with the Elders, in fact your own ability to deal with them through diplomacy this year alone has put you in higher graces. You're the head of your clan, a Count and your ability to govern your property, your family and indeed your many deals are inarguably astounding... you can do more with just your mind than I can with four of my vassals. You have troubling qualities though, a touch of ruthlessness that can be seen from your association with the bane Taliesin Vilmore, I can see that calling your seeming 'uncle' such has already vexed you. But also, you show a violent streak in the face of danger and a cruelty that has meant I must ponder it all carefully... then I came to the conclusion that each situation was done in defence of your family... family is very important to you and any wife would be given unquestionable loyalty and faith from you. I note though, you don't bare ill manners and you do not show affection, at least publicly... yet I know that in choosing a bride for you from my own daughters, I have been given a heavy burden and a great act of trust between our clans. This choice, this marriage, it will mean there will never be a moment when the future Count Viper's decisions do not reflect upon my family. It's a heavy burden... but the burden of all Noble Marriages..."

"I understand that well, dear friend, hence I sought no other family but your own, my neighbour and my friend. You were an ally my father respected above the Pipistrello and I too have more faith in you then I do the Italians." Thibaut stated firmly, his voice low and his eyes sparkling with a flame of fury that Phillippe noticed and could not help but smirk over. He knew Thibaut could be a shameless flatterer for the sake of business relationships, but that sparkle spoke of a hidden fury towards the Italians that the Frenchman assumed would be related to the matter of Theodosius and that seeming shame upon the household. However, Thibaut just breathed a soft sigh and then lowered his eyes, seeming to take a moment to reflect that Phillippe appreciated, though he had no idea of course that it was because Thibaut was trying to overcome the pain in his body. Internally, Thibaut was begging for the pins and needles to kick in, the numbing to occur so that he could just bear it better. "This decision has been holding sway over my mind lately... I hope you understand too Phillippe that any wish for me to rush into the actual wedding and the aftermath is unlikely. Whatever wife you have chosen I will court properly through an engagement before I wed... then you can see the kind of husband she will be getting."

"Heh... I don't doubt you want it to be a steady situation... you're not a vampire to take anything on a whim, it's one of your best qualities and why we work so well. I cannot pull the wool over your eyes... and it would seem the girls cannot either. Nor can they confuse me..." Phillippe stated with a soft sigh of despair as he turned away from them all to lean over his desk. He shook his head as if the burden had been terrible and Thibaut eyed him cautiously, as did his daughters and his latest wife... who appeared rather uncomfortable with this reaction. Thibaut was amused though, clearly Phillippe had picked up on the latest rumours regarding his daughters too, but then Phillippe just sighed as he stood up again. He spun around to face them all with his hands behind his back, looking incredibly proud though his face seemed hard as if pained, though his nose was twitching from picking up a curious scent that was making him almost want to crack up with a giggle. "The choice is simple, I would be a cruel father to put a brainless woman with a wordsmith like you... dear Serpent... but alas Marie is not only dim but her tongue never knows when to stop wagging and I'd fear you'd remove it from her slighting your dear younger brother. Heh... and well, Michelle? I would have said her to be more sensible... but sensible girls don't get pregnant from horse grooms or conspire with their adoptive mothers to urge me to pawn a bastard child off onto a serious ally. So, it looks like Jacinthe alone is left..."

The Madame dropped her cup onto the floor with a resounding crash that made Phillippe shake his head in dismay before lifting the little bell upon his desk and ringing it for the servants to come in and clean the matter up. He did not even seem to blink despite the calumny in his words about his own daughters and Michelle just burst into tears at having been found out and clearly disgraced. Not only was she in tears but Marie's mouth was dropped open and she looked to say something but she could not, a first that Phillippe turned to view with a firm grin. He could not stand the chatter either, but his eyes then turned towards Jacinthe who was blushing crimson, trembling on her seat and looking as if she might burst into tears herself. Phillippe flicked his eyes towards Thibaut, rather shocked that for all his usual composure and pride, the young man was just staring straight at Jacinthe in shock, his eyes wide and his face looking as if he'd been slapped… but in a good way. It reminded Phillippe of the first day he had visited the Viper's Island, brought the girls and the two fools had gone to bother Gaston and Thibaut, but though Gaston had been eager to make friends, Thibaut had given that same look of shock towards the nervous little girl that had been clinging to her father for safety. Phillippe recalled though that the moment they were introduced, Jacinthe had been scared and too nervous to say anything and though it had sounded as if Thibaut had been unkind to her, when he had said that ill manners befitted ill breeding, she had suddenly introduced herself and he had said even then 'you're clearly more interesting than your sisters'. It perhaps had been fated and then Phillippe gave a soft little titter as he looked to the still stunned looking girl, his most intelligent daughter, his most simpering perhaps, but one that would complement Thibaut's harshness with her tenderness.

"Heh… I doubt if she were loose in tongue and leg like her sisters that you would even care, Thibaut. Though the Italians claim to know love they only know its extravagance… the French know its tragedies, its true romance and its subtlety… I have seen all I ever needed to see each time you have come into contact with Jacinthe… and flowers do have voices. I hadn't assumed you to be interested in such a gentile hobby as floriography, though your greenhouse is a place of envy amongst the gardening fanatics I hear… but you know, I saw Jacinthe come in one day from town with a firm blush that made the white carnation on her head stand out like a beacon." He turned about to face the room as the two figures still seemed too stunned for words, unable to even move in case this was not even real. Michelle and Marie however had lifted their teary faces to look at their father in confusion, recalling the day Thibaut had put the flower in Jacinthe's hair after complaining that she looked too plain compared to them both. Their eyes darted back and forth from Jacinthe who looked about to cry to Thibaut, the sisters believing he looked like he was in agony and clearly upset with the decision as their father yawned and continued. "Forgive the yawn, but if I recall… a white carnation is not just for 'good luck' but for 'pure love'… heh, you made your first confession right under the nose of her sisters and then today… well, I do tend to like looking down into the maze and you can't hide the strong scent of white hyacinth. Well… I wish you great happiness…"

Phillippe had looked to turn back to view outside when Thibaut had made a sudden noise and then to the shock of everyone present, lithe little Jacinthe launched from her chair and straight into Thibaut. His chair was flipped onto its back, his legs in the air and he was winded as Jacinthe gripped him tightly, bursting into happy tears although the other females in the room and the servant come to clean up were staring in total disbelief. Jacinthe was in tears, sobbing with joy against Thibaut's chest as he remained rather stunned, too happy and in shock to focus on pain elsewhere in his body as everyone else just remained staring out at the pair of them in total disgust for such a display. But when Thibaut gave a soft cough, Jacinthe suddenly realised what she was doing and leapt back to sit and stare at him in anxiety before grabbing at his face.

"Oh Thibaut… oh Mon Beau… forgive me I forgot that you do not appreciate such things. I am sorry but, but I am so very happy…" Jacinthe still could not stop herself from sobbing softly and Thibaut just gave a snort of amusement as he pulled himself up off the floor, lifted the chair back up and then stretched his hand out to her. Jacinthe took his hand, standing up swiftly and was rather shocked when he then brought his other hand to her chin, stroking at her beautiful skin as he bent forward and tenderly placed his lips upon her forehead in a tender kiss. Jacinthe practically gasped in surprise, her skin burning with pleasure, her heart almost stopping to finally receive a kiss from the man she was so very much in love with. But then Thibaut stepped aside from her and then swiftly hooked a beautiful little box out of his pocket and bent on his knee, startling the family even more. "But Thibaut… we are already engaged…"

"Perhaps… I have an arrangement with your father but, Jacinthe… I want to know if you will accept marrying me. If you do not want me, I will not force you to marry me for the sake of an alliance. Marrying me is a heavy burden, its marrying into my family and every expectation… understanding too that I am a cold person and I am sorry that being my wife might leave you more as my companion and friend rather than my lover." Thibaut stated with a genuine anxious expression, pain eating into his entire body for daring to bend onto one knee and awaken that horrendous pain within. But Thibaut endured it as he opened the little box and presented the rather delicate looking silver ring bearing a gorgeous little diamond at its centre. It was beautiful in its simplicity and perfect to show just how much this meant to Thibaut and the kind of person he was, but he could not stop himself from smiling up at her. "But if that is what you can endure, dear Jacinthe... I would have the honour of your hand in marriage..."

"Thibaut... I know the man you are and the way you are and I know how difficult being your wife will be... but I could not even imagine marrying anyone else." Jacinthe stated, tears suddenly skimming down her cheeks as she stretched forward to jerk him straight back up onto his feet and she almost did not let go of his shoulders. Her family were watching in fascination, although they did suddenly feel as though they were intruding on the matter and yet... none could ever recall Thibaut ever looking so curiously emotional before or indeed Jacinthe being so bold. It certainly intrigued her father who was grinning away at the thought of them both together and how ridiculous they could indeed be within the confines of their own home. But when Jacinthe stated 'yes' and then presented her hand to him, Thibaut very tenderly eased the ring onto her finger and then he bent his forehead down to lean against hers. Their hands held onto each other tightly and where perhaps any other couple might have kissed away forever, the pair of them just remained in this seemingly relieved pose for a moment before he kissed her forehead, she shuddered in joy and then he straightened up to look at her with a tearful expression of bliss.

"I'm very grateful Jacinthe... I will do my best to keep you happy, comfortable, and safe... I'll do my best to give you everything you desire..." He began and it was still quite a shock for the Vulturie to hear these kinds of things coming from Thibaut's mouth. For a moment, the twin sisters were even looking at one another as if they had been hoodwinked this whole time, indeed his reputation was terrifying and he'd never once really shown a romantic bone in his body and yet Jacinthe just sighed. She lifted a hand to his lips to stop him, gaining a surprise kiss to her fingers to make her blush before she'd grabbed his hands again tightly and then looked up at him firmly.

"I don't want anything but to be your love, that is all I wish." Jacinthe stated and then she received a shock as Thibaut bent forward as if to kiss her, only to blush and pull back, suddenly very unsure of himself and it made Jacinthe give a soft giggle. It would not be Thibaut if he were not so unsure of something as simple as how to kiss someone, she could tell he was trying to think of the right angle to go in for and the right way to motion his lips as well as thinking about their audience. When he tried to make some semblance of apology Jacinthe lifted her hand, caught his tie and jerked him downward to ensure he crashed into her lips for a firm little kiss before she let him go and then held his head. "I look forward to our wedding day…"

Part One: The Unwanted Couple

L'île Pourrie, Channel Islands (Within the French Veil), France,
January 1926

Gaston had just finished packing the rest of the luggage for the honeymoon into the back of the car, still not quite sure he trusted the automobile over the horse, but then again he had never really been much for travelling places where he could easily walk. His whole body was still tingling with delight, his mind a little hazy because it still felt so unreal to be married for a few hours already! He could hardly cope with it, the fact he wanted to keep grabbing every person he met and telling them that he and Lynette had married at last! It did not matter that he was also the first in his family to get married properly! He had never really known before if his family would have agreed to him marrying the werewolf love of his life, but none of them had protested it and none of their friends to have attended did either. They had all been so loving and endearing and the island had rocked with the howls of joy from their community as the ceremony and the party had been held there for all. It had been just what the whole family had needed after such a trying time and now at last, the pair were finally going to enjoy some privacy in the south!

"Mama… has Thibaut said if he'll be running late? I can't imagine leaving without knowing exactly what happened at the Vulturie's last night! Oh hello again Vittorio… Mama, let me hold him please!" Gaston had just turned away from the car when he'd noticed his mother strolling around in her long black dress and coat amongst the still crunching layer of snow with the baby in her arms. Gaston could have squealed to see the baby dressed in a great big winter coat that he was far too small for, he was just so adorable! The moment Adelia brought her grandson over to his uncle, the little baby gave a few grunting sounds and a little sneeze as if in greeting and Gaston was quick to hook him up into his arms, whether he had permission or not. Like everyone else in the family, Vittorio's birth had been the height of the winter months and been hailed as everyone's early Christmas present! Now he was a little bigger and Elaine was trying to encourage some distancing on her part so the transition of him going to Valentino and Dio would be simpler, everyone was getting the chance to hold the baby and fuss him! "Awe… look at those little cheeks… you know, with that golden hair and the amber eyes, it's impossible to think he's Valentino's at all! But for those curls, he reminds me so much of father... no one is ever going to think he's not Dio's! But is Elaine sure she'll be alright with this?"

"Theodosius has been at her side since his birth, he's slept in the same room as the baby practically all the time, he sits beside her as she feeds him... you'd think he was the one who'd given birth to him! Elaine is quite content, she says, not to be mean, but she did this for her brother and when Tonauac returns in August for the ceremony here, she says it's the first thing they'll think of for each other. If it could have been done, I would have carried Vittorio for Dio's sake, but its best it's his twin really... she and he just have the same mind and same thoughts when they're together and with him hovering over Vito when he's not finally passed out from the stress of it all, Elaine says she's just currently the feeder." Adelia stated, she knew that no matter what her eldest daughter said, the whole idea that she had birthed this thing and it was not to stay with her was still disheartening. Especially when Tonauac had stayed behind for the birth and been very eager to be beside her, to hold him and then been so downhearted when he'd had to pass him into Valentino's hands. There was no doubt it was going to be seriously painful for them, but that was why Vittorio was being urged onto the bottle and at six months would then be taken to Italy with his fathers... and why Dio was making sure Vittorio was comfortable with him. "To be honest, I don't even think Vittorio recognises Elaine as mother anyway... when he cries, it's not Elaine that he cries for but Dio."

"That's going to be a confusing situation as he grows though... but it's the beauty of a close family... we'll all be in each other's business so he'll assume we're all his parents!" Gaston teased as he then nuzzled his nose against the baby's and Vittorio gave another sneeze. As if on cue, from the house Theodosius came skidding over on the icy steps with a steaming blanket in his arms and a warm handkerchief. Before Gaston could say or do anything about it, the blanket was suddenly wrapped around Vittorio and his face was being cleaned with the fabric. Suddenly the baby's face was almost hidden in a scarf that was suddenly looped about him like a boa constrictor and Vittorio seemed to give a visible grimace at the situation. Gaston was then giggling as Dio then hooked the baby up into his arms and then kissed at him as the baby gave a heavy sigh. "It's just a sneeze, at this rate he's going to be overheating... ah, that's Thibaut's carriage!"

"Finally, by the way… who did you bet on? Me, mother, Selene and Odette all put a hundred Decker on Jacinthe. Apparently, Noel, Elaine and Beauregard put a hundred on Michelle, Lynette and Brennan all put money on Marie." Theodosius queried as he nuzzled at Vittorio with his chin and the baby gave a soft grunt wrapped up amongst a multitude of fabrics as Gaston gave a chuckle. Adelia cleared her throat gently, she was not usually one to endorse gambling but since it had been made clear from Vulturie's first impression of Thibaut that he was going to force him to marry one of the triplets, the betting pools had been held in secret amongst the staff and amongst the household. Adelia had assumed of course it would be Marie or Michelle, they were the ones most likely to suit the social standing that Thibaut was developing… yet she'd been compelled to choose Jacinthe because long ago Theo had watched Thibaut showing Jacinthe around his little garden and his favourite amaranth… something Thibaut had never even let the gardener touch! Still, they were all quiet as the carriage pulled up and Ashford stepped down from the driver's seat, the dryad far happier in this line of work than being the under-butler and swiftly opened the door with a smug expression as Thibaut stepped out and the family almost passed out. "Oh dear God he looks lovestruck…"

"Hello, dear brothers… dearest mother… I'm very happy." Thibaut had stepped out of the carriage with an aura about him of utter joy and benevolence, some kind of euphoria written within his eyes as he held his pocket watch in his hand and was sighing at it. There was a secret compartment in the watch, one that suited a little portrait or a lock of hair and that was what the others assumed to be within the item. However, they were completely shocked by just how relaxed he was as he stepped over to them, gripping Adelia in a hug before kissing her cheeks and then doing the same to both his brothers and even to Vittorio, who gave another sneeze. Thibaut dared to give a soft chuckle at this and gently took the cloth from Dio to wipe Vittorio's nose before the baby gave a grunt at the attention and Thibaut then heaved a heavy sigh of relief. The others remained staring at him expectantly, just who had he been given? "Well… I would say this is a subject for the living room, but as you are about to depart Gaston, I will whisper the answer to you alone…"

"Hold up! I'm your mother, I should be told first!" Adelia snorted in frustration, stepping forward and gently smacking at Thibaut's shoulder in frustration as he turned about to give her a sudden peck on the cheek. He then wrapped his arms about Gaston, nuzzling into his shoulder and breathing a sigh of relief before telling him how much he loved him and how happy he was for him. Gaston was thankful, gripping Thibaut back in a firm hug of his own before he was then whispered the answer and he suddenly pulled his head to the side in utter disbelief before he suddenly grasped Thibaut's shoulder, asking him firmly if this was what he wanted and Thibaut gave the most loving expression possible.

"Oh yes… I could not have hoped for such wondrous luck… God has decided to be very kind to me, not only has he given you, my dear brother happiness with my dearest friend Lynette… but he's given me the chance to woo the one woman I've ever met to ever make my heart tremble." Thibaut sighed gently and Gaston's eyes crossed before he received a kiss to each cheek and then Thibaut returned to climbing the steps into the household, leaning onto his cane to do so before shuffling into the household, only for Lynette to give a squeak as she was grabbed and given a sudden swing. Gaston gave a grumble that Lynette was his wife, not Thibaut's and his elder brother chuckled before hurrying back into the household to look for Selene and Elaine. Theodosius was grinning as he held his baby tightly to him and then Vittorio gave another soft sneeze as Adelia pinched Gaston's arm roughly to find out.

"Ah… mama…" Gaston fussed, swatting at her to back off as he was certainly not going to tell! Adelia then gripped her arms about Gaston in a tight hug, nuzzling into him, sighing in adoration as she then grasped his cheeks. Before he could do anything else, Adelia was suddenly peppering his face in kisses and fussing how much she loved him and hoped he would be a good husband to his wife and look after her on their honeymoon to Normandy. Gaston just chuckled at his mother's fusses, he knew she was not going to have the time to worry about it when she still had Theodora to prepare for her schooling and well, it sounded as if everyone was probably going to be involved in fussing Thibaut and his love life. Gaston could hardly believe it as he then kissed his mother's hand lovingly and then turned to spot Lynette skipping down the steps in her bright blue dress with matching bonnet and her hat box as her last bit of luggage. "We'll telegram through when we arrive in the town, you should not worry Mama, we're not leaving the country and we won't be more than two weeks away. I doubt anything too dramatic will occur now Thibaut's making sure he's going to have his work cut out to woo someone properly."

"Well, if he hasn't told me by supper, I'm going to call Phillippe myself to find out the answer. But I suppose he's waiting for his uncle to call before he tells us anything." Adelia sighed in frustration, before returning to squish at Gaston's cheeks. Of all her children, Gaston was the one that looked the most like he was her son, all the others had developed some kind of blonde hair and their father's looks, but Gaston had his mother's dark hair and darker features that just made him stand out alongside his strength and bulk. He'd been such a steadfast member of the household that the thought of him going away for two weeks was almost unbearable, but everyone was happy for his marriage and hopeful that soon enough, Dio would not be the only parent amongst the Viper Clan. "Stay safe, both of you. I trust Macron as your driver but I don't trust anyone else… enjoy yourselves."

"We plan to mother, I'm very thankful that my friends were eager to house us for our honeymoon. After everything that's been happening, it's going to be a breath of fresh air to visit the beaches and enjoy the surf where it's a bit less cold." Gaston teased, kissing his mother's cheek before grabbing Lynette suddenly about the waist, lifting her up as she gave a sudden squeak and he then swung her about. When he settled her down he brought his lips to hers firmly as she blushed and apologised to the countess before Gaston ushered her into the car. He waved goodbye to Theodosius and Vittorio gave a sneeze in response to it all before Gaston climbed into the vehicle. Settling in the back and clasping his arm about Lynette's waist, he pulled the door shut and then the vehicle was off with a clunk and then a honk. They were soon waving out the windows to say goodbye to their family before they drove out of the courtyard and on towards the ferry. It was only when they were out of sight of the household though that Gaston noticed the look of concern upon Lynette's face and tenderly, he kissed her. "What is wrong my darling?"

"Oh… mon Beau… I was just thinking… Normandy is strictly posh vampire country; they were the ones to remove werewolves from their lands and well, I know it was something of nearly forty years ago but… I am nervous of how they will react to you and me. The Veil has not really changed in the past decade…" Lynette muttered anxiously as she thought about the stories her father had told her of that place and how any damage to the livestock in the region had been blamed on their kind and how there had been the need to hide away from threats to drive them into the sea and drown them. She was scared that the moment she stepped into the Veil regions there, they would know what she was in one look and they would react, but Gaston could understand and he shook his head gently as he grasped her hands tightly and then nuzzled his face to hers as she blushed. "Mon villain…"

"Don't be afraid Lynette… you forget, I am Gaston Viper and I'm a damn good fighter, they'll take one look at me and zip their lips so a surgeon won't have to do it for them." Gaston grinned, irking her to giggle slightly as she then settled back against him, cuddling into his arm. Gaston sighed lovingly, considering they had been married only a little while, he was pleased that the only difference from how they had been before was the lack of secrecy, they did not need to run into the woods to their secret little cabin to be together and then Gaston gave a chuckle to himself. He thought about a piece of paper that Thibaut had passed him yesterday and he lifted open his jacket to pull it out and give a smirk. "Well… Thibaut said he was going to take a little while to arrange our wedding gift, but considering he's going to have his own wedding soon enough, I have no clue what would be suitable when you see what he's given us…"

"What do you mean?" Lynette questioned, gently lifting one of her well-worked fingers to pick up the piece of paper from her husband as he smirked down at her. When she pulled it to her face, her eyes bulged in shock and she gave a firm gasp at the list on this legal document and then her eyes darted to her husband. Gaston gave a wink, yes this was definitely the real thing and he made a soft motion that it was for being the 'first' to marry and Lynette chuckled. She knew too that it was also because of her friendship to Thibaut and her kindness to him, but considering it all she could hardly believe it as she had to say it aloud. "He's given us not only free roam of the household, but the Warden's Cottage he's granted for us to live in if we wish and… and he's given us the cottage on the Shepherd's Island as a holiday home complete with servants at both sights… our own carriage or car depending on preference and is that number right? How come he's giving us such a massive allowance each year? This is… this is too much… he shouldn't be…."

"He's a soppy old fellow when it comes down to it really… my brother is a very adoring creature and you're incredibly romantic too you know…." Gaston growled softly in amusement as he hooked his arms about his wife, pulling her in for a loving snuggle as she gave a sudden giggle of amusement. She was soon lounging on her back in the car as he stretched over her, cuddling her up against him and peppering her cheeks and neck with kisses as she giggled away. He gave a sudden sigh of utter delight, pressing his nose to hers to nuzzle it slightly before she gave a soft moan and wrapped her hands about his cheeks, pushing him down for a passionate kiss. The pair moaned together softly in delight as Gaston then sighed. "This is it… our future starts here… we can have children and then watch them grow, see grandchildren… oh, it will be so wonderful. As long as I have you, Lynette… everything is wonderful!"

Lynette gave a soft chuckle at the words as they kissed again, but she felt a slight pang within her chest for his words. The pair of them had been fornicating for many years, they had rarely used protective sheaths and though they always tried carefully to miss her cycles, there had been several moments where Lynette had thought she must be pregnant. Indeed, she had been very sure to have been pregnant once but then something had happened and it had suddenly stopped… now her cycles were taking longer and her scent in season not as strong as it used to be. Indeed, Lynette was rather upset at the thought that maybe she might have missed her chance completely and well, vampires might be slow to reproduce but werewolves were not immortal….

"Mon Villain… tell me please, if we did not end up having children, would it upset you?" Lynette questioned gently and she looked suddenly very embarrassed and concerned. But Gaston just continued to kiss her lovingly, shrugging his shoulders and stating calmly that he had her and that was all. She gave a sigh of relief as they kissed at one another lovingly once more and then Gaston sat himself up before pulling his wife up and into his lap. She was swift to wrap her arms about his chest, to sit in his lap and just sigh and swoon as the car bumped along the road and on towards their destination and Lynette was happy. "Oh Gaston… everything's going to be so wonderful isn't it?"

"It will be…"

The pair reached their destination by the later hours of the night, Gaston awake but Lynette fast asleep in his arms, sighing lovingly as she gripped at his waist, her head nuzzled to his shoulder. Gaston was pleased the Veil corridors made the journey faster than for humans, but when they pulled up in front of the fancy little hotel with views of the beach but wide grassy slopes and a refreshing sea breeze, he gently patted her back. Lynette gave a soft groan as she woke up, pulling herself upward and then staring in confusion until she rubbed her eyes and then spotted the beautiful looking hotel and gave a sound of excitement and delight. Their driver stepped to the door, gently opening it up for them as Gaston stepped out of the vehicle and was startled to see a gathering of eager looking Turned and Blueblood vampires waiting to greet him, some minions already on display to take their luggage to their room. Gaston grinned at them, then stretched his hand out to Lynette, her little soft white gloves sitting into his hand and then was gently led out.

The staff had taken a deep breath of expectation, looking at how handsome Gaston was, knowing he was a Viper and very powerful, so they assumed his wife would be just as beautiful. Indeed, she was a very beautiful figure as she stepped into the room, but the moment she smiled at them in greeting, their breath was lost in disgusted gasps. There were no fangs and they could smell she was a werewolf! Immediately there was the whisper of confusion, would such a high-ranking vampire really marry a worthless carpet? Lynette ignored the sound immediately, she'd heard all that rubbish before whenever she'd been seen with Gaston but to her great surprise, Gaston's fangs were suddenly on display and he produced an aggressive hiss that made the staff step back in anxiety before the owner, Madam Blanchard, stepped forward with an appeasing smile.

"Forgive the crude words of the underlings, sir... we were rather startled that she was not a vampire. But of course, Madam Viper is astoundingly beautiful and I am very honoured to welcome you both to our humble establishment. We are at your service." Blanchard was a vampire on the way out, the death of her husband had dropped her low in the rankings and knowing that unless she passed on, no one would ever respect her son taking over the name of the establishment, she was starving herself. She looked haggard, weak, little more than a skeleton wearing skin and a grey and white wig in a bun as she stretched her hands out to them both. Gaston relaxed, taking her hand and bringing it to his lips in a gentle greeting that made her blush before she rather suddenly spun on her heel, rather than hold onto Lynette's hand in greeting. "Come along then, the minions shall deal with your luggage, but you must be starving..."

"We are indeed, Madam Blanchard... I've heard you're the best cook in Normandy and I'm very eager to partake..." Lynette beamed softly in delight as she gripped hold of her husband's arm and leant against him. The vampire turned about to look at her before giving a soft snigger, one that was smug and said that she certainly believed that Lynette had probably never eaten anything more than raw lamb or deer. Lynette could sense the disregard as the vampire beckoned them inside, her eyes locked only on Gaston, who was standing tall and stern. Lynette did not know how to feel about it but she could tell that this was not going to be as relaxing a time as they had hoped. She gripped Gaston gently and then looked up at him as he turned his head down to her, lifting his hand to stroke her face gently.

"It will be fine." Gaston whispered gently to her, kissing her forehead and then leading her to follow after the Madam as she beckoned them again to follow her. Stepping into the building they felt it was something grand and fancy yet somehow quaint and pleasant. Perhaps it was because everything was sparkling, the building was modern and well, it smelt curiously cosy and delicious all at once. Lynette and Gaston were led to the large dining room where there were two other guests settled and eating their meal. The sight of the meal made Lynette's eyes swell in delight, it looked delicious and the smell alone could make her mouth water. As Madam Blanchard settled them at the top of the table, they greeted the other guests and there was the usual exalted greeting towards Gaston before they suddenly realised that Lynette was not a vampire. All the same, Blanchard clapped for her servants to come to her and bring out the starter. "It's a beautiful place… I was a little worried it was going to be a little too elitist like Paris and Rennes…"

"I've got no experience in such fancy places, mon Beau, but it is very cosy here and I like it very much. But I like being with my husband even more…" Lynette chuckled, grasping his hand in her own and squeezing it gently as Gaston brought her hand to his mouth and gently kissed her knuckles. She gave a soft chuckle of amusement before the food was brought out to them and they began with a soup. Happily, they enjoyed their soup and then they were served a hearty beef meal and then a beautiful dessert and Lynette sighed and fawned over how beautiful it all was. Gaston enjoyed it, but it was only more pleasurable because she was loving this moment and when they had finished their dessert, Gaston had stroked a dollop of cream from the edge of Lynette's mouth before licking it off his finger as Lynette giggled. "You're such a strange fellow…"

"Yet you married me knowing this full well…" Gaston grinned, showing off his wicked fangs to make her chuckle rather cutely, bringing her hands up to her face as she giggled. She then gently brought her hand to push his shoulder, only for him to snatch her hand and pull it to his face. His fingers eased and massaged each of her fingers and her knuckles, squeezing up her palms as he then kissed the tip of her digits with a loving sigh of pleasure. He then even dared to gently clasp his lips about her ring finger to make her give a firm blush and excited gasp before he released her. He then leant forward, nuzzling her nose with his own as he purred and she sighed against his face, thinking almost to kiss him until they heard the soft coughing of the other guests at the table. Gaston turned to look at them for a second and his stomach filled with fury.

These snobs were looking at Lynette more than him, they'd been eyeing her eagerness to eat during the meal and he could feel them judging her. If his father would have been there, Theo would have continued to fuss regardless and then made a subtle point that he always worried that people might be jealous of how clearly the pair loved each other. Gaston wished he had the intricacy in speech to give them the telling off they needed without literally snapping at them and then pushing their heads into the table. But when he heard them whisper a word… Fur-Licker… Gaston almost launched up from the table, his fangs were out and his jaw clenching as Lynette snatched her hand about his tightly, holding him back and he turned to look at her cautious, anxious face as he could sense the fear she held that he might hurt her.

"Perhaps we should settle in our room, darling… I think we're both quite exhausted still." Gaston growled calmly in response, holding her hand tightly, almost crunching it within his great strong digits as the fury started to dissipate. But when Lynette nodded her head, they were both startled when Madam Blanchard stepped over to them with a smile upon her face and a question on how they enjoyed the food. Gaston thanked her, insisting it was the best he'd ever had and Lynette nodded her head, though Blanchard once again seemed to ignore her as if she were little more than some prostitute Gaston had brought for a fun weekend. But then she clicked her hands for her son, the head butler, to step out with the key and then bow before beckoning them to their room. Gaston and Lynette stood up and followed the figure, but they could both still hear the whisperings going on.

As they were led to the third floor, the butler was silent and Lynette could smell the disgust coming off him because of her presence here and she and Gaston both overheard one of the cleaning maids whispering they'd have to change the sheets every morning to stop the stench of dog getting stuck. Gaston would have turned about and stormed out then and there, but Lynette gripped his hand tightly and just leant her head to his shoulder. The thoughts of others did not matter, they loved each other and that was what was important, that was what they needed to remember and be happy about! The butler finally brought them to the far door and opened it, the ceiling was low with the arches of the loft and it looked airy and spacious, beautiful floral patterns all over the place and a soft scent of flowers filled the room. There was a bathroom attached with golden taps and a showerhead, it was pristine and large enough they could both just about squeeze in together and Lynette knew what she wanted to do straightaway!

When the butler turned to leave, he made a quick request on whether they would like breakfast brought to them or to come down for it and for a moment the pair stared at one another in fascination. But Gaston could read within Lynette's eyes that she did not want to suffer such an embarrassment amongst the other guests and so Gaston requested the information on what was on offer. The butler insisted he would return with the papers they needed to fill out and when he disappeared, Lynette gave a soft whistle towards Gaston before lifting her hands up to the sleeves of her dress and then pulling them down to bare her shoulders. There was a coy expression upon her face and with a snarl of pleasure as his fangs appeared, Gaston leapt to her side. He hooked his big arms about her and then plastered her shoulder in his kisses as she giggled and chuckled at his actions, before he paused and gently they brought their lips together, her hand tenderly stroking his dark hair.

"Oh... mon Villain... will you humble me with a simple request this evening... as it's supposed to be our honeymoon..." Lynette whispered softly as Gaston lifted an eyebrow before tilting his head to the side in curiosity for the request. She grinned up at him before gently stroking down his sharp nose to watch his lips clip about her finger before she gently pushed the finger to his fangs. Gaston froze, his jaw vibrating in a painful manner for the sudden pressure as she prodded the revealed items before she gave a soft little chuckle. Gaston was not sure what she was about to ask of him, but he was slightly scared that it would be something he did not wish to give in case it hurt her. Indeed, when she requested, his face paled. "I want you to mark me."

"What?" Gaston was startled, in all their time together, they'd never once thought to follow the old ways of their kinds becoming mates. Where a werewolf might howl with her mate under the full moon light, which Gaston would love to do no matter how awfully comical his howl, for vampires it was far less... equal. Indeed, traditionally the role of women amongst vampires was little more than a glorified concubine and well, the right of the vampire's bride to hold dominance over all other females her husband dared to bed or imbibe blood from was to bear the mark of his fangs upon the left side of her neck. They were permanent blue-looking bruises, the saliva of the vampire being repelled within the flesh of another to cause these marks and scars, but on a werewolf it might never heal properly. He was scared it was something that could do damage to their relationship and yet Lynette stroked his cheeks gently.

"Perhaps it's my vanity and pride… but I would rather bare a mark that none could ever think to question than just a wedding ring that others can mock." Lynette knew it was scaring him, but she stroked at his cheeks still, watching the way his eyes drooped and he looked terribly scared and anxious for what she requested. He gently brought his big hand to her chin, grasping it firmly as he bent to kiss her lips softly and then rub his nose to hers as she breathed a sigh of pleasure. She could see from the expression within his eyes though that there was something else bothering Gaston and gently she slid her fingers about one of his thick black locks and swept it behind his ear. "That is my one request of you… what is your request of me?"

"It's not really a request so much as a decision I have made… a decision I have only discussed with Thibaut before now…." Gaston began, but once again the figure of the butler returned to take their breakfast order, ignorant to the intimacy of the situation if only because he saw this as just a vampire playing with a toy then of a husband and wife. Gaston's teeth clenched, his fists balled up and he looked as if he might turn around and beat this figure to a pulp, but for Lynette gently taking the piece of paper. She showed it to Gaston, tapping his nose with the pencil to calm him as he gave a soft snort, his anger dissipating because of her confidence as they scratched a few of the boxes for their breakfast and then passed the paper back over. The butler bobbed his head before departing and this time, Gaston grabbed the little paper hangar for the door stating 'do not disturb' and then closed it before lifting one of the heavy chairs up without little effort and wedging it in front of the door. He turned back to see Lynette giggling sweetly at his actions before he clapped his hands over a job well done and then scooped Lynette up within his arms as he kissed her lips and she queried his decision.

But when Gaston thought about the decision in his mind, he was brought back to the moment he'd mentioned it to Thibaut when his brother had been in his greenhouse tending his beautiful flowers. It had been the one place that could guarantee Thibaut's utter calm and then, when Gaston had revealed it all to him, he recalled the way Thibaut had dropped a flowerpot onto the floor and turned to look at his brother, body quaking and eyes suddenly streaming tears. Thibaut had then wobbled towards him anxiously, his hands stretched out to grasp his shoulders before Thibaut had then dropped his head to Gaston's chest and sobbed. It had been the first time since their father's loss that he'd ever known Thibaut to cry or ever needed to comfort him and it had nearly killed Gaston to know that his decision would cause such a reaction. But then Thibaut had made a promise to him in return for it, rather than trying to dissuade or stop him and Gaston was thankful as he stroked Lynette's body and then eased her to sit down beside him on the bed.

"Dearest Lynette... I know that your life is fleeting, and current laws forbid me to turn you fully or take you as a Pet when we have married instead... so I have decided that, for the sake of our life together, I will not drink a single drop of blood and when you pass on, I will pass on with you. We'll go together as silver-haired and wrinkled old fools..." Gaston stated softly, but he could see Lynette's eyes widening in shock, fear written upon her features for ever once forgetting that the biggest difference between them was mortality. A vampire lived eternally as long as they lived the life of a parasite, but a werewolf lived a human lifetime aware that they may always turn no matter their age and steal lives by giving in to their hunger. She would die, could die from any disease imaginable to mankind... he could not unless he starved himself of blood. After everything they'd been through so far, she began to shake her head furiously and even thought to punch his broad chest as he looked at her anxiously. "Belle?"

"How could you decide such a thing? In doing so you condemn your family to suffer when age takes you, to force your mother to know that she will bury a son alongside a husband long before she ever goes. You are cruel to them Gaston... you are cruel to decide that they will suffer like that..." Lynette stated pitifully, she was glad of his statement though, glad that he wanted to be with her forever and she loved him very, very much to make such a sacrifice, but it seemed a trend in the males of this household. Theodosius willing to go to hell alongside Valentino because he would never be parted from him, saved instead by his father sacrificing himself so that none of his children could suffer. The whole thought of it, of losing the second son who was so much more the rock of the family these days with Thibaut under so much stress, and because of her, she felt wretched for it. But as tears formed in her eyes, Gaston's hands grasped her cheeks and he kissed her lovingly before nuzzling his nose to hers. With the softest of sighs as he kissed her lips as she stared up at him pitifully, realisation hit her to see the tear dribbling from his own eyes. "You… you already told Thibaut, didn't you?"

Suddenly Gaston's mind was locked with that image of his brother weeping and Gaston had to grasp his own face to stop himself from sobbing too. In seeing this, knowing too that Thibaut knew and accepted, Lynette wrapped her arms about him tightly and nuzzled her face into his chest with a soft sob of upset before kissing his chest. She apologised, telling him it was a very beautiful thing for him to do and then his big hand covered hers, gripping it tightly to his chest so she could feel his heart hammering within and understood just how much he loved her. Lynette leant up on her tiptoes to firmly smack her lips to Gaston's and then his mind seemed to switch, the sadness gone and instead happiness gripping him. He hooked his arms about her, making her give a squeak as he swung her to his chest like the bride she was and then peppered her cheek in kisses as she gave a soft giggle of delight before being carried out to the bathroom and she gave a soft snort of amusement.

Once in the bathroom, Lynette hopped out of his arms and practically galloped across to the taps, pushing the plug in firmly and then turning the water on, giving a sigh of pleasure to watch the steam roll out and into the tub. Gaston grimaced as he looked at the size of the bathtub, he'd fit but he was quite sure he'd have to sit with Lynette opposite him and he was not exactly happy with that thought. But then she turned to look at him with a soft grin, kissed his cheek and then grabbed a little box of bath oils and salts, throwing it in before swirling her hand in the small bath to check the temperature thus far. With a grin she turned about, pointed her finger to Gaston and gave a soft flick as she stretched her finger up and down and Gaston's face flushed in embarrassment. He certainly was not used to Lynette giving him the order to undress and he swung his arms about himself, giving a coy reaction as he slowly unbuttoned his shirt before teasingly lowering his shirt down his sleeve though Lynette swiftly smacked his shoulder.

"No teasing… you're to strip down and get in the tub." Lynette giggled in amusement as she twirled her fingers for him and then he turned his back to her. He then very slowly began to slide his shirt down his back, making the kind of silly music that they had heard people mime to indicate the dancing in some cathouse. Lynette gave his backside a gentle pat to make him jump and then stick his tongue out at her as he then threw his shirt aside before looping his arms around her, kissing her lips lovingly as she then went to grasp his belt, unclip it and then tug his trousers upward before letting go. They landed down with a soft thud before she looked down and then shook her head before gently pressing his nose with her fingers. "Mon Villain… what did I tell you about teasing…"

"Is it teasing? Do you want it that much?" Gaston growled playfully, but then Lynette stepped aside adding just a pinch more of the bath salts into the water, turning the taps off completely and then cleared her throat, throwing her thumb over her shoulder to get him in the water. With a soft sigh of acceptance, Gaston quickly dropped his underwear and then lifted his feet to remove a sock, wiggling it at Lynette's face as she gave him a lecture on how he did not need to tell her how bad his socks smelt when she had stronger olfactory senses. He stuck his tongue out at her again before kissing her cheek and then making a fake dive for the bath to make her squeak before he then lowered himself in with a soft moan of pleasure. "Aaah… heaven…"

"It's warm enough for you, my darling?" Lynette chuckled softly as she watched him sink deep down into the tub with a soft moan as he stretched his legs and then patted the water to beckon her to climb in. Lynette sighed softly, peeling the clothes from her body before gathering them up and dumping them casually on a chair near the bed, giggling at the curiously exciting feeling of being naked outside of their usual places. To be fair, for a while it had been so strange that she had been allowed to kiss him freely in the household, to join the family at the dinner table sitting beside him and well, lounging in the library beside him without feeling as if they might be told off or shunned. But coming here she sensed it again and yet… yet she was so happy as she clambered into the bath with him. "Hold yourself… I don't want to cause an accident…"

"Heh… I was going to ask you something about that…" Gaston grinned in amusement as the water rose with her added weight and as she gently lowered herself between his opened legs as he held himself protectively, Lynette gave a curious expression. She settled down against him, chuckling as she felt that firm form push gently against her backside as she leant back into his chest, letting the last of the water rise and splash out over the side. She mumbled that they were not supposed to soak the floor as Gaston bent his head down and kissed the bridge of her nose softly as her face went red and she cackled in amusement. Gaston wrapped his arms across her chest and then whispered softly to her. "Lynette… did you ever want children?"

Lynette went deathly silent, she let him kiss at her ear and across her face as she stretched her legs down and became weightless within the tub. She remained motionless as she let herself consider what he wanted and indeed what she thought over the matter. Lynette was not bothered either way about children, she knew that werewolves had a reduced fertility unless it was with other werewolves, vampires had low fertility rates as well, but she was not sure of herself and her situation. Considering how often they'd coupled and how they'd never once even considered to take precautions, she grit her teeth together and heaved a sigh of frustration.

"Gaston… don't you think… don't you think that after a decade of being 'unguarded' on the matter… don't you think we'd have had a child by now?" Lynette stated anxiously, a grimace upon her face and she was thankful that the oils in the water and the steam in the room stopped anyone from seeing her face, especially him. It was not that she did not want children, but she had been quite sure she might as well have given up any thought to it. But Gaston gave a sound of fascination and gently he dropped his mouth to her shoulder, kissing at her soft flesh to make her chuckle and lean back against him. Suddenly a grin was on her face as she looked up at him curiously. "Or is this a subject you want to use to excuse me not leaving the bed for the next fortnight?"

"Could be…" Gaston grinned, but he guessed that the subject had to come off the table and be discussed at home. He had thought over the matter before, when he had first talked to Thibaut about their relationship, his brother had asked if he wanted children and Gaston had said he did, but only if she wanted it would he care. But with Vittorio around it was a more attractive possibility and yet he pondered her words.

Time was not on their side, though born a werewolf, Lynette was only second generation and it seemed longevity belonged to the tenth and beyond… vampire meddling no doubt. Already she had aged where he had not, a tired expression starting to live upon her face on a busy day to make Gaston worry. But they had a good ten years still to try and he would not press the matter. His great arms swung about her as he purred and growled at her shoulder. His soft warm lips grazed her tender flesh to make her giggle as she brought a washcloth to her body. Gaston grinned, taking the cloth from her hands and stroking it about her shoulders and her neck as she sighed lovingly. He rubbed her back as she leant forward and he did the same to kiss her back.

"I can wash myself, husband." She grinned in amusement as she grabbed another washcloth and he snatched this and then dipped it in the water to scrub at her face. She gave a sudden cackle at him for being so naughty as he growled gently by her ear and then nibbled her lobe slightly. With a grunt, Lynette grasped hold of the flannel and rolled around to lounge within his lap. He gave a sort of coy wriggle of his eyebrows as if she'd just fallen into his trap, but before he could do anything suggestive, Lynette slapped a wet flannel over his face with a snigger. "You, however, never know how to wash properly… let me help you…"

Lynette grinned wickedly before lifting the flannel to scrub at his face as he grumbled and spat at the soggy nasty taste of the damn fabric as it rubbed over his lips. She then cleaned his eyes and up to his forehead, scraping any dried in sweat aside before pulling it down to wash behind his ears. He gave her a firm scowl; he did not need to be taught how to clean himself and yet Lynette just gave a snigger as she then dropped the flannel to his shoulders and rubbed softly around them and back to his neck. This made Gaston give a different expression and he sat up, leaning forward towards his wife as she scrubbed at his big muscular form as he smiled lovingly down at her before brushing his lips to hers. She finished his back and brought her hands to his chest, rubbing in soft circles only to gasp gently as he used his cloth to do the same to her bosom, making her shudder.

"Villain…" She teased in amusement, leaning forward against him and letting their lips come together as she moaned softly as he rubbed at her nipples to make them strain outward. Then he had to drop the cloth just to gently flick his fingers against them to make her give a shriek and drop back into the water with a heavy splash. One of her feet bounced off his shoulder as she shook her finger and insisted that such things were not to be considered within the bathtub and Gaston just snatched her foot to kiss the damp sole.

"I'm not going to let this beautiful skin prune... come on darling... lets enjoy our honeymoon!" He growled softly and pulled himself up out of the bath as she giggled in amusement. She watched him almost slip on the puddles on the floor before he had the towels about him. He shook his rippling muscles like a drying dog as he gave a soft bark to amuse her. Lynette just ducked deeper into the water as she chuckled at him stomp back into the bedroom.

She was waiting for him to charge back in and yank her out and up into his big arms. But when nothing happened, she remained cautious although sceptical as she slowly clambered out of the bath. She then went to the towel rack near the door and it popped open. With a squeak a big towel snatched about her middle and Gaston hoisted her up under one arm as she gave a yelp and kicked about as she giggled.

He sat on the bed, swinging her into his lap and then crashing his lips to hers. They kissed with low growls before sighing softly as he rocked her little naked body in his arms as he stroked her cheeks. Their time together might normally be a serenade of heat and bodies ravaging one another with an unquenchable thirst, but now the passion was tamed by love and relief. His nose brushed against hers and she knew the words resting on his tongue that made her soul shiver to guess and to read as he moaned against her, lips grazing her wet shoulder as she groaned.

"I'm so in love with you Lynette... my heart couldn't beat if it weren't able to time to yours. Without you there would only be rage... you tame me, little guardian... Ange..." He moaned each word as his lips devoured the droplets upon her neck and Lynette shivered. She could feel the skin sink down around the pulsing jugular... or had it just been lured up to his now bristled tongue that burnt the skin but made her all the wetter. "You're mine... I'm yours and now... now you'll bear my mark upon your neck for all to see..."

"Whereas the other scar is known only to your eyes..." She shuddered in excitement, letting him turn her to sit on his lap. He grasped her legs, spreading them and pulling them back to try and wrap about him. Her back arched naturally against him, her arms swinging back to hold his neck and moan softly as his tongue still strafed her flesh. Then she shuddered, his thick hot shaft leaning menacingly against her quaking entrance. He pulled her legs apart more, making her give a soft whimper as she felt his manhood probe into position as she quivered against him. With a low moan she relaxed her body down, swallowing his form, feeling it pull her wide yet satisfy her utterly with its heat. "Will you be gentle?"

He didn't answer, her nostrils burnt for the sudden expulsion of pheromones that drowned all senses but pleasure. It heated her blood and soon she was moaning softly as his form stroked and dipped into her, pumping in and out as she gave a low sigh of utter pleasure. She leant back against him, gasping swiftly as his pheromones soaked her body in joy, her blood was burning, her body already starting to sweat as she groaned and felt him stoking the fire even more. Lynette was moaning softly, giving a gentle gasp of pleasure as she felt his hands suddenly upon her breasts, her nipples straining out to his touch as her body rocked and rode him with ease. She was gasping, sighing in a higher pitch, she felt drunk and dizzy, utterly overcome by the hypnotic suggestions within the scent, screaming at her that this was perfect.

She almost felt like she was falling away into some strange dream, that none of this was really happening as she felt a question whispered into her mind by his voice and yet he continued to stroke her neck with his tongue. It was a strange question, she was not quite sure she'd heard it right, but when asked her only answer to him could ever be yes. As Gaston chuckled in amusement to sense it, he opened his mouth so wide his jaw stretched down like a snake's and seemed to almost wrap about her whole neck with seeming ease. Then his great canines shifted, they seemed to pull back as the great needle-thin fang beneath slid down to suddenly curl into her flesh. The pressure and warmth of his mouth over her neck made the vein lift up to make it more suitable as the fang suddenly slid with ease into her shoulder, only to produce a strange violet coloured liquid to make her moan. It seemed to burn into a bruise like form within her flesh, marking her forever as his mate and would never be expunged!

Gaston felt her blood bubble up into the hollow form of his fang, spilling into his swelling gums and then his desperate vessels sucked the blood right down into the rest of his body. It sent prickles of excitement into his body, his thrusting became more intense, he moaned into her neck as his eyes rolled back and he felt her strange blood hitting every sense of pleasure within his being. As she was moaning and gasping, trapped in an eternal orgasm that would not depart until he withdrew his fangs, Gaston gripped her body tightly to him. He whispered softly with his mind to her, asking her if they could indeed try for children, but Lynette's mind was lost in the joy and the question did not pass through, though he continued to pump into her until he pulled his mouth away, lapping the wound to seal it as she continued to moan and then Gaston reached his end with a soft groan of pleasure.

Her sweaty body fainted against him, her hips shivering and jolting against his body as he felt his body trembling against hers. The blood was clearing away all pain and agony within his body, soothing away any sense of hunger, thirst, and exhaustion. He felt more alive than he had ever felt before and it scared him that his fangs did not want to pull back and he gave a groan of pleasure as he lifted her within his arms, easing her from him as he carried her into the bed. He settled her into it, feeling her moan softly in pleasure as his lips then came to hers, grasping and massaging at them as her eyes flickered open softly and then her arms swung around his shoulders. He gave a gasp of surprise as she moaned up at him with a chuckle of amusement….

"You couldn't do that again… could you?"

Lynette was sighing lovingly as she lounged over Gaston's back, her fingers teasing and stroking gently through the thick coils of black hair that sat neatly across the top of his back and arms. She sighed lovingly, kissing him on the back of the neck sweetly after peeling the hair aside, before rubbing her nose into his dark hair and producing a soft sigh of love as she gripped about his body tenderly. She gave a giggle as he rolled about with a groan, clearly exhausted within the soft sheets as they heard the door knock gently. Lynette stood up and then stuck the duvet about herself, stealing it from the bed as Gaston gave a groan and flopped his head back into the pillow, his back littered in bruises and scratches and nibble marks from their marathon of love. Lynette opened the door with a giggle to the servant, only to have the figure leap back in shock.

"Don't worry, I'm covered…" She teased, but she could see that the eyes were not being averted from her body but rather they were locked upon the mark on her neck. There was such disgust and shock to see it, a marital mark to say that she was in the position of any vampire's wife, maybe even more! She realised this with a grimace of anxiety, then she stepped back and beckoned him to bring the food into the room as Gaston turned his head and also beckoned. The figure did, but then promptly left, a disgusted look upon his face before Lynette closed the door and then turned to look towards Gaston with a grimace. "I don't think he liked realising we were married."

"Don't take it to heart my love… come and eat…" Gaston growled softly, watching her step back over to him and then they settled for their breakfast. The pair cuddled and kissed as they did so, Gaston sighing lovingly as he nuzzled her and then, when they had finished, he got up and insisted she should take a wash. Lynette mused she would go for a walk on her own after her wash and he nodded his head, insisting he needed to go and talk about dinner. Lynette mused he was trying to see if they could stay in bed for the whole holiday and Gaston stuck out his tongue. "Maybe…"

When Lynette washed and dressed neatly, she strolled down the stairs and then, when she passed a maid, there was a quick whisper of 'Lap Dog', which made her pause for a minute. She sniffed gently, the maid was not a vampire but a ghoul, typical vampire staff and it made Lynette curl her lips in frustration. However, she continued down the stairs with a soft sigh upon her face before she strolled out to the main hall where a few other beings were wandering around. They looked at her for a second, before whispering something about her being filthy… that no one would want to kiss a werewolf's mouth! It made Lynette grimace but she stepped to the door, looking to the figure in the cloakroom expectantly to get her coat. The figure though, ignored her and she grimaced in frustration as she was ignored again until she decided to be obnoxious and turned into her wolf form.

She scratched at the door until the figure, terrified that she'd cause damage, hurried to go and open up the door. Once he opened it, she was out for a gallop around the grounds with a grin upon her face. She couldn't believe the way these beings were acting about it, so what if she was married to a vampire? She then grit her teeth in irritation, the marriage of interspecies in the Veil had never been illegal unless it was with a full demon, why were they thinking it was so bad? But as she galloped about in the woods, clarity came to her… werewolves were the lowest of the low in the Veil-Born and vampires were the top. They were treating it like she'd married way out of her league and well, she had, but love meant it should never matter, Thibaut had allowed it!

Inside the building, Gaston had been beaming with the chef and the serving staff, all of them pleased he had enjoyed breakfast and to get their lunch and dinner taken to the room, he noticed something odd. He was looking at the other guests that were whispering with the butler, utterly shocked to hear that a werewolf was wearing the Master's Mark, the sign of a vampire's wife. They were all being posh snobs about it, scoffing that she was probably married to a Turned, the only way it could happen. After-all, there had never been a werewolf and a vampire child ever born and it was deemed incredibly unlikely. But when Gaston sensed them pointing to him, and everyone knew the handsome second son of Theo Viper, Gaston grimaced to hear them gasping.

He ignored it though, focusing on talking to the Turned chefs that were far more eager to help him out. But as soon as he heard the whispers about Gaston being a fur-licker he had to pause. He had never been deemed as such ever, never when everyone knew he was with Lynette and that even when he had made a point to flirt with other species before, no one had ever called him something so derogatory. It made his lips curl and his fangs show, but he sucked it in deeply and then gently waved that he would see them later before going to the gym. He settled with boxing in the gym, hurrying to punch the bag and imagining it was these people irritating him, but also he considered how he acted around the werewolves and he scoffed at the assumptions of the people, especially when he had practically grown up amongst the werewolves and if it weren't for their ferocity and strength, he might have killed someone with the rage built up after his father's death.

With a groan after a few hours punching and ignoring the universe as a whole, the sweating, glistening figure decided to go to the room, showing off a glistening chest just to make everyone look and gasp at the sight of his body. He hoped they'd be jealous and maybe give a little more thought to the fact he was not someone that should be insulted, but his ears caught the sound of paws scrabbling at the glass doors near the dining room. He spotted the pretty red and white wolf, looking more like a husky than a wolf, spinning about and looking adorable for her master's attention and he grinned. He strolled over to the door, easing it open without care to the other guests and their indignant expressions as she bounced in and then galloped up to their room, leaving muddy paw prints behind her.

"Ah… I'll pay extra on my bill for the cleaning… apologies." Gaston grinned to the maid that was nearby, staring horrified down towards the muddy paw prints. Gaston did not care though, he could hear them insisting that it was disgusting, a mutt running around a fine establishment, but Gaston knew they were speaking rubbish. He strolled up the stairs, finding paw prints all over the building and he grimaced before stepping to the room and grabbing the sign for 'do not disturb' on the handle. They might be getting kicked out of the hotel tomorrow, he could already sense it coming but he was still going to enjoy today as he looked to the familiar outline of his wife hiding amongst the bedsheets, a big fluffy tail wiggling around as he sniggered. "I think you made your point… bit unfair to your fellow maids, but whatever, this place is getting too rude for us to enjoy ourselves much longer anyway."

"When we get back, I want Thibaut to then send Mhulder here to collect the rest of the pre-paid holiday money and give them the fright of their life. I can just see your brother losing his head over this… its funny, I don't think he's ever looked down at a werewolf before…" Lynette giggled from amongst the sheets as Gaston slowly advanced, he looked ready to pounce and have a bit more fun. However, the sudden shriek in the hallway from the madam alerted him to trouble as the door was suddenly pounded upon. He shook his head, she could bash it as much as she liked, he was going to have the noisiest, messiest time with Lynette right now and really make the old crone pale over what her establishment was being turned into and Lynette peered out from under the covers with her wolfish grin. "I bet Thibaut's going to inform people how good it was to cater for werewolves and really drop her reputation…"

"Oh… I pray he will!"

"Mhulder brought back a square of carpet where the wolf prints had really stuck in. Made sure to cut it from the very middle of the floor in front of all the still astonished guests and then, when she was squealing about it, he said if the cleaning 'could not be achieved' he'd just cut out every wolf print from the building. She relented into giving the money back and I gave her a phone call this morning, expressing my dismay and wrote a little to her local Noble to inform them of my disappointment. I hope it should get the message across…" Thibaut sighed in frustration, gently passing over the piece of neat red carpet to his brother with a smirk and a letter of apology pinned to it from the terrified staff of that place. The fact the cow had gone and had the bed in the room thrown on a bonfire upon their departure had been an insult too far and well, even if it had only been just a long weekend away, Gaston and Lynette were utterly bemused and happy to stick around the mansion as everyone was cheering up. "I'm sorry… I thought it was a place you both could have enjoyed… maybe I should send you to Sardinia with Beauregard…"

"Lynette and I don't need a holiday, just to be loved and respected for our choice by our family… that's all we want. But uh… I wanted to ask if you found out from the blood test if… if it was possible…." Gaston had been glad to come home but one thing had being weighing heavily on his mind and it had been before the wedding. He'd sent the requested blood and semen samples to a demon that could perform tests that were apparently almost a century advanced on current medicine and he'd sent some of Lynette's fur as a sample too. Apparently, the test would reveal if they were compatible to reproduce together and of course, Gaston was hopeful that maybe they could just have some luck.

"I'm surprised you're asking… I think… I think considering what we knew of father's tenacity, it would have happened by now if it was meant to happen. You've been with her so long and you never once wore a sheath… despite my nagging and don't lie, you have still got all the original ones I had to get surreptitiously for you… unused under your bed." Thibaut stated, and even

Gaston could understand the words that were to come next and yet Thibaut's face softened. His brother straightened up and then shuffled to his brother with open arms, gripping him so tightly and lovingly that Gaston nuzzled against Thibaut's shoulder and he sighed. "The tests came back... of your health there is no concern... but Lynette's body has no compatibility to it. I do not know if it is from the werewolf curse or the dragon blood within us still... but I'm afraid it is not possible. But... but if you wished to adopt a child, you may, I would welcome any child you and Lynette chose to care for!"

Gaston hooked his arms about Thibaut even more tightly, noting the slight sob in his brother's voice because he knew very well that Thibaut had hoped that Gaston and Lynette would have a child to make the household happy. But Gaston sighed, stroking his older brother's blonde hair gently as he considered the matter and the conversation he'd had before with Lynette. It was nice to know that Thibaut would agree to any adoption they felt was necessary, but Lynette did not want children, did she? Gaston pulled from the embrace and then he looked to Thibaut cautiously, if only because his next words might break his older brother if Thibaut dared to truly understand it.

"Will you send your little attorney-emissary whatever he's called to visit me soon, brother. Considering I have married, I shall need to adjust my will to ensure things are properly sorted, don't you agree?" Gaston stated calmly and Thibaut stared at him cautiously for a moment before nodding his head and simply writing a note for himself to contact the fellow. Gaston then stood up and insisted he must go to his wife, but then he paused as he reached the door and turned about with a beaming grin of delight. "So... wedding set for the 28th of January in four years?!?! Honestly brother... Jacinthe is a ridiculously patient woman!"

"Indeed... but with Noel to marry in February and Selene and Elaine to depart that spring... there is much to deal with. Not to mention Beauregard and Odette need some care, as does Theodora. It also means Phillippe can arrange the two twits to appropriate nitwits for the pair to marry before us... then the sisters can claim something else before their sister. After-all, Michelle would be due sooner than married if Phillippe doesn't work fast enough." Thibaut stated calmly, no emotion falling across his face and Gaston stared at him for a moment in utter amusement before giving a soft chuckle before departing the room as Thibaut gave a soft sigh. However, his eyes flicked towards the note and then the piece of paper regarding Lynette's health... she was not immortal like the vampires and she was already nearing her fifties and the health charts were not fantastic in their review and their understanding of werewolves. But then again, only the luckiest of humans lived past sixty in this day and age.

Gaston strolled out down the hall with a soft chuckle of amusement as he padded towards the section of the house that was given up to them until the cottage was ready. Gaston was aware that Lynette had gone shopping with all the women of the household for clothes of the latest fashion and other such things and it amused him. Even Sorina had been added to their group and Jacinthe of course, it made him exceptionally amused to think that the house was finally starting to grow and then he found himself staring at the neat portrait of their father in the library, squatting above the chair he had favoured that even Thibaut tried not to sit in. Gaston paced to the image and then sat on the ground staring up at him, knowing that his father was alive in hell, trapped but not really gone and probably struggling to get out and it made Gaston's heart burn.

"Father… I feared telling you for so long that I was in love with a werewolf, I recalled how your mother had been murdered by one before your eyes, that though you were kind to all I feared it would disgust you should I let one step into our family. But mother told me about your thoughts before, that it would not matter as long as we were in love and happy and then I thought of Dio and Valentino. Heh… you went to hell so that my brother could love another man, you'd have done the same if that were the cost for me to marry a werewolf." Gaston smiled softly as he looked to the proud image, to anyone that did not know him they would have assumed that Theo Viper had been a very proud and powerful being, always he was referred to as a being of great cunning and manipulation who took out the heir of the Pipistrello for the sake of his own family's growth… with Vittorio it might have been true, but it was not the image to Gaston. Instead, he recalled that painting had been done when the boys had been showing off that they could look just as proud and stay still just as long as their father, that expression was softer, the eyes glowing with warmth because he had looked upon his boys and known in that moment as he did every moment he had taken the time to observe it… he loved them all so much! "Father… Lynette is mortal and when she departs this world… I will follow. My vow at our wedding was 'till death do us part' but like you my heart is so loyal to her that death will not be able to do such a thing and my soul will follow hers. It is my choice… it is a harsh decision, but it is as it must be and it might be sooner than I'd assumed."

"No…" Gaston jolted at the soft male voice that reached his ears, broken with tears and he turned about in shock as he realised that Thibaut was standing behind him. Tears were streaming down his brother's face and Gaston turned about upon the carpet, only to suddenly feel his brother collapse onto him, sobbing heavily and holding him tightly as Gaston grit his teeth tightly. He held his brother to him and sighed, he had not wanted anyone but the attorney and their father to know that even he assumed it was soon, but Thibaut always had that habit of being in the wrong place at the wrong time for Gaston. He grimaced as he held his elder brother to him, rocking him softly and Gaston groaned.

"Tibbs… you know what rage overwhelmed me every time I was unable to be beside her and you know that if she were to perish, I would be nothing but fury and despair. I cannot be as strong as our mother and hold out for the hope of meeting that soul again… you knew how much we were connected, or you would never have kept our secret, let us be together without daring to judge. You did not even judge when you knew I was leading her to the barn to take her innocence, you even helped us several times and I knew you stood nearby ready to throw me off should I have forced it from her. You have always protected me and Lynette and shown us both great love, more than you ever showed the others once you joined academy… you know this is what must happen, when it happens... starvation will take too long." Gaston whispered softly into his brother's ears and the sad fact was that Thibaut understood it so completely and he hated it too, what would he be without them? The thought that instead of accepting the steady death from not drinking blood, Gaston was going to do something far worse, made Thibaut want to scream. But Thibaut pulled back giving Gaston a soft kiss to the forehead before then pulling himself up awkwardly before wiping his face and growling that there was always too much dust on the carpets in that room and Gaston watched him walk off with a soft grimace of frustration. "Thank you for understanding… you always do."

Lynette rushed into the bedroom with three hatboxes hanging from her arm and three dresses flapping about madly with their thin paper covering as she galloped to the wardrobe and pulled it open. She then turned around with a smile upon her face to see that Gaston was busy lifting weights gently on a chair looking to the mirror, fascinated by the bulging vein in his muscles whenever he pulled the weight up. Lynette chuckled in amusement at the sight of it before gently going out of the room and grabbing the collection of other clothes and boxes before then pulling out a sweet little violet crème from a patisserie box before bringing it to Gaston as he opened his mouth and she pushed it in, sticking out her tongue!

"Mon Beau... you would not believe what I just saw... just as we ladies returned, Thibaut was waiting for us at the steps and when Jacinthe emerged, he was right to her side. He was actually stroking her cheek and he kissed her engagement ring three times! She was so red even milady's face went scarlet at the adorable scene. It makes me so happy... doesn't it make you happy?" Lynette beamed in delight as Gaston nodded his head firmly before he put the weights down and dealt with the sweet within his mouth. He was not as keen on the sweet things as much as his wife, but with Lynette learning that she had all the access to his funds she needed to try whatever she might not have been able to before, it was rather common for her to get two of everything just to try it with him. It was adorable, she was so used to getting something for her and her father that she couldn't help but get just a bit too carried away with her excitement. "But you know what Gaston, I was actually worried at first when he touched her. Do you recall before the way he would always just touch her hand or hair or clothes just to scold her? I feared it was the same thing here... but when he was able to show his true feelings... it made me want to cry."

"But of course it would... my brother has only been able to show such affection and such hope in love because of your friendship and the love all of our siblings have shown to our fated mates. But it was because of you Lynette, because you were unafraid to rescue him from his agony that he was able to be in love with Jacinthe. You should be very proud of yourself my love... you're a true friend to my poor old brother." Gaston smiled softly as he stood himself up and then gently swung his arms around Lynette's slim form, pulling her into him in a tight hug. She gave a soft 'wuff' sound of surprise as he hooked her right up and cradled her in his big arms, kissing her lips tenderly before then settling her upon the bed with a soft chuckle as he looked to the clothes upon the bed. "Dear Lynette... did you know it was you slapping him in the face and telling him to think of the family above his shame that pulled him from that agony... that you telling him that he could endure hell for the sake of the family was what allowed him to protect us all? I only wish your words had touched me like that to stop my time fighting... I'm ashamed as your lover that your words have not hit me so hard."

"Huh… you are a strange one my love… of course my words did not work on you like that, Thibaut reacts to the words only of those who are not blood and are unbiased… yet you would always listen when I touched you with my lips." Lynette whispered softly, leaning into her husband to gently press her lips to his as Gaston smiled lovingly, bringing them together and stroking her neck with his large fingers. They moaned softly against one another before they cuddled together on the bed and Gaston stroked her hip tenderly and lovingly. He sighed as he looked towards the collection of hats and clothes… he hoped that she would always enjoy herself this much and always be happy with him. But then Lynette gave a soft chuckle. "Your mother did an amazing thing today… we were at one of the garment shops and I stepped over to be measured and dressed, but they insisted they did not dress dogs… your mother then informed them that if there was a dog she could understand, but that I was her daughter and that was all that should matter. Then, Sorina and Jacinthe insisted that if their new sister were to be disrespected, then they would take their business and their family's to better manufacturers. Suddenly I was being apologised to and they were rather eager to help me dress. We all got our clothes for free… but then Adelia insisted she wouldn't go there again and I had to laugh… now I know where you get your stubborn manner from."

"She's not half-dragon for nothing! Heh… but dearest Lynette, I'm so glad you are my wife now no matter what others think. You are my Lynette and I will never allow anyone to treat you so poorly nor will my family. You're a Viper now and that's all that matters!" Gaston smiled tenderly as he kissed her lips as she sighed softly in delight. But as she snuggled up to him with a soft giggle, rather eager to enjoy the attention, her heart fluttered and swelled in joy as Gaston then kissed her lips again gently. "You're the first of the wives to join the family… I hope you won't be the last and all my siblings will be as happy in their romance as I."

Part Two: The Modern Couple

Tonauac's Kingdom, Sierra Gorda, Mexico, September 1926

Once again, the time scale had changed with regards to the Elders and at the end of August, the traditional boat had arrived from Tonauac's kingdom to collect all the chosen brides. It had been a shock for everyone to receive the call from the beings to turn up, but thankfully, a priest had been permitted to go along as a missionary and ensure a Catholic marriage, though the Protestant and Muslim brides chosen, were not overly keen on the thought. Elaine had no worries, Selene was confident with the journey and they sat together with Selene telling everyone what to expect in the land beyond as Yoloti and Tizoc steered the boat and insisted that everything was going to be fine and even used the word 'dandy', which he thought was a very funny word.

When the journey seemed to pass on with great speed, seemingly getting across the Atlantic in just a week, Selene was excited, but Elaine had spent the entire journey curled up on the floor feeling sick. This had made Yoloti laugh, he'd reminded her that Tonauac was the same whenever he crossed water because water marked the boundary of his greater powers. He'd teased it meant they suited each other, but Elaine had not been as grateful for the knowledge, though Selene had mused if Elders had started the rumour that vampires could not cross running water. Elaine failed to comment, but when they reached the familiar water and Yoloti led them to the tiny hidden stream, the plants and landscape opening up to let the boat reach the hidden kingdom of moss and vine covered stones, Elaine was far more settled.

The women were all in awe of the place, seeing its true beauty in the way Selene had too, smelling exotic flowers, wild sounds, beautiful animals and the strange ancient beauty of the jungle kingdom. They were met by Xiuhcoatl standing by the stream as the jungle returned to normal and the massive boat was sitting calmly in the middle of a grassy plain, making the women gasp in shock. Selene though did not care for rules or etiquette, as Yoloti sniggered for her eagerness, even Elaine was smiling to herself as Selene leapt out of the boat and then rushed up to Xiuhcoatl. His arms were out, he caught her in a hug, swung her around in delight and was then nuzzling against her happily as Yoloti gave a sigh and then hopped out of the boat too.

"Alright ladies… if you would all care to follow me into the main part of the temple, I will let you all settle in and have a good rest. Oh, Selene… do you mind taking Elaine to the moon lake, she has to have a cleansing bath because of the, well… 'disruptions'…" Yoloti was trying not to laugh for the fact that Elaine still looked like she was going to vomit again, but Selene straightened up to agree before she turned towards her sister with a happy smile. Elaine thanked Yoloti as he then beckoned the women to follow and Xiuhcoatl also stepped forward to help lead everyone out of the boat and on to the deep passages below. Selene grabbed her sister's hand and began to drag her off towards the forest, only pausing behind Xiuh to pat his backside beneath his skirt as he gave a soft grunt. Selene then giggled as she dragged her sister off and on towards the pool.

They marched through the jungle at a steady pace, Selene beaming and waving her hands to some of the animals that appeared to watch her. Elaine watched sister in confusion, her eyes were also trying to drink in the entire nature of this world of trees, green, brilliant colour, flowers and a scent of mildew and rain ever heavy in the air. She was shocked to see so many things that she'd never even imagined could exist before Selene paused for a second and gave a squeak of greeting as Elaine turned and drew her talons, ready to fight as a large spotted cat stepped forward.

"This is one of Tonauac's friends, Elaine. He's the top jaguar around, he likes to guard the Moon Pool from non-Elders so he just wanted to check us. Yoloti said he'd let the animals know about us, maybe you want to say hello?" Selene beamed sweetly as the big cat stood beside her, staring with its massive head towards Elaine and then back to Selene. It almost seemed to be double-checking with Selene that her sister was alright and Elaine straightened up, letting her claws relax. Elaine preferred cats, they had a much more sensible lifestyle and she held out her hand whilst looking towards the jaguar in her naturally domineering fashion.

The jaguar seemed to pant for a moment in concern before Selene patted his shoulder and the spotted cat pressed his massive jaw against her hand, snuffling curiously as Elaine's fingers curled around its head. The fur was so soft, a yellow gold like clear honey with glorious rosettes that seemed to mimic the shape of flowers. Elaine knelt and gently she stroked the shoulders of the big animal as it sat and lifted its head, she rubbed its cheeks and under its chin, taking on its precious scent and in doing so, becoming accepted by the cat. She then stroked his whiskers and lay her forehead to his, listening to the sound of the cat's harsh breath and his beating heart in a manner she would any cat.

"It's an honour to meet you, I intend to protect Tonauac and your peoples here too... do not concern yourself with my anxiety, I am afraid of nothing." With that, Elaine straightened up, her composure returning as Selene beamed at her before she stepped along after Selene towards the lake. The cat strolled off calmly without a second look and she was thankful that Selene was standing there patiently to help her out. Selene stretched her hand out to hold Elaine's as she led her on through the trees and past the calls of the various canopy animals until she felt them climbing a hill and then Selene stopped. She had stopped by a large stone that had moss on its top and curious looking etchings onto its surface, Selene stroked it and then beckoned her sister to do the same, only to watch the forms flash as Elaine eyed her sister up. "Why this?"

"Oh... it lit up? It never did that before... but I'm sure it's just the earth recognising you... or that you've touched something connected to Tonauac. It's quite likely your future hubby is currently one with the universe as he prepares for tonight." Selene stated with a grin of amusement towards her sister and Elaine just gave her a cautious expression, Selene was startled she hadn't blushed though. But then Selene gave a sigh, Elaine was not a romantic person, she really could not understand what everyone else in the household even understood and she shook her head. Elaine watched her continue on as she stared towards the rock, then she gave a soft grunt.

"Tonauac and I understand each other... he is romantic and affectionate and I am not. He knows I tolerate him and I feel an interest in physical contact with him... but love is difficult. I value him and I suppose I love him like family but... I don't believe or feel like there is a difference. He's as good as family so that's all there is." Elaine stated firmly as she looked towards her sister and Selene gave a curious expression and then gave a soft shake of her shoulders. She was not going to have this conversation again, she and Tonauac understood each other and well, at least it would ensure that their children would be the most well-loved children in the world. Elaine could tell it bothered her sister a little and she stepped over and grabbed Selene's hand again with a sigh. "Selene... just understand that Tonauac and I understood when we were with each other that we felt there was never anyone that could replace the position of family within our hearts but someone that was close to family. It was only surprising for both of us when I realised I wanted to kiss him and have physical contact with him when I'd been bored with others… and he wanted to cherish me."

"I'm not complaining… it's just luckier that you both found each other because, I love Tonauac like family too and yet… I know he suits you. Now come along, come and see the Moon Pool!" Selene beamed, squeezing her sister's hand as Elaine rolled her eyes over the sentimental statements and was then pulled in through the various tall trees. They passed a few more stone monoliths that hinted to the connection with the rest of the temples as Selene finally brought her sister through the foliage, they came across a massive pool with water so blue it was almost ominous. "Meet the Moon Pool, now strip down and let's hop in and scrub! We need to soak our bodies, Yoloti said it's the purifying ritual for the marriage ceremony."

"Ah… but Selene… are you going to be married?" Elaine asked suddenly, only to smother her mouth, realising her natural catty attitude she kept for her brothers was unfair to Selene. Her sister turned about to look at her and then, stripped off her clothes and revealed something that made Elaine give a gasp of disbelief. But as she looked at the golden loop hanging from her sister's nipple, she suddenly gave a grin and then started to chuckle as Selene slipped straight into the water. She sat herself right down into its deep mineral form, letting what would be poisonous to humans fill her pores and ease away the toxins upon her flesh. Elaine clapped her hands in thought as she peeled her own clothes off and then leapt into the water, making Selene give a yelp as Elaine almost leapt out of the water, trembling in the darkness but suddenly beaming. "My God… I've always wanted to bathe naked out in the wild… this is my home now, no one's allowed to tell me I have to wear anything in this universe! How about we convince them to ceremonial burn our corsets to banish those undergarments and liberate ourselves!"

"Hmm… I think you've spent too much time reading books about the French Revolution! I'm quite sure I need my corset… but the clothes they'll give you here… you know, Yoloti said traditionally women never had to wear anything and clothing was only for status and warriors… women and kids could do what they like… eyes shouldn't be wandering." Selene beamed and Elaine gave a soft chuckle of amusement, not sure if Selene was buttering her up or telling the truth. She mused at being in a place where her naked body had no value and she pondered her time here in amusement as she waded over to her sister with a chuckle. Selene giggled, she was quite aware that her sister was going to have some fun here and hopefully she would be happy here too. "I know he'll make you happy, I just hope you don't try to make things... odd here."

"Odd?" Elaine teased, swinging her arm about and splashing water into her sister's face as Selene gave a squeak of delight. The pair continued to slap their hands about in the water, coating each other in the liquid, diving down and swimming about to try and tag the other. Elaine was quite aware that she felt more energetic, happier and surprisingly healthier too after being ill on the way down here. She raced about in the water after her sister, but it was clear that Selene was quick to slip away from her and she was grinning as she sat back up until they heard the sound of heavy feet moving towards them and Elaine stood up with a sneer. "Who dares to..."

"My eyes are bound, I've merely brought up some food, fresh water and a change of clothes... are you enjoying the pool?" Xiuhcoatl had emerged from the jungle with such calm that it had only been the loud footfalls made on purpose to have alerted them to a presence. Elaine looked at him cautiously for a moment, checking that he was indeed covering his eyes before she sat back down into the water thoughtfully. Then suddenly, Selene launched out of the water and rushed over to Xiuh, grabbing the items, setting them down and then hugging him tightly. He was blushing even without seeing she was naked and Elaine had to give a soft snort; she really was startled about how sensitive such a hulking warrior could be and it told her how different this place was. "Lord Tonauac will see you when the sun rises on the top of the ruins, so when you are washed and ready, I will guide you there. Traditionally, Lady Viper, you will be expected to sit in front of the monument of Tonauac's mother and ask her blessing."

"Monument?" Elaine questioned cautiously but then she paused and gently stroked at her chin. She realised that she'd been told that when an Elder died, they turned into a stone monolith telling its story within its carvings. She was curious to know what story Tonauac's mother would tell of his life, but she had a feeling that it was likely to be something exceptionally sad. She thanked Xiuh quickly for the matter and he bowed his head, before turning to leave until he realised Selene was still attached in a hug. He bent and gently nuzzled his nose to Selene's as she giggled and Elaine watched them with her stomach twisting in disgust. She really could not understand that kind of thing, it was like watching dogs nuzzle, it didn't seem natural to her. "If you'd go wait nearby, we'll call you when we're ready."

"Alright… love you Xiuh… I'm going to bring the food over to Elaine… wow, your hair is glittering!" Selene beamed as Xiuh departed and she settled herself down on the ground beside the pool, still naked with her silver hair soaking in the moonlight and shining. Seeing that and hearing her compliment made Elaine snort, sometimes she wondered if her little sister even realised how beautiful she was herself. But Elaine looked to her pale blonde hair, only to realise it was glittering and more golden than ever before. Her eyes widened in surprise as she looked towards Selene and then gave a soft chuckle that it did. Selene beamed and beckoned her over to the side and Elaine followed.

The pair settled with the food, grains made into flat breads and some local vegetation including some rather bizarre looking corn that was very pleasant, but Selene informed her it had outgrowing roots covered in slime. Elaine had to look at her cautiously for a while, hoping her sister would realise not to say such things when they were eating but Selene lifted her head to look at her sister blankly. Sometimes, mainly because their mother did not feed on blood or flesh and their father ensured the girls did not have to witness the actual butchering of prey, she forgot that things were not that easy out here and Elaine then looked about her with a soft grunt as she asked where she'd get her blood from here, but Selene beamed.

"You don't need to worry… you will have Tonauac's blood to drink. That's how it works, the Elders give energy back into the world that they drink in from the air, they purify things and when you mate with them, their blood is all you'll ever need. It also apparently means you get an instant sharing of their feelings… though you don't have to bite each other as sometimes just joining flesh can…" Selene began, talking so matter-of-factly before she froze for a moment and then blushed heavily as Elaine curled an eyebrow and gave a look that was more like Thibaut! Selene forgot that Elaine had known about the attempt to have intimacy with Xiuhcoatl, but she had not known that the pair had actually achieved it much later on and Selene just gave a soft mumble under her breath. "That's what Yoloti says…"

"Yoloti is a surprisingly open person, he has no fear of answering questions and he does not dumb things down and I'm intrigued by the attitude they have to women here. Then again, that's what made Tonauac so curious to me." Elaine stated, dipping her feet back into the pool with a soft chuckle as Selene beamed at her and nodded her head. She insisted firmly that the only difference in equality within this universe was the position of the husband, but that women widowed inherited their husband's position and right to speak but women were not to fight unless the children were at risk. Elaine chuckled at her sister, gently stroking her sister's silvery hair before kissing her cheek softly and then heaving a soft sigh. "I'm glad you found these people; they are curious and they are what I had hoped to find. I know though that I will have to bring some kind of modernity to this place, encourage them to have more links to the rest of the Veil for their own protection... because we cannot trust humans or some of the elitist Veil-Landers not to see all this beauty as potential construction sites or tombs to plunder."

"I think that's one of the reasons Tonauac chose you Elaine, he knew you would get things done and help guide him in an area where he really knew nothing. He also knew you were responsible, caring even if you like to be a little stoic and grumpy, but he knows you look after everyone weaker than you and that's incredibly important!" Selene stated and Elaine smiled sweetly to her sister, knowing very well that Selene knew Elaine did not understand the romantic ideals of other people. Elaine was quite blind to romance, but respect, physical attraction and the desire to be around someone more she understood very well and Selene just nuzzled against her sister's shoulder gently. "He also loves you because the moment he met you, he told me he realised that you were the one for him because you were not shocked by their arrival."

"Heh... what a curious thought, but you know... though father would roll in his sleep to hear me say it... I never understood love that was not familial... I could not love 'friends' but Tonauac is curious for slinking into that position within my mind. Xiuhcoatl is the same, but only because I see him and you as little siblings, Valentino too... he's curiously close because I see that Theodosius is so in love with him that there is nothing but happiness there. Seeing Dio so happy and you smile again, they're close to the only things I can look at and say 'they must be in love'. Does that make sense to you?" Elaine questioned gently and Selene gave a curious expression but she gave a soft chuckle, Elaine had been the child that had always wanted to be a little boy because then the other little boys would stop asking her to marry them! It was just how Elaine was and trying to put it into words was almost confusing but Selene just knew Elaine was Elaine and then her sister gave a sigh. "You know... it was how he reacted around Vittorio that changed everything... I could see that he was almost, part of my family already... the way he was beside him and even willing to fight to keep the baby as our baby... I never cared about children before, but I seriously want to have Tonauac's child!"

"Vittorio is a treasure... that face, those squishy cheeks and that giggle... I mean, you look at him and he's a Viper but he's also like Valentino. You really did something wonderful for Dio you know and I'm glad doing that helped you want something of your own." Selene beamed in amusement and then Elaine gave a soft scoff before she stretched her hand forward to poke Selene in the forehead before she asked about Tonauac's mother again and Selene gave a shrug. "Might as well go and sit in front of her pillar then. Did you know that apparently, this is the only way that most people even know that that Elders have even been there before? Yoloti said that there used to be a network of tunnels under the Veil where the Elders from all parts were able to come together and meet and mingle, hence they have knowledge of all languages. But then the Mastemma found that Lucifer had been using the tunnels to get demons into the Veil and Beyond it so they sealed them up and the Elders lost their connections, but there are maps in each underground catacomb under the temples to show the tunnels to the world and the other colonies."

"You learnt a lot whilst you were here with them, didn't you? I'd always just assumed that you'd spent your time here drawing Xiuhcoatl or making Tizoc smile." Elaine chuckled as she grabbed the cloths to help dry herself and her sister before they both re-dressed and then stepped away from the lake. Selene then shuffled down the path and then took a turn to the left where there was a ridge and Xiuh's great form was sitting there expectantly. Elaine snorted as Selene leapt onto Xiuh's back and he gave a soft grunt before grinning at her as she kissed his ear and nuzzled against him. Then the figure stood up straight like a mountain, letting Selene hang from his shoulders before he stepped to Elaine, bowed and then calmly hooked her to sit on his elbow and arm. She grasped Selene's arm for some kind of stability and then she was gripping more tightly as Xiuh began a slow march up across moss and vines covered rocks that merged around his feet to give him stability.

He carried them out towards the higher steps of the great pyramid that was almost engulfed by the jungle and looked almost lost amongst the stone and the trees that were almost hanging off the ridge and growing onto the pyramid. Here, Xiuhcoatl stepped onto the great strong limb of the thickest tree and then steadily clambered onto the hard stone of the pyramid. Here he froze and the let both girls down before he stepped further down the great steps to where a curious tree, reminding them of a magnolia grew, then settled down. He leant against the tree and breathed a gentle sigh of affection before seemingly joining with the bark and falling asleep. Elaine stared in fascination but Selene pointed to the larger tablet of stone in front of them with unique pictographs upon it and Selene beamed.

"This is for you… read it, guess what it says, touch it, talk to it… think of it like the mask in mother's bedroom… female knowledge only passes properly to females doesn't it?" Selene beamed, grinning in that manner that said she was quoting Elaine. Her elder sister looked up at her fiercely for a moment before she watched Selene skip over to Xiuh and then sit beside him, leaning against his shoulder and the tree and seemingly falling asleep. The sight of them was so charmingly sweet that it almost made Elaine feel sick, but she knew it was right for them. With a sigh she turned to the monolith before her but grimaced at the initial sight of pictures that were almost gruesome of something like a baby being pulled from someone's body and held up by the ankle to the sun! There was the image of something like a snake or maybe even some kind of jaguar opening its mouth for a figure that wore some kind of skirt made of what looked like arms in its mouth and being wrestled. She really could not understand until she looked at the centre image where it clearly showed the figure in seeming repose as if it had been asleep, although it did not wear any clothes and was more like just an attempt at drawing a naked woman.

"Hmm… I guess this is about Tonauac's mother and this is where it starts, the basic that it's a woman but then…" Beside it was something that was rounded with spikes but slightly swirling, the sun perhaps? Was she bathing in the sunlight perhaps? Elaine scrunched her lips together as she looked at it before slapping her face, Tonauac had said his mother was Tonalli, which meant 'warmth of the sun' and the Elders liked to draw the meaning of the name to identify the individual. It startled Elaine that the centre image might actually be as easy to read as a travel document, name and gender, simply put in a picture and then she worked her way out from that. Elaine thumbed at her chin as she read it over, Tonalli it seemed had been a busy girl growing up who was surrounded by what looked like weaving equipment, obviously clothes were her thing and she started being shown in the skirt only when she was put beside someone else. This being was masculine with the jaguar headed thing beside him, then she looked at the image of Tonalli 'wrestling' it before it seemed to go onto this scene with the child being yanked out. "Did she fight Tonauac's father?"

Elaine could not help but smirk, it seemed Tonauac was truthful when he said he'd grown up around very brave women, but she felt cautious too as she looked at the images that must have announced her death. It seemed her body covered the form of her son as arrows were shot into her and then she seemed to put the body into a hole and that was it. Elaine stood up, automatically dusting at the growths and vines around the bottom of the stone and she was startled that her fingers found something hard, sharp and clearly shaped into an arrowhead. She pulled it up, a black stone so smooth and sharp it shone as it sat in her hand and she grit her teeth… someone had tried to kill her son and she'd taken every arrow to protect him, despite the fact they'd been made of obsidian, the Elder weakness. Elaine then put the stone down and stretched her hand further back, suddenly finding a narrow chute half-hidden in a grown patch of fern that fell deep down into the pyramid but was so small only a very little child, no older than five perhaps, could have gone down there.

Elaine heaved a sigh of frustration, as she considered how young he'd been to lose his mother, for perhaps the first time since it had happened Elaine considered how she'd lost her father. He'd gone to save her own twin brother, he'd been just as brave and willing to sacrifice himself and even Valentino had been willing to be killed by Tonauac if needed for Vittorio to have been born and passed to Theodosius. She thought about her mother as well and those images she'd seen, how Adelia had been pushed aside with her father for their sake. It was strange, parental love held such power and she could understand, but then she sighed gently. She placed her hand to the centre of the monolith and then rolled her eyes before whispering softly to it.

"Help me ensure that I can love him as much as he seems to love me, that I can comprehend it fully and never disappoint him. I can see him as family, as a father to my children but… the context of a husband or even a mate… I can't see how it separates, how it has more meaning…" Elaine felt terrible now she considered what was to happen and what she might be robbing Tonauac of. There was all the possibility that he might find some other woman far more suitable to be his mate than her and she was just going to make him understand only the affection of children and a relative… not a partner. It made her grit her teeth, she'd given no kindness nor forethought to the women she'd performed sexual acts with because sex had nothing to do with love to her, she could not comprehend what her parents had experienced between them as even being possible for her.

Suddenly there was a strange sound, she sat up swiftly from where she'd been leaning against the rock to ask for advice and to her surprise it was a harpy eagle that had caught her attention. Her eyes focused on the bird and the other one next to it, larger and clearly female. They looked to have a nest nearby and they seemed to be hunting for a monkey or sloth, Elaine was startled to see them out so late and yet she considered how, when a child was hungry, the parents must feed it. Then she pondered it over, birds had no real concept of love, yet many chose to pair for life to secure the raising of young… they did what they did for the family and family she could understand. She heaved a sigh as she stroked the stone once more, this time her sigh almost drawing her to slump back, but she shook her head and then heard a soft giggle from nearby. She sat up and looked to where Selene and Xiuhcoatl were cuddled together and she recalled how Tonauac had been when Vittorio had been born and how much she wanted to give him a child.

"I suppose that's the key to it, when we go through the process together, with him beside me instead of my family and him understanding my needs, then things will be very different. We may have the bond we need because we'd have forged it for the children." Elaine stated, feeling a little more relief for the situation before she curled up on the ground in front of the stone. She would sleep here until she needed to go to Tonauac and maybe, just maybe she might inherit some more wisdom from the past. But she barely got a moment to sleep it seemed, before Xiuhcoatl was beside her, gently beckoning her up onto her feet and pointing a large finger up towards the top of the temple. She turned to him curiously for a moment, about to ask if she should go alone when he just stared forward and so she nodded her head.

Stepping up the stones as delicately as possible, trying to move fast so that she did not miss time or make a mistake, she noticed how black the world was around her, yet her eyes could see things in a kind of grayscale thanks to the starlight above. She picked her way up the stones, avoided the flowers that were closed up and came to the top of the first set of stacked stone to see another staircase, but Tonauac waiting at the top. He was wearing a black cape wrapped about his body, a crown of turquoise upon his head that she'd never seen before and the box that had held the two daggers Xiuhcoatl had protected that had led to this moment, sitting upon a flat stone between him and her.

Elaine reached his side gently, pacing carefully around the loose stones at the top that she could hear creak and chip down into an empty room below. She grimaced as she felt the wind buffer against the top of the temple, it almost felt like it would fall down with it, but for the trees and vines that seemed to be wrapped around it so protectively. She looked about, they had reached the height of the canopy and she looked out across the jungle at night to the pale lights of the humans in the distance and their growing town, to the river that cut a wide swathe through the jungle and then to the east, the high cliffs that were spewing out water from a thunderous fall. She could not see what was Veil and what was beyond it, but it was a strangely beautiful sight as Tonauac sighed softly.

"When dawn light first lifts in the east, it will skim across the edge of the Veil and you will see the extent of my empire as it once was. The river and the falls are the eastern border and to the west a deep gully that breaks the land from one cliff to the next. It's a large area that must be kept as natural as possible... the humans are permitted where I tell them..." Tonauac stated firmly, as he looked out across the landscape the air was starting to heat up and with it would come the power of the sun. Elaine nodded her head in understanding, she would see the village soon enough, learn what they did and how it related to this kingdom and she would help Tonauac as she said she would. But then Tonauac cleared his throat and opened the box, passing an obsidian dagger to her and then holding one himself over the stone. "Now, we cut our hands, hold them together and keep holding as the sun rises... if the sun burns me as we stand here, then the jungle has not accepted our relationship and we must separate."

"Huh... such a traditional view, surely we should be together because we are happy together." Elaine stated as she watched him hold the stone blade to his hand, cut it and then let it bleed quite vigorously. Fearlessly, Elaine did the same but she had no fear of being rejected and she'd never abandon him even if he wanted her to. They clapped their hands together, smiling at each other as Tonauac agreed he was happy when around her and Elaine gave a soft snort of amusement. "Good, because I intend to have all those children you read on my palm and you're going to be the father. Don't think I'm just going to run away in shame because you haven't kept up on your blood sacrifices."

"Heh... that's why you make me so happy, when I'm with you I have more confidence in my own beliefs and desires, I do not feel like I'm stuck in my father's shadow. I want you to make me better, to make this place better, to help me help the people and give everyone the same chances… equality is more important to me than rank… its only for the duties of a high priest anyway." Tonauac stated, copying the comment she'd made to him about his position after the first time he'd returned to Mexico from her home. It had seemed so far and long ago and yet so much had happened. Tonauac gripped her hand tighter and as the sun began to blink and a golden line seemed to crease the sky on the horizon and around, Elaine ignored it. She leant forward to press her lips to his, their kiss was loving and soft and they held it as the sun came over them and filled their bodies with heat that mingled with the heat of their kiss.

Suddenly, Tonauac's hands lifted up to clasp her face, ignoring any previous thoughts on matters like the risk of the sunlight burning him. He just held her face as he kissed her more lovingly and then Elaine began to shudder as she felt something different. She could not explain it at first, a feeling of complete joy and happiness, a feeling of content and comfort, anxiety for the sake of another that mingled with the sheer triumph of them touching… something she could not even think of describing to anyone else. She could feel that it made her heart flutter, she could feel her body tingling for the touch, but rather than just the giddy excitement she knew occurred with sex that she felt enjoyable, the feelings did not get washed away in a wave and yet the anticipation was not violent and spine-crunching, it was like a warm body wrapped around her. There was a sensation of safety and happiness… that things were the way they should be and that for this, Elaine was very comfortable, even if this new sensation confused her as she gripped his shoulders gently.

"Tonauac, when your kind shares blood with others… they can share their emotions and feelings, can't they?" Elaine questioned as the warm rays of the sun seemed to bathe the bottom of the step pyramid and slowly clamber its way up and amongst the canopy of the jungle. She was sure that the emotions she was feeling right now were not her own, they were wonderful, but they were foreign to her as she looked to the smiling form of her husband as he slowly closed his eyes in acknowledgement. The sensation filled her with even more happiness that mingled with the relief she was creating to know that they were on the same wavelength and she was not going crazy. Elaine had to give a soft chuckle before she leant her head into his shoulder, heaving a sigh of relief and nuzzling against him before he bent to kiss her golden hair that was shining white in the sunlight.

"I haven't been burnt… so the marriage is complete and it appears that we've been accepted as a couple. Thank you, Elaine." Tonauac stated calmly and Elaine sighed heavily again in relief as he chuckled and held her to him lovingly. For a while they were still standing there, cuddling each other before there was a familiar chirpy call from lower down the vine-coated pyramid, asking if they were alright. Tonauac gave a soft snort of amusement, sharing the feeling with Elaine and amused that Elaine was feeling almost irritated by the question as Tonauac pinched her hand gently within his own. "Elaine… this feeling that you can feel in the background, warm and secure… that's the sensation of my love. Its unique only to you, no one else makes me feel like that and no one will produce the same feelings for you as I do. Do you understand?"

"I do…its strange, there is something familiar about it, wholesome… but there is just something so… it seems almost stupid to say 'personal' about the sensations but… unique. Yes, unique is the better word for them. They're pleasant, but surprising." Elaine chuckled gently in amusement, almost laughing out loud at how silly she felt and could feel Tonauac felt over the conversation. She could sense that he was doubting the clarity of his explanation, but she rather liked the feeling that he could be wrong or anxious. She sighed as she stroked her cheeks gently, they felt hot and there was no doubt they were rosy now, but she looked to her husband with a pleasant snort. "How long will this last?"

"Not long, about a day… but then when we couple this evening, I'll let you drink my blood and I'll mark you too… we'll share our most intense sensations and I will be able to show you how much more satisfying the physical motions of love can be between lovers." Tonauac stated wisely, but he could feel the scepticism and the almost smug sensations about him being a virgin. He would not deny that he'd never been tempted by the flesh of another, nor indeed kissed before he met Elaine… but that did not mean he had no understanding and could not make her feel something. Elaine picked up the irritation and the growing confidence and she licked her lips gently before looking down towards the bottom of the pyramid where Selene's silver hair was waving like a banner on the wind and shimmering like some glinting gem under water. Elaine then sighed but Tonauac could sense her question. "She and Xiuhcoatl have never shared blood… I never taught him that much because it is not appropriate for him to have a mate. Selene is just an exception."

"I don't know if it's an exception… but she's got a way around her to get everyone smiling and musing over her. But I don't think it will be long before the pair eventually figure that part out… they always seem to figure things out!" Elaine groaned softly, hands to her hips as she shook her head and Tonauac nodded, though they could both sense the similar feelings each other had for the pair… love, humour and complete exhaustion!

With the ceremony complete, Elaine and Tonauac came down the edge of the pyramid and to Elaine's great amusement, Tonauac's happiness beckoned the passionflowers to burst out of the vines and cover the side of the pyramid in a mix of purple and gold, regal colours as they both marched down to where Xiuhcoatl and Elaine were patiently waiting for them. They were both grinning in delight, looking at the beautiful flowers that opened out with a sigh as Tonauac's feet touched the earth. His hair had erupted into brilliant golds and soft blue shades to match the way the sky was shaping above. Together the group walked down to the strange scar on the surface of the pyramid, the seeming bat cavern that they all slid into comfortably before the lights on the walls within seemed to erupt in sharp white spurts of flame.

"Now the pyramid recognises you as part of it Elaine… you will find whilst we share blood, you will be able to make certain aspects of the pyramid move and you will be able to merge with the stone. Heh… you share my powers for that time." Tonauac chuckled gently and Elaine was amused, Tonauac's powers of strength and his ability to manipulate the stone around him was certainly an exciting prospect to play with, but Elaine just sighed. He could sense that she had no intention of playing about or bullying others, instead they marched through the corridor into the hall where the grooms sat on one side of the room and the brides on the other, waiting to be wed by their leaders.

Once they stepped into the room, Selene rushed to grab the two feather cloaks, wrapping their rainbow design around Tonauac and then Elaine's shoulders. Xiuhcoatl then produced the box with the daggers and Elaine's eyes widened in disbelief. She wanted to muse on how fate really seemed to have pulled them both together; one of these daggers had been the cause of Selene meeting the Elders and now, to see what it was used for, it was almost like Selene had been sent as heaven's matchmaker for the pair. She was certainly reminded of how lucky Selene always was as she turned to Tonauac expectantly as he opened the box.

The daggers shone in the firelight, brilliantly black and yet the crystal surface seemed so glassy it was almost impossible to see the intricate designs upon them. Tonauac took out one and laid it calmly and quietly into Elaine's hands, he then took the other and then beckoned her to bring it with him to the large burning pool of oil at the centre of the hall. Together, they heated up the blade into the fire to clean it, before they stepped back between the couples and then beckoned them to step forward to them. Yoloti and his mate, the other daughter of Sahib, stepped forward and Yoloti was beaming as Tonauac gently cut his palm and then turned to Elaine, who did the same to the slightly shivering bride. The pair were then beckoned together and Tonauac then joined their hands together, held his hand over them and then muttered something in a language Elaine could not understand before he released them and then, Yoloti was about to move off when Elaine gave a smile.

"In our culture… this last part's usually spoken aloud as a vow and then sealed with a kiss…" Elaine stated, though Tonauac and Yoloti tilted their heads to the side in disbelief for a minute. To them, the idea of a kiss to seal a deal of any sort was a link to the demonic powers of Lucifer, but it seemed the kiss was to initiate the giving of innocence to the partner. After that brief discussion, Elaine then swatted her hand with a gentle chuckle. "Alright, we'll just do it this way… do you swear loyalty and devotion to your partner for as long as you live? Yes… then you may kiss the bride."

"I see… it's also so society can witness that the union holds consent, alright." Yoloti clicked his fingers in amusement, but Elaine just beckoned him to kiss as Selene was grinning. She quickly lent up to whisper to Xiuhcoatl that talking like that spoilt the sacred notion of a wedding, which was just curiously typical for chatty Yoloti. But then Selene stepped out to one of the halls where there was a camera that Tizoc was setting up as Yoloti kissed his bride and then the next couple were brought forward. Selene had to make sure that Tizoc was aiming the camera properly, had prepared the film as they were going to take one big photograph of all of the couples together and they needed the negatives to be good because there were going to be many copies made. Tizoc insisted that it was all ready and so, as the weddings continued, they remained waiting patiently in the beautiful golden looking room.

Elaine said the same thing for the second couple, making the brides feel more relieved to hear something they accepted as normal marriage protocol and each came up to be bled and placed together without question. Elaine could feel the joy that filled Tonauac to see everyone so happy and to sense their love for one another and Elaine accepted it, but she was still rather surprised. Everyone did look exceptionally happy, even if she doubted that within the brief time between with just letter writing and telegrams, that love could really have formed so firmly. She knew it was just her general disinterest and confusion over love, but at the same time she could feel Tonauac's happiness and that made her confusingly happy too.

With everyone then married, Xiuhcoatl beckoned everyone to go into the other hall together, where Selene then settled them all to their places before she and Xiuhcoatl got behind the camera with Tizoc. Everyone else was blushing and grinning happily as they stood together, holding hands and beaming in happiness as Tonauac and Elaine stood in the middle. She looked towards him for a moment, not sure what expression she should make at this point, but he leant forward to kiss her lips, making her give a soft sigh. As their noses gently stroked against one another, there was the brilliant flash that made them all hiss suddenly in surprise as their eyes took a while to calm down. But with the photograph taken and the weddings held, it was time to feast and Tonauac had a surprise for everyone as he lifted his hand to speak.

"The locals of the town and the villages have been eager to meet you all and so they have prepared a massive celebration through the whole day for you all to enjoy and we shall go join them now." Tonauac stated and Elaine was excited, she was eager to meet the locals that she needed to make friends with, especially when Selene had enjoyed their company. Within the time since Selene had awoken them, the Elder had gone out to meet the Veil agents and the locals and gifted them with good crops, helped clean the rivers and aided in recycling any material that was broken. They'd come out to help them rebuild their settlements and shown an interest in sharing more with them over the coming years as long as they protected the growth of the forest. Everyone had been eager to get the chance to meet the new members of the community and show their respect for the forest beings, as well as to show where they could help the young ladies who would be leaving behind their luxurious surroundings. This was something that Elaine was looking forward to, as she was eager to share her own thoughts of female enlightenment and development, as well as combating illiteracy!

As they wrapped themselves up in their feather, fur and plant cloaks, the ground began to march off out of the tunnels as Selene ran off ahead of them, ready to rouse the villagers if they were not up already. Though the vampires had been cautious of stepping into sunlight, Yoloti had reminded them that sharing Elder blood gave them strength against the sun too. With that understood, Tonauac and Elaine held hands tenderly, smiling at one another as they marched through the loud chorus of cries and roars from the beasts of the jungle as they saluted the marriages as the Elder marched through. The ground seemed to grow flowers out just for them and the various ants and insects that might buzz them held back till the procession passed before they continued on their way. The birds and monkeys came down to the lower branches of the trees, whistling and clacking their beaks in delight to watch them all walk through and Elaine found herself almost sensing a strange thrumming sensation… a melodic low hum that she was convinced was coming from the voices of the trees!

When they came in view of the first few houses on the edge of the forest line with their pigs and goats, the houses were painted with paper flowers and chains, coloured grains were scattered upon the ground to make a rainbow pathway for them to follow and the windows were open. People came out when they spotted them, hurrying to the edge of the road and beaming in delight as the flowers grew ahead of the party and the people plucked one each, placing it in their hands and holding it like some kind of saluting object to the procession. They continued to pace along the rainbow pathway, with the mortals stepping behind into procession with them and the more they passed and joined, the more that songs began to be sung by the excited and music began to start up.

The procession became loud and joyous as they marched through the farms and into the interior of the community, seeing the docks, the river, the hotel and the various other town buildings that looked fresh and colourful with great fabric and paper banners welcoming and congratulating the others. When everyone reached the square, the township stood in front of a large wooden structure that held a literal square of coloured, risen wood that was for dancing and around it, a massive set of fires where people were cooking away like mad! Great big vats of drink and alcohol were being made and combined, beer had been brewed in preparation for this event and as the mayor stepped out to bow before Tonauac and Elaine, he introduced the people and the fiesta started in earnest!

There were lots of screeches of delight, music, dancing, hands being shaken and cheeks being kissed! Gifts were brought out to the newlyweds and flowers erupted out of the earth as if it were some ancient fertility ritual! Food was passed around, people laughed and talked and everyone that arrived at the dock was invited to the party. Emmanuelle, the were-jaguar leader of the Veil Agents in the region made a point to greet Elaine and thank her for falling in love with Tonauac. She was impressed by his respect and how happy he was, though he went and gave Selene a hug that made Elaine suspicious but caused Tonauac to giggle at her. The whole event was ridiculous, loud and yet the wild animals even came out to join in despite their natures, shocking the locals but then bringing them even more delight as the snakes gathered to enjoy the heat and dance to the vibrations, the deer came out to prance and perform as the pigs enjoyed the food and helped carry things where the cats emerged and lounged about, enjoying conversation and the attention of the children of the village. It seemed the marriage of the Elders after their awakening was to herald in peace between the wild world and the human world, the Elders were returning to their guardian nature and this place would certainly be a place to behold in time!

It was certainly exciting and as the day wore on into the evening, Selene and Elaine had even danced together with one another before Tonauac had stood up, his hair jet black and beckoned for the party to end. There were many drunk people around, but all of them were joyous and safe, no one was harming anyone and with the animals on hand to stop it, everyone was behaving. But as Tonauac beckoned for the Elder to form up, many of them were carrying their exhausted and tired wives… wives who'd not even thought to question how they had survived in the sunlight out here after they'd stepped into it and just found themselves engulfed in joy. Elaine was thoughtful on the matter and as they waved goodbye, she thought to ask before Selene hurried up to her and gave her a hug, Emmanuelle right at her side as Selene beamed.

"I'm staying here, the next ship from the Veil Agents arrives in the morning so I'll be going home with them. But if you need anything here, Emmanuelle is who you go to, but you can also go to the priest, Father Gabriola, will also help you out. He's a vampire hence he hasn't come out to see you, but I'm staying with him tonight with Xiuhcoatl at my side too, but he'll be back once I've gone. Promise you'll stay safe, won't you?" Selene was almost out of breath, she'd not stopped dancing most of the day and Elaine chuckled before grabbing her sister tightly to her and then snuggling against her. She was keenly aware that the love she felt for her sister certainly was not like the love she felt Tonauac had for her and curiously, it made her feel incredibly joyful. As she let go of her sister, kissing cheeks, they waved goodbye as Tonauac then stepped forward and kissed Selene's forehead gently.

"You will always be welcome here… you're the Emissary of the Elder, after-all." Tonauac chuckled and Selene gave a grin of amusement before leaning forward to kiss his cheek before then patting him on the shoulder and then skipping off herself. They watched her go over to Xiuhcoatl, he held her tiny little hands in his huge ones and the pair of them stayed for a little while longer before it was indeed time to go. Tonauac and Elaine then stepped over to the rest of the procession and as they followed the trail back, the jaguars stepped in behind them to guard them on their journey back. As they moved on, Elaine questioned Tonauac about the effects of the sunlight and he gave a smile. "The blood of their husbands has protected them, but it is only for the day… but to see and feel the sun for the first time… it's probably made them a little tipsy."

Elaine nodded her head with a smirk, but as she looked more curiously towards the procession and how they were all snuggling within one another's arms, she was feeling unsettled. Perhaps she should be acting a little more effeminate around Tonauac? But no… she'd never change the way she was purely because it looked like tradition, tradition was her enemy after-all! But she knew for some of them it was because the beer had got to them and yet there were lots of kissing sounds and loving sighs that almost made Elaine feel sick until she realised something that actually disturbed her quite a bit. The sensation of panic reached her partner and he held her hand gently, looking at her with an anxious eye as she opened her mouth to speak but somehow, she found herself going quiet.

Though Elaine wanted to inform him that she was not going to have sex on her wedding night because of tradition, she realised it was embarrassing if she announced the reason to be because she was 'not ready' for it. In truth, she was reminded of the awkward mess of her first time with Valentino and how it had certainly left her feeling a little like the process would be… uncomfortable. But if she were to say it out loud to the other women, they might either panic or they might assume she was someone pathetic and weak, unworthy to be their protector. She knew they looked up at her here, she felt the pressure and she knew that if anything went wrong then it was her job to look after them and deal with it… it was her duty!

"You don't have to be scared Elaine… no one's encouraged to do anything tonight… but if its permitted to share the bed so I have the honour of waking up beside you and knowing that we are married… that's enough for me." Tonauac stated gently and Elaine gave him a sideways look before rolling her eyes. He could sense that his words had made her feel a little sickened, but the pure intentions and the truth of his words had echoed across to her along with this overwhelming sensation of love and she had to just settle her mind down. She kissed Tonauac's ear gently, making him blush slightly and then she was shocked to feel that sudden tingle copy across to her own ear and Elaine gave a soft snort.

"It would be intriguing to say the least… I would like to know much more about how you are as a husband and how this sharing will be passed into the act. I mean, you're shockingly passionate and your thoughts and words are always truthful… you're careful with your words, but I'm certainly intrigued. I think, I might not let you have a quiet night." Elaine beamed softly, but she felt that sudden shiver of excitement from her partner that passed through to tickle her spine and, amusingly make her groin throb. This made Elaine grin, she actually wanted to know if there was a difference in their sensations as she did things… this might even be the best way to find out what it felt like for the other party in this situation.

They marched on through the jungle and the cats then stood around the deep lower entrance into the kingdom that had now been cleared and turned into a clever hatch. As they stepped down into it, the jaguar lined up around this doorway, ready to battle anything that might dare to interrupt the actions of the night and the completion of the seeming ceremony. As they all marched on towards the bed chambers, they separated out and steadily everyone filtered into the rooms to leave Tonauac and Elaine alone.

The pair marched up the slightly sloping levels of the pyramid interior, following a path that was patch-worked with light filtering in past the passionflower vines that bloomed even now. The sweet smell filled the air and Tonauac was feeling romantic as he drank in the scent, which passed to Elaine as a soft warming within her belly, a sensation like her skin was burning to be touched and automatically he stroked his arm. It sent a sharp shot of boiling heat into their groins, making them both blush and turn aside from each other, their bodies reacting so much more clearly than their minds. But Elaine realised something curiously simple in this matter, if they both knew the thoughts of the other… what was the need for words anymore?

The pair stepped into their room, a square room of stone with a large and surprisingly modern bed that was purple and gold in fabrics although the natural grey of the stone and the mosses gave the room the correct feel. It made Elaine wonder if Selene had somehow had an effect on this, or if perhaps this was Yoloti's mad attempts to try and get them all prepared to welcome their brides. Either way, she was glad she was going to have a comfortable sleep on a soft mattress before she marched over to the bed. Tonauac waited, he had the feeling she wanted him to wait and see as Elaine stepped to the edge of the bed, turned to face him and then calmly shed her clothes. She stood there naked, tall, strong and elegant with her perky breasts and her neat shape. She looked beautiful and Tonauac bowed his head down, waiting for her to give a sensation of acceptance.

When he felt it, he calmly removed his own clothes, his groin throbbing and organ almost bouncing as Elaine could sense the anticipation that had mingled with her display to encourage an erection. She was shocked by her mate's girth however, having assumed something large but not assumed that she might experience what Selene had. But as that slight anxiety passed across, Tonauac bowed his head to her in acceptance and then stepped over to a collection of strange looking, trumpet shaped plants that were clearly unique to the Veil. They were green with red veins bulging around a thick lip-like opening that was sticky and glistening, Tonauac dipped his hand into it, pulling it out and showing it was now coated in something that was almost slimy.

For a moment, Elaine was a little concerned about what this was for, but then she recalled something about the creams used to make it… easier. She'd played with some of the body butters that had been made, but they were not to be used in such a delicate place and this was fresh from the plant. She looked at Tonauac in anxiety over the cleanliness of the situation, but he just bowed his head gently and his confidence shot across to her that she would be safe. His hand seemed to shimmer slightly, his fingertips going black before returning to normal and Elaine recalled how these beings could purify anything they touched. She smiled and then sat on the edge of the bed, letting him sit beside her, the pair of them kissing before his hand went to her soft warmth and she shuddered in pleasure that he shared with a hot, moist breath.

His fingers stroked and glazed, learning from the thoughts and sensations of her body just where it liked to be touched and just how much pressure she would accept. Elaine sighed and moaned, her head pressing to his shoulder as she kissed at him gently and his fingers delved deeper. He searched but moved carefully, feeling where she got tight, feeling where it stung if he tried to push, but feeling every groove and fold that exuded delight to make her purse her lips and sigh. He moved his fingers carefully again and again before they were kissing one another in firm smacks again and again. Soon, she could sense his building heat and her own growing pressure that was filled with tingling pleasure and Elaine shuffled to lie back on the bed as Tonauac clambered onto the bed beside her, leaning over to kiss her before she opened her arms and let him lie upon her.

His warm lips pecked and pinched at her neck, gently feeling his way around her chin with soft brushes and licks. She shivered, enjoying the warm little marks to cover her skin as well as the reverence that seemed to ooze as Tonauac touched her. As she relaxed back beneath him, his mouth then came up to kiss her lips again, one hand holding her face to his as the other stretched back to touch her body. Their soft kisses mingled with soft sighs and then gentle motions of his hand to awaken her interest with fingers guided by the sensations she shared with him. Her breath caught, feeling the warm digits stroke and caress, twirling around every area that sang and rippled with pleasure as she groaned into the motions as his fingers sought the burning warmth.

His fingers reached for every part that made her body shiver, drinking in her pleasure and panting hotly onto her neck as she craned it back, arching her spine to lift her hips and help him search. There was that familiar pressure building up, that anticipation within to reach bliss that Elaine was aware of and enjoyed. However, the more she moved and enjoyed herself, the more these waves of extra intensity, of a determination to make her feel good and to be the one to do it... a strange kind of pride, glittered into her mind. It made her body hotter, her fingers quivered as she grasped for her husband's shoulders and pulled his body firmly to hers, fed up of foreplay as she snatched his chin and forced him up for a kiss. This kiss forced her tongue into his mouth to roll and touch every sensitive part of the gum to make him drool and sigh, mimicking the motions of his hands until he was panting and she could feel the desperation glowing between them both.

"I think we're ready..." Elaine whispered softly, wrapping her arms around him and then guiding his shoulders up over her body as her legs looped around his hips. She felt his heat caress her own with a delightful purr of satisfaction before their bodies united and her mind was overwhelmed with the stretching, but also the burning heat that made them melt into one another. She cooed and sighed until she felt he was settled within her, her feet stroking at his hips as her hands twiddled into his hair that turned a brilliant burst of red. She nuzzled to his neck, her fangs out as she scraped their sensitive forms against his skin to make him shiver, the sensation rattling down into their cores that seemed completely joined. She knew it was the effect of his blood, but for the first time in her life she could not tell what part was her body and what was his, drowning sensations of affection, pleasure and a hunger for kisses and the union to continue filled her mind as she gently pierced his throat with her fangs.

His whole body seemed to take in a deep breath, lifting her as the pain was subsided with purest ecstasy that Elaine could feel too. His body began to move, his motions gentle and rolling, moving with the heights of the chemicals flooding his body as she drank only slightly and let her tongue roll and press against his wounds. Their motions seemed to be imitating his motions within and for the first time, Elaine was able to feel what it felt like for him to be inside her… what it felt like to have such a thing and it only made her more grateful to be with Tonauac. That kind of understanding seemed to make them both sing in delight as their hands grasped and gripped at one another as they continued their snake-like writhing dance.

The scent of sweat filled the room, pleasant and familiar, wholesome as the pair heaved and wheezed towards the building pressure as every part of their insides were on fire and felt melted. They were nuzzling and kissing, panting and pressing lips together and moaning to each other in the pleasure, Tonauac's neck bruising where Elaine's fangs had touched him in the traditional "Mark of the Mistress", as the pair continued to move on and then they felt the pressure mingling, coming to a head with ecstatic tingles of delight. Lightning strikes of utter joy were willing them, drowning their senses and with it came that sensation of happiness to have been able to cause such a thing within one another. It made Elaine pant softly as she gripped hold of her lover tightly and finally, she began to feel her own pleasure breaking through, something she doubted she'd experienced quite like this before as Tonauac took the moment to press his own fangs to her neck, pinching in to leave the permanent mark of a mated couple as Elaine gave out a sharp cry of delight and their bodies pinched and squeezed together. There was a wild burst of energy between them, a sudden slapping wave of pleasure and exhaustion that caused them both to groan out in the shock before they felt something trickling away as they felt themselves collapsing together.

Despite the fact the process was over, the pair were soon still grasping each other and kissing lovingly. Elaine had never been interested in kissing or affection between one another, but with Tonauac she could not help it. Every touch of his lips to hers filled her with happiness and a warmth she was not quite sure to be the same kind of love she'd felt with her family, if only because it was more intense. Elaine still could not quite grasp it, but she stroked his darker skin, kissing it lovingly and rolling her hands through his long, beautiful hair before she leant back and then kissed his lips as he nuzzled against her and then Elaine gave a sigh.

"I love you." She sighed softly, though Tonauac's eyes widened in surprise and then he smiled, pulling her closer and happier for it.

Four weeks after her arrival, Elaine had Yoloti take her back down to the town and she met with the vampire priest that was eager to shake her hand and muse how he was pleased to meet another of the Viper Clan. Selene had returned unexpectedly and was in the village already, chatting with everyone, learning as much about the fish as possible and drawing people. Elaine was glad to meet the figure and the Veil Agents that came out too as she was brought to the local meeting point, the town hall that was a traditional long building on stilts near the edge of the river. It also doubled as the church, the real community hub in these regions and with the local leaders they settled down and began to discuss the situation with connections to the Viper Clan and what could be done to aid the Elders.

The situation was simple enough, Elaine was aware that the family of the other women to have come with her to marry would be more interested in coming to visit and they would have high expectations. Elaine stated that there could be a good deal of money in improving the hotel to suit these people and organising local festivals and events into calendars to help them arrange times to encourage the visitations to suit the income for the village. There was also the need for transport improvements, getting a more frequent ferry arranged between their community and the next up the river, as well as exploring the jungle regions to learn more about what was here and any of the other temples still held under Tonauac's control. She stated these things, but very quickly the eldest member of the local council tugged at his straw hat and was shaking his head about frantically.

"Whatever must be done it cannot destroy the forest around us, or we would be harming the ecosystem that supports the tribe. The people here have always kept to a quota of how much land can be cleared and what can be farmed here, chickens, goats, and pigs but we do not want to raise cattle that would require more than the land could give just for visitors to be fed. The fish on the river are the mainstay, the river needs to be kept clean so too many boats would upset this… we even have dolphins in the water that we share the fish with…" It was clear to see that the balance here had been maintained well enough with just respect for Tonauac's clan and Elaine had been a little irritated to be told there were things that they did not want her to interfere with. At first she assumed that they were being unkind because she was a woman and a foreigner, but then she calmed herself as the Veil Agent nodded his head and looked to Elaine with a smile.

"Everything we did of course would have to be with Tonauac's permission. Setting up radio towers can be done by building huts on platforms in the old, dried river ways and if we think of building something exciting to please the visitors and encourage them to understand the balance here, it could be useful for everyone. We can call in people with this sort of experience to help, but that of course would only be with the Permission of the Tribe. I would assume that Tonauac would do a morning sacrifice to read the calendar and learn what we can do…." The figure stated and for a moment Elaine was still stuck thinking that this was them deciding they did not want to discuss the matters with her gender at all, but then she gave a sudden jolt of confusion and surprise as the Veil Agent then pulled out a typewriter from a massive heavy case and then lifted a finger. "I'll take down these notes… firstly we should all consider the amount of people you would be expecting to be brought in. All the families could not be brought in at once of course…"

"…we'd need to figure out a calendar that works with the movements of the boats and the seasonal changes. Tonauac mentioned there's flooding, hence I assume we're on stilts, but also that there are seasons when the river dolphins arrive. Dolphins are assumed in vampire culture to be messengers of the angels and are treated almost as holy relics. Selene told me that the people here feed them and they're only found within the Veil waters… we'd certainly gain the most interest from vampires to visit around then and pay for guides and someone to supply fish." Elaine stated suddenly and the figures all nodded their heads in delight as the Veil Agents began to clatter away on the gawky writer. It made Elaine amused to see him work, but she was also fascinated by the machine and how much she'd not even considered using one in the past. But if she wanted to help with educating people and getting communication through without having to take blood to overcome a sore wrist, she would certainly need one. "Oh… I would need to acquire my own typewriter in order for me to write up my ideas and my correspondence to help us out."

"Ah… not a problem, the Veil Agents can have the machine sent and the Elders will surely know how to make a natural paper from shed bark to use. There's actually a big industry for authentic Elder-made items and that can help improve matters here. The Veil Agents certainly could do with funding for the kind of resources needed to protect this community… though it does beg the question what the vampires will do with the family allowances as Elder do not use commerce." The Veil Agent stated and for a moment Elaine's lightning-bolt brow raised as she eyed the figure up. If he was looking for some way to acquire that kind of money, Elaine would want complete transparency over what he was using it for and would rather have it paid into the Veil Agents as a whole. But to her relief and indeed to the relief of the village leader, the priest lifted his hand with a common goal that everyone could adhere to.

"The Elders can perform cleansing and healing for other… but for most here it's a riverboat journey down to the nearest doctor and at least two days by boat to the nearest hospital. I feel we should look into preparing a hospital here, especially considering that birth for vampire females can be exceptionally risky. We don't want to lose anyone just because we had few resources. It will also help give future potential to the locals if there's a hospital to bring in more trade with neighbours and a place they can learn skills and move to the cities for. Not to mention… the plants here have amazing powers." The pallid being stated with a calm smile upon his face and Elaine smiled in relief to hear it, nodding her head and insisting that it was something they could certainly press the vampire households to arrange money towards and to gain assured doctors. This seemed to make even the Veil Agent nod in delight and soon they were busy discussing other matters as the typewriter clacked away busily to get the information down.

As they worked, Elaine was eager to learn how the device worked and she made notes as they all did before questioning something. Perhaps it was an ignorant and impertinent question to ask, but she enquired about the literacy of the locals and it made the leader give a grimace. He explained that the situation here meant trades were learnt on the job and reading was limited to childhood basics and work. Those with good brains would go and learn where they could but families had to raise money for it and this was something Elaine knew she and the vampire women could deal with easily. She turned to the priest, the Sunday school was the only sort of curriculum the children had to work on and Elaine smiled.

"Amongst the women of my group, we are all elder sisters who learnt much and taught our siblings. Teaching is something we can do with money only needed for supplies. We can all find some way of helping out like this and we can easily help with other things like assisting healers… vampires are very good at removing venom from blood, let alone the Elders are likely to encourage us to do things too." Elaine stated, smiling thoughtfully towards them as they all nodded their heads in approval before the old man of the village made a point she'd have to get permission from the women of the village as well, as they controlled what happened with the children. Elaine had to give a smile at the thought that the women here were respected too, she hoped it would be an easy enough victory to gain and with that, notes were made and everyone was ready to continue their work.

Elaine stepped over to the old man of the village, he had been from the native people of the region, but like many in and out of the Veil, his blood had mingled with that of the invading Europeans and with it the Christian names had been enforced upon them. He liked to be known as Iago, with some of the tribe telling Elaine that he never liked anyone referring to him under the name he'd grown up with, out of respect no one did but Elaine was amused at the thought of such irritation over a name. Iago though made it clear when she pondered it that his mother had chosen a very silly name for him, in his opinion, that was far too common and so it was better to have nicknames. Elaine had to agree, back at home there were six werewolves called Jacques and only one of them was ever referred to by that name, the others were Jax, Jackie, Jack, Jay and even Grumbles! They both mused on it as Iago led her over to the collection of women that were sitting outside one of the wooden houses with their babies, some half-naked because they were busy breast-feeding or just too hot and Iago insisted that the heat here could make anyone shed their clothes, so no one was too bothered.

Amongst the women here were the three eldest women, one was busy sewing, one was chewing some kind of grain and then spitting the mash into the mouth of the grandchild she was holding, whilst the third was busy piercing the ears of one of the young girls that was doing her best not to flinch. These three were the women in charge and apparently, they held the collective knowledge of the region, especially about the actions of Tizoc and Xiuhcoatl's mothers, hence they insisted the magnolia tree, the passionflower and a brilliant red flower that grew only on the boarder of the Elder land, were sacred and being sewn into the images of the quilt. If Elaine had their approval about the children's education, then she could do anything in the village, but she could see the way they eyed her up and were not impressed by her grey skirt and white blouse, let alone her hair in its tight bun, that it might not be easy.

"Good afternoon ladies…" Elaine was thankful her Spanish was top-notch, but she was aware too that these ladies mixed their own dialect and words into their speech and she was worried that her ability to understand would not be as simple. But she knew that from being paired to an Elder her ability to communicate would increase somewhat to at least know the words he knew, it was part of the reason anyone could pair with an Elder and language never was a barrier. Besides, in order to cope in the vampire court, French was still the main language along with Italian and Romanian was also highly valued, so learning new languages was natural for her and Elaine turned to Iago to make sure she was alright to speak before he grinned. "Right then, I've come here to ask for your permission to set up evening school for the children around the area to help them read and write. This will increase their likelihood of good jobs in the future and will help when we have guests from Europe that will likely ask a lot of questions and not always bother to learn the language."

Perhaps she was being too haughty as she spoke to them, they were looking at her with a firm expression as if they had no interest whatsoever in listening to her. She grimaced, she'd found the older a person was, the more set in their ways and with the elder women it was even harder to get them to understand the kind of things they actually needed. Most people with low rank in the universe just tended to grit their teeth and carry on through, aware that though they deserved help, help usually came at a high cost and troubling times. She could understand their reservation to respond so quickly, but Elaine then tapped her chin with thought to try and say something that would be more welcomed perhaps.

"We want to get our vampire families to focus on building a proper clinic and maybe even a hospital nearby… so the children here would have to grow up to know how to work it and how to treat people. You know the people around here need easier access and there is land that the Elders have permitted us to use for improvements. But… I don't want to overstep the mark and do something that you would not approve of. I also want to know what you feel the children need to learn here, what you hope for them to achieve and how we can make that happen." Elaine stated firmly, not really willing to sound meek or to beg for this kind of change, she was stubborn in knowing that this change needed to happen no matter what, but she could see too that it was not going to happen if she did not give the right level of respect. In fact, Elaine sat herself down onto the ground in front of them, ignoring the thought of getting dirt on her clothes and just staring up at them expectantly for some kind of instruction as the old women gave grimaces and then the one piercing ears paused.

"Our children are good children and they need these chances… but we do not want them taught in the way of the vampires and the non-humans… there are few in this region that are not human, it was why this region of the Veil was such a pristine sanctuary protected by many creatures so that we would never feel the domination of your kind. But all of that changed and we do not want our children to feel they must remain tethered to the east more than to their own history." The old woman groaned, gently gnawing at one of her teeth that was obviously loose and uncomfortable. Her words made sense to Elaine, they'd been through a lot here and the old ladies were already expecting Elaine was going to create some kind of hierarchy to make them all slip to the bottom of the ladder under all the Veil beings again. She grimaced at the thought of such a thing, reminding herself of what her father had done by letting people be themselves and Elaine nodded her head.

"Of course… we don't want to teach your children that they are any less than the next being… my father was very firm in his belief that there should be equality at all levels in some form, whether it's that a woman shares the same job possibilities as a man, or a child and an adult require the same protections in the law. We don't want to teach anything you would not, we just want to give them the chance to write their own histories for the next generation." Elaine stated, only to notice the three women gave her sharp looks as if they were being told their knowledge over decades was going to be replaced just like that. Elaine was not sure how she could explain these thoughts now, gritting her teeth and then looking towards their work and then considering that she would have to make sure that these women were part of the process, that they did not feel like they were being kicked out… they needed to have some kind of control over what was happening and she grimaced as she considered how much easier this would be if only her father were standing by her and encouraging her. She then smiled, thinking about how he'd mused that pride and ego were troublesome things, but they should be dealt with carefully as they were shockingly fragile and Elaine smiled. "Of course, we'd need you to teach us too, we'd need you to teach us to cook and sew in your style to help our own families as, you can tell I'm sure, the brides and myself are all a bit too used to other people doing it for us. So we thought we could all work together like this."

"Hmm…" The three women stated together, turning to look at each other before then seemingly having a conversation that was all eyes. Iago held Elaine's shoulder, a warm smile on his face to encourage her that it was going well, but Elaine was not sure he was involved in the same conversation. She knew she was forcing a lot of new things very quickly, but she was sure the benefits outweighed any real complaints and then the old women pointed a finger towards Iago, asking if he had agreed to all of this.

"Yes… we have all spoken, we will bring more trade and money here, more medicine if we work together and of course, a better opportunity for the children to spread out and remain connected. Old ways will be kept, but these newer ways are simply to fix problems we could not have otherwise had a way to deal with… such as if some boat of Europeans were to arrive again and this time demand to take over… we would be able to show them that they are not needed." Iago stated in his rather more jovial and firmer tone, though it was clear the women only had a little more respect for him then they had towards Elaine. But they accepted the situation as what it must be and they bowed their heads in agreement before the one to pierce ears grabbed Elaine by the wrist and yanked her onto the ground beside the little girl.

Suddenly, her hair was pulled out of the bun and the women fussed at its golden shade and its straight form. They mused at how it got greasy in the heat but was still shockingly beautiful as they stroked it out and then wagged their fingers at Elaine. They insisted that she must keep her hair long, wear thinner clothes against the heat and walk with either wooden sandals or barefoot like the Elders did. Elaine almost laughed at that, considering she would not be poisoned or bitten by anything in this landscape, they were probably quite correct that wearing boots around the place was not really needed outside of the market area. Then the women leant her head back as she relaxed into their grip before they grasped at her ears, noticing her very basic piercing with its blue gem earring before they noticed the necklace she was wearing.

Their hands stroked around the little dagger, reminding her that it was very important for her to keep it safe and then the women pulled up a collection of little turquoise stones they'd shaped into various forms. She could see that they wanted her to look more appropriate for her position and to her shock, she gave a sharp yelp as two large needles from one of the ragged trees in the region, were pushed through the lobe of each ear. They sat beside her little gemstones and they stung quite badly, her body unable to push them out and heal as quickly as the women hurried to decide upon the jewel that best suited her. They then chose two little snake shapes before bringing out two long hoop earrings that they'd made from gold that had been passed on for generations it seemed. There must be Elder magic to them, for they flexed and bent smoothly as the turquoise snakes were added before they were brought to her ears and with another sharp needle hooked to the end, fed into her ear to come out the other side before they then removed the wood needles.

Elaine grimaced, she could feel the weight pulling on her ears, but the snakes lay calmly just above her shoulders, showing off the elegance of her neck before a necklace was brought out and wrapped around her neck. It was made of some crystals rubbed smooth by the river, quartz and they were colourful as they were wrapped around her and she realised it was to help ward off demonic beings. She was thankful for it, about to sit back up and thank them for their kindness, before she saw them bring out wooden bowls with some rather earthy smelling pastes as she found a smooth, creamy solution plastered onto her face and revealed skin that was said to help before another wooden needle was dipped in what appeared to be damp charcoal as little black dots were drawn about her forehead. Another of red was mixed in before one the colour of gold and then finally, a gentle line of an ochre paste was smeared down the centre and rubbed under each eye and under her lips. Elaine was quite sure she looked terrible right now and that this was perhaps some kind of joke to them, but the old women beckoned for a tin pot to be brought over and Iago fetched it with a grin.

When he brought it over, he showed it to Elaine and she was able to see that the paint to her face had a curious effect of colouring her forehead like the scaled top of a snake's head. She then was informed the ochre paste was to keep flies away from her face and Elaine thanked them greatly, before they told her that this was the paint on the face of a female Elder that should be worn during formal meetings. They explained too the large earrings were the same and to make out some animal guide to the wearer. It made Elaine smile to hear these thoughts before they finally gave their soft grunts of approval, so long as she'd let them paint her face each time she came for official business… Elaine had to agree.

When she'd returned home the women had been excited by the words and the thought that they would be able to do something more useful, but certainly the make-up had intrigued them and shocked the males. Yoloti had gone in search of the items to help them wear the cream to help their skin from sweating too badly under the heat of the day, let alone the help the paint stick. Elaine was pleased though when Tonauac had come to see the change. He'd brought her to their room and licked and kissed her sore ears and then gently used his powers to take them off and put them back on too without causing her pain. He'd then found himself pulling Elaine to their bathing area and together, Elaine curiously surprised how eager she'd been to share such a private space with him, enjoyed the evening within the cool, refreshing water with her lips pinching and pressing to his as they had not connected their bodies and not needed to.

Time seemed to slip on by with the regular contacts from home and the news of the weddings of her other siblings and their luck. It seemed the chaos of the Veil society was not affecting them in this section of the world and it made things much easier to cope with. There was regular contact too from Theodosius on the development of Vittorio at home and with a package even coming with photographs and drawings the little boy had done for his aunt, Tonauac and Elaine had found themselves locking hands and sighing lovingly at the thought of sharing these experiences with their own child and, in 1929 just a week after her own birthday, Elaine was busy at the school when her own body decided that work was over for the day.…

The old ladies of the village and the other young vampires were all filling out the tiny room within the temple where Elaine was experiencing something she'd already gone through once and shockingly was glad of. The other women, some of them heavily pregnant too, were watching with wails and grimaces of agony at the faces and the growls that Elaine was producing. Her feet were smashed firmly into the stone of the floor, her hips relaxing back as she clenched the hands offered to her and focused on her breathing. She took in deep breaths, panting it out as the rolling waves of pain filled her body and she growled out at the universe for making her a damn woman! There was nothing the Elder could do to soothe her pain in this moment, but they were also waiting in the hall near the birthing chamber with the male representatives of the community were also looking excited to be present.

This was the first Elder born in over two hundred years, it was also Tonauac's first child and would be his heir... the situation could not be any more symbolic of the good shift in the region! With the hospital being funded and the school working well with children from other communities that were human and non-human coming in, there was a lot more commerce and a lot more communication. Even two leaders of the next two villages along and the Chieftain of a Veil tribe of were-jaguar had come for the occasion and brought offerings for this momentous occasion. Tonauac though was still looking uncomfortable as he was being held against Xiuhcoatl's shoulder in comfort, being reminded how Elaine knew what to do and everything would be fine. He reminded him that he'd read she'd have five children and yet it made Tonauac all the more fearful that there could be some kind of injury to his beloved. But Elaine's firm growls kept them all grinning and aware that things were going very well.

"Ugh... last time I had my stupid twin in the room... I can't believe I wish Dio was here right now so I could break his wrist!" Elaine grimaced, her voice squeezed and barely audible as she recalled when Vittorio had been born and how she'd made sure Theodosius had been in the room. The memory of her brother going pale and fainting before pulling himself up only to faint again was making her grin and want to laugh. She was quite sure that her brother would have made an amusing pregnant figure, if only whatever deity he believed influenced his fate had permitted it and oddly, she found herself thinking about Selene too. As she groaned and grit her teeth to push the baby's head free of her body, Elaine considered her family and how Noel and Sorina had just learnt of their own pregnancy, Selene would be helping the youngsters out, Adelia would be waiting on the phone call regarding her second grandchild, Gaston and Lynnette would be cooing in delight at the tale and Thibaut would be annoyed that once more he was being beaten to the punch!

But Elaine found her mind going back to that moment when she had first seen and held Vittorio, that sudden explosion of love she'd felt for a child that had grown inside her had been unbelievable and undeniable. She mused how, her growing situation with Tonauac had meant that she'd certainly felt that same high and desperately clinging emotion to him and the more she prepared for this child to come into her arms, the more she felt that overwhelming happiness bring tears to her eyes. With the final groan of agony as the baby was freed and the elder of the women hooked him up by the foot, lifting him up so he spat out fluid and squealed in fury, the gender was obvious and Elaine gave a loud messy sob of delight with her arms out.

The squeal from the baby echoed around the stone temple and everyone stood up on edge within the hall as Xiuh released Tonauac and he darted towards the room. The great guardian stepped in front of the door, guarding it from any potential intrusion as the women inside were cooing and fawning in utter delight at the sight of the baby with his reddish skin that was perhaps even darker than his father's and the dark coils of night-blue upon his forehead. He was squealing and shrieking as his chord was severed and the afterbirth collected by the eldest women, before they brought the naked baby to sit upon his naked mother's chest. The baby snorted messily, taking in the scent of his mother he would remember forever as Elaine wiped his nose and held him close as the women cleaned her. She pulled her son to her face, her tears dribbling down her face freely as she sobbed and kissed the baby in total joy.

"Oh my baby… my baby… oh I love you, I love you so much and I'll never let you go!" She whimpered, nuzzling into the screeching ball that still did not seem content. His little limb strained out, fingers slowly stretching and curling as he realised that the tight protection and warmth of the womb was gone… which he did not seem to approve of. Elaine laughed at his fussing, kissing him and pulling him close to her as ruby-red eyes to match his father's blinked up at her as she shivered slightly. One of the old women brought water mixed with some plant juice to her lips to help her recover as they mused they'd let her hold him just a little longer before they bathed him. Elaine laughed at the thought of it, she could not believe this little one, only now just calming down, would submit to being cleaned by someone other than her. But she drank in his smell, shocked by how addictive the newborn smell was as she let the reality overcome her that this… this was **her** child!

There was the sound of the women parting and whispering to themselves, the brides seemingly unwilling to leave the three old women with the baby just yet, but they departed. They were urged by Tonauac's arrival as he thanked each of them by name for being there and the vampires smiled lovingly towards him for showing such respect. He then hovered in the doorway, hands hanging on the arch as he pulled back the urge to just bolt in and hold them both, tears visible as they ran down his cheeks for the joy that both had survived. The old women seemed to want to leave him hanging before they recalled tribe tradition and brought the clay bowl bearing the shed placenta to the Chieftain, musing they'd recalled some of the old traditions they'd heard stories of. With that, they passed it over and left the room as Tonauac dropped onto his knees.

"What is it you're doing?" Elaine questioned softly, cleaning some mess from the grumbly looking babe's mouth as it pinched its lips and seemed to relax against her warm skin. Tonauac lifted his head up to her and then bowed his head gently, before then showing off his arm and that was unmarked and then laying his hand onto the shed item that had linked mother to child. The blood seeped into his skin, the icons forming upon his body to tell him something of the child's future and most importantly, his name. When Tonauac saw it, he smiled and then held his arm out to Elaine, approaching slowly as she tilted her head to the side. "It looks like someone with a beak like face, feathers and they're locked within two trees? I do not understand."

"It's a slightly unusual one, but it tells me his name should be Ehecatl for the wind… this beaked figure was how the god Ehecatl was sometimes drawn, he brought music to the world as well as aided the creation of humanity. He also apparently turned into a tree with a beautiful goddess that intertwined to… embrace… which is where some of our stories say the Elder were the children born from those trees in the Veil. It's a suitable name for a first son and a new time for our people. Elaine… I could not explain to you how happy having our son makes me, but even more so knowing you are alive." Tonauac stated as he watched Elaine's face skew up before she mouthed the name for a moment and seemed to smile. She bent down to kiss their son's head again before bringing little Ehecatl up to his father's face. Tonauac took him gently, pulling his son close and then kissing him, although the baby decided to give out a sudden screech of fury not to be with his mother and Elaine chose that moment to admit something that Tonauac only slightly heard above Ehecatl's bleat.

"I love you Tonauac…"

Part Three: The Odd Couple

Aurora Castle, Italy in the Veil, August 1926

"You know… if ever there was a woman I would choose to marry that would not dishonour my beloved's memory… it would be your mother. Your face tells me everything, but what vampire would not want a countess that controls them with just one look, whose disinterest in any touch and dismissiveness to my advances makes conquering her all the more exciting? The thought that someone was able to not only marry her young, have nine children with her and capture her heart to the point she will reject all others… is there any greater challenge?" Mircea was beaming in delight as he watched Adelia leading off Theodora and the youngsters with Selene to the wings where the female vampires were to wait in the Aurora Castle. The Romanian Count had found himself just staring out after the elegant, dark-haired woman whose natural olive skin had paled since her husband's loss and never returned properly to its original lustre. However, he'd decided to declare this to Gaston, Noel and Thibaut just before the Noble Circle meeting was about to start and suddenly he had the most vicious series of glares focusing upon him as he gave a chuckle. "Did you ever know that you've all inherited your mother's vicious glare but your father's dominating aura?"

"Thank goodness for that!" Gaston scoffed, though Thibaut made a gesture to scoop something in the air with his hand and squeeze it. Gaston assumed it was a rude threat, but Mircea felt his heart ache slightly in the memory of Thibaut's unpleasant technique in holding his heart! He grit his teeth in frustration as he watched them both move along, before spotting Noel waiting to see him and looking awkward. It was not unusual for Noel to look awkward, but it was instead rather adorable to see as Mircea patted at Noel's cheek and then hooked him about the shoulder, pulling him close. The moment he did, Noel looked suddenly sad and it was only because he could sense the mood coming off Mircea and it was a definite no should he ask for permission to marry Sorina just yet.

"Noel… you understand the importance of an only child, don't you? I mean… with Sorina I question whether I could even pass her to just any vampire, let alone someone whose family would be on a lower level than her own. The big issue with it is that I would have to know her children would have loyalty to me, not to any other Count. I'm sure you could understand such a thing, after-all Thibaut's children will be loyal to their father for the sake of their future rather than to their grandfather Vulturie… with Sorina, I'd need to make sure that even her partner knows that our role at the top of the Romanian bloodline means I stand above all others in loyalty… save loyalty to my daughter." Mircea was beaming playfully; it was quite clear though that Mircea was putting out a challenge for Noel to understand. Indeed, the third son of Count Theo Viper was aware that Count Blestemat was still on edge after the betrayal of the Hungarian Count and was aware that anyone marrying his daughter would be looking for his title. It was obvious to Noel that this was what Mircea needed to know before he considered anyone, then he called out to another. "Bogdan… dear nephew… come here and meet Noel!"

Immediately Noel felt like he was being rejected even more, Bogdan was the cousin that everyone assumed would be taking the position from Mircea in future and many were suggesting might as well produced a child with Sorina to unite their bloodline again properly. Cousin to cousin marriages amongst the highest ranked of the nobles were very common, especially if the youngsters had grown up together and made a close connection as Sorina and Bogdan had, but it was clear to them that they only saw each other as siblings. But when Noel looked to the tall, dark haired, olive skinned and brilliant bronze eyes of the figure who was taller and slimmer than Noel and certainly handsome in his fancy dark blue velvet suit with his neat short haircut and just his aura of beauty that came over with him.

Noel felt pathetic; he could feel though that there was only joy coming from Bogdan as he approached, hugged his uncle, kissed his cheeks and then turned around to grab hold of Noel around the shoulders and beamed before kissing both his cheeks and pulling him into a hug as well.

"Greetings Noel… it's such a pleasure to meet the man my little Sora won't stop talking about! Oh… but she mentioned you had a tail last time… you haven't been showing off, have you?" Bogdan was grinning from ear to ear, his whole body just blooming with delight to meet the figure that made his cousin so happy. Noel was pleased too to hear the word for sister being used both as what he felt Sorina was, but also as a loving nickname. He felt oddly relieved although embarrassed at the joking comment that made him blush and made Mircea give Noel a sideways glance as if he'd not heard that himself. But

Bogdan wrapped his arms around Noel in another hug, pulling him in tight and then beckoning him to come with them. "Come with us Noel… you'll sit with me in the rafters in our booth, we're going to watch the council and you're going to meet the rest of the Romanian noblemen… eh, there's only seven more so you can see how restricted our bloodlines are… and why Uncle fusses so!"

With his arms around Noel's shoulder and a clear aura of protection now falling from him, Mircea was pouting as Bogdan urged Noel away up to the spiral stone staircase, which would go to the curtained booths in the rafters that looked down upon the amphitheatre below. Noel had never been up there before, there was not a booth for the Viper Clan, there was only booths for the ten highest families and often they were never really filled although ten people could sit opposite one another in each booth and listen in. Tradition stated that the Heir of those families should always be present to see the situation and as Noel was brought up, it was clear to see that there was quite a crowd waiting at the top and he could see Vulturie's sons, the Fratello, Sahib's sons, the Chinese figure's sons, the Gala's grandsons, Hermann and the top brass of the German Bund, Hernandez's cousins, the Japanese nephews and sons, the Ubitsya of course were utterly absent and then there was the cluster of the remaining Romanian men.

The seven of them had been wating patiently for the chance to meet Noel it seemed, as they rushed over to introduce themselves and shake his hands in excited joy. First, he was to meet the three cousins from Wallachia Alexandru, Mihai and Apostol, which all kissed his cheeks, clapped his shoulders and fussed that Sorina was enamoured with him and he had good taste to know a good strong woman when he saw one. It made Noel blush, before the three from Moldavia stepped forward, these the cousin to Sorina's cousins from her mother's side… Constantin, Dănuț and Dacian. They grabbed his cheeks and his hair, checking him all over and musing about how strong he looked as they clapped at his back and even his buttocks before the final cousin, very distantly related but very important came forward. This was Radu, the last of the Romanian noble blood from the region of Drobuja, he was the cousin of Nikifor from the bloodline of the region that, for territorial purposes, always paired into Romanian or Bulgarian blood. Radu was nothing but smiling as he grabbed Noel's hands and squeezed them tightly with a grin.

"You have no idea how happy we all are… our parents were forced to flee the country because of the warlock battle within the Transylvania region that used to be our shared grounds with the Hungarians. When it happened, the Hungarians tried to claim that region but were forced out by the werewolves, it was only because Mircea was able to befriend the werewolves and give them a position of power as the local police and army with permanent jobs and equal position to every other non-vampire that we were able to fight back the witches and maintain our region." Radu beamed, clapping Noel's cheeks as he gave a soft grunt before grabbing him in a tight hug as the others looked to be beaming in delight. From what Noel had learnt, all of these children had grown up with Nikifor's family and Sorina's mother, their parents killed in battle or in birth and when Sorina's mother was the last killed in the last attempt by the witches to take power, her death had brought them all under Mircea with their loyalty as clear as if he'd been their father because his wife had been like their mother and all of them had been big brother to Sorina no matter what! Noel could see the importance and closeness of this clan, why they all sat in the booth together as they led him in and then Radu clapped his cheeks firmly. "Don't you worry… we've all joined together to pay for you and Sorina to have a wedding, whether Uncle Mircea agrees or not, we want happiness because its deserved."

"Look at your shocked face! You couldn't have thought any of us would have stopped you, right? Hell we want Sora to have all the happiness she deserves, people have been unkind to her so we want to make sure she's going to be treated well and she just can't stop talking about the son of Theo Viper!" Mihai beamed in delight, his face very close to Sorina's in its round shape but his hair a curious charcoal colouring, almost grey and almost black but not exactly either. He was very pleased to have a connection to the Viper Clan and as they settled down, ignoring the usual roster and the agenda being announced below, they were eager to tell Noel about everything they were hoping for with the marriage. The most important thing it seemed was to have a clear decision on the heir and also to have young life that could claim old seats back home when ready. They were very talkative of how there was classically sixteen seats in the Romanian Vampire Diet and that though Noel would not be able to take one, any of his sons and grandsons produced would have such a position. It amused Noel to think that he would please Thibaut if he told him that, but he was still nervous on the idea that he and Sorina would have children.

"We're all currently looking through the market for our own wives, but we all wanted to wait until either Sorina or Bogdan had been married and with Bogdan having a lady he wants but Mircea being a grump, we all were hoping the Elder meeting would be the moment and well, you won't believe how glad we are that we can finally actually turn around to girlfriends and say 'you wanna get married'?" Constantin beamed in delight, sticking out his tongue and showing off one of his fangs that was actually broken. He was the youngest of the lot it seemed and was about Selene's age and clearly as cheerful and cheeky! His words came with a few grunts from the others to muse that he was far too young to be ready to marry just yet and they were all giggling in amusement. It made Noel laugh too as they all seemed to settle down, enjoy some blood that was brought to them and just to listen to the usual deliberations.

This time the missing likes of the Ukrainian, the Caucasian, the Bessarabian and Belorussian vampires along with news of the Russian massacre thanks to the dragon known as the Krimorsky awakening, was the main topic. Listening in made everyone uncomfortable, but the Bulgarian Count was able to stand up and state that the Ukrainian Warriors, once nicknamed it seemed as the Kievan Knights, were maintaining their stronghold, but that the Bessarabian court was not getting through to the Romanian or Bulgarian Courts with any form of contact. In their booth, Dacian informed them all about the fact the Bessarabian's had been the ones to classically accept the warlocks and witches exiled from the Romanian lands along with the Hungarians, but how Count Agyar, after taking power, had exiled them back out to flee to Bessarabia. Knowing this, Noel understood that there was a likelihood that the Bessarabian vampires had been removed by the same Coven upon seeing the weakness caused by the demons in the east. It seemed that the Ubitsya influence in the entirety of east Europe had kept many of the battles at bay once Vlad and Mircea had confirmed their alliance, but this was the first time no one could see or smell the bald and aged Vlad anywhere!

The concern about the Caucasian vampire having been possibly wiped out was brought up swiftly by the Turkish vampires, their Count looking distraught as the countess of the region was his own sister and the two regions had always been as thick as thieves and content neighbours. With the understanding of apparent 'Soviet' factions beyond the Veil, it was discussed that the Krimorsky's powers extended into both sides of the Veil and this meant from Finland to Siberia, would be Red Veil… demon territory. The room was quick to start grumbling and worrying at the thought of so much territory becoming seriously dangerous and unfriendly for vampires. There were rumours that there were still little pockets that would be able to resist, but grumbles about how it might turn out like the Nordic Veil that had wiped out all of its vampires and rejected all of them. The fusses were loud and unanimously obsessed with their money and their power. It irritated everyone watching and listening, but Mihai gave a grunt.

"It puts us at more risk of infiltration too… we'd have to get the Veil Agents involved to secure a Mastemma barrier and getting the Circle here to understand that will be impossible. The old guys really don't understand it's important to ask for help when you can't control something!" Mihai grunted, making the others nod their heads, he also got a soft grunt of agreement from the German booth next door that tapped at the wall to let them know it had been heard. Mihai slapped his head, he had spoken in French rather than Romanian for Noel's sake and not thought to be more secretive, but the others still nodded their heads that he was right. But as they were watching, they were all surprised when Noel's tail appeared from seemingly nowhere and was whipping about as his eyes narrowed and he gave a growl.

"Something wrong Noel? Can you see something?" Bogdan questioned, staring out across the same place as the Viper and seeing nothing. He sniffed the air too as he saw Noel drink it in, but he was not sure what was going on. The others pressed to the window too, gathering and poking their heads out so everyone below could look up and notice them watching. It caused a few faces to lift and grumble, Thibaut spotted his brother and his lip began to twitch as he sat with Gaston on the lowest level of the benches as was expected of them. But Noel's body was sensing that someone was determined to kill and it was not a vampire! His eyes scanned the groups and he noticed one of the gargoyle guards was looking just a little bit shifty near Count Yīnyǐng and certainly he would be a big target for these incursions in the east.

Without caring about the protocol and running on instinct, Noel climbed up onto the balcony banister and his companions gave bleats for him not to. Their hands snatched out to hold him, but he slid out of their grasp as he hopped down onto a thin patch of stone that was holding onto the various flags that represented some of the members of the noble circle. All eyes were turned towards him and he could feel Thibaut's furious twitching look searing through him, but he was calm and purposeful, even if his speed might be beyond them to notice as he reached a hand to grasp the Italian flag of the vampire nobles. It was flag of green, white and red that might be recognised outside of the Veil but with the bat insignia in the middle with a crown hanging above its head! He swung with it, making the Pipistrello sputter and swear for the disrespect before his feet pushed off the stone wall and he launched himself amongst the guards.

The guards gave bleats of confusion, opening their wings ready to jump and snatch, but Noel took a second to turn into a small bat, dodging through the snatching claws and then turning into his human form in a flash. His body slammed into the gargoyle he sensed the dark vibes coming from, smashing it hard into the ground with an ear-splitting crash like glass being shattered and to the surprise of all, bits of mirror flew into the air. Noel's face, shoulder, thighs and hands were sliced by the shards, but he stomped his foot down aggressively onto the seeming human hidden behind a wall of mirrors! The gargoyles shrieked in fury, scraping away the glass and hissing at the deception that a Veil Agent might be showing, but Noel's nose would not stop twitching.

He hooked the human up around the collar, spotting the little shield badge upon his chest which bore the wolf and the lamb reared up with hooves meeting within and the wings of either an angel or a dove in the middle. This person was dressed smartly, smelt human and had all the familiar looks and groans of a Veil Agent, but he should not have been an enemy to the gargoyles or to this moment within the Circle, but everything was strange. Noel looked at him firmly and his eyes flickered with a few flashes of green that made the human ease and soft pheromones were used to calm him. The nobles crowded over, eager to see what was going on as Noel spoke to him calmly, sweetly.

"You're a Veil Agent… why are you here? You smell like you want to kill someone… is that why you're here?" Noel questioned and suddenly the vampires were able to look at this human a little more. He was not too tall, rather lean and his face had an expression that was very much a mix of fury and anguish, but he looked and smelt British… why was he here? As Noel spoke, his pheromones and the flash in his eyes seemed to make the figure relax and then become hypnotised as he seemed to stare off in a daze, a soft smile upon his face as he spoke.

"It was for my sister… that Oriental bastard's son took her and killed her… he didn't do it for blood… I had to get revenge and send him to hell where he belonged. But if I got a chance to take more vampires down with him… I would take it." The figure stated and gently he placed his hand into his jacket and the gargoyles immediately growled and turned into their human forms, indicating that something with the power similar to sunlight was being removed. Straightaway Thibaut barked at everyone to get down under the tables and throw their capes over themselves. It was an automatic and swift reaction as the Vipers stood up all the same and the human pulled out a large glass ball with a brilliantly bright and hot light within, developed by the exorcists working for the Veil Agents. The human gave a wry smile and then dropped it, hoping it would smash onto the ground.

Noel's hand caught it gently, he let the gargoyles grab the human and then calmly pulled his jacket off and then wrapped it around the ball before passing it over to Gaston who gave a wink. With that, Gaston strolled out of the amphitheatre and then jogged down the hall, he was going to drop it outside in the moat as hard as he could so it would not harm anyone. He then jogged back inside when it was gone and Thibaut and Noel helped everyone stand up whilst the gargoyles cleaned up. Magic mirrors were not common and usually meant that someone had links to the witches, but it was obvious a Veil Agent could be in contact with anyone. As they settled down, the meeting was called off with a request that everyone needed to be checked and thankfully, nothing had happened in the rooms with the women or the children, but the Romanian vampires were ecstatic.

As the room started to clear, the men in their booth came galloping out and down the spiral staircase, hollering their praises for Noel with as much hype as if they'd been watching the Vampire Football! It was shocking as they barged into the main room, gaining a slew of multi-language slurs and swears from everyone filing out as they screeched Noel's name and seemed to crash into him. Noel was not expecting it as he was tackled onto the ground and firmly pulled up onto his feet again before having his hair ruffled, his cheeks kissed and clapped with his back as they hollered out their joy at his amazing skills to identify the enemy and take him out. They were hardly letting his family get close to him, or let Mircea go to touch him… Mircea just looked stunned as Bogdan gave Noel a firm kiss on the lips to make him pull back before clapping his cheeks hard.

"Marvellous! Magnificent! You sensed that all whilst sitting next to Mihai and his mouth-breathing noises!" Dacian scoffed in disbelief, only for Mihai to give a grunt and smack him on the ear. They were all then laughing and though Noel was generally shy and nervous of this, he blushed and nodded his head with a smile. Finally though, Thibaut cleared his throat loudly and the Romanians backed off with a few grumbles about how they were only being nice as the Viper Count eyed them all dangerously, his face in a grimace as he was leaning greatly onto his walking stick. He shook his head at them until Mircea stepped through with a big grin on his face, looked to Noel and then shrugging his shoulders gently.

"Alright… so as far as proving the kind of person you are… you're certainly impressive… but loyalty-wise…" Mircea began, only for the young males to glare at their uncle for thinking that display alone was not good enough, he chuckled. He grasped hold of Noel's hand firmly and then pulled him into his arms for a tight hug, squeezing him rather aggressively until he heard a slight wheeze before letting go. He clapped Noel's shoulders firmly with a vivid grin to show off his amazing fangs as he gave a soft sigh. "So… yes… sure… marry my daughter, why not? She seems to love you."

"I love her very much… thank you sir." Noel began, only for Mircea to make a chuckle that he *could* call him father but Noel had already passed him at that point. Noel ignored his brothers and his friends as he took on a sudden amount of speed, picking up his legs and jogging as far as he could out down the hall to where the women and children were being collected. Sorina was standing beside Jacinthe and Marie, Michelle was ignoring her to talk to Adelia and try to insist she should make a point to Thibaut about choosing her instead! But Noel was looking firmly towards the chubby vampire that was getting excited over her invitation to Jacinthe's wedding when Noel gave a bark. "SORINA! MARRY ME!"

"What?" Sorina questioned suddenly, looking towards his charging form in total confusion as even Adelia's eyebrow curled in total confusion at the sight of it. The news of the assassination attempt had not reached them properly yet and they could only assume that it was for this fact that Mircea had allowed it, and that the figure was galloping towards them. But when he hollered out for her to marry him again, ducking down as his shoes were skidding on the marble floor and his arms were opening out to snatch her, she stepped aside clapping her hands with a chuckle. "Of course I'll marry you!"

Just like that, Noel smashed into her with a sudden sweeping motion of his arms, throwing her over his shoulders with a loving moan. He cuddled into her broad hips as she gave a few hollers of surprise as he spun her around gently and she fussed at him to keep her skirt pressed down. He obeyed, he could not help but cry slightly with joy to be holding her like this and Sorina just shook her head at him, he was certainly a silly one and Adelia had to just grin in amusement.

Though there had been hope for a marriage to take place in Bucharest, the situation to the east encouraged Mircea that they should marry as Thibaut would in the Cathedral of Notre Dame for the entire family to attend. It was not a big wedding, there was the traditional pale blue dress of a vampire lady followed by a white veil that was laced with the colours of her country and family. There was also the large train with fabric flowers upon it that dragged down behind her and well, Theodora had been asked to hold it to help out but she'd sulked about wanting to be a flower girl and was instead scattering rose petals onto the train with a grin. The family, the Romanians, the Bulgarians, the Hungarians and indeed the French and shockingly also the Chinese nobles had all arrived to it, a small contingent anyway and Noel and Sorina were granted many gifts before joining the Romanians on a train heading home as he kissed his mother goodbye at the news he was going to a small castle on one of the so-called 'Seven Hills' in Transylvania that had been the property of Sorina's mother's family. There was hope that it would later be given to their eldest son and the mention was enough to make them both a little aware of the pressure suddenly upon them for their first time sharing a bed.

Thankfully, they were too busy for the first week of their marriage in getting to the Romanian Veil, somehow meeting the terrifying black-armour clad warriors of the Ukrainian vampires, meeting the werewolves, making friends of the Covens of the region and the various other groups in the region. They were very busy, so much so that Sorina was often going to bed before Noel was allowed to leave the other men or even explore the busy castle. The local people worked it, all of them dividing their weeks between their farms, stores and working in the castle, some of them a little worse than others at the job but all of them insisting their delight to see vampires back and to meet someone as unique as Noel. He was very tired from too much social activity and the need to be on his best behaviour to cope after their wedding, to even know anything more than how nice it was to share a bed with a warm body, didn't matter.

Their first two months went by in the same sort of chaos, with both of them lying that they'd been together just to stop any more interference before they'd needed to return to Paris for Thibaut's much more grandiose wedding. It had been a surprise to go there and then to stay at home with his family again for a week and suddenly feel that there was no longer any stress over what they were expected to do and where they were… so one early night when the sky was just turning indigo, Noel led Sorina out to the woods and to the hunter's cabin that had once been Gaston and Lynette's spot with a small bottle of wine as they decided that here there was only going to be just them!

When they gone inside, the place had been stripped of most of the violent equipment, which Noel had believed to have joined Thibaut's dungeon, but there was the soft carpet that was looking a little mossy along with most of the building and yet the wolf furs remained hanging nice and clean. It made Noel smile as Sorina hooked one down, dusted the grey fur off and then lay it upon the carpet before beckoning him to sit with her as he did so, leaning against a creaking box of unknowns. They cuddled one another gently, popping the cork from the sweet Hungarian wine that Agyar had given them and taking a swig each before sighing and nuzzling against one another, glad that it was finally quiet and they were finally alone to do as they wished.

"You know, I think this is the first time I've woken up since we married and not had an agenda pushed in front of me. I would have hoped we'd have had more room to ourselves, but it seemed everyone just wanted to say hello. If you'd been born in a more country-owning clan, you'd probably be more used to it… I was always less interesting to people so even I wasn't prepared." Sorina chuckled in amusement, snuggling up against her husband's chest as Noel sighed softly and nuzzled her head, peppering her with a few kisses before he gave a soft groan.

"Thibaut and Jacinthe had such a huge wedding… but they wanted one like ours if not one as quiet as Gaston's… I feel bad for them, they've not had a good week despite their marriage. I could sense so many uncomfortable feelings around them…" Noel sighed gently, having sensed that something was up between the pair and not at all sure what had happened on their first sleep, but Noel had sensed that Jacinthe's nervous hands and clumsy fingers were related to it, whereas Thibaut was snapping more easily at others. He was not sure what it was, but he shook his head as he took another swig of the wine before passing the bottle back to Sorina to swig before she gave a giggle and he kissed her lips softly. "But at least we don't have to do anything much when we get home… just live and be happy…"

"Heh… well, there is one thing we have to do… but we don't *have* to do that at home either." Sorina blushed softly, taking another, deeper swig before then passing it to him and giving him a slightly clumsy kiss to the lips. He gave a chuckle, kissing her back softly before then taking a deep swig himself and then putting the bottle aside. He brought his hands to her cheeks, stroking them softly to pull her lovely hair back before he pressed his lips to hers again and this time they massaged their tender flesh against each other for a moment. They paused to breathe, their cheeks flushed and giggling with excitement and embarrassment before they then leant into one another again to kiss once more and this time she stroked the slightly alcoholic taste from his bottom lip and he pulled his head back with a sudden giggle of delight. He was rubbing at his lips suddenly, they felt like they were tingling and Sorina grinned before she gently unbuttoned her sleeves and then her shirt, shifting the dress down her body before climbing out into her silken underwear.

"Uh… Sorina?" Noel questioned in surprise as she giggled and then dropped onto her knees, unbuttoning his neat puce coloured shirt and then jerked it down his shoulders as he gave a sharp grunt. He then blushed as she clambered onto his lap, pushing him back down onto the wolf fur with a grin before leaning forward to kiss him softly. He gave a soft chuckle of amusement before lounging back and gently slipping his hands onto her tan thighs, rubbing them gently and making her giggle before she asked him to take her underwear off with a quick grin that made him gulp heavily. "Alright…"

Carefully, he grasped about her thighs, taking the hem of the fabric and then slowly easing it down before she stood up and lifted her petticoat to show herself. He'd never seen a woman's lower half naked before, it was not what he'd expect to see either… it was different but that was what it was supposed to be like. She awkwardly placed a hand over herself, blushing at the way he was staring before she sat back down but a little further back, grabbing his button and zip, undoing his trousers and then pulling them down to reveal his white underwear. It was not flattering at all and made his form look rather funny as if someone had just tried to make a pair of shorts and then replaced the front of the crotch with a sock. He was quick to blush but just as she peeled his underwear down, his eyes were widening with anxiety as she looked at him and then pulled her head back with a look of surprise.

"Is this what it looks like with a foreskin?" The word made Noel's face go so red he found himself pulling his hands forward to protect himself before he gulped and told her to close her eyes and hold him. She blinked but did as he said, giving a giggle to feel him before Noel held his hand over hers and then led her to stroke up and down as her eyebrows lifted. She was almost willing to give him a commentary on the matter, but she kept quiet as she felt him get bigger and the shape and heat of it change to something longer and hotter before he let go of her hand and she was able to open her eyes and take a look again, only to blush and lean forward to kiss his lips. "Is it a bad thing to say I like how it felt in my hand?"

"No… I like that you like it too…" Noel gulped, his ears going scarlet as he tried to keep focus on the situation as she continued to touch his form with a look of utter fascination. He then brought his hands to her thighs, slipping them past her own hand as she gave a sharp gasp and he gently stroked his fingertips against the fabric of her undergarments that still seemed to bind her by the knees, glad she'd already rolled up the petticoat to sit upon him. Sorina was giving a soft grimace of anxiety at his touch, squeezing him just a little to make him give a soft growl before he strained forward towards her. "Can I kiss you again?"

Sorina pressed forward, smiling at the idea he thought he should ask but he leant back as if to avoid her. She let go of him, shifting higher up his body and bending down as his hands carefully teased her underwear down a little more so his flesh could just touch hers. For a moment, it felt like two parts of them had shared the soft brushing of a kiss and Sorina's eyes widened as she went bright pink to match and then covered her eyes with a little warble of anxiety as Noel heaved a gentle snort and then beckoned her to trust him. She gave him a funny expression, why shouldn't she trust him as he gently twisted his fingers around the fabric and gently pulled the fabric downwards enough it would not rub him or hurt her as Sorina gulped heavily.

"So… so this is… the big thing… is it?" Sorina whispered fearfully into his ear, her whole-body fidgeting and shivering because she could feel his heat at such a delicate place. Noel gave a soft grunt of acknowledgement, he then brought his lips up to hers again and she wrapped her arms around his shoulders. She then let his fingers touch her fragile place, gasping loudly and taking sharp intakes of breath as she heard slight sounds that were uncomfortably wet and certainly not lady-like before she felt the burning hot heat and her body went stiff in anxiety. She felt him gently press at her, tug just a little to make her bite her lip before he licked at her neck and she gave a soft blush. "If you mark me with your fangs… it's supposed to reduce any pain… can you… can you bite me?"

"I'll try…" Noel whispered, knowing his fangs were not as delicate as other vampires' and knowing he might injure her more… but if she would prefer this pain to any other, he'd obey. Tenderly, he rubbed at her body with his hands and her neck with his tongue, kissing and stroking at her as she shivered more gently and her skin began to feel like it was boiling. A wave of pheromones seemed to ooze from her neck as she snuggled into his body, beckoning him to take a bite and irking his fangs to become as aroused as the rest of his body. Tenderly, still stroking her delicate form to help her body prepare as she gave soft little moans of her anxiety, Noel pressed his teeth to align with her jugular and then gently pierced through into the skin.

The sensation was hot, more painful than Sorina had expected but thankfully it had made her lower body tingle enough that Noel was able to let her weight guide him into union. She was too focused on the hot sensation in her neck, the way she could feel warm blood oozing around it, but then something pulsing and drawing the pressure out whilst something else pumped into her blood to make her whole-body sigh with pleasure. She wrapped her arms about him as carefully as she could as his jaw was stretched out and his tail suddenly looped around her back as his arms finally came to hold her. They did not move for a moment, he let her whole body relax about his, drinking her blood and learning so much about her body and her health as he did so, just waiting and soaking within her boiling body before instinct begged to have control.

The air seemed to start reeking of the pheromones, echoing with Sorina's soft pants and moans of pleasure and the shuffling of their bodies against the fur beneath. Their motions were gentle, but kept a steady enough pace that there was pleasure running between them to make both moan out in delight. Noel was soon moving with more energy into her as she relaxed over him, swallowed up in the pleasurable sensations running up and down her spine like a finger. Noel was able to remove his fangs and then focus more on slowly rolling his hips with hers, dancing alongside her as they began to kiss and sigh instead, hooking about one another more frantically and groaning with more passion as their lips kept pinching and puckering and they panted together as they continued to fulfil their roles as husband and wife.

It came as no surprise to the family when the second pregnancy announced just before the birth of Elaine and Tonauac's first son, was that of Sorina and Noel. The entire household was excited by the thought of having another grandchild that was a bit more closer to home and it was the talk of the

Romanian nobles. Noel and Sorina had been showered with gifts inside their little castle and had been informed that her marriage had permitted the males to settle as well, it was rather exciting but as the time got closer to the birth, there was anxiety too. Mircea had not mentioned anything about the fate of their child if it were a girl, clearly unless they produced a son then Bogdan would still be trapped taking over, not that he was too uncomfortable with the idea of having Noel as his ally for it, but there was also something else that bothered others about this child and it was Adelia who was most aggrieved to overhear the conversations at the Noble Circle on the day she was going to meet the baby for the first time!

"I hear it would be a frightfully ugly baby… that Viper son is not exactly the most handsome, had it been from Gaston or even young Beauregard, then it might be a particularly handsome baby… but instead its Noel and mixed with Sorina? Oh darling, I'm afraid I can only imagine a pug in a Christening gown!" The snorting laughter and the high tone that reminded Adelia so much of Victorian England was coming from the rather pompous wife to the Dutch Countess' eldest son, whose name Adelia had decided not to remember. The woman was called Cordelia, of English heritage with a link to the grandmother of Count Taliesin's bloodline and she often put on a pronounced English accent when talking with Lakshmi Gala, the current wife of Count Gala the Indian Vampire. They were not being quiet about the topic and were talking specifically near to Selene who was holding onto Vittorio, who was bouncing on her knee and trying to get Adelia to snuggle him.

Adelia's head shot up and her lips curled, she wanted to breathe fire onto the haughty women that would dare insult her family, but whenever she looked angry, Vittorio would give a suddenly loud squeak. She'd drop her eyes down to his amber ones, be reminded of Theo and then manage to hold herself off from killing whilst Selene would make a point to blow bubbles onto the little boy's belly. Vittorio could speak and certainly had opinions, but he used his happy squeaks and giggles to keep everyone content and well, he was very cheerful to have around. Odette and Beauregard though were not looking comfortable, and Beau stood up, leaning to his mother's shoulder and insisting he would talk to Cordelia privately a little later.

Adelia was getting a little concerned with Beau's behaviour lately, at twenty-one he had finally graduated the academy but since turning eighteen his beauty had become more apparent and his odd coloured eyes all the more intimidating. He always had a woman beside him, not always the same but even if they saw him with others they appeared and flocked to him desperately, loving him and well… many of them were married or engaged that swooned over him. Adelia did not approve of her son being so dangerous, but Beauregard seemed to always be careful with his actions and thought she insisted he not say something so foolish, Adelia noticed the way Cordelia was looking towards her son with a slightly flustered face. Sometimes, Adelia was more disgusted by the women that went after her baby boy!

"Mother… Noel's just arrived; he's heading up with the others now – are you joining him Beau?" Odette questioned softly, this was her last time coming to the Noble Circle, she would be going to Paris to learn how to be a nurse with beings that did not care about rank as much anymore. Beau lifted his head and then tapped at his lips… he was not looking eager to go and with Gaston always sitting beside Thibaut in the stalls, it was rather obvious that there was nowhere for Beau to go as even Theodosius was sharing with the Germans because the Italians still did not like him amongst them beside Valentino. But then Odette gave a sudden shriek of excitement as she was hanging in the doorway and rushed out, telling them all that Sorina had arrived with her baby!

Beauregard settled back down beside his mother, holding her hand gently to reassure her that everything would be fine and Adelia gave him a sideways glance. She then almost jumped out of her skin when Vittorio sat beside her, grasped her hand and looked up at her with the same sort of expression. Adelia shook her head at him, really he should be playing with Theodora in the children's nursery but, Adelia did not want to go there and see Theodora ruling the roost and play acting a pharaoh getting slaves to build her tomb… which had been the case last time.

"Good evening everyone… sorry to be running late, Draga was a little fussy with her dress this morning and she seemed to want to wear the brighter colours!" Sorina shuffled in, looking oddly a little less round for having her baby but dressed in a more traditional black and white dress with colourful sleeves as she settled into the room. Her face was a brilliant smile but it was not her that everyone was stuck staring at as the whole room of relaxing noble ladies and countesses, found their eyes locked onto the baby within her arms. Though only two weeks old, the baby in her arms was wearing a brilliant smile, had a beautiful round face with big brilliant reddish amber eyes and soft coils of dark and blonde hair upon her head. A beautiful little girl was smiling towards the universe in a lovely red and white dress that Sorina had clearly made for her daughter that was so beautiful. With a little beauty spot just above her lip that made her look even more gorgeous, Adelia opened out her arm with a gasp of surprise as Sorina chuckled. "I had to call her Draga, it means dragon of course but, her full name is Draga Mea Viper, because Noel thought it was adorable to have her first two name to mean 'sweetheart', he's so gentle with her."

Sorina beamed as she snuggled her daughter's cheeks as the baby's eyes lit up in delight, before passing her gently into Adelia's arms. Tenderly, Adelia hooked up her first granddaughter, bringing her to her face and then feeling those soft little hands stroking as her tenderly. Baby Draga's face was making that strange grinning to say she was still learning how smiles worked but recognised it was a good thing. Adelia found it adorable as she leant forward to kiss her granddaughter and then pondered over the name, Draga had the tan skin of her mother, almost the olive shade Adelia's held when she was freshly fed and, in her arms, she could feel that curious confidence of all babies. Adelia was glad that Draga held her blood, then she did not fear hurting the baby as she kissed her again and the baby continued to touch her. Dragon it had meant... with that darker hair, maybe there was a reason for that name?

"Goodness... she's the most beautiful baby I've seen all year!" Lakshmi Gala had to suddenly cover her mouth, she had not expected to say it aloud and yet even Cordelia was looking a little abashed for her earlier talk. Sorina was ignorant to them, just gently stroking her daughter's pudgy cheeks as Adelia turned to look at the others with a smug expression. She was very happy to have such a beautiful granddaughter of course, but even more pleased to know that her son Noel was happy and content and enjoying being a father. But then a curious expression of anxiety fell upon Adelia's face, about to question the situation with Mircea and the succession but Sorina wagged a hand towards her mother-in-law.

"Papa said he'll wait and see what happens... he can't think about retiring for at least twenty-five years, especially when I'm quite eager to have more children and, birth was actually easy for me... it was like... uh, what was it Noel called it? Like 'shelling peas', I think?" Sorina stated and the other women present had their eyes open wider in surprise, having never heard a single woman to have given birth ever say it so casually like that. Adelia was rather shocked, but she then mused about the way some said that Sorina's wide hips made her look unattractive... clearly they had a purpose and it was pleasing to hear that she was content to have more and Adelia chuckled as Sorina then leant in closer to her. "Noel said he'd want to have as many children as would be safe… he said he never liked the thought of a lonely childhood and I'm just as content to have a happy, safe family."

Adelia was happy to hear such a thing, though she was already wondering how she would ever cope with Noel producing as many children as she'd ever produced, but it was certainly nice to think she'd have many grandchildren and Theo would be pleased. Indeed, as time would go by Noel and Sorina would produce a son named Wadim whom Mircea would take on to train as his heir in time, before two more sons in Aurel and Ferka, followed by Narcisa, a girl even more beautiful than any of the other daughters born in this new generation… at least, in Adelia's opinion!

Part Four: The Forbidden Couple

Tonauac's Land, Sierra Gorda region Mexico in the Veil, 1930

The household of Tonauac's tribe was alive with children and pregnant women, there was a lot of noise and the village was lively with its newly developed schooling program and hotel for the vampires. It was louder, more colourful but still happy since Selene had last come here and as she hopped off the boat, followed by a few of the nobles that were coming to see their grandchildren for the first time, Xiuhcoatl was waiting for her. The ghoul and gargoyle servants to have worked the boat and travelled here under Selene's direction were soon gathering up items as the upper-class beings stepped onto a wooden platform that creaked. They were quick to spot the mud, smell the fish and see the wild place they'd walked into and looked to Selene's exuberance in anxiety, but she did not care for them.

"Xiuh! I was hoping I'd get to see you first, have you missed me?" Selene chuckled as she leapt up onto Xiuhcoatl's huge broad shoulders and he hoisted her up into his arms as they rubbed their foreheads and noses together before a soft kiss. They cuddled happily and then Xiuhcoatl turned to look at the anxious beings before noticing the mud and rolling his eyes at their disgust before he turned to the soil and tapped it with his foot. He beckoned the plants and grasses within to form a layer to hold the mud and make a green carpet to the hotel for the figures to walk upon. They seemed to straighten up in appreciation before Xiuh let Selene sit calmly onto his shoulder as she sighed. "I'm looking forward to visiting and seeing Ehecatl. I've brought a camera that apparently takes better photographs to show off to everyone back home. I also want to take a lot of pictures of you too."

"I would like it if we could have a picture together, like in those papers that the others sent in. They always look so happy and beautiful together." Xiuhcoatl stated calmly as he started the steady walk on towards the tribe temple. Selene sat there comfortably for a few moments, considering what he meant and then swinging her luggage onto her lap properly and then giving a chuckle. She assumed just the modelling pictures showing off the new fashions or the celebrity images were what he might be. Perhaps he wanted a wedding photo? Selene chuckled in delight as they strolled onwards towards the jungle where she then slid down to be carried in his hands and enjoy the familiar scent and sight of the flowers as they rubbed their cheeks together with loving sighs. "Everything seems more alive today…"

"I've missed this smell, this feeling of the world being alive and wild… but at the same time I miss home because… I miss my siblings greatly. I've been visiting Dio and Vittorio a lot lately, he's grown so big now!" Selene beamed in delight as she lay back and rubbed her head against his broad chest to make him chuckle softly. But she was feeling oddly depressed at the thought of being separate from Xiuhcoatl again after this and she heaved a sigh. He noticed and he kissed her head gently and mused over how beautiful her silver hair was as she stretched her hand up to touch his dark golden hair with a chuckle. They both beamed in amusement at one another before Selene then looked towards the temple in the jungle and she gave a funny expression. "I don't know what it is… but something feels… different."

"If it helps… you're in what would be referred to as 'season' amongst the animals." Xiuh stated so calmly that it made Selene's eyebrows lift and her amber eyes widen in surprise. She certainly had not expected that there was something about her body going on that he could react to like that and she blushed as she brought her hand back to her face. She was quick to look up at him in fascination, but he gave a soft chuckle. "We're bonded… I can tell… though Tonauac can as well as the leader so he would not probably want us to share a room."

"Oh… does he not believe in prophylactics?" Selene questioned, only for Xiuh to give an expression of utter shock and then a grimace as he turned his head to the side. Selene looked at him thoughtfully for a moment before considering the sizes of the products that were issued. She rather doubted there was a suitably sized sheath for him… but sex was not the only reason she was happy to see Xiuhcoatl again and gently she gave him a kiss to the chin. "Don't worry about it, it was just a joke. I know the rules."

Xiuh smiled happily to her as he continued to carry her onto the familiar ground that lay before the temple structure and included the secret hatch that brought her to him. He set her down and gently lifted the hidden opening up as she chuckled and then leapt inside, sliding down with a loud shriek of enjoyment as Xiuhcoatl chuckled and then sunk down through the earth to his original position. Once here, Selene bounced against his foot as she halted her slide and then was sitting there with a wide smile upon her face, her dress scuffled but she did not care as she stood up and held Xiuh. They cuddled one another for a while, snuggling against one another for a time before they kissed and there was a soft giggle from nearby that made Selene jump in surprise.

"You're looking happy together… it's good to see you again Selene." Yoloti was standing in the passage with a grin on his face, glad to see them both and beside him, his wife was leaning out with a slight belly showing as she giggled at them. Selene pulled backed from Xiuh, rushing over to the daughter of Sahib and cuddling her tightly. They kissed cheeks and Selene explained how she was so excited because Sahib had sent the girl's younger brother to greet her and learn about the baby. Yoloti was beaming in pride as he ruffled Selene's hair to make her jolt before she hugged him suddenly and he gave a grin. "Tizoc's getting married soon too you know, once word had gone out we were about, a female from the rainforest of Brazil was sent to us. She arrived with her face painted half-red and ready to fight if she needed to, Tizoc was beaten by her and made sure to get the same agreement Xiuh had made with you!"

"Really? I was not expecting myself to be such an influence, but I'm glad he's found someone worthy of him. Shall we get in and I can see my sister!" Selene squeaked, hopping on her feet but showing obvious signs that she was actually getting excited to see another baby! Yoloti was sniggering as he led her in, but Xiuh insisted he was on his guarding shift for the rest of the daylight and so Selene gave him a quick kiss to the ear before she turned and trotted inside with the others. The temple was brightly lit inside, there was no longer the feel of various eyes boring into her or the whispers to say someone was with them. Instead there were giggles and the sounds of happiness and a busy community as Selene strolled calmly into the hall where the children were all playing happily when it was clear Yoloti had been trying to teach them about the heritage of the Elder.

As soon as Selene stepped inside, all nine toddlers of varied ages stopped giggling or playing and were suddenly staring directly at her in total fascination to see a stranger. She was carrying her bag too and the eyes were looking from it to her silver hair, trying to figure out whether they were looking at a stranger or just something interesting. Selene beamed, she understood but she was most amused by the oldest child, an eleven-month-old child, pulled himself up onto his legs. He grabbed hold of the nearby seats and then began to ease himself along, gripping the side of the seat towards her, his red eyes almost magenta and burning with his head covered in a thick crop of blue hair. There was no doubt in Selene's mind who he was and swiftly she waddled over to greet him, knowing that Elder children were usually more advanced mentally than non-Elder children and so she went down on her knees and opened out her arms to greet the figure as Yoloti chuckled.

"Are you… Eh-he-kar-tul?" Selene sounded the word out as she assumed it to be and the baby paused, his face pinching up into a scowl as he seemed to sniff the air expectantly, not really sure of the figure in front of him. Selene was a bit worried, she did not want her nephew to be fearful of her and she made sure to drop down onto her knees and open her arms out as wide as she could. But the baby then seemed to give a grunt and waddle into her arms as she gave a delighted sound of praise for his walking abilities. He swung his arms to hold hers as she lifted him up and then suddenly pulled him into a tight hug, which made him go suddenly limp and panic her. "Oh no… have I hurt him?"

"Not at all Selene… Ehecatl has developed a dislike to cuddles from somewhere and just goes limp whenever his father cuddles him too much. He's quite a character already." One of the other women had called out to her with a chuckle, making Selene give a wheeze of relief to know she had not done something to hurt him but she calmly stopped squeezing him and he readjusted his position. She sat down holding him and he pulled himself into a sit and was suddenly grasping at her face. Selene opened her mouth, let her fangs show a little and let him explore as she had the other babies of the family, Vittorio and Draga! But Ehecatl then grasped onto her silver hair tightly, focusing on it intently before looking up at her amber eyes with a grunt of surprise.

"You're interested in my hair, right? It looks like it belongs to an older woman but I'm young… its strange, isn't it? I don't know why I have silver hair; all my siblings have blonde hair like your mother… my sister. Except Gaston and Odette, they have your grandmother's black hair." Selene chirped, she'd always been at a loss for her hair colour but with the knowledge there was demon in their bloodline, odd hair colours went hand in hand with natural variance in eye colour of vampires stemming back from their demonic nature. Ehecatl then seemed to stroke at his blue hair and it made Selene grin, of course the Elder's hair, eyes and skin could be any colour… she'd even heard there were green-skinned Elders in the Polish Veil! "Your hair is beautiful… I'd love to have blue hair."

Selene beamed at her nephew, and he seemed to take it in and made a brief show of a satisfied smirk to state she amused him. Selene then let him go to do what he wished, but he slumped back against her, the prince deciding upon his throne and Selene completely stuck where she was. Selene was not bothered and she pulled out a special picture book for children from her bag that was in French and presented it to Ehecatl to choose what he wished her to read. A little book on the kinds of jungle animals seemed to make sense to him and so he patted his hand to it and she began to read to him.

The other babies soon shuffled over, pulling close to her to look at the pictures and clap their hands as she told them in French and then in Spanish what the words were. Hearing the different names and the language change seemed to be of more interest to the babies than the pictures and Selene was intrigued by the way Elder children seemed to learn and understand. Selene was quite content by the time Elaine arrived with a basket of bread she'd brought from the village, only to spot the scene and chuckle. One of the other male Elder arrived to take the food from her and as she settled down beside her sister, Selene turned to give her a kiss on the cheek before Ehecatl gave his mother a very affectionate look before scowling.

The baby looked from his mother to the book and back again, his mind confused over what he wanted to do as the urge to greet his mother was too strong to disobey. He turned towards the book and then towards Selene, his beautiful red-brown skin turning crimson as his eyes began to fill up with tears and suddenly, Ehecatl began to bawl heavily because he did not wish to choose between them. Automatically Selene was looking panicked as the other children began to look stressed, however Elaine hooked up her son, cuddled him lovingly and then sat back around the group of children as Selene continued to read and Ehecatl calmed down. The children were soon looking sleepy, and Selene got to help put them all to bed, including Ehecatl.

"I was told he's a character, but it's astonishing how much he's like you and mama... Elaine. He has this self-assuredness and this attitude." Selene began, watching her sister chuckle as she settled her son down into his woven basket within the collective nursery. It seemed during the night was the only time the baby went into the parents' room, apparently to encourage them to understand what bedtime meant and what bedrooms were for, but it made Selene amused to see Elaine coping so well with a baby as she beckoned her sister out to sit down in a small cave filled with a soft, cooling air that made Selene slump back with a smile. "I've got to make sure to take a photograph of you holding him for mother, she's desperate to know what he looks like and acts like... your letters take six months to reach us and the telegrams are never exactly as fast as they should be!"

"Heh… you all expect too much of me, I'm here in Mexico, I'm not Theodosius or Noel in other parts of Europe! The world's a big place." Elaine chuckled pleasantly, patting her sister's shoulder and making Selene stick her tongue out at her. Of course, Selene understood that… she'd come here first after-all, but it was clear that Elaine felt a kind of superiority for her time here over Selene's and it made her younger sister feel a little forgotten. But the two were soon chattering away with each other and laughing over everything they'd been experiencing at home and abroad. There was a lot to talk about, the issues outside the Veil thanks to an economic collapse that was affecting the Veil with more migrants and less work to go around. There was also the rise of a group that had been producing pamphlets that most people just cast aside… the Purists they called themselves.

The conversation continued on with Elaine nodding her head slowly in acceptance to all of the news before Selene had pulled out a booklet from her bag. Within were wedding photographs that Elaine had not been able to see as well as pictures of Vittorio as he was growing at five years and then also the only photograph of baby Draga. The black and white image had Elaine clapping her hands in excitement, insisting that she'd never seen such a beautiful baby before Selene had told her all about the way Sorina had thrown it back at the women to have given her callous comments over the years. The two of them were very pleased to share that opinion and pride in Sorina's strength, as well as how beautiful they both felt the child was. But then Elaine's hand had tapped on the image of Gaston and Lynette.

"Nothing from them yet? I would have thought they'd have a house full… then again, I thought she would have been pregnant during their secret liaisons… those two were worse than dogs in heat!" Elaine scoffed, making such a rude observation that Selene lifted her hand to refute it. She reminded her older sister that, as Lynette was a werewolf, there was an issue in any reference to dogs around her and Elaine clapped her hand over her mouth with a grunt of apology. Selene was glad though that now Ehecatl was born, Elaine no longer looked at the pictures of Vittorio with Theodosius and Valentino with a touch of sadness or jealousy… Ehecatl seemed to have removed all questions on who her children were. But Elaine still looked to the image of the pair together, noticing uncomfortably that Lynette was in her forties now, mortal and then she grimaced. "They say conception is hard between our species?"

"I hear but… I think Lynette never wanted children to begin with… I could never say if she was doing anything about it but, she never seemed to exhibit the monthly symptoms like others and Gaston made her go to a specialist last year as a final time only for the doctor to inform him she was barren from the beginning. I didn't know how that could be possible to assess but… Gaston's focused heavily on being a good uncle and good brother. He's happy though." Selene stated, but it gave them both a lump in their throat; it was sad enough that the law forbade a werewolf being turned and that most werewolves were mortal with only a seventy-year lifespan at best. It also seemed extra painful to think that there would be no child born from the pair and yet they had to agree that being together was something the pair were more than happy with, until Elaine looked to the pictures of Jacinthe and Thibaut and their awkward expressions.

"Poor Jacinthe… I can't imagine how she's doing as Thibaut's wife… his expectations for her are probably exceptionally strict and of course… have they had any luck trying to…" Elaine was going to ask if there was any sign of a pregnancy between them yet, but there was a strange expression upon Selene's face to say that it was not a subject to discuss. The pair went silent, an uncomfortable sensation fell upon them and Elaine was able to read that there had likely been a miscarriage and she did not want to comment and wound either of them. However, Selene gave a soft grunt of irritation to think that Elaine still thought their brother would be cruel as a husband, though it had been obvious only to a few about how in love the pair really were and so Selene lifted a hand and cleared her throat.

"To be fair, they're a very content couple… it's just the stress about an heir that's troubling them. Jacinthe is desperate to give him a baby and Thibaut is just… he is giving up his weekends completely to give her as much attention as she wants and well, he's very romantic with her. He's always buying her gifts, kissing her… in fact it's made us all worry a few times that this is actually someone in disguise…" Selene explained, thinking to how she would see the pair holding hands, sitting in Thibaut's private garden and just stare into each other's eyes thoughtfully. She had to admit, she did think she did that when she was alone with Xiuhcoatl, but it was hard to tell if there was anything that could be said staring at each other that long. Surely it was just some romantic hogwash and even Elaine was looking rather disgusted at the idea for a little while as Selene sighed. "Thibaut shocked us all though… Taliesin teased if he'd be unhappy to have a girl instead of a boy and he mentioned… he'd keep going to get his male heir but, he would be the happiest Count alive to have a daughter. I never even thought he liked children."

"That is a little… well… no, he was always attentive with Odette and Theodora, whom he particularly spoilt but… who can say? Maybe he's far more enlightened about gender issues than I ever thought he was." Elaine chuckled softly and the pair of them were soon giggling about how they were likely to have little Jacinthe's running around the place and Thibaut murdering any of their potential lovers because no one was good enough for them. They laughed at the thought, it was so easy to assume their brother's possessiveness as well, when it came to Theodora there had been troubling developments now that she was ten and playing kiss chase! "Heh… its funny, being away from him there's a sort of sense of loss… like I actually miss the stoic bastard."

"Really? I'll tell him you said that…" Selene grinned and suddenly she was being tickled and wrestled by Elaine as they tugged at each other, pulled hair and were just playing around in total delight for a while. Their giggling soon calmed as they hugged each other tightly, sighing heavily as they considered how long it had been and how much they had missed one another. But before they could have a chance to talk about anything more, dinner was called and they both got up to eat. Everyone greeted Selene happily when she stepped in, but Tonauac was missing and as everyone began to eat, Selene could almost sense that something odd was going to happen, that something was up as she continued to eat away in delight, chatting as everyone did before Tonauac appeared.

He stepped in and the lights of the fires seemed to roar louder as he stepped in with a smile and a grumpy looking Ehecatl within his arms. It was clear the yearling was unhappy with something but in his father's arms he was relaxing until he noticed his mother. Selene had been informed by her sister too that Ehecatl was being weaned off milk and that he would get hungry and clingy but he was on a strict rule not to have anything from her. Tonauac stepped out with a bottle of prepared milk from a goat that had been donated to the community by the villagers and was a very pleased goat indeed. Tonauac was soon bringing it to his son's mouth as he greeted everyone and then strolled over to the end of the table with the happiest of smiles upon his face to see his favourite relative.

"Little Selene… Moon Child… it's so good to see you again!" Tonauac gently fed his son as he bent to nuzzle cheeks with Selene as she giggled and then Tonauac gently kissed Elaine's cheek before he settled to eat too. As he sat, his nose started to twitch intently, catching something curious that then made him shake his head firmly with a grunt… but his hair went pitch black as if he was angry. The entire tribe noticed and went pale, freezing as they ate as Tonauac continued to feed his son and drink in the air, Selene looking to her sister for some kind of understanding, but Elaine lifted her hand up to keep anyone from saying anything that could irritate the figure.

"Do you smell something rotting?" Elaine quizzed him, her expression calm and stern so that he knew there was nothing to panic about. It was not that Tonauac had an explosive nature to him, but knowing that if he got upset, Elaine would remain calm, he was quite thankful for it and took a deep sigh. He turned to her, sniffed deeply and then kissed her lips lovingly, his expression utterly adoring. Elaine noted the flash of pink and red within his hair, knowing very well that it hinted to arousing thoughts and she'd begun to understand that there was a certain manner to the things that happened here as she gave a soft chuckle of understanding. "Ah… well, I'm content to try for another, I do love our boy very much but I have to wonder if we'll have a girl I can raise properly."

There was then a relaxed chuckle within the group and it seemed to settle down slightly to encourage them all to just chat about the idea. Selene was relieved, it sounded like whatever she had sensed was calming, until Tonauac continued to sniff at the air. He passed Ehecatl into Elaine's arms, letting her give her son a lecture on why he needed to behave himself… it was something almost amusing but for Tonauac standing up and sniffing the air. The room went still once more and Selene could see a look of aggression forming upon Tonauac's face as the other females shrank down and something became obvious….

Selene had learnt from the werewolves that if two females were in season at the same time, the more dominant might attack the other to ensure she mated first. It was to keep hierarchy in the pack, numbers under control, but also to make sure that there were no rivals for the materials on display and no unworthy bloodlines started. It made Selene worry a little, she thought about what Xiuhcoatl had mentioned about her being in what might be called a 'season' and then the conversation between Tonauac and Elaine just then. Was she the lesser wolf that had come into season and was making herself a rival purely by accident?

When Tonauac reached her side and snuffled at her, he straightened up with a low grunt of understanding and a sad expression upon his face. He was shaking his head firmly and then heaving a sigh that almost made him seem a disappointed tutor. It worried Selene and Elaine was starting to look a little irritable that something was happening between them that was not to her liking. But then Tonauac patted Selene's shoulder knowingly and cleared his throat as Selene prepared to be shouted at or told she would have to be locked away from anyone or even sent out to the village with the other vampires. She was an honorary member of the tribe; she did not want to be cast out for any reason and yet Tonauac was calm as he spoke.

"Selene… I'm afraid it appears that you have come to us at a time that could be awkward should you be left around Xiuhcoatl. I would request that once your meal is finished, you will go to the Moon Pool area and stay there for the night. You will be alone but it is to ensure that you and he do not make a fatal mistake." The words 'fatal' made Selene a little anxious as she dared to ask him what that even meant in the situation, and he took a steady sigh and then looked towards Elaine. She was holding her son close, trying to judge if there was anything sexist in this conversation… but the traditions of the tribe she could not be interfered with in this situation, especially when it was Selene's own protection and then Tonauac said something that caught all the non-Elders by surprise. "Xiuhcoatl is of the lowest rank… tradition states that if he were to produce a child, that child would have to serve as the sacrifice for the tribe to maintain a balance and prevent the curse of sunlight falling upon us. For the sake of the tribe's survival, we have to honour that the lowest is the lowest."

"What?" Selene questioned, but Elaine lifted her hand, she'd heard something about it before and knew very well that there was an ancient link to this and she mentioned one word that kept everyone quiet… the Nephilim. By all histories of the Veil, the Elders were the descendants of the last of that kind of half-angel, half-human giants with brutish manners and violent tempers, beings that should all have been drowned in the flood. The children to depart had agreed that the strongest of their kind born within a tribe was deemed the most akin to the sinful Nephilim… if they were to not take a punishment as guardian of the tribe and the willing sacrifice should anything happen, they must be purged so the curse of the Nephilim and another Great Flood did not occur again. By essence, if they had a child then it must be sacrifice to Moloch to reject the demonic aspect of their nature and from it, traditions of sacrifice and the devouring of humans that broke rules and entered their grounds had come about. To ensure the Nephilim never fully bred back to humans, this was the belief and Selene found herself confused.

She said nothing in response but a soft 'oh' and then bowed her head in acceptance as everyone returned to a quiet meal. Selene's heart though was confused, she believed in God and angels and demons, but she believed that within the Veil there was no fear of beings like the Nephilim ever holding that kind of power again. Here, everything was safe and there was no need for this kind of superstition… but as a member of the tribe she had to obey and gently she just settled back to eating until she was full. Elaine gave her an anxious look when she finished, trying to think how to help her sister in this situation, but even she had to admit that she believed in the barbarism of the Nephilim of legend and if this was what the tribe had done to prevent such an action, then it was all they could do to prevent such superstition… but it tasted bitter.

"Ah… I'm lucky, I get to see the stars in the night sky tonight and see the Moon Pool in its full glory… goodnight everyone. Goodnight nephew… goodnight sister, goodnight Tonauac." Selene beamed in delight, hurrying to kiss them all and cuddling them until she paused to meet Tizoc's mate. She went to kiss but got a bear hug of thanks that made her smile before she departed, her head down as her stomach began to knot in discomfort for the first time in a very long time. She could not think of anything to have made her feel so disappointed and confused before, yet she obeyed them as she strolled out with her bag and past Xiuhcoatl's guarding post, followed by one of the others to ensure she got there when she paused beside Xiuh. "Darling… I'm to stay at the Moon Pool tonight, you're not to come near me, understand?"

"Yes… I understand." Xiuhcoatl bowed his head but then Selene almost shook her head in disbelief when she witnessed him give her a wink. She was not sure what it meant, but he would obey the rules as he should and gently she went out and up the clambering path with its firm vine to the ground in front of the temple complex. She paused to take in the broken step pyramid carefully, noticing the way it seemed almost shadowed and unwelcoming this time and with a sigh she strolled on through the hills and the thick jungle undergrowth as she paced the familiar trail towards the pool as the sky was growing dark, before she was interrupted by the appearance of a large jaguar that strolled her way, a female that was swishing her tail.

It made Selene pause for a moment, she smiled at the cat as it whipped its tail and then let out a low groaning sound that was to attract a mate to her. She watched in fascination as the female strolled on, giving Selene a knowing look before it seemed to pick up into a jog and there was a hefty grunt behind. A big male jaguar, smelling of blood from a few whacks to what appeared to be a bloodied nose, frothing at the mouth, appeared. He was clearly just eager to keep up with her no matter what because this was his chance with her… his chance to complete what people always seemed to say was the cause of life… to pass on a part of yourself to the next generation.

It was more a way to gain immortality than any other method and Selene found herself just watching the pair catching up and hurrying off together. But she almost wanted to turn on her heel, rush back and grab Xiuhcoatl and pull him away with her, make him chase her like the cats and yet she sighed heavily. Selene had caused enough trouble and risk with him by being intimate, she was happy with what she had with him… was she just feeling a bit left out because everyone else in the family had babies….

"Huh… its simple… just the womb in my body trying to convince me that its time and it isn't." Selene stated, making a lowering gesture with her hands as if to calm down that organ as she continued to stroll with her bag to the familiar form of the Moon Pool and the trees alongside it. Selene sighed, stripping naked automatically and then slowly dipping her feet into the water, taking the pins out of her hair that had held her fringe back. She let her silver locks roll around her body and then sighed softly as she looked up to the moon itself that was shining out over her, making Selene then gently slide into the pool. Once she was inside, she settled back against the stones and then watched the moonlight suddenly fall upon the pool and turn it as silver as her hair as she closed her eyes and sank down to her nose with a soft sigh.

As she lounged within the pool, she almost felt like the water of the moon was merging with her own body, twisting and filling it with something more. She felt herself wanting to cry out like the jaguar had for her mate to come and join her and she brought her hands to her head, holding it gently with a groan. It was not a headache; it was like there was only one thought in her head and she wanted to leap out of the water and find Xiuhcoatl… maybe this was why she had been told to stay away from him? Selene groaned in frustration and then she settled back into the pool as she splashed around and kicked about a bit, feeling better for the splashing before she then sat in a more meditative position.

For a while, Selene was sitting there with her hands together and looking up to the sky with a groan of frustration, feeling at a loss as it grew darker and unwilling to go to sleep because her body was not tired. She remained within the water, letting her skin eat up the minerals as she then paddled to the other side, leaning over the edge and staring down below at the scene of the temple and the rest of the landscape. Warm fires were glowing through the varying levels and in the distance there was the flickering of lights from the village. Bats were soon out dancing in the air, hungrily grabbing their prey and the night predators were becoming loud in the heavy warmth that began to fall upon Selene and make her thankful for the coolness of the pool as she stared out to the horizon where the sun had set.

There was then the sound of the brush and fern pulling back, not being pushed but almost sliding away and Selene gave a sigh. She assumed that Yoloti had been sent to keep an eye on her and keep her company, but she was not in the mood for his jokes and not really in the mood for anything but the warmth of Xiuhcoatl's body. She was feeling such a keen loneliness and distress that she could almost smell his warm, almost sandy scent in the air around her, until she heard someone step into the water and the pool seemed to rise. Her skin was crawling in excitement as she felt the waves of a big being swim over to her side and then she sighed happily to see the tanned skin and the loving expression upon the face of her mate as he bent his pierced lip to her for a loving kiss as she sighed and held his shoulders.

"It's really you, isn't it?" Selene questioned gently and Xiuhcoatl bent his head about to give her another kiss before she stretched her hand out to stroke at the ring upon his lip. She then sat back, giving him a curiously sceptical and yet somehow coy expression that made Xiuh smile knowingly as her soft hand then gently stroked over his chest to reach the nipple that was still pierced. Here she licked and stroked at it gently, making him shudder as she looked up at him with a thoughtful smile upon her face before he bent to kiss her again before lifting one of his big hands. He gently stroked at her breasts, stroking the left breast and down to the nipple where the opposite ring sat rather comfortably to her now and she gave a chuckle. "Alright… it's you… but what are you doing here? Aren't you going to get in trouble?"

"Maybe… but I'm quite willing to accept castration if I can just spend this rare time together. We don't get to see each other already because of our fates and our families… so why would I give up that time? Besides… Tizoc and his mate have taken up my guarding job for the evening and have told Tonauac that I will be near the village… he will not leave Elaine tonight." Xiuhcoatl stated gently, but Selene could see from the way he lowered his head and slammed her hand right to his chest, that he was showing his sincerity. It was clear that it was a risk for him, but perhaps like Selene he had felt that strange desire of their bodies calling out to one another. He then sat down into the pool, beckoning Selene into his lap as she gave a blush and then settled there, nuzzling her face into his broad chest, sighing happily as he wrapped his arms about her.

But then, rather suddenly as if to make the mood just a little more light-hearted, Xiuh lifted a hand, put it to Selene's head and gently plonked her into the water. She pulled her head up, her hair smothering her face from view but after a few spitting sounds, he could tell she was grimacing at him for doing that. Xiuhcoatl then ducked into the water, only for Selene to splash water right into his face, which did not faze him until he splashed back and the pair began a little war against one another, giggling and chuckling away heartily. It was probably one of the few times that Xiuhcoatl had a chance to be so playful and then, rather suddenly, Selene disappeared into the pool and did not resurface.

"Selene?" Xiuh questioned, standing up and wading about the pool until he felt something poke the top of his submerged hip. He spun around, arms snatching into the water, but he missed her. He chuckled as he squatted in the water, feeling for Selene until he heard her surface behind him and he turned about with a grin, only to have water spat into his face. Selene then ducked right back into the deep pool and, in the moonlight where the surface shone back silver, it was hard to see where she might have gone and so he stretched his arms out again… only to feel a sharp pinch to his backside that made him leap with a yelp. "That's not playing fair!"

He grinned as he dropped onto his knees, letting the water bare his weight as he paddled gently through the great pool in the cliff, feeling for Selene wherever he could. He thought he caught her ankle, trying to snatch it until he felt a tug somewhere more private and bolted upright, his big hands covering himself as his innocent nature beckoned him to go scarlet. Selene's head popped out of the water beside him, a wicked and even dirty look on her face that made him chuckle as he pulled her into his arms, kneeling so they were nose to nose. Gently they kissed each other, and she swung her arms around his shoulders, feeling him lift her chest up from the water as their lips wrestled and massaged… that ring tingling and tickled each time it touched her lips.

Then, Xiuh's head bent to her neck, he licked and kissed lovingly at her neck, lifting her up so she could lean over him as Selene gave a sharp gasp of delight. Her spine was tingling in delight as she felt his tongue exploring the ring he'd given her, the soft tug, the way it made her nerves bite with pleasure as she groaned in her pleasure. He nuzzled against her chest, even rolling and pinching his lips against it to change the sensation as she groaned and shivered and nibbled her lips before grasping his head tightly to beckon him to stop the intensity. He paused, pulling her down into the water and then lounging upon his back, letting her lay over his chest as he gave a soft chuckle of affection.

"Having these moments with you are priceless… it just saddens me that once more, we'll have to be alone with our memories." Selene stated with a heavy sigh as she lounged onto him, feeling more than a little excited to feel their naked bodies touching again. Xiuh let the water hold their weight, the pair of them just gently floating and bobbing along with smiles upon their faces before Selene gave a soft snort and kissed his lips, making them dip in the water again. But as their arms looped about one another lovingly, the distant roar of a male jaguar made Selene's skin shudder in excitement as she then looked at him firmly. "You know… if we just ran away from here together… went off into the jungle and founded our own tribe… we'd never have to be separate from each other."

Xiuhcoatl suddenly sat down into the water, pulling Selene in with him so that she had to kneel into his lap to be face-to-face as they both looked at one another anxiously. His cyan blue eyes were screaming that he would love it but there was something that was holding him back completely and Selene grimaced as she pushed her head against his chest. She was hateful, she knew what he was going to say and that it would be a no in the end, but she gripped his shoulders and insisted she did not want to hear his answer at all. She did not want to hear the refusal and yet he brought his hands to her soft cheeks so delicately that her eyes looked to him mournfully and they both shared a miserable expression as Xiuh sighed.

"I would love to run away with you… there are moments each day where I contemplate abandoning everyone to have my own happiness. But we cannot be selfish… because, if I left, then Tizoc would have to take that role and he has a mate and an important position now… it would mean another would have to take on this burden." Xiuhcoatl stated and Selene groaned in frustration, she wished that she had found someone just like her other siblings that were more willing to throw aside such ideas of duty or care for the future as long as they were together. She wished that Xiuh and her could both have the strength of Theodosius and Valentino… but though their love was as strong, their love for their family was just as strong as she cuddled into him tightly. She wanted to weep, she wanted to scream out that life was not fair and they should not have to carry the burden of a culture that would not let them be together… but it wasn't the culture, they both loved all of the people in their lives and running away would only hurt them.

"I guess we can't help but be the people we are… the fact Tonauac allowed us to be a couple in the first place was wonderful… but hoping for the chance to just have children without risk was always going to be a separate matter. I don't want anyone to think any child we have is damned or troublesome… but I do not, *not* want to have a child with you." Selene grumbled against him, hating the fact that Xiuhcoatl was holding her so calmly and once more able to hold onto his own sorrow and dismay about their situation. His stoic face was always good at hiding his despair, but he nuzzled into her wet hair, kissing her gently and then slowly he began to wade back to the side of the pool and settled her down on the edge of it before pulling himself up.

"I was thinking… there are many orphaned children in this world that we might be able to take in, maybe the child will not be ours together but we can treat it as such and it will always have our affection. I do not think that would be against the rules, especially if it lived with you. I do not know how that would work, but time is something we have a good amount of." Xiuhcoatl stated gently, reminding Selene that he'd been orphaned and raised alongside Tizoc by Tonauac and Yoloti, they'd been very lucky in fact. Selene smiled up at him lovingly, nuzzling against him, kissing his chin and then slipping off his lap and stepping out into the jungle, completely naked as Xiuh tilted his head to the side but followed after her.

They both walked naked under the moonlight, above them the sky was painted in stars that shone out as if to compete with Selene's radiant hair as she skipped out to the grassy clearing between the next patch of jungle where a house had once stood. In the moonlight her hair was waving about and Xiuhcoatl strolled after her, a glorious smile upon his face as he hurried to her side and then grasped her by the wrist. She spun around, clapping into him and for some reason, he chose to drop back down into the long grass.

She lay upon his stomach, the grass swaying in the moonlight around them as they listened to one another's heart before their lips came together. As they continued to kiss together lovingly, their bodies began to grasp one another, intertwining their forms and nuzzling against one another. Then Xiuhcoatl rolled to be above Selene, his lips coming to her as their chests touched and their bodies began to burn with a growing desire. His big hands stroked along her body and she sighed lovingly as she kissed the hand that came to stroke her face. Then the big hand stroked back down her body, stroking her wet and soft thighs before moving to a more sensitive spot. Selene caught her breath in surprise as Xiuh bent his body down to smother her with a passionate kiss as his fingers dared to try and satisfy the craving in their bodies.

At his motions she was writhing and groaning out beneath him, her legs spreading wide to let his fingers touch deeper as he moved gently. He made sure that she felt only the most pleasure as he sought the spots that made her hips jolt and her back arch. She moaned and sighed, her hands smothering her face for a moment, though he kissed her to encourage her to reveal the desperation upon her face. As their tongues then stroked at one another, she lifted her hips to his fingers, letting them get deeper again until she pulled away from him with a sudden bark as Xiuhcoatl looked to her anxiously… knowing this was the best way they could make each other feel good without risk.

"I can't… it's not… it's not good enough… please Xiuh… we're with each other so rarely, it really won't do any harm…" Selene begged and Xiuhcoatl could not refuse her when his whole being was screaming for total union. Their arms wrapped about each other again, they kissed more firmly and desperately as Xiuhcoatl then pulled back to kneel down over her, taking in a deep breath to try and calm himself before he looked down. Selene's body was tingling with heat and twinkling in the moon, her starlight hair glittering as if to make her into some sort of moon goddess to tempt him. Her body was quivering with excitement, her beautiful shape and full breasts so beckoning as she panted up at him, a smile on her face as her lips seemed to glisten. "Come Xiuh… let me bite you…"

He couldn't deny her and he could not deny himself as he bent over her and wrapped himself about her. She gave a playful chuckle and then a strained grunt that then began a quivering gasp of pleasure. Their bodies came together with more eagerness and ease then before, as their lips joined and their tongues massaged and mimicked the actions of their bodies lower down. She held his shoulders, pulled back to pant gently, her breasts heaving and rubbing up against his chest, making their rings tap and tingle as they moved in steady rhythm together. They sighed and moaned in pleasure, stroking each other's faces ad hair before kissing again, pinching their eyes shut to focus more on firmer motions, before Selene let her fangs show and dared to bite into his shoulder.

Xiuhcoatl permitted it, letting her fangs sink so deeply into his neck that he hoped the bruising would remain forever. She took in some of his blood, the pair of them soon sharing the ecstasy the other was feeling and then moving more. They became drunk on each other, Selene moaning and groaning as her fangs drank in his blood and made his body breathe for her own. Xiuhcoatl growled and panted, the air getting so hot as it rolled past his lips and the hunger becoming desperate. They moved faster, firmer, touching every part of one another that sang until finally, Selene removed her teeth and together they roared and screamed out to the moon at a time the jaguars seemed to roar around them.

The earth seemed to have moved for them and the animals of the wild began a louder night chorus as if to protect them as they rested together....

An hour or so passed, the moon was still high but Xiuhcoatl was sure he needed to wake up and return to his position on guard, but he did not want to separate her warmth from his. He held her tightly against the chorus of night frogs, kissing her shoulder tenderly until she gave a grunt and slowly woke up. Her hand stroked his face and she was still feeling satisfied as he sighed.

"It's time to go, I don't want to risk you being in danger." Xiuhcoatl spoke firmly, but his heart was aching as he held her hand away and rolled aside. He sat up and looked about to start walking when Selene wobbled onto her feet and slumped over his back. She kissed the little circular bruises on his neck with a loving sigh that made his heart sink. She stroked at the great heavy golden hoops on his ears, kissing the back of his neck and then sighing heavily.

"Why don't we just runaway and be happy together?" Selene's tone was depressed, she was clearly unwilling to bring up the topic but both their hearts were aching. An awkward silence sat between them and through it, each rationalised the reason to go. If they abandoned the others, if they went out on their own then they could start anew. There would be no society to bind them under crude constraints and no family to honour or uphold. They could chart their own course in the jungle and cast aside old hates and rules for this new world and new time. They could thrive and they would survive it too....

"But..." Xiuh said the dreaded word first, the word that was a refusal in disguise but all the more devastating. The three-letter word chastised her thoughts even if they had just been wishes and she lay her head to his back. She listened to the heaviness of his heart as he took in a deep breath and spoke the words that felt like doom but were sensible. She felt guilty for mentioning it, but they both knew the other's heart in this matter. "Neither of us could stand denying our loved ones of more love. We would only blame one another should we run and their lives change for the worse. It's harsh and unfair, but we wouldn't be happy or whole without them."

"It's so strange isn't it, for my parents there was no such loyalty because it stopped their happiness. Our happiness is affected but, it makes our love stronger." Selene stated with a grimace, she did not want to have another dictating if she had children or not. But she knew it would hurt them in the end, the guilt would eat them away inside. Gently, she nuzzled into his back and gave a soft sniffle, only for him to turn about and hold her close. "I love you, no matter what, I'll never be with anyone else or accept anyone but you at my side."

"Thank you, Selene... I love you too and I know, sometime this will end and we'll not have to feel this burden." Xiuhcoatl stated lovingly as they kissed again. For a little longer they nuzzled into one another, sniffling and cuddling, until Xiuhcoatl had to leave and Selene returned to the pool. She sat back down into the waters and held her hands to her stomach as she looked to the celestial body to share her name.

"I just wish it was not always so lonely..." Selene stated, but she would regret those words soon enough only, that is another story....

Part Five: The Happy Couple

28th January 1928, Paris in the Veil

The wedding at Notre-Dame was exciting, the congregation had been large with the Highest Nobles at hand and even Taliesin invited. The lesser nobles had arrived too that had formed friendships with Thibaut, such as the new Count Agyar, and Theodosius, Valentino and little Vittorio had come too with the toddler dressed to the nines. The ceremony had all been in French and amusingly, Vulturie had almost refused to let go of Jacinthe at the altar, till she'd given him a sharp look. Then she'd stood there with Thibaut and they'd shared rings, shared vows of fidelity that had included Thibaut insisting he'd kill himself before touching another and then they'd kissed. It had been sweet, soft and as delicate as a butterfly landing, Jacinthe had then cried in joy as they'd been announced and the Viper Clan had a new Countess.

At the after party held in Vulturie's family estate just south of the Palace of Versailles and boasting a copycat hall of mirrors, everyone had been giddy bar Jacinthe's uncomfortable sisters and stepmother. Her brothers though were all very happy, all of them shocked that since she'd started down the aisle, the stoic Thibaut could not stop smiling. Her brothers, like her father, knew it was a love match and they hoped for nieces and nephews from their baby sister as soon as possible.

Jacinthe was radiant in her blue dress as she moved around the party, seeing to every guest and thanking them for their gifts. She was quite shocked to see such extravagant gifts for her and her husband, but even if it had been a closed ceremony as for Gaston and Lynette, she'd have still been smiling as much as she was now! But as she stepped past Sahib and his covered wives and daughters, she overheard the familiar voice of the Principessa speaking in hushed tones to Donatello who was looking very uncomfortable and it drew her near.

"I always feared that Dio was not the only Waste in the family, with his cold manner I was sure Thibaut too must be a little queer... but it's clear he and Jacinthe are in love. Heh, Enrico would have been in tears!" The old female grunted and Jacinthe stepped behind a nearby curtain that was right beside the Italian matriarch and listened. She wanted to scream at the old goat that Thibaut was not a Waste and not some cad either, but the mention of Enrico made her oddly uncomfortable as she listened more. Donatello queried why his cousin would have been upset when he'd probably have congratulated Thibaut, but his grandmother just swigged her champagne laced with virginal blood and scoffed. "Because he once asked me if I'd sanction him to bed that creature... instead Jacinthe will. Always jealous of those beings he thought of as pets..."

The giggle of Vittorio nearby alerted Donatello to a conversation he was far more eager to have, his face clearly showing discomfort at any such idea. Jacinthe watched them mosey over to the youngster that was waving his hands as if trying to fly, desperate for cuddles as he called out names and swung about within Valentino's arm, the two-year-old desperate to try and get some attention from the Viper Clan. Jacinthe should have felt relieved the conversation was over, but her stomach was twisting in knots as she considered everything the Principessa had claimed about her husband and she swiftly shook her head and muttered as she recalled the way things had been!

"It was probably just a joke to upset Thibaut, something he could brag to try and keep his friend close to him and on his toes. She's right, he was always so jealous but that's all it was... nothing else!" Jacinthe grit her teeth, no one would ever believe that Enrico would ever have shown interest in a male, it was such a different subject when compared to Valentino and she shook her head again. But she was surprised when Selene stepped to her side, patting her shoulder and she turned to look at her with a blush and a gentle smile. Selene's face grimaced slightly, she was worried something was wrong but Jacinthe was just looking suddenly flushed and it was clear she was enjoying herself as Selene beckoned her to the cake table to cut it with Thibaut. Jacinthe's eyes widened, it was the first time since Lynette and Gaston's secret wedding that Jacinthe had seen a wedding cake and she was blushing as she was pulled along. "This feels exciting... but what if it topples over when we cut it?"

"You're cutting it with Thibaut... he'll have a ruler out and dot the line for you both to cut!" Selene mused, Jacinthe sniggering softly in amusement at the idea as she noticed the way Thibaut was suddenly limping against his cane to the cake, but unwilling to sit down when Dara and Brennan tried to offer him a chair. He seemed almost irritated, a figure too proud to ever really accept anyone thinking he could not achieve things on his own, especially when he hated anyone noticing his limp. All the same, Jacinthe shuffled over to his side as Gaston straightened up and beckoned everyone to come and witness the cake being cut. There were a few murmurs and jokes about whether there would be a situation with a garter being flung, only for Thibaut's eyes to narrow viciously, though many just chuckled. "Thibaut… your… wife's just coming now."

It made Thibaut suddenly blush, shocking everyone into grinning to think that he would react in such a way to just being told he had a wife now. But he held out his hand to her as Jacinthe stepped over, only to have his hand hang around her hip as he pulled her close and their eyes locked. Jacinthe's freckled face was turning pink and Thibaut's paler face was flushing too as they kissed each other gently. There was a soft cough from the crowd to remind them that they were being watched and both of them went red as Brennan then brought over the knife to cut the four-tiered cake, which bore something surprising that made him look at Sabine.

"Well… candy couples are boring… I thought two blood chocolate snakes entwining was more fun. I put some chocolate bars on too, otherwise it's just four Victoria Sponges covered in marzipan!" Sabine stated with a chuckle of amusement as the whole crowd chuckled and Thibaut beckoned her over, giving the ghoul that had been a permanent nanny and ally to him, a gentle kiss to the cheek. But then he passed the knife to Jacinthe and held his hand over hers. Their eyes locked, they seemed stuck staring at one another for a while as they took the moment to cut the cake in a neat slice before making another.

Carefully, they both scooped up the slices and brought them to one another. Jacinthe tenderly fed it to him, making sure not to push the hard marzipan in so he could take his time to eat. Thibaut though was rather more awkward feeding her, his hand trembling as he practically drew the cream and jam centre over her mouth as lipstick. She was giggling as she took a few firm bites and they placed their pieces onto the plates Brennan brought out. They were both cackling in delight afterwards, both messy but they kissed each other to the clapping hands before they stepped to their seats at the table again.

Everyone was happy to see them looking so joyful and in love with one another, using forks to feed each other as the cake was shared to Theodora's growls of joy. They kept their hands together, fingers intertwining and Thibaut was startled; right now his heart was filled with nothing but happiness as he sat there. He considered how carefully he'd spent the years before flirting with Jacinthe in secret, testing her boundaries to test her devotion and whether she could stand someone as cold as him. But to be beside her, to know that they could never be pulled apart was wonderful. He'd never felt so safe and secure before, never felt like there was someone who was more important than his family sitting right beside him and that she could keep him calm no matter what! It was a bizarre way to judge his wife, but he truly loved her and he was glad, she loved him.

The party moved on late into the morning with lots of noise and lots of happiness. Everyone was giggling and dancing and Thibaut could hardly care about it as he sat outside near the venue's fountain, snuggling with Jacinthe. The magic kept her safe from the sunlight's power, but watching the sunrise together they were surprised, it was strange seeing a new day and realising it was the first day they were married. Their hearts were fluttering in pleasure, but there was a growing sense that something was to happen now as Count Vulturie stepped into the garden and cleared his throat gently.

"Hello dears… I believe it's time for the couple to retire and everyone to see them off… the carriage is waiting to take you to your destination." Phillippe was smiling sweetly, clearly happy that his youngest was finally with the person she loved, Thibaut clearly loved her and it was clear that he had a very advantageous alliance in pairing with the Viper Clan. Phillippe was also hopeful that by having strong links to his bloodline, should Thibaut decide to go against the Noble Circle and become the dominant vampire family, he might not think to wipe out the Vulturie. Jacinthe gave a slight jump as she'd snuggled into Thibaut's arm and then looked at her father with a gentle smile before nodding. She stepped up in her neat pale blue dress with its design of different coloured roses going down the sides and Thibaut grasped his cane. "Do you need…"

"He's fine." Jacinthe beamed, stopping her father from asking something that might have gotten his head bitten off as Thibaut was reminded once more of his impairment that could never be healed. He grasped the cane and pressed it into the paving stones, gritting his teeth that the smooth bottom did not really grip the way his shoes did before he pushed his weight to the unharmed side and used the stick for balance. As he stood up, the shooting pain in his other side made the bad leg refuse to lift and he almost roared for the sudden hot spasms running up and down before Jacinthe gently held him in a hug and kissed him. She carefully pulled his hand to her hip and bore his weight to let the spasm calm and his bad leg settle on the ground as they kissed sweetly and he whispered thanks in her ears.

Then they stepped steadily over, Jacinthe wrapped about him looking adorable but giving him all the support he could need, as the crowd calmed and then prepared to farewell the couple. Jacinthe was almost giggling, her honeymoon was going to a very special place within the Fae World, a place that was filled with beautiful gardens that Jacinthe was excited to see! More exciting than anything else, was the fact they were going to a world within a pocket of Veil that was off limits to anyone that was not permitted and Thibaut's kindness to the Fae had meant that they had offered it as their best chance to give him thanks for all he'd done for them. The room was soon waving and saying goodbye as they marched out to the door and the carriage was waiting, a large white canvas tunnel leading them to it and the pair marched down as everyone waved them off.

When they reached the carriage, he let Jacinthe sit inside first before turning back to look towards his family, looking curiously towards Vittorio who was waving them off with a mouth he was trying to stuff with cake! It was funny that the first thing that came to his mind as he was stepping as strongly as he could into the carriage, was about a child. He knew it was his duty to produce a son and heir with Jacinthe, but as he closed the door and Theodora started howling that she didn't want her big brother to go, he could not help but think about having a little girl. He settled into the carriage with Jacinthe, turning about to gently caress her cheek before they kissed lovingly.

"Jacinthe… I know that we have expectations to produce a son but… you do know that any child I have with you, I will love and adore no matter the gender." Thibaut stated, grasping her hand tightly and bringing it to his face, kissing her knuckles one by one to make Jacinthe blush before she nuzzled into his shoulder. They sighed again, utterly content to be with each other with no expectations as he then gave a chuckle of amusement. "I still wonder how you can be so willing to marry someone as grumpy as me."

"Hmm… well, whenever you snapped I could tell it was because you were worried about me, but you did not want anyone to see you worrying about me and so you would be visibly torn. In fact, even when you complained, you were the one who always fixed my problems, you sewed up holes in my dress, you stopped my hands getting burnt, you fixed my hair and always made a point that I was equal to if not more than my sisters. Like father said… you were speaking in your own language and well, I can't help but be in love with you… I was in love when I first met you and it was me you spoke to first, not them." Jacinthe stated, blushing heavily and then pulling up one of the bags of luggage sitting in the carriage. She pulled a book out and then showed him something that made him blush heavily, a pressed flower and not just any flower, but a sweet little trio of forget-me-nots; the first flowers Thibaut had ever given her, though he'd pretended not to know what they were or their meaning and Jacinthe sighed. "I couldn't forget…"

"That's ridiculously sweet and would normally make my stomach churn… but when I hear it from your lips, somehow it seems ever so truthful." Thibaut stated with a sigh, his hand knotting around hers, unwilling to let her go as they continued their journey and then the carriage steered off the track and onto the grass. It was bumpy, but they held each other firmly and were chuckling with each other as they bounced around gently upon the seats and watched the carriage steer off into a grass mound where there was a familiar patch of mushrooms… a fairy ring! Once there, there was a sudden sound like a gulp and they were brought into a beautiful thriving garden maze where the carriage stopped and Thibaut gave a chuckle before then opening out the door and climbing out before grasping his cane and placing it on the ground.

They both suddenly chuckled, the cane exploded with flowers and yet did not stop Thibaut moving it or leaning, instead it seemed to set in roots and give him more stability as he chuckled and then beckoned Jacinthe down and out. The maze before them was beautiful, glittering with flowers that were ivory white with golden pollen dancing from them as a twilight world seemed to surround them yet the landscape was alive with flowers. Jacinthe rarely saw flowers that were not cut or closing against the moon, marching with her new husband, they strolled down the hedges that opened up for them, steering them down beautiful alleyways of flowers that smelt of heaven and both of them adored.

Each time their hands touched the flowers, the plants seemed to grow out to touch them, to bless them with pollen but also luck in their marriage. It was calm, quiet, there was great peace here that made Thibaut's sensations of happiness increase as they followed the maze to a small summer cottage that was covered in ivy where a few of the mossy fairy hounds were bouncing around and barking at them in greeting as Thibaut stroked their faces and Jacinthe tickled at their green bellies with glee. She could not believe their luck to be permitted into the Fae Realm, but to be given a honeymoon there and she knew it must be because Thibaut had such love for flowers and such a keen mind for making friends and deals.

"The dogs will keep us safe if strangers come, there won't be any but I asked if it could be done this way. There is fairy dust inside that we can use to create whatever we need or want... when we're done here, I will give them my prize milking cow as thanks for their help. I wish I could explain how I ended up becoming friends with the Sidhe and not the Unseelie, but let's just say it was all a case of curious luck." Thibaut stated with a chuckle, remembering his visit to Taliesin's dungeon where he was introduced to his demon-possessed aunt and uncle who were locked in a pit and made Thibaut's stomach clench. He'd wanted to kill them to ease their suffering and this embarrassment to the bloodline, but Taliesin seemed to have some deranged symbiotic relationship with them, needing to speak his crazed mind to them and torment them to keep his own sanity. It had been as Thibaut had stepped aside to smell some lavender to ease his sickness that a gentle hand from a dark cage had requested a drop of the oil and Thibaut had dared to take a great risk against his uncle. "It's not a pleasant memory."

"You have a curious sense of compassion; I knew it from the moment we met... any other vampire would have turned their nose up at me and certainly no one would have given the time of day to the werewolves that you do. I know there are many things you hate in this world, many things you cannot express... but I hope you will always be honest with me and be compassionate towards me." Jacinthe stated, the words of the Principessa somehow bobbing to the top of her mind and she remembered the aggression Enrico had shown towards her and his constant taunts that he and Thibaut would marry the twins and swap them between each other and Jacinthe would be nothing more than the spinster raising her nephews! It made her feel upset and her face paled as Thibaut then clasped her cheeks gently, his hands oddly warm for once as they locked eyes and he kissed each of the adorable freckles about her cheeks.

"Jacinthe... I will only show compassion and love to you..." Thibaut stated, stroking her cheeks and pressing his forehead to hers as he stroked at her neck. She shivered to feel his slightly long nails with the tip slightly hooked, as was Count fashion, stroke and tease around her flesh. She could imagine the sharp edge of the nails were close to his teeth and her hair stood on end. Her breath seemed to snatch as her heart began to pump hard, her blood shoot around her body as a heat filled her stomach with fear and anticipation. She shuddered against his face as he brushed his long nose against her more petite one with a soft chuckle. He then kissed her lips ever so gently before sighing. "Do you want to view the room?"

Jacinthe's blood was boiling in excitement, she could not stop her palms from sweating or the shaking that filled her body. As Thibaut opened the door and beckoned her after him, she gnawed at her lips but then tried to stop herself as Thibaut had taught her to. He stepped inside, she followed and within they both viewed a room of beautiful red colours, a bed that filled the room with four posters where cobwebs lounged across like netting with beautiful flowers stuck within the strands. Rose petals were scattered around the floor and there was a soft scent of lavender and valerian from the pillows filled with the softest cotton fibres. The room was not overwhelming in scent, it was perfect and Jacinthe was surprised when Thibaut's hands sat about her waist.

"Does it please you?" He purred into her ears, but there was always that strange almost threatening edge within Thibaut's voice. It made her excited as she nodded her head and then brought her hands to the edges of her dress. Calmly, Jacinthe wrestled herself free of the fabric, leaving only her flat bodice with its thick strings and the great silken underwear that on one side had been rather awkwardly crinkling into the groove of her backside. She trembled and stood there, patiently awaiting his response until she felt his mouth gently hold her shoulders, kiss her jugular but she could feel the tremble in his own form.

Thibaut knew that now, he would be expected to perform a task he felt was vulgar, incautious, invasive and utterly disgusting. Since the first time he'd understood the physical need to reproduce within books and then, unhappily, been informed by his father about the facts of life when he'd been twelve, Thibaut had known that there was no interest within his body for carnal activities. He'd never experienced any desires, dreams or motions that urged him to have the reactions of his brothers and friends. He had recalled the first incident of erection as painful, humiliating and thankfully after pushing through puberty with a vicious temperament and cold attitude, he'd kept his body under utter control. It was not a matter of gender or sexuality, or perhaps… maybe a little about sexuality for although he knew he was interested in women, he was not interested in sex itself. He could not completely explain it, only that it meant nothing to him… even now the desire to kiss and hold was present… but what after that?

He knew what the process was… he knew the invasive and painful act that was to be performed… part of him did not want to subject Jacinthe to such a thing but, there was no other way for him to secure his position. Thibaut knew that his position was already under a timer, if he did not produce an heir quickly into his marriage, then his power would be under serious scrutiny. Thibaut grit his teeth and then gently kissed at her shoulders and her neck before clasping her hands in his, leaning her against his chest and holding her tightly as he whispered fearfully to her.

"Jacinthe… I'm quite out of my depth here… my desire is to hold your naked body to mine, to bite you and share the warmth of your body… but I do not want to hurt you and I'm… I'm afraid of the… the lower half." Thibaut stated, worried that he might not even rise to the occasion to please his wife as she shivered but then gave a soft chuckle of amusement. A flash of anger filled him to hear her laugh, before she turned around to face him and her beautiful, warm hands lay upon his cheeks as she sighed lovingly. They locked eyes and he found himself melting into her understanding expression and those adorable freckles as she gave a gentle snort.

"No fear, my love… let us lie together then and let the mood take us… we have all the time we could desire." Jacinthe stated, a curious flash of confidence in her eyes as she gently grasped the buttons of his shirts and began to undo them. Thibaut's heart shuddered in excitement, he was oddly enticed by her confidence and for once, he felt he was ready to let Jacinthe take control and lead him where he was so fearful. With a chuckle, she then peeled the shirt from his shoulders, making him sigh as he leant forward and they kissed each other gently. When she pulled his shirt away, she stroked at him, surprised that he had more muscle than she could have expected, though she'd always known he was broad chested and strong, to see that there was definition, only made her mouth water. Jacinthe could not believe how exciting it was to think that she would be the one to be with him, she would be the one to produce his heirs and she would be the only one he would ever want to touch!

Her hands went to his trousers, she unclipped them but suddenly he grasped her hands, his own shaking with the fear she'd never thought to sense from him. She lifted her head up to see how he blushed and yet she leant forward to kiss him, taking his hands and steering them to the straps at the top of her shoulders. He gulped, gently unclipping them as she then sneakily shuffled his button out and let his trousers start to slide downwards as he let the silken fabric slide down her body. Then she stood there, naked but for her bloomers, her breasts finally revealed to be a lot larger than they had appeared, her body though skinny as a twig, ginger freckles dotting her body like a map to pleasure and her skin a curious peach shade and Thibaut gulped.

Somehow, seeing her stand so proudly before him, almost naked and far more vulnerable than she let him see, Thibaut found that his revealed underwear was now tightening as arousal seemed to finally occur. He was pleased it was appropriate, though still a little uncomfortable as something in his mind warned this might offend her, he stretched his hands out to her, stroking her naked shoulders and then pulling her naked body to his own. As she wrapped her arms around him, Thibaut released his pheromones to soak into her body, heat her blood and let her know she belonged to him and would be the only one to know his perfume. Jacinthe sighed in pleasure, but sneakily managed to yank his underwear down and to his sudden gasp, her hands were soon fondling him as Thibaut shivered against her and then whispered in her ear.

"Is… isn't that unpleasant to do?" He whispered, all thought of the organs there rather disgusting to him because of their function, but Jacinthe kissed his neck. She then teasingly grazed her growing fangs against the edge of his neck, causing the hairs on his body to stand up on end, his mouth to open and fangs to grow as his body reacted and he gave out a moan. Jacinthe shuddered, teasingly licking his neck as she watched his skin turn beetroot red, loving that she was the only one to ever hear him make that noise and touch him here. She then pulled her hands away, letting him hold her, their bodies rubbing and nuzzling against each other as they drank in the warmth, the pheromones and shared scents as their bodies touched and teased with anticipation starting to tickle at them both.

Steadily, they walked to the bed and clambered onto it, Jacinthe lay upon her back with her arms open wide and her legs slightly open. She beamed as Thibaut lounged along the bed beside her, his physique so curiously beautiful, his fair skin seemingly highlighting his innocence here as Jacinthe had to blush to think that she was the one corrupting such a powerful being. Thibaut's face though was wearing an expression she'd longed to see in the bedroom, that relaxed but intense love… something that held some passion to it but most of all told her she was precious to him. He lay over her, their bodies wrapping up together as they kissed and licked at one another's flesh. Their hands stroked and touched one another's chests and back, exploring as Thibaut tested his weight upon her body and against his leg.

"How is your body? Is it only comfortable on your side? I can move to that." Jacinthe beamed, her face showing great happiness and eagerness to do whatever he wanted and Thibaut shifted onto his side with a chuckle, stroking her face tenderly before Jacinthe leant forward. They kissed intimately, their lips massaging against one another, their sensitive fangs tickling at each other's lips to make them moan as Thibaut stroked her cheeks tenderly. He pulled her into him, lifting one of her legs over his shoulder, stroking her thigh and gently grasping at her backside that made her give a shiver as he chuckled. They paused, he nuzzled noses with her and was grinning with a curiously youthful expression that Jacinthe had not seen before, he mused how she perfectly fit in his hands and she slumped her forehead to his chest with a grunt. "Don't be so naughty…"

"Why not… we're married, we're in love and we can be naughty with each other if we want…" Thibaut teased, making Jacinthe blush to hear him talk as cheekily as he would normally speak with a snarky edge. They kissed again as he massaged her backside in his hands, loving the way the flesh was warm, soft, springy and then stroking up the beautiful curve of her spine as Thibaut moaned and sighed in delight. They continued to kiss passionately before he pulled her leg over him more and slid himself into position, Jacinthe wrapped her arms around him and then… then things seemed to go suddenly quite wrong.

Jacinthe had expected that her body would have been welcoming, but when he brought his hot form to her, her body felt like it was hesitant and unwilling to accept. When he tried to enter, there was resistance, but Jacinthe just nuzzled into his shoulder hoping Thibaut would not think he was hurting her. He tried to move in, feeling a tight, snatching sensation and feeling anxiety start to reach him as he tried to push in further, only to feel something seemingly tear and Jacinthe gave a sudden little yelp of pain. It was enough to make Thibaut's mind spin, remembering extreme pain and pressure and suddenly, he pulled himself out as carefully as he could and then practically leapt off the bed. He dropped onto the floor, pulling himself up by the bed post and then giving a frightened, strangled sound of horror to see spots of blood on the sheet and on himself. He looked down at the treacherous organ with fear, his eyes wide and shaking as he gripped his talons into the wood of the bedpost, his shoulders suddenly quaking as he began to sob.

"I'm so sorry… I'm so sorry… I didn't mean to hurt you… Jacinthe… I'm so sorry!" Thibaut seemed to gag and retch, utterly sickened but terrified too and Jacinthe shifted onto the bed, against the pillows with an expression of concern as she looked out towards her husband. Her heart was trembling in terror, she had never once heard him sound this depressed or scared before and she wanted to stretch out her hands to hold him and soothe him. Instead, she could see the way his shoulders hunched and, as he stood there, she suddenly became aware of a pair of puncture marks that were nearly permanently bruised upon the bottom of his shoulder… the kind that said someone had tried to claim him but had hit the wrong place. Worst of all, she saw that there was a vivid, ragged pale line that seemed to climb up from the crease of his buttocks and could only have been made by skin being split there.

"Darling… my darling… you did nothing wrong; this is what happens with a virgin woman, you have done nothing wrong to me. See, is not even that uncomfortable, come back to the bed won't you… just let me hold you…" Jacinthe stated, realising that this was the first time she'd ever seen his back exposed and his reactions told her that someone hard hurt him very badly. She was reminded of the attack to have made him lame, the thought there was damage somewhere against his sciatic nerve, but no one had ever questioned if he'd been stabbed there or something else. Now Jacinthe's mind tickled uncomfortably with the words of the Principessa and she gave a soft hiss. "Thibaut… we're married and should have no secrets; you trust me and I trust you… so I want you to tell me the truth about what happened…"

Thibaut had stayed as still as he could, grasping the post for dear life and taking in ragged breath, his eyes flashing a reddish shade that turned them amber. His nostrils could only pick up a disgusting smell that made his stomach lurch… a smell he had only experienced once and brought with it every memory of pain, humiliation and the desire to die he'd never wanted to experience again. His body was prickling with fear, his bad leg twitching painfully and at her words, he slowly turned his head back over his shoulder, eyes wide and terrifying for just a second before he pressed his forehead to the wood, wanting to bite it so he never had to speak, but Jacinthe was right. He couldn't lie to her and yet… he could feel her soft eyes upon his body, staring at his wounds and he wanted to scream at her to stop looking, but he could not.

"Then… then you will think less of me and you will see me as something wretched and weak, but I am NOT!" Thibaut whimpered before suddenly barking at the bedpost, his talons digging in tighter and his arms shifting slightly to form wings before they stopped. He rubbed his sweaty, hot forehead against the post as he hissed and sneered in anxiety, unsure if he could really talk to her. He knew what she could see and though terrified, his body trembled as he turned around to face her properly, slipping to keep behind the post as if it gave him protection as Jacinthe looked at him with nothing but affection.

"How could I ever see you as anything but my beloved Thibaut? Slayer of serpents and threats to the clan… Count of the Viper Clan and protector of your siblings and friends! You are many things my darling, but none would ever believe you weak or wretched. You're heroic, stern and the only person who could ever have given me the time of day." Jacinthe stated, throwing out compliments to make him feel more comfortable as she smiled and looked at him with that shy expression that said she wanted to kiss him. "You're the only person I could love."

"I… I love you too but… please, don't think different of me if I tell you the truth." He almost whispered it, his face burying against his arm as he seemed almost to turn into a frightened child. Jacinthe could only imagine what had happened, how much he'd been hurt and when he began to speak, her heart sank to think that her beloved had experienced this. "One night… Enrico had taken more drugs than before… he'd had an argument with his grandmother and was very wound up. He… he dragged us all to the brothel, but when he was with Ada… you know the werewolf at home… he started choking her! Knowing she was mortal, he seemed to want to kill a woman… I pulled him off and pushed her and the other girls into the back. I blocked them… and told him he was not right in his head and needed to go back home… but he was furious that I interrupted him and attacked me! We fought and I knocked him away but he set the others on me. I was smashed into the snooker table, it collapsed beneath and then Enrico pinned me against it…"

Thibaut's eyes started to glaze over, he did not want to say anything else, his body was shaking violently as he tried hard not to think about what had happened next. He did not want to go back to that moment and yet that whole experience held so tightly in his mind. He remembered the scent and sound more… the sounds that were unreal and he looked towards Jacinthe with an even more fearful expression as he took a gentle breath and gripped the wood more tightly, tears starting to glitter out from the golden eyes that were usually so fierce and controlling.

"I remember he said 'it's all your fault, so you'll take their place… make as much noise as you want, I know you'll love this.' Then… ugh…" Thibaut turned away from her view, retching and flopping onto the edge of the bed, pulling up his legs to his chest and shaking violently. Jacinthe shuffled over, hurrying to hold his shoulders and pull him against her, nuzzling her face against his as his salty tears dribbled into his mouth and he spat the squeezed words through them, his throat aching and tightening to let the words he'd hidden for so long have life. "I wouldn't make sound, I was... I don't have to say it, you know what he did... but I wouldn't make a sound and when it was over and I was a bloodied mess... his friends begged him to let me be and that this was wrong. He didn't care, he kept grabbing my throat and telling me I had to say I loved him... then he went to bite, even through the agony I covered my neck and he only bit into my shoulder. But it only made him more furious... you could see his eyes were bloodshot and the veins in his body were so visible... those drugs had turned off all sense and then he said... 'I'll make sure no one else will have you'... then he took one of the pool cues, smashed it and... I just remember a sound like a rabbit being killed... I didn't know it had come from me... then I was left, dying."

Jacinthe went quiet, unable to say anything more than stroke and kiss his cheek. She had never thought such a thing would happen, although after hearing that conversation at the reception she found herself far more aware of the circumstances that had led to it all than even Thibaut might be. She gripped him tightly against her body, unwilling to let go of him as she whispered softly to him that he was alive now, he'd survived and he'd done amazing things and proven he was a better male than Enrico had ever been. But now she could understand the reaction to Theodosius' homosexuality, let alone his relationship with Valentino. Knowing this, she realised how hard of a situation it had been for Thibaut to accept without fear of his brother being at risk of the same and, they'd both experienced horror thanks to those Italians!

"I survived because Ada and the women of the brothel saw me as a friend, they all gave me their blood, used their only emergency portal to get me home to Doctor Garou. Only Lynette and he knew the real story, until of course she later shared it with Gaston, and now you know it all." Thibaut stated, looking miserable but seemingly relieved as the tears continued to fall but his body stopped shaking as much as it had before. Instead, his skin seemed to heat up even more, he was snarling suddenly and grinning like a maniac as she gave a violent hiss and looked to his talons as his fangs came out and a demonic growl joined his voice as Jacinthe stared at him in horror. "I made sure when Enrico went out on a walk alone with me after I healed, apologising like the fool he was, I led him to where I knew his Strix drug supplier would be. I had intended to kill the Strix in front of him so he would be without and then watch him suffer from withdrawal… but his apologies were as false as everything with Enrico's treatment of me. He dared to pin me to a tree, try to kiss and insist that I was his and… I don't recall much but the feel of his blood on my tongue and his organs being ripped apart within my teeth and claws! Then that Strix ran over to try and stop me, I turned my arm into a wing and sliced him in half then ripped him to pieces too… I hurt myself a little as I turned them both into pulp… I'd won… I'd made them both pay!"

"You did my darling, you made sure that no one else would suffer from either of those monsters… I told you, you are heroic!" Jacinthe stated, feeling no remorse for either but looking at the manic expression upon her husband's face, it was clear to see that the event had broken him. Somehow though, he'd always kept that broken side hidden from everyone and until now, Jacinthe had never once thought that her husband could ever be like this. She had never thought that Thibaut could ever experience such pain, shame, hatred and insanity as this event seemed to have caused and Jacinthe heaved a heavy sigh and wrapped her arms around him tightly, kissing the mark on his back that made him flinch and hiss. "It's over now, you've survived and now, it's time you throw away the control and agony they put upon you Thibaut. Firstly, you won't and will never hurt me and secondly, you're going to live your life, father children, raise them well and continue to keep your family safe. But… whenever it's too much or you feel you cannot cope or you need to say it to someone in total confidence, you will come to me and I will hold you to me and I will protect you."

"Ah… dearest Jacinthe… my beautiful blossom…" Thibaut sighed, tears starting to slow down and his reddened eyes and face seemed to lighten with relief. Jacinthe kissed his ear and then shuffled back up to the top of the bed, lounging back and grasping the blankets. She patted the bed beside her, beckoning him over and, as his pains were starting to develop and he knew he needed to sleep and give his body time to cope as the shock began to hit, he scrabbled over to her side. He crawled up to the pillows, his wounded leg hanging limply and dragging as he pulled himself to the bed and was wrapped in the blankets by Jacinthe. She snuggled into him and then he nuzzled against her neck as she kissed his ear.

"If you just bite me and leave the mark that we are one… then we can say it was done and none can ever question it. I will keep your secret to my grave my darling." Jacinthe stated, holding onto him tightly as he whispered sweetly if she would bite him in return and, as she could feel his body shaking violently after such a shock, she nodded her head. Together, they bore their fangs and sunk them deep into the bottom of the neck, drinking one another's blood and letting their sensations and their comfort flow through to one another. As he drank her blood, Thibaut's shock and horror seemed to soothe and as Jacinthe drank, she felt the pain he had experienced and the fear, but she was strong enough to overcome it with the comfort that seemed to merge between them.

Finally though, they had bound themselves to each other and together, they spent almost half the next day cuddled together in bed.

The rest of the honeymoon was different, they spent most of the time exploring the gardens, eating and laughing with each other. They'd made picnics and lounged under a sky made of sparkling blossoms and even climbed trees and flown around the area. They'd been frivolous and carefree, even swimming together, which was something Thibaut seemed to have much less pain in performing compared to anything else. They had then spent their evenings cuddled up on the bed, drinking herbal teas blended with blood and either reading to one another or talking about their secrets. Jacinthe had a lot she had never thought she could say because women were told to keep quiet about it, but Thibaut wanted to know everything he needed, even if it was clinical or embarrassing. He shared just as much of his pain with her, telling her his fears as he snuggled into her chest and then, when they were getting tired, they would hold each other naked and kiss and touch and learn about each other's flesh.

Thibaut's lack of interest in the final act meant he was much more interested in learning things she liked because he liked how it pleased her. He learnt where she liked to be kissed, where she liked to feel his curved talons scratch or stroke, where she liked to feel his fangs and what sounds she made if he touched her ever so gently. She would shiver and tremble, blush and insist it was all embarrassing, but he spent the time learning and then, he began to pleasure her in every other manner that did not involve that part of himself that was so… shameful. Then, on the final day, he finally felt comfortable enough to embrace her properly and after ensuring that she was fully sated and not in any pain as he took his pleasure in just making her satisfied, Thibaut experienced the rapture that others spoke of… but it was not as addictive to him when he reached his climax as it was to see Jacinthe sweaty, dewy eyed and looking up at him as if she could not love him anymore if she even tried.

Confidence returned to him; he had taken hold of his fears but they were always there at the back of his mind just like the scars upon his back. When they returned, he felt the task was done and focused heavily upon his work, Jacinthe found herself suddenly a little alone with Thibaut only present for guests or dinner. He used the room he had given Theodosius and Elaine to hide in as his sleeping room for the brief hour-long naps between work during the week. His addiction to working and keeping control returned and he remained the harsh but protective Thibaut they all knew, even though they had hoped he would soften after marriage.

However, whenever he sat with Jacinthe he was filled with joy and the pair were almost quite adorable to watch, though extremely restrained in public. When he would not have anyone to trade with over the weekends, then Thibaut would spend his time sleeping beside Jacinthe, kissing and cuddling her and spending his entire weekend doing anything he could to make her comfortable. There were a few sessions of lovemaking, but it was rare and though Jacinthe savoured every moment, to Thibaut it was always a moment that required him pushing away his fears of hurting her or being hurt himself. If his leg should be acting up however, the situation did not occur and yet they were comfortable all the same.

After a year though, there was no sign of a pregnancy and Thibaut found himself being questioned over and over again at the Noble Circle about how long until there would be a pregnancy. Thibaut was concerned that his masculinity as well as his power were being questioned and so, every weekend she was willing, he embraced her with the desperation that it would be over soon and they would have their child. For several months there was no sign of anything until Jacinthe's cycle seemed to stop and then Thibaut became excited and so openly affectionate towards her that everyone in the household began to be excited to see how Thibaut would be as a father.

However, within two months the cycle was back and Jacinthe watched Thibaut bury himself in work for two weeks, barely sleep or eat and ignore everyone as his heart seemed to need the time to heal from it. Jacinthe felt bad for him, but when he returned to her again, he decided they would keep trying and so, by the third year of their marriage they had tried and tried but to no success. At this point, Thibaut was getting more looks of concern as his siblings already seemed to be producing children and yet there was nothing for him.

Thibaut began to take longer breaks between being with Jacinthe as his workload altered, he was busier and busier and their whole fourth year of marriage they barely shared the bed and Jacinthe was fearful. She confronted him about feeling abandoned or punished, but Thibaut apologised and instead revealed he'd been working hard to find doctors that could do something to help them out. But the methods to try and help out seemed no different from the methods they'd been using, except it was more timed to her cycles and yet, even during their fifth and sixth and seventh year, there were brief moments between where something seemed to happen, Jacinthe would watch Thibaut get excited and joyful once more and then, somehow it would go back to normal and even Jacinthe could not understand what was happening to her... she felt nothing happening inside her!

During their eighth year, Thibaut had seemed to turn exceptionally cold to everyone but the children in the household, he was barely home but always away working on something even when he was. Jacinthe felt even more abandoned than before, something she had thought he would not do and yet, even Adelia had soothed her on the matter. For Thibaut, who'd seen his siblings have such luck and had come from a big family, whatever was stopping them from having a child was making him think it was his fault, but Jacinthe knew that the situation was different.

Within vampire society, and most societies still, when a pregnancy did not occur then it was the fault of the female and, approaching their eighth year trying without any luck, vampires would rule Jacinthe as sterile and it was not long before her father understood the situation and took it as seriously as he needed to, arranging to see both of them separately.

"Hello child, I hope you don't mind us talking openly with one another... I know it's not something you're used to but, I can't ignore the situation any longer when it's risking the alliance I have with the Viper Clan." Though Phillippe Vulturie knew in his heart that Jacinthe and Thibaut were in love with one another, the traditions of the Noble Circle could be strict and when a good deal of money and power were at risk for the French Nobility because they did not have a blood bond with the Viper Clan, Jacinthe had been their best bet. Her situation meant that at any time, the Vipers could switch allegiance and with Theodosius already in with the Italians and the Germans, a switch to either side could undermine the Vulturie position amongst the Elite of the Nobles when the

Iberian Nobles were looking shaky and too focused upon themselves. "Please daughter, sit."

Jacinthe had not wanted to be called up, her sister to have disgraced the family had been married off swiftly to a Turned vampire that had been hoping to get some position with them, but her other sister was still single. In fact, Marie had overheard of her sister's lack of ability to reproduce with Thibaut and had already told her father she was still a possible substitute. Jacinthe was aware her position was in trouble because she was risking being called sterile, but she did not know what had been happening with her body and as she took a soft little seat on the sofa beside her father, he offered coffee as he took in a deep breath. She drank it calmly and then looked oddly miserable for a time before she then listened to her father take another heavy sigh.

"Jacinthe… little one… I don't want to end your marriage with Thibaut because of a lack of a child, I know you both love each other greatly and that he has treated you with nothing but respect and love, so I'm at a loss here. The best I can think is for you to allow Thibaut a mistress to produce a child with, preferably your sister." Phillippe did not want to upset his daughter like this, but the traditions were the traditions, any of the other nobility would do the same if there was not a clear sign of a pregnancy within the first eight years of a marriage. Like all the teachings of the time Vulturie assumed it was to do with Jacinthe, but as Marie was the twin to Michelle who'd birthed a Dhampir through a sneaky affair, he had no doubt Marie would produce a child quickly. "Your sister would only need to be in the house until a little after the birth, then a wet nurse would be hired… it would be no different to what happened with Elaine in fact."

It would, Jacinthe knew it would but she kept her head lowered and her lips tight. She brought her hands together and adopted her usual anxious and fearful expression, hiding herself away from the conflict she knew was building up. She did not want her sister to have Thibaut's child, this was not the same as with Elaine… Theodosius had been a man and unable to bear a child! Jacinthe wished she could explain what it was that was doing this to her, but her father just stretched out his hands, patting hers as he gave a knowing and kind smile that sadly, Jacinthe knew to be one of his ways to manipulate her.

"See my dear, it is the best way and no one would question the heritage and Marie would be looked after well…" Vulturie began, glad that Jacinthe was such a pliable girl at the best of times and easy to encourage to do the right thing. After-all, this was a matter of nobility, heritage and alliances, something older and more important than simple matters of a husband and wife having trouble. Vulturie straightened up, patting his daughter's hand and then getting a real shock as his hand was suddenly slapped away, the coffee almost smashed onto the table and Jacinthe was towering over him.

"NO! I will never let such a thing happen; Thibaut is mine!" Jacinthe had rarely shown her vampiric side, rarely shown her voracity but she was as much a predator as any other and her body changed shape immediately as she towered over her father. She took on the form of a soft ginger coloured horsetail bat standing on its hindlegs like a human with its wings stretched out but its face distorted and showing a massive jaw filled with horrible sharp teeth and large canines. She gave a violent shriek that made the glass windows crack suddenly, making her father drop down onto the floor in surprise, staring at her as if she had gone crazy! Jacinthe looked furious and to the surprise of both, the door was forced open and the servants were scattered about the floor as Thibaut's own monstrous bat-like form launched into the room.

He gave a violent roar and launched onto the back of the chair beside Jacinthe, his looks far more demonic, his golden eyes shining and his muzzle not exactly bat-like but more like some kind of lizard. His teeth were huge and horrifying and his wings were curiously coated in a strange iridescent layer as if wearing scales. He looked stronger, more able to rip Vulturie apart and devour him than Jacinthe but together… together they could take down a demon! Phillippe pulled back, dropping onto the floor with his hands up in the air, waving them and beckoning that Jacinthe calm herself, knowing that alone would make Thibaut less dangerous before Jacinthe turned towards the window already cracked and then spat out another screech that shattered the glass.

The dark night stood beyond and Jacinthe launched into the air, hurrying out the window with a roar of fury towards her household. Thibaut paused a moment, bringing his muzzle towards Phillippe and giving a voiceless warning that he would have no trouble killing him and Phillippe had to admit he could well believe it. After-all, his eldest son and heir had already made good friends with Thibaut and it would not be a new thing for a father to be killed for a new count to take control. But he watched as Thibaut launched out of the window faster than Jacinthe and was soon flapping in the air to reach her side. He went below her in the air, flying calmly at her pace though she was hurrying towards home and furious that there could ever have been such a suggestion.

In the cold, dark night where the wind was gentle but the moon was hidden beneath clouds, Jacinthe's energy was starting to lag and she was crying as she flew. She knew her husband was beneath her, preparing to hold her up if he needed to and slowly, she drooped down until she lay upon his back, her thumb claw hooking to his shoulders and her body so light it was no trouble for the flying Count to carry her. Thibaut just continued to fly in the direction of home, letting Jacinthe get as much cool air as she wanted as she nuzzled into his back with soft sobs of upset over what had been said. Thibaut did not know what had upset her, but he was determined to make sure she was content and he remained quiet for a time as she nuzzled and sniffled onto him with her pretty little bat face as she sucked in air.

She nuzzled against the soft fur upon her husband's body, glad that Thibaut was not angry with her or unable to hold her as they flew. She wished she could ask him if he would ever pair with Marie for the sake of a child, if he would think of it as similar to what had happened with Elaine, but she was afraid of the answer. Thibaut had to think about the best for the clan, the best for their bloodline and she knew he was too practical and aware of the traditions to think it was not a possibility. She wondered if he'd even brought it up to her father and yet, she swallowed down that thought, unable to cope if that was even remotely true because it could not be true!

Thibaut spotted an abandoned watchtower on the edge of a waterway below that had once been attached to a bridge. He could tell that it was abandoned and guessed that this was the safest place for them to settle down and talk. He could sense the sun would rise soon enough and within the tower he could protect Jacinthe if needed before calling on Dara for help sending them back home. With a soft sigh he dropped his wings and she gripped hold of him tightly in fear as he dropped down suddenly and then opened up, delicately twisting to latch his talons onto the edge of the opening and then swinging them inside.

Jacinthe had not yet returned to her human form, yet somehow Thibaut was able to use his speed and dexterity to spin her around to lounge in her bat form against his human. He kissed her soft face, stroking her gentle fur and holding her against him as she sniffled and cried and then shrank down into a tiny little bat. Her anxiety was obvious and without question, he opened up his shirt buttons and beckoned her to slip onto his chest and even drink his blood if she needed it. Jacinthe just pressed her nose to his chest, licking and snuffling at him as he stepped about the empty belfry and then noticed a few of the native bats settling above them and he bobbed his head to them in greeting, which made a ripple of excitement run through the colony.

Thibaut then calmly sat himself down upon the floor, taking off his cloak and then laying it upon the ground, lying along it himself and sighing. He lay his hand protectively over Jacinthe, kissing at the air above her and sighing softly as he felt her licking at him and decided that he would try to sleep. In the back of his mind, something was complaining that he had papers to write, invoices to check, payments to make and work he could not quite guarantee that Gaston would get right and certainly did not want their mother to feel pressured to do. But despite that, the thing that pushed these obsessive thoughts about having such control were swept aside by the thought of Jacinthe being in distress and needing him. He kissed at the air above her again and gave a soft chuckle and then spoke to the room.

"Petal... I did not know what your father had called you in for, but as I was waiting for you, Marie had strolled over and suggested something hideous. Then I marched to the room but was not permitted to enter, when I heard you yell 'no', I had to get in there and rescue you. But of course... you never needed rescuing, you're stronger than even I am." Thibaut smiled sweetly, sighing and stroking over the area where the bat lay upon his chest and Jacinthe shivered against him. Her anxieties seemed to be soothed when he called her flower nicknames and then, she listened to him whisper to her with a sigh of love. "I don't expect you to tell me what occurred just yet, but know that I'm willing to listen. But dearest Jacinthe, I want nothing more right now than to hold you properly in my arms and shower you with kisses. My dear, brave darling... I'm so proud that you stood up to your father."

Jacinthe began to stir upon his chest, she started to shuffle out of his shirt and he opened it out for her, taking off his jacket and then wrapping it about her shoulders as she returned to normal. She was shaking a little in shock, her expression dour and the misery obvious as Thibaut lifted his hand to stroke her face softly before leaning forward to kiss her cheek. He could only imagine what had upset her this much and mostly his mind was thinking about the lack of a child thus far. He would not deny he was jealous his siblings had achieved it already, but when he loved Jacinthe so purely and truly, he did not even care about it. He would be with her forever and surely, at some point, they might be lucky!

"Thibaut... I want to have a baby with you. I know you're probably going to laugh it off and say, 'of course we'll have one', but you don't understand! I don't want anyone else to have our baby, I'd rather we never have one and one of your nephews become your heir than think of you using anyone else but me. I'm being selfish, that's what my father was trying to make me think, but I am not and I do not want you to touch any other woman but me." Jacinthe had straightened up, taking in a deep breath and then made her statement so firmly and harshly that anyone else overhearing might have thought she was having an argument with him. But as her face went red, her freckles shone through and her shoulders raised as the heat of her fury crunched into her hands as she growled and shook her head in utter rejection over the thought he'd chose someone else. But then she opened her eyes to see the loving expression upon Thibaut's face.

He took her hands together and brought them up against his own, locking their fingers about one another as he took in a deep breath and insisted that he wanted no one else. She stared into his golden eyes, seeing the love and affection within that were rarely shown to anyone but her and Jacinthe gave a soft sniff, insisting she was not proud that she was so sensitive, but she refused to change the thought of being sensitive around her husband. Thibaut found himself chuckling softly as he stroked her hot cheeks and kissed from one side of her jaw to the other in a crescent over her forehead before then pressing his nose against hers.

"You know... I fall in love with you more and more each day.... But forgive me, I'm not a good husband and I leave you alone more than I should. I wish I could say that I will change, but you know me well enough to understand that I do not feel the same as others. If I were perhaps like any of my siblings, I think I'd be the mate you deserve." Thibaut stated, knowing full well that his own aversion to the carnal act was what had brought them into this situation, but with his body being so unwilling because of his traumas and his own distaste for sex, he felt there was nothing he could do. However, as they snuggled up against each other, Jacinthe insisted she would never have someone else and then lifted her head up, pondering maybe if she might stir a bit of jealousy within her husband after-all... though she feared too it might stoke a murderous rage.

"You remember my friend la Lame... he's been back and staying at my father's house for a time, my father suggested I could stay in his company whilst you dealt with the matters. I did not know what it meant but I was fearful that his reason for not marrying is because he's been keeping an eye on our situation…." Jacinthe spoke anxiously, not sure if Thibaut might return to the form of a bat and leap out into the air, returning to slaughter her father. But she watched his eyes narrow violently as he looked past her head and seemed to envision the moustachioed Casanova with his harem of concubines back in Tunisia and Jacinthe being pushed amongst them. It made him curl his lips in fury, his fangs appearing and Jacinthe was a little worried before he wrapped his hands about her, one hand stroking his mark upon her neck.

She shivered, giving a sudden moan of pleasure as she smelt and felt her husband's pheromones pouring out and swarming around her. She was drowning in his scent and the more he stroked her neck bruises from their mating bite, the more her body was becoming aroused. Her whole body was starting to feel hot and she gave a soft moan of pleasure before trying to produce her own perfume to perhaps arouse him as much as he was arousing her. Thibaut pulled her close, his possessiveness taking over as he growled and then rolled his tongue over her neck mark, making her give out a sharp gasp that came with a wave of pleasure that only made her body more desperate before Thibaut's claws appeared and gently he cut her clothes open as he began to lick down her body.

Jacinthe shuddered violently, she was not used to her husband showing such a sudden moment of passionate fervour and yet his face was soon nuzzling into her warm chest, licking at the skin betwixt her bosoms and listening to her excited heart rate. She shivered, unable to move within his grasp as the pheromones seemed to engulf her and whisper to her that there was no need to fight him. It was strange, her husband almost seemed to be predatory as he licked and growled and rubbed his fangs against her flesh, making her hair stand on end and her voice come out in a squeaking hiccup. Then he brought his head down to her belly, lying her upon his cloak as he seemed to kiss and lick at her stomach as she shivered.

"Thibaut darling… that's so embarrassing…" Jacinthe's face went rosy, her freckles standing out visibly as she rocked and shivered beneath the slow rolls of his tongue beneath her navel. His pheromones became stronger and she could feel the motions causing her body to burn, her skin sweating madly and her stomach tightening in anticipation. She was feeling alive in such embarrassing places that she feared this growing excitement would cause her a little moment that her husband might tease her for. But then she felt a fang dare to tap about her outward facing belly button and she gave a sharp whine. "What is that feeling?"

"It may hurt… but… just a quick test…" Thibaut purred into her belly, making her jolt and give out a sudden cry of pain to feel the fang penetrate the primal flesh that had once connected her to her mother. She jolted and writhed beneath him, the strange sensation seemingly setting her nerves ablaze and she could not even tell if it was pain or pleasure before the fang was removed by a strong stroking of his tongue. She relaxed and tears were in her eyes as she looked at him. She was confused, scared because he'd promised he would not hurt her before he licked the tear to dribble from her cheek and then licked her ears before growling deeply into her neck. "Did you know… that little action of mine has told me that it's the right time to conceive."

"What? But… how…" Jacinthe shivered, only to be silenced by one of her beloved's most passionate kisses. She moaned and sighed, her mouth soaking as his tongue stroked and teased every sensitive groove of the top of her mouth before tickling her fangs. Her fangs slid out, vibrating and making her hips jolt as his tongue teased and stroked those fangs playfully, making her gasp and moan out loudly. Jacinthe pulled back as she then felt his lips pinch and kiss down her chin, her neck and then down her chest once more. He seemed to hover over her breasts, kissing and licking at them both as she giggled and shivered in excitement, stretching her hand out to stroke his shoulder as she gave a grunt. "But how do you know…"

"One of the reasons I've been away recently… I had a friend teach me how to tell the difference in the blood… I thought it might help." Thibaut stated with a few heavy pants, his wet tongue almost hanging out of his mouth as his fangs twinkled with the desire to bite any part of her body. Jacinthe blushed heavily, her heart beating faster and her body more giddy as her mind seemed to sing… he was thinking about them all the time! But she was soon distracted when his kissing moved southward and soon she was arcing her back, her legs straining out as she whimpered and covered her mouth as her husband showed off the skills he'd been developing with her.

Feeling her writhe beneath him, smelling the arousal that was starting to drown them both as she moaned out desperately as her hips shook almost violently, Thibaut growled in pleasure. He was glad that the actions had awoken his body and that he must be ready now and that they must have greater luck, he'd not wanted to use artefacts or potions to achieve this, his whole image as a masculine vampire relied on doing this without aid… at least in his mind it did.

As he felt her body shiver with the orgasm that had been building, he grinned wickedly as he lounged over her body and kissed her freckles adoringly.

"Are you willing to let me hold you… in this quiet place?" Thibaut purred, lapping at her freckles and the edge of her lips to make them crinkle from the pleasure. Jacinthe was practically naked now beneath him, exposed to the empty tower and clearly unsure how to react should someone see them and yet, Thibaut rarely started these situations. She gulped heavily, she stroked at his face and he rubbed his cheeks against them, giving soft sounds of pleasure and growling in his arousal as he seemed to rub himself against the body to make her gasp and then smile with a blush.

"Aren't I always, my darling?" Jacinthe sighed, Thibaut leaning down to kiss her, their hands rubbing and stroking at each other as her legs splayed out and Thibaut shifted into the position that was generally so awkward. Jacinthe knew their positioning could change at any minute, that her mate could feel pain and be unable to maintain himself without having to switch back, but Thibaut did not seem to care. Their bodies connected and their arms wrapped around each other, Thibaut no longer scared to unite with her but always so steady and gentle in his movements, moving his hips to find her best spots and making her cry and moan out in pleasure as he kissed at her neck and her breasts as Jacinthe moaned.

Together they danced steadily back and forth within the dark, cold tower… the cold air outside forcing steam to seemingly rise off their sweaty bodies even as the sun was starting to shine out over the lands about them. The sunlight seemed to threaten them, but Thibaut pulled out his arms from holding her and let them turn into their bat form, wrapping them about them both like a tent as he pulled Jacinthe up onto her feet and against the wall. She clambered onto his shoulder, lifting herself up against a seeming ledge that was just enough to hold her backside as Thibaut protected her from the sunlight and still lavished her in love.

Her body weight against the wall, the fear of slipping down and needing to cling to him making the situation even more exciting for Jacinthe. She was starting to moan out loudly, her skin crawling with Goosebumps in pleasure as she felt her husband's fangs scratching at her chest, his tongue lavishing her with warmth as their insides were burning with pleasure. Thibaut was startled at how much she held onto him, how much she seemed to pull him in tighter, how close they felt and as they kissed each other lovingly towards the end, the climax hit them both quite harshly.

Thibaut felt the spasm of pleasure rocket up his body, but then trigger the damaged nerves in his body, he did not dare pull away and instead lifted his leg to try and ease the sensation. He felt the need to keep them both attached to one another, not to dare think of parting and losing this chance as Jacinthe's body still quivered and shivered with the heat of her pleasure and the feel of him within her. She kissed at his neck, stroking him as he kept her protected from the sunlight until Thibaut gave a wheeze of pain and Jacinthe gently shifted her hand down to touch him… to pull him away. Suddenly Thibaut pressed her up against the stone with a violent snarl and display of teeth as Jacinthe gave a gasp of shock, only for Thibaut to give a groaning whine of fury at himself before cautiously separating from her as they both shook and trembled at the fearful moment before Thibaut groaned.

"I'm sorry… I… you know I can't stand being touched anywhere like that…" Thibaut groaned in pain and confusion, unable to let his arms return to normal as he kept her protected and Jacinthe took in a deep breath. She knew it had been a bit risky of her, she was reminded that there were still problems for her partner that would mean certain things she could never do for him. But as he relaxed she leant forward and kissed his lips gently, making him grunt in surprise before she pulled up his clothes for him, trying not to touch him but letting him be covered before she kissed his ear sweetly and nuzzled his shoulder.

"You'll want to call upon Mhulder to collect us… he won't be shocked and I won't be embarrassed if he's the one to collect us." Jacinthe whispered softly, kissing at his lips tenderly, nuzzling at him lovingly as he gripped her tightly all the same. He growled gently, licking at the bruises on her neck where his fangs had pierced her before and then, he gave groan and opened out a wing slightly, calling out to Mhulder on the wind. It would take a while, but the hound would find him even in the daylight and they would hear the mad howling and barking of the pack followed by the charging horses. All the same, Jacinthe found herself stroking her husband's chest and shoulders, kissing at his neck and sighing happily. "Do you think we will have a child now?"

"I hope we will… I want nothing more than to raise a child with you my darling…" Thibaut whispered sweetly against her neck, licking at the bruises softly, encouraging her to giggle before they heard a maddened howl not far off. Thibaut turned his head upward, looking towards the sunlight that he was shielding Jacinthe from and he gave a soft chuckle of amusement before he turned back to her. Then she stared in surprise as he pulled his arms from his wings, but his wings remained open and Jacinthe was not only scared but excited as no vampire could do such a thing and surely, this was from his mother's demonic blood! "Come darling, I'll carry you…"

With that, Jacinthe was blushing as Thibaut pulled her up into his arms, cradling her before then wrapping his big wings tightly around her. Within them, Jacinthe realised that these were not the wings of a bat, they were closer to those of an incubus or worse… she could not tell and she did not want to think that Thibaut might be some terrifying kind of creature. She cuddled up close and he carried her out, his trousers slipping uncomfortably, but he was hopeful that this time he'd done his duty.

Indeed, almost ten months later, the entire Viper Clan household that was in Europe, hurried to come and witness the birth or at least be present for the birth of Thibaut's first child. Despite his desire to be in the room with her and ensure that Jacinthe would survive no matter what, the midwives made it very clear that he was not welcome to go instead. It was April 1937, he and Jacinthe had been trying nearly ten years for their first child and within that time, Vittorio was already lively and had insisted that his uncle would have to call him over the phone as soon as they knew. Gaston and Lynette had produced nothing and insisted they would have nothing, which meant this birth was all the more important for Gaston to interact with a child, across the sea Elaine was on her third child by Tonauac and her first daughter, but Thibaut had decided that it was only right that an Elder Emperor should have heirs as soon as possible. Noel had a daughter and a son, Wadim the seeming heir to Blestemat now and Sorina was only four or five months away from birthing her third child and even Selene had produced a son!

It had taken him so long to come to this point and the family were all on edge should it not be a boy and Thibaut would go through difficulties that Mircea could understand. But as Thibaut sat outside the room, grinding his teeth and claws against his cane that was now being scratched to death, Gaston sat beside him with a nervous expression upon his face as they heard the sound of Jacinthe screaming in utter agony. Gaston knew it would be far too easy for his brother to turn on his heel, leap in there and kill his own child because of the pain it was causing, Gaston could read it clearly on his brother's face, but he grasped him by the wrist and gave a hefty grunting sigh.

"She's going to be alright; it's going to be a male and you're going to be able to do things at your own pace together. There will be no more worries about your future and you'll just be able to heave a sigh of relief and go back to work, knowing that no one is going to question you or your abilities." Gaston stated firmly, only to get a shock when Thibaut pulled out of his grip and then snapped his hands around his brother's neck, making Gaston give a gag of horror and snatch for the hands on his neck. He gagged and gasped, his brother's hands squeezing so tightly around his neck he could feel the bruises forming as Gaston groaned out. There was then a much more violent scream from Jacinthe and Thibaut pulled a hand up, his golden eyes pitch-black and horrifying as Gaston swore, his brother's hand turning into the blade of a wing, ready to strike him until the gurgling screech of a baby filtered out from behind the door. "Hear it… do you hear that brother… that's your baby…"

Gaston's heart was beating away like mad, running around his chest the way his whole body was screaming that he needed to run away, but he was trapped. Thibaut still had his claws around Gaston's neck, no longer squeezing and the raised hand had lowered, but his brother was facing the door, his bat ears had emerged and he was listening in. Gaston could feel the fury and the panic within his brother's grasp and he understood that Thibaut was waiting to know if Jacinthe would survive. Gaston hoped she did, because if that child ever wanted to be loved by its father, it had better not kill its mother! There were a few sounds and then the door opened and Adelia poked her head out… Thibaut immediately dropped his brother back into the seat as Gaston gasped.

"What on earth were you… never mind, Thibaut, come see your son and don't worry, Jacinthe's barely lost a drop!" Adelia chuckled, insisting she was going to fetch Sabine with some fresh blood for Jacinthe all the same, but Thibaut practically knocked his mother aside to get into the room. Gaston rubbed at his ragged throat, the bruises visible as Adelia straightened herself up with a grunt of confusion as she looked from her second son towards Thibaut, wishing she'd known what he was feeling more than relief but sensing terror coming from Gaston as she turned to him as the door closed. "What happened just now? Are you alright?"

"Mother… you ever… you ever wonder if there's just a tad more 'dragon' in Thibaut than the rest of us?" Gaston grimaced and Adelia tilted her head to the side in confusion. She could read that Gaston was being serious, that the thought scared him and yet Adelia was not sure how to respond. He was the oldest, whether she'd taken enough venom when carrying him, but she stepped over to hold Gaston to her, kissing his cheek and patting his back as Gaston grimaced slightly. "I don't want to admit it, I know he wouldn't have killed me because he did stop… but he's not safe, is he."

"I don't know… lately it's hard to tell… but hopefully, having a son should calm him down." Adelia stated with a visible sigh of relief at the sound of Thibaut praising Jacinthe within. It always sounded a little patronising, but considering what he could have been like, Adelia was rather pleased that her son was sounding relaxed. Gaston gave his mother an anxious look all the same, his heart quivering in fear to think what was going on inside his brother's mind as he stepped in there to see his wife.

To see that Jacinthe merely look exhausted and happy all the same, sighing and fawning over the newborn pink-red flesh wrapped in fabric within her arms, filled Thibaut with ease. He watched as the midwives backed away from him, all of them sensing danger in his presence though Jacinthe was blissful, joyous and had no reason to think anything dangerous could ever happen here. Thibaut shuffled to the bed to her side, sitting upon it and leaning in to kiss her forehead and then her lips. Their noses nuzzled against one another, her face was sweaty, her cheeks clammy and yet she heaved a sigh of exhaustion against her husband as he looped his arm about her, nuzzling into her lovingly as she presented their son to him. But as Thibaut looked down to the boy, he could see dark roots with pale blonde strands, something similar to his own hair and he could see a writhing unhappy baby that seemed to be displeased with its existence. When the eyes opened, they were golden and somehow as Thibaut looked into them, only one thought bubbled into his mind.

I hate you.

The thought was kept hidden of course, Thibaut stared down blankly at his son, lifting his hand to touch at the babe's face and yet feeling no sensation of delight or joy as he had done for any of his siblings or even when meeting Vittorio. Was his son lacking in something? Was it because he was in a stressed situation right now and unwilling to accept something that had clearly hurt Jacinthe? Thibaut's mind was spinning, but he did not let it show and then he turned to Jacinthe and kissed her lips tenderly, nuzzling against her and thanking her for producing something so wonderful.

The baby continued to writhe and shriek, so Jacinthe beckoned Thibaut to hold the baby and this time, a disgusted expression fell upon his face and Jacinthe was unsure. She was aware that normally a man would not be expected to hold onto the child, but the family's general reaction was a lot more... eager... she was worried she'd done something wrong. Thibaut noticed though that his wife was looking anxious and so he calmly hooked up is son, who stopped shrieking and slowly he pulled him close and was staring at him for a while. The pair seemed to take the time to observe one another and it was clear that neither liked what they saw... but Thibaut still could not put his finger upon the problem.

Familiar faces then appeared at the door, Odette and Beauregard looked eager to come in and take a peek and then, when Theodora strolled into the room without fear, Thibaut chuckled. He beckoned his youngest siblings in, seeing the elder two still as teenagers rather than the adults they all were now. Theodora gladly hooked up her nephew from her brother as Beauregard gave Jacinthe a kiss for doing so well before he then looked to his nephew and made faces at him. Thibaut heaved a sigh of relief, suddenly feeling guilty for his reactions around Gaston and he stood up, stepping to the door and about to beckon Gaston to come in and see the baby, when Odette said something that made Thibaut's ears tickle.

"He reminds me a lot of Taliesin's pictures of his father... except the gold eyes... don't you think so Tibbs?" Odette questioned, standing gently beside the bed and looking down at the rather angry looking baby that Theodora was holding with pride. Beau tilted his head to the side too, looking at the baby before then noticing the uncomfortable expression upon Jacinthe's face and then lifting his hand as if to apologise. Jacinthe had been made aware during their courtship of the true relationship between Taliesin Vilmore the Second and Theodulus Viper, she'd been shocked, only to muse that Theo had been very much a Vilmore in looks, but in aura something wholly new within the vampire society. The words had given Thibaut great relief, he'd been fearful at first that she would have called everything off and blurted the truth to her sire, though Thibaut was rather sure most of the Counts had probably guessed it.

"Actually... now you mention it... perhaps that's what I can see in him. It's interesting really, but its only features... his heart will be his own and I'm sure he'll be a Viper like the rest of us." Thibaut stated, rather startling the others but Jacinthe just chuckled and insisted Thibaut was right, both their fathers had been blonde so there was more chance of them having a blonde son, not to mention he shared Thibaut's golden eyes. Thibaut appreciated the comment and kissed Jacinthe lovingly before being a little more reassured about his feelings over the baby. But there was still something about the boy he was not overly keen on.

As time went by, the boy named Cesaire Theo Viper, turned out to be unlike any of the other babies born to the Viper Clan that anyone could remember. As a baby he was generally unhappy unless with his mother, he hit Thibaut numerous times with toys, bit him and even defecated on him once or twice, which made the other siblings rather amused as Cesaire grew into a more disobedient brat than could be imagined. From demanding everything, getting nothing and yet Thibaut being too afraid of the violence Taliesin had undergone as a child to dare raise a hand against him, Cesaire was unfortunately spoilt. The other Counts made it worse, mixing him in with their family members of similar age, Cesaire started to comprehend his future role and became incredibly self-entitled. He picked up a lot of the language around the noble court too, commonly referring to Theodosius and Valentino as Wastes and refusing to recognise them as relatives, even though he was only six years old!

What was more, he found himself more drawn to the North African vampires and their sons, always intrigued by the fact they kept old traditions of harems, concubines and murdering the weakest born children. It made Thibaut incredibly ashamed to think that so much effort to have a single child felt wasted upon this brat that seemed to be more Vilmore than Viper! However, despite it all, upon turning seven and becoming horribly aware of the actions of the Purist Movement that swept across the European Veil as the nationalist movements beyond it, Cesaire seemed to pull back from his thoughts on Wastes. He stopped talking about werewolves and other species as subjects and it seemed for a while, he had changed… Jacinthe though knew it was down to one moment Thibaut had rather hoped no one had observed….

"I'm asking you because I'm scared for you… if the movement spreads over there, I want you to abandon that island and come here. I've already tried to persuade Dio, but he and Valentino are staying strong and protecting who they can. I'm terrified though, uncle… Hermann's being kept prisoner to keep the Bund compliant and the issue with the Krimorsky dragging the circle into other areas of concern, I fear this will be a moment they will aim for you too.

Please… I don't want to lose another like father…" Thibaut had been on the phone to Taliesin as usual, it was done in the middle of the day and in utter silence on a landline that connected through the outside of the Veil to Slater Island, especially since the French Veil Parliament had been occupied by the Purists and all lines of communication were monitored. It was only at this time of day that he could call his uncle and ensure that Taliesin was still safe, but his uncle tended to insist he was just panicking about everything and needed to relax.

The conversation from Thibaut's side was becoming more and more frantic as time went on, he was getting fearful that he could not do anything to keep all of his family secure, especially when one of Jacinthe's own sisters had dared to marry one of the leaders of this dictatorship! He had rescued Noel and his family from the Krimorsky and with Lynette looking quite sickly lately, Odette in England learning to be a nurse and helping the Veil out with the attacks there… the only people he could not secure were Dio, Elaine and Taliesin. He wanted to keep them safe, he wanted to make sure that they were not at any risk and though Elaine was safe, Theodosius seemed to be in a different situation and unable to move, but Taliesin….

The conversation finished and Thibaut had to put the phone line down, knowing that his uncle was bound to be in danger and feeling as if his inability to secure Hermann was completely his fault. Somehow the world had fallen out of his control and it scared Thibaut, without having any ability to manipulate and steer the course of things, suddenly everything he loved and had worked hard for was at risk. He was fearful that something dangerous might befall his family, that Jacinthe would be in some kind of danger because of her sister and Thibaut gave a hiss of fury as he buried his head into the desk, wrapped his arms about his head and suddenly started to sob quietly, glad no one was around to hear it now that Dara and Brennan had retired over to Mhulder's Island and Renard was doing the work of a butler for the meantime and doing well, along with Ashford's help.

As he sat there sobbing, he was unaware that Cesaire had woken up and decided to sneak around. He was hoping to find one of the maids and bully her into giving him the treats he wanted, they were so easy to order around and he liked it when he got what he wanted, but then Cesaire had thought to go to his father's office. Cesaire was not usually permitted to go there, he liked to sneak around though and was convinced that it was within his father's office that his

Christmas presents for next week might be hiding! But as he'd shuffled down from his room next to his mother's, where he'd learnt that his mother only slept when his father was having to work very hard, Cesaire realised the lights were on and there was someone inside.

He'd only snuck into the office once, but when he'd gone in there his eyes had locked upon the hideous painting above the fireplace and he'd pulled back. The scary sight of a being upon the cross with blood spurting out into a cup held by something that reminded him more of a Strigoi was horrifying. He'd been scared out of his wits when he'd felt the eyes of Christ staring right at him and he'd wet himself! For doing that, he'd been caught and warned with one stern look from his father that he was not to come into that room, but he was feeling braver on this occasion!

Carefully, Cesaire stepped towards the door and noticed that the door was slightly open, enough for him to spy into it and so he peered in. His golden eyes glimmered to see something he'd not seen before and so young, he could not quite comprehend. He was looking at his father, hearing him sob but more importantly the sight of tears on a red face and his father clasping a picture was worrying. Cesaire's brow wrinkled in confusion as he wrinkled his nose and then heard exactly what his father was sobbing about.

"Why did you have to leave us at that moment? Why did you have to think that their love was more important than the rest of us? I can't be like you father... I can't keep them safe!" Thibaut sobbed into his arms, feeling totally weak, totally unable to do anything and finding it unbearable. He growled and snarled, opening his mouth to show his nasty fangs and preparing to bite himself in his rage and distress. His eyes were flashing so brilliantly gold that it seemed to mimic the fire coming from the great furnace roaring beside him. The sight of it made Cesaire terrified, he watched his father's wings stretch out behind him, even when he was snarling and growling towards his hands... it was not normal and Cesaire felt almost as if he might wet himself!

His father looked like a demon!

Cesaire quickly turned away and hurried out of the room, his heart pumping in terror and he rushed to find the bathroom before thinking of bed. He hopped inside, hoping that he would not be noticed as he slammed the door shut and locked it, knowing it was the only place that would be completely safe. He used the toilet, sighed in relief and yet the image was still fresh in his mind of something that did not feel normal and yet was his father! His stomach knotted all the same as he took the chance to open the door, hoping to leave and sneak back to his room and have the rest of his nap… when he realised someone was standing in the hallway.

It felt like a shadow at first… a terrifying shadow that was overwhelming him and behind the door! He felt that if he dared to step away from the door or close it, he would see the monster hiding behind and he could not stop himself from quivering. All of his usually bolshiness was leaking away from him as he trembled and tears began to form in his eyes as his lips pinched together but wobbled too. Before he could make a decision, the door was pushed closed behind him and he turned to face the being that had terrified him only moments ago.

"Cesaire… are you alright? Are you fully awake or just… you look sad?" Thibaut squatted down to his son, a look on his face that was concerned but those his eyes were reddened and his face stained from tears, he did not seem to be the same creature as a moment ago. Cesaire just continued to tremble in front of him, unsure if he could even say what he'd seen to be scared, but Thibaut wrapped his arms around his son's body and pulled him in for a tight hug. Cesaire remained stiff with fear at first, but then his father snuggled into him, cuddling him tightly before kissing his ear softly. "Did you have a bad dream?"

"Yes Papa…" Cesaire blinked a few times… could it have just been a bad dream? He did not know but as his father continued to nuzzle up against him, kissing his head and patting him, Cesaire relaxed his body. His father was always kind if he thought Cesaire was ill or sad, but aside from that their interactions were somewhat limited. Maybe Cesaire had just been imagining monsters as his father brought him to the bedroom where Jacinthe was fast asleep. Cesaire was more relieved to see his mother, but Thibaut placed him on the bed beside her and then slipped onto the bed too.

"How about we all try and nap together? If you have me and mama beside you, then whatever you saw in your dreams won't come back. Agreed?" Thibaut questioned softly and Cesaire bobbed his head, only to snuggle up against his mother. Jacinthe gave a groan, turning around and opening her eyes then her arms to him as he pressed right up against her, knowing he was safe within her arms. But Jacinthe looked up and noticed Thibaut too and her face slid into a loving smile as he bent down to kiss her, then Cesaire's head before lying down beside them as she beamed sweetly.

"Did he have another nightmare? Thank you for bringing him in my darling... you look tired." Jacinthe stretched her hand out to stroke her husband's hot face. Thibaut sighed and nuzzled into her hand before then settling down in the bed and cuddling Cesaire too. It scared the boy, he could feel his heart beating away like mad inside his chest and he wanted to stifle his breath, unaware his body was screaming there was a monster in the room. But then he heard his mother's heart beating away calmly and his father's was calm and steady too. Cesaire rolled to face his father and gave him an anxious expression as Jacinthe stroked his hair gently.

"Papa... what should I do if I see a monster?" Cesaire questioned, wondering if asking the question would confirm his father's true identity or whether it would just be something his father would laugh off. Thibaut was silent for a time, not too sure what his son was asking but he gave a soft sound of thought. Thibaut pondered if Cesaire had been overhearing the difficulties going on in the world around them and mistaken his father's disgust for the Purists as monsters. He stroked his son's head and then spoke very calmly.

"Whenever you see a monster, run to your mother, your grandmother, your uncles, aunts or to me. We will all protect you... I wouldn't let anyone hurt you." Thibaut stated, feeling curiously relieved to have the chance to redeem his earlier upset by making this promise to his son. He stroked his son's strawberry blonde hair back, musing that it was starting to turn a more gingery shade around the roots than his brown as he kissed his son's forehead and Cesaire shivered slightly but nodded his head as Jacinthe nodded her head too.

"Of course darling, no matter what, you can always count on us to protect you. Now rest, Renard will wake us when it's time for your nap to be over." Jacinthe stated happily, her heart starting to flutter as she noticed her husband's golden eyes fluttering towards her thoughtfully with affection and love. Whenever she caught his attention, she was happy and having this family moment together made her feel special. Thibaut felt pleased that she was smiling, but his heart felt just a touch of relief to know that he could at least keep the mansion and its residents safe.

Time went by and in 1944, it was revealed that the Purist movement had been invented by a dragon that had two heads and infected one man outside the Veil and one within. The information was snuck out of the German Bund where the nobles had been split in who was infected by the dragon and who was not. The actions of Hermann von Nebelblut to escape and alert the Noble Circle caused a riot and war, but Thibaut and many other Counts stood up and declared war on the Purists within their region. When he did, he learnt of what Valentino and Theodosius, but mostly like Vittorio had been doing to save others and the entire Veil outside the control of the red dragon dropped into violence to purge the demon dragons, finding that the presence of one in their part of the Veil later revealed a second that was hunting the Iron Wolves.

For three years there was instability in supplies and communication throughout the entire world of the Veil, but though the Krimorsky infected Red Veil and the Scandinavian Veil remained disconnected, even the Antarctic Veil that was run by Reformer demons came together to help. They removed them all, businesses began to reform and there seemed to be a sudden relaxation within the Veil by April 1946 and things for the Viper Clan were back to usual, but for Jacinthe everything seemed… lonely.

With Cesaire having just turned nine, he was now of the opinion that his mother had no position in his life and having to go through three years with all his usual luxury lost, he had not learnt to be grateful but more belligerent. With Thibaut away regularly, the staff had been fearful to discipline him and he had resorted to biting quite frequently whenever Jacinthe, Adelia or Gaston tried to deal with him. With Lynette now often at home because she was sickly and unable to move very well, Gaston was rarely able to help his brother with the running of the mansion and Noel's own children kept him very busy too. Cesaire was running reckless, Jacinthe could only ever seem to control him by threats of telling his father!

But Jacinthe was rarely able to see Thibaut, he had not been able to share her bed for three years, save on their anniversaries and her birthday, and his insomnia had been rather extreme, matching his lack of interest in anything much more than a slight cuddle and a kiss. She was feeling shockingly lonely, but Jacinthe had been aware upon marriage that she and Thibaut would not see each other too much no matter how much they loved each other. However, with Cesaire barely around her because of his schooling and her own family rather more wrapped up in their own problems rather than willing to talk to her, even speaking with Selene and spending time with the snakes in the household only increased her loneliness. Thibaut too had admitted that the bombing of the opera house in Paris that had taken out the head of the Purists in France, not to mention her sister married to his second, had been under Thibaut's instruction. He had been avoiding her over that too and yet, after what she'd heard had been done by the Purists, she'd lost all sympathy for the foolish Marie.

But what saddened Jacinthe the most, was that she did not just want company for the sake of company; she wanted Thibaut to return and to love her. She wanted him to climb into her bed and show her the tenderness he had shown in the past. More uncomfortably, Jacinthe wished for the same kind of passion that she had experienced when she'd been weaning Cesaire. She was not sure what had triggered it then, but at that time she and Thibaut had spent every other day in bed together for six months! She'd been quite sure that Thibaut had hoped they might have another child then, she knew he loved the thought of having a daughter… but they had not been so lucky, or at least it had not fully developed to the point she could have said they were lucky.

The loneliness she felt seemed to make her clothing change; before Jacinthe had thought to dress sensibly but however she felt before when she left the house, now she tried her best not to wear anything that wasn't plain when Thibaut was not around. Then, when he returned from business, she would be dressed up as if it were a celebration to gain his attention and though he would stroke her face and say she looked beautiful, he would disappear into his work again. She knew it was what they had agreed to understand of one another after they married… but Jacinthe was shocked to think she was frustrated sexually.

Jacinthe had taken Cesaire and Adelia across to Paris to see her family for a party. It was her father's birthday party and the children were all enjoying themselves and playing under the watch of the gargoyle servants with Cesaire taking control as he always did. The men were in their smoking room enjoying themselves thoroughly and the women were all within a separate drawing room enjoying themselves and talking about the latest gossip. To be fair, Adelia was rather bored, her interest instead focused upon something she was working on towards Jacinthe's birthday next month. Jacinthe though was uncomfortable in her situation and dared to ask the women or her family their opinion of what to do, but the response was not very helpful.

"I don't think anyone can help you on this matter, none of us have any idea what makes that husband of yours tick and to be fair, I really would not want to know what was going on in it!" Her stepmother scoffed, shivering and shuddering in a display of just how sickened she was by anything that was mentioned about Thibaut. Jacinthe looked to her with a sigh, she was hoping that someone might have at least a clue and yet the women around her all looked anxious. It was not news to them that Thibaut had no interest in sex, they had all assumed that Jacinthe would have realised once she'd produced his son, that was her only job and then one of her elder sisters-in-law gave a chuckle.

"Get yourself a lover… Thibaut probably would not care as long as you were being satisfied and did not produce a child to them. Knowing him, as long as it was someone discreet, he wouldn't notice!" She chuckled heartily and some of the other women gave a few giggles as if they understood it, but Adelia just gave a soft little chortle as she listened to it. All eyes slid nervously towards her, most of the women in this household still very uneasy about the being they had all been told was half-vampire, but some had heard killed a member of the Pipistrello family. Adelia just gave a pleasant sigh as she placed her work to the side, showing off it was a sketch before turning to them.

"With the ghost hounds and the gargoyles Thibaut pulled in to guard the entire household, let alone the complete loyalty of the staff… everything that happens at home, Thibaut knows about. It would be risking death to take on a lover… especially as it would disrespect him." Adelia stated gently, but she noticed that the women were pale and yet Jacinthe was shaking her hands, embarrassed enough her freckles were shining through on her cheeks and her coiled hazel locks were jumping about as she shook her head wildly.

"Non! I would never do such a thing to him! I love him and that's the problem… I don't want anyone else, I just want him!" Jacinthe stated, sounding miserable as she lowered her head downwards and brought her hands over her face. She could not believe it, she had thought they would understand her feelings of frustration were because of how much she loved him, instead it just seemed that the ideals of love really did not exist amongst elite households. She began to understand the stupid actions of her sisters with other men, the flirtations of her stepmother as well as why her brothers felt they did not need to hide their own affairs as long as their wives did not flaunt their own.

It made her stomach churn in distress and she rubbed at her belly, wishing perhaps that maybe they'd have another baby and then Thibaut would fuss and protect her the way he had with Cesaire. Maybe… when it would be time to wean the next baby, he'd be as passionate again as before? Jacinthe grimaced and rubbed her hands over her face again, the room was quiet as the other women just seemed to be amused over her. They seemed to find it naïve that she felt that way, especially when they all viewed Thibaut as something unwanted, despite his beauty and his power, but one of the family members seemed to understand.

"I understand Jacinthe, I feel the same about your brother and we are very happy, in fact I am glad that Laurent and I agreed not to have other partners and just be together… but when he does go away for business with his friends in Hong Kong, it can get incredibly lonely. Sometimes he comes back so tired I don't know what to do because I want him to rest but I'm so desperate to just be held by him and well… I think it's just as much about our thoughts on being valued as much as our desires." Samantha was about the same age as Jacinthe, she had been a surprise wife that Jacinthe's third eldest brother Laurent had fallen for out of nowhere. She was from the Bordeaux vampires, a small clan that rarely pulled themselves into politics and worked on providing products, but when a business meeting had them come together, it was love at first sight for the long-time bachelor. Hearing her say these words as she stretched out her hand to pat at Jacinthe's filled the other with a sigh of relief to know that she was not so strange.

"So… what do you do then?" Jacinthe questioned, though she could sense the quiet in the room was being caused by the fascination of the other women but also their amusement. They were thinking that Samantha was just as innocent and naïve as Jacinthe, but to know what the wallflowers of the group would do or attempt was intriguing as Samantha gave a smile.

"I tell him before he leaves that I'll be waiting for him and think about him just before I go to sleep so I will always have good dreams. He then gives this sort of look that says he just had an image of me swooning over the picture of him beside my bed and when he comes back, he thinks he has a job to do to remind me he's still there. It's funny… almost like he's jealous of my dreams of him!" Samantha stated gently with a smile and the others looked at her curiously and shrugged their shoulders. That tactic tended to work for their lovers more than their husbands and Jacinthe was intrigued as Samantha continued. "Then, when he returns home… I make sure his favourite meal is there for him and in bed, I make sure to be wearing the outfit he likes the most to see me in."

"I see." Jacinthe stated, only to hear the sudden soft chuckle from Adelia in the background. They all turned to look at her expectantly, eager to know what the mother of nine children had to do to inflame her husband's heart. Adelia just smiled at them, shaking her head as she considered her romantic relationship with Theodulus and how, he'd been the one putting in that kind of effort when she'd just been happy enough when they were together.

"Heh… I actually had it from the other side, Theo would say these thing to me, or turn up in the room dressed like a butler and make me breakfast in bed or he would just… well, be himself. I don't see Thibaut as the kind who would accept you trying to seduce him… he hasn't really got that kind of… passion." Adelia stated, knowing full well that Thibaut and her were the same in this manner. They did not crave or want sex, it was just a means to an end and though, on some occasions they'd enjoyed it, mostly it was all about the contact. "But I think… if you tell him that you're going to miss him terribly and hope he will think about you… that might make him more eager to see you. Honesty is wholly more attractive to Thibaut than gifts."

"Explaining his interest in Jacinthe's ugly freckles…" One of the other women at the back whispered but made sure it was loud enough for a few more to hear and giggle about. Jacinthe took in a sudden breath, lowering her head and not sure how to respond or react to such a comment. Sometimes, she did not doubt that in the looks department she was plain, her hair curled and was chestnut in colour, her skin would tan in the summer and her freckles would stand out across her face in a manner that embarrassed her greatly. She rarely had fashion sense either, she wore what she thought would look suitable, not what would make her stand out and she sighed heavily.

"I haven't got any pretty dresses or fancy clothes he might be drawn to… I don't tend to dress up… but perhaps I should." Jacinthe stated calmly, fidgeting with the sewing in her hand and then looking towards Adelia thoughtfully. With them having nothing to do the next evening, Adelia read the sign and insisted they would go out and shop the next day, which made Jacinthe smile happily as she lowered her head again and tried to be a little more excited by what was to come.

The next evening saw them going around the Paris Fashion district with Ada, the now old werewolf female that Thibaut had saved so long ago. She often played the role of Adelia's servant so that when someone called Adelia's alias of 'Ada Viper' out to the world, the wolf would turn and she would too. But hearing Jacinthe's concerns, Ada had been eager to do anything to aid the woman that made her master so happy. She had added her own thoughts on the matter, that Thibaut might find a good conversation about an interesting book or fact enough to make him more eager to spend time with her, but also that honesty would help. Jacinthe was thankful, especially as Ada was able to keep Cesaire's attention when she spotted some toys.

"Whilst Ada has Cesaire occupied, this is a very special room that I once caught Theo inside and initially, I was stunned thinking he was up to something… only to find that he was in fact, looking at the enticing clothes for men to wear… it was incredibly embarrassing and amusing all at once. He was trying to find something he could wear that I might find… enticing but, in the end I just bought some ribbon from here and explained to him how I didn't need anything or anyone but him." Adelia chuckled sweetly, then there was a sudden pained expression as she heaved a soft sigh, but that was to be expected whenever she found herself remembering something wonderful about Theodulus. Jacinthe though was blushing heavily, not sure how to respond, until she was brought into the room and her eyes widened.

Jacinthe had heard before about the curious things behind hidden doors within the vampire culture, their "toys", which were supposed to increase the likelihood of them producing offspring in some cases and then in others just to satisfy fetishes that were often used with hired succubae rather than risk scaring a female. Jacinthe stared at them… from negligees and other such lingerie to whips, chains and gags… things that scared her as she looked towards that area. Adelia just cruised around without thought, she had known there were such things in the world, her and Theo had once found a book of such things in Taliesin's house and sat down reading through it, giggling at some things, blushing at others and rather learning more than they'd expected… until Taliesin had spotted them and had a sulk about them reading his books!

"Do you… do you think any of this would work with Thibaut?" Jacinthe was scared, she did not want to miss out an opportunity to entice her husband and make him excited to see her in such attire or interested in such things, but Adelia just patted her shoulder. She steered the trembling, thin vampire towards the collections of beautiful silken nightdresses, pointing them out and especially one that was a soft lavender colour, had straps over the shoulder and barely just covered the thighs. Jacinthe saw it and blushed heavily, turning towards Adelia with an anxious look. "Are you sure this would be enough?"

"Of course… it's something new… when you next see him, tell him you bought something new and you want to show it to him, then wear it and beckon him in… see if he wants to touch you. Ah! Maybe some stockings that he can stroke around your thighs to entice him…" Adelia clapped her hands, suddenly excited at the thought of dressing Jacinthe up as the woman blushed nervously. Adelia hurried over to some of the white fishnet stockings, some garters and a nice pair of white 'French Knickers' that were very popular at the moment. All of these items had been impossible to get during the time of the Purists, this kind of place had been considered perverse so had gone underground and now it was happy to be back and needed once again. Jacinthe was surprised that Adelia was so excited about the situation, it was embarrassing but she was glad that Adelia seemed to think this was enough. Back at home, she heard a lot of rumours about how vicious and brutal Thibaut could be, that he tortured those who went against him and sometimes it was just for fun rather than to make them regret coming near his room. So she was thankful that Adelia thought only these things would be needed and she was happy when they purchased them.

The items were wrapped in black and gold tissue paper, tied up with string and slid inside a paper bag that was purple in colour and almost looked like it had come from a cake shop. Jacinthe was startled when Ada and Cesaire returned with Ada looking a little embarrassed because she was carrying several bags containing items from the cake shops, sweet shops and even a toy shop. She'd been spoiling the young master again and Adelia shook her head in frustration, but Cesaire looked to his mother's bag. His hand shot out for it, insisting he was going to take a peek until Ada mentioned it was for his father… immediately Cesaire recoiled from it and then they pulled away.

They headed back home to the household and were very happy when they reached home and found that Thibaut was present, though only for a short while. The excitement was enough for Jacinthe to gallop up the stairs to the bedroom with her package as Cesaire greeted his father with a hug, a kiss to each cheek before being given a new book on the curious creatures of the North African Veil, something Cesaire found fascinating, he galloped off with it in delight as Thibaut turned to his mother with a curious look and Adelia thought to tell Thibaut to go upstairs and see to his wife. He was confused, insisting he had to leave at dawn, but Adelia swatted at him to go up already.

Thibaut slowly strolled up to his wing with a curious expression upon his face, a mix of puzzled and amused. When he strolled to her room, he knocked on the door gently and there was a sound of concern from Jacinthe. There was then an elastic snap and Jacinthe gave a yelp, causing Thibaut to barge in to see her wrestling with garters. He did not even look at what she was wearing, as he calmly held her hands away and gently adjusted the straps whilst Jacinthe was blushing to the ears.

"There... don't you look beautiful Jacinthe, the purple looks nice with the white... is it comfortable?" Thibaut spoke so sweetly and lovingly that Jacinthe could not help but blush brighter and then looked downwards. She felt as if Thibaut had completely missed the situation for what it was, but only because she'd fumbled and had not gotten it right at all. But as she sat there, he could not seem to help but stroke at her thigh and lean his head against hers. It made her smile a little and she turned her head up to ask for a kiss and was given a gentle one before he wrapped his arms about her and held her close. "Is this something you're preparing for your birthday?"

"Uh... perhaps..." Suddenly Jacinthe felt her heart trembling, her stomach doing somersaults to think that Thibaut might have picked up on something. She then shivered gently in excitement as she felt his hands gently stroking at the netting on her legs, musing that they made her thighs look very lovely. She was hopeful, her senses tingling and her stomach now heating up with the pent-up desires that she hoped to be expressed, before Thibaut just smiled and stroked her shoulder, leaning in for a tender and loving kiss.

"It will look very beautiful... but maybe you should change into something more suitable for dinner. I can only stay long enough to eat and settle you both to bed at dawn before I must return to work. I would not be back till possibly your birthday." Thibaut stated gently, stroking through her chestnut hair suddenly, something he tended to do to suggest that he felt sorry for not being with her as long as she perhaps hoped that he might be. It made her immediately flop down into his lap and give a grimace and even a light sob of dismay and frustration. The action startled Thibaut greatly and he held her by the shoulders, gently easing her into a sitting position and looking at her with anxious eyes. "Darling, what's wrong?"

"You would hate me if I said it..." Jacinthe whimpered, feeling utterly dismayed that her husband could be so oblivious and yet she knew what Thibaut was like. When it came to this kind of thing, if she were not honest about it then how on earth could he even try to guess? With a whimper as he stroked her cheeks and insisted he would never hate her, Jacinthe heaved a sigh and yet her head dropped. "I... I want to have sex with you."

"Right now?" Thibaut stated in a confused tone that also insisted it was neither the right time nor place for such a thing. It made Jacinthe even more frustrated, but she straightened up and heaved a sigh. She kissed his nose and then shook her head, insisting she was not in the mood for dinner nor in the mood for anything more than to go to sleep. She pulled the covers up off the bed and slipped inside, leaving Thibaut to stare at her for a while before leaving.

Jacinthe just felt miserable... her honesty and her attempt at seduction seemed to have failed.

Jacinthe was enjoying the warm air current that had chosen to grace the English Channel in the early hours of the morning, just before thinking of heading to bed. She had been watching the light forming in the east, lounging on the stone bench on the balcony outside of her dorm as she sighed lovingly. It was so beautiful, so wonderful and yet she had hoped that tonight her beloved would return and come to her side, but that was always such a silly thought. Thibaut only returned from work when he was done, not just because the time seemed right for Jacinthe as Cesaire was away in Rennes with her family visiting his grandpa. She wished though that he might receive the message seeping from her heart, her hope to be held by him and to be loved as it would be her birthday soon. He would not forget her birthday, he never did and he would smother her in affection and love then but... he would abandon them all after to hide in his uncle's kingdom where there was only darkness. Maybe she should not be hoping for him to come to her now, she could wait until the fifth of May... she was sure she could!

Just as she sighed and stood up, watching the sun start to lift, she stepped into the north-facing French windows and into her bedroom, sighing softly in her long silken nightdress as she prepared to close the door and shut up for sleep. But... a shadow loomed over her against the pale light and silhouetted upon the wall was the shape of a giant bat-like form that shifted suddenly into a man with a great cape sweeping about in the wind behind him. Jacinthe froze, her heart hammering with excitement and her mouth wanting to utter a cry and swoon back into waiting arms... but she could never be so impetuous. She could see the red cape flapping about near her, could smell the scent of amaranth in the air and she trembled as he stomped off the balcony wall and then stepped into the room and behind her as she quivered and waited for him to greet her. But to her greatest shock, the cape was suddenly swung about her, shielding her eyes before soft pale lips caressed her neck, one hand dropped to her stomach and she leant back against his body. Her eyes were shimmering as she looked up into the golden eyes of her husband as he lifted his head to look down at her before lifting his hand to stroke her neck as she shuddered in pleasure and mouthed his name before his lips came down to clasp hers.

Then Thibaut's arms pulled back, throwing off his cape to reveal him in just a neat white shirt and slacks before he turned to close the glass doors behind them and pull the heavy black curtains across. Jacinthe was scarlet, moaning softly as she turned to look at him as he then approached her, standing behind her and kissing at her neck more, his tongue stroking over the marks he'd left as he worshipped her in silence. Jacinthe moaned lovingly, sighing and almost purring as she stretched her hands to his, feeling them lift up to sit over her breasts. She gave a soft chuckle as she cooed at him, starting to unbutton the clippings upon her chest as she pulled them down to reveal her bosom to the air. Thibaut then turned about to face her, hooking her up into his arms as his lips caressed hers and they moaned loudly together in a firm, passionate kiss as Thibaut carried her to the bed and then lay her down before crawling over her.

He then lay on his side against her chest, one hand lay over one breast, stroking and massaging it lovingly before his mouth came to the other breast, his tongue teasing her nipple to make her moan before he began to suck lovingly at her. As he twisted to lay down on one side, stroking the top of her chest as he held and squeezed at her hand, the free hand then grasped at her body as he suckled obsessively upon her nipple, his groin grinding and moving up and down her leg as she could feel his excitement growing. She moaned lovingly at his attention, leading the other hand to the forgotten breast again to massage it as she stroked the hand, gasping and moaning beside with the motions. Her other hand stroked the back of his head and she could not help but let her hips roll, feeling him against her leg make her stomach coil with pleasure as she gasped, her fangs out as she then turned to him.

"You… you can take my blood if you wish darling… all I want is to please you…" Jacinthe purred and then the blonde hair lifted, his soft lips departed from her breast as he strained forward to kiss her lovingly. She melted into the kiss, feeling his body align more, his hips began grinding and rubbing against her body as she shuddered away from the kiss. His kisses pressed softly about the edges of her mouth and for a moment, as she moaned loudly to feel him pushing against her body so eagerly, she had to freeze and grab his face. Rather harshly, she'd grabbed him by the head and pulled his face up to look at her to ensure it was indeed her husband as the golden eyes flashed and Thibaut produced an aggressive hiss that showed his fangs. For a moment she almost wanted to scream to have angered him, but suddenly Thibaut shuffled up her body and kissed her forehead through his fangs with a low hiss of pleasure.

"I'll take your blood… but forgive my perversions beloved… my Petal I'm sorry to seem so ravenous after abandoning you so long…" Thibaut purred softly and Jacinthe almost wanted to squeal like an excited child. He'd never said it in such a manner and yet she was joyful of it as she giggled to herself and then blew him a kiss as he then lowered his body down again. Swiftly, he dared to use his own talons to shred his clothing aside before ripping it away and revealing his arousal as she blushed more profoundly. But then he made sure her clothing was neatly sheared away from her hips as he lay over her and then seemed to crouch awkwardly. As his groin aligned with hers and she was forced to stretch out against the mattress with her hands hanging as she moaned aloud, he joined their bodies with a soft groan before he seemed almost to bend double. He grasped a breast, pushing it as far up as he could so as not to hurt her as he lowered his head to it and extended his jaw, his fangs swiftly stabbing into the soft caramel coloured areola as Jacinthe gave out a low groan and Thibaut began to move.

Jacinthe fainted back against the bed, moaning and sighing, feeling nothing more than pleasure in her body as every motion teased nerves that danced in happiness and his body pumped hormones into her blood that blocked out pain and filled her with an ecstatic haze better than opium. She lowed softly, deeply, her hips relaxing back and lifting with his motions as his body danced with hers in a seeming frenzy of delight. His mouth was filling with blood, his skin drinking it in as feverishly as her body welcomed his elegance within. As they danced on and on as the day brightened outside, Jacinthe lifted her hands to his dirty blonde hair, stroking and teasing through locks as he detached from her bosom and lapped it, sealing it before he came to her neck. As he groaned and his body moved more into a great pleasure that would make Jacinthe think she had screamed out in joy, his mouth kissed and stroked over the mark upon her neck that was from his fangs alone.

Tenderly, he slipped his sharp fangs under the bruise and she moaned even more as her hips began to shudder and tremble of their own will. His fangs pulled in blood and he seemed almost to sink into the flesh of her neck and shoulder, Thibaut's body struck a match within her own and she gave a sharp gulp and stared upward for a moment, unable to breathe as muscles tightened suddenly and then seemed to flush back and soak the bed. Thibaut gave a gurgling growl of upset at his own end before pulling away swiftly and rolling onto his stomach, writhing and moaning in agony as his left leg began to kick and shudder in unwelcome convulsions.

"Oh… oh darling…" Jacinthe sighed softly as Thibaut swung himself off the bed and grabbed the hard oak pole, pulling himself to his feet and standing as the leg stopped trembling but Jacinthe could watch the nerve from the top of his left hip to his left thigh pulse and twitch, making the muscles jump. He was blushing and grimacing, trying not to appear childish and yet feeling utterly defeated despite himself. Jacinthe sat up steadily, only to faint back a little when the loss of blood hit her. Suddenly Thibaut was back onto the bed in a flash, right beside her despite his pain, pulling the bed sheet up and rolling it into a tight folded corner to press to the wound and hold it down as he whispered fearfully over whether she was alright. Jacinthe just smiled up at him, stroking his arm tenderly and blowing kisses at him lovingly as Thibaut then gently lay down beside her and leant against her, kissing her shoulder and then checking the wound was not still bleeding before he then kissed her cheek. She sighed as she stroked at his chin and he kissed at her lovingly, a piteous expression upon his face for fearing he'd wounded her, but she chuckled. "It always surprises me when you have these moments with me… but are you alright?"

"I'm fine my love… I'm fine… as long as you're fine… I only ever want to make you happy." Thibaut growled softly and Jacinthe sighed and then gave a gentle chuckle as she stroked at her stomach thoughtfully. He shuffled down to hold onto her, to pull her close and kiss her, lying on the unharmed side as she chuckled and insisted he always made her happy. But Thibaut gave a soft sigh and lay his hand to her stomach, stroking it alongside her and then kissing her lips. He settled back down against her as she teased that he'd come back to the house in a very 'cad-like' manner but he'd dared to stick his tongue out about it, only to sigh again. Thibaut was curious though, would this give them something special?

There was an hour of them snuggling in the bed together before Mhulder was sent for, bearing a fresh blood concoction for Jacinthe to drink. She took it in with ease and then watched as Mhulder offered a needle and syringe to Thibaut, who then stood up and gripped the bed post again as Mhulder then injected him with something that stung and became awkwardly hot as it seemed to rush within Thibaut's blood. With that, Mhulder left and Jacinthe watched in surprise as Thibaut returned to the bed and then stroked at her stomach again, nuzzling her neck as she looked at him in confusion before finishing her meal and staring at him thoughtfully.

"It's a painkiller, it will numb my leg for a while but also mean I cannot move too much. I used it once before but there's an embarrassing side effect that you'll see soon enough." Thibaut grimaced, looking bashful but then kissing his wife's lips tenderly again before he lay down and clasped her hip then her back, beckoning her to clamber onto him and as she did so, the side-effect was obvious as Thibaut blushed. "I was ashamed of it... so I wished never to take it again but, I had been neglecting you so foolishly that... I thought as long as you did not mind me just enjoying watching you enjoy yourself... then for as long as it lasts, I will not be in pain and you can truly feel... satisfied."

"Oh... darling..." Jacinthe cooed, knowing that this was something that Thibaut would share and ask only of her. She was grateful, fearful she might hurt him but, it did not take long for his pheromones to stoke her ardour again and her belly to grind with a hunger she was desperate to fulfil. With his hands caressing her sides, her hips, her legs and watching her dance upon him, the pair coupled more times in that brief three hours of dulled pain than it seemed in their entire marriage, both of them happy and hopeful that this chance would lead to something else.

Indeed... the following April, they were quite startled when another little boy with his mother's chestnut curls and hazel eyes that seemed to flash vividly gold in the light, was born to them. They named him Acelin, "little noble one", he was hated by his jealous brother immediately and though disappointed not to have a daughter, to have a true love child within their household was wonderful. Though of course Thibaut's relationship with Acelin would not be clear to others, just as his love for Jacinthe, he would love the new child greatly... though wish for one more chance to have a daughter.

Part Six: The Forgotten Couple

Black Candle Region of the London Veil, 1940

The family were not pleased by the decision, but Odette had made it clear that she did not want to be anywhere close to the Purists or to step over to mainland France and accept the hideous regime that they had begun. She'd qualified as a fully trained nurse, but she was not going to be lectured to about whom she should heal and who should die. It was not the way of a nurse and though her family utterly respected her choice not to work in France, her decision to go across to England was something they'd had more difficulty with. However, Thibaut had travelled at her side along with Taliesin and they'd met the last remaining member of the Ecclestone family, named for his beloved uncle Richard and the only one who had tried to save his uncle… or rather Emma… from the family. It was Young Richard, as he always made sure he was called, that seemed to be the reassurance for Odette's position the family needed.

"She'll be in the dorms with the other nurses here, it's perfectly safe and no men can get in, besides several are Turned vampires so it won't be a situation where they can't get along. Taliesin's got the old gargoyles posted around that will keep an eye on her and have been working well with the witch's magic to keep the effects of the bombing outside the Veil minimal. But that's why we need nurses like her, ones who are tougher and can step in amongst the rubble without fear to help others. Odette has strong opinions and ideals and is more than capable of doing this." Young Richard was about the same age as Selene, his own son.. another George… now mature enough to be looking around for a wife. At first, Taliesin and Thibaut had been cautious that this was the reason for his interest in the matter, but with Taliesin having less influence over the London Veil than he used to, Young Richard Ecclestone was the only one with enough power to be listened to and protect Odette.

"You're a wise young man, Richard. But you should be concerned that should anything happen to my younger sister, I'll remove whatever's left of your family from existence." Thibaut had stated firmly, with Taliesin beside him wearing a hooded robe made of blue crushed velvet like some curious kind of monk, the image was rather unsettling to Richard. He could see Thibaut's huge fangs as he spoke and the scowl that seemed permanently fixed to Taliesin's face these days, only seemed to add to his concerns whilst speaking. But Odette finished passing her luggage over to the gargoyles that were helping her out and gently stepped to Richard's side with a firm expression.

"If there is an incident, it will be my own doing. You cannot go seeking someone to blame for everything that happens in life, especially when most of the problems are caused by one's own self." Odette stated gently, her expression firm, her manner rather haughty as if she'd fight anyone with words and oddly, it caused a grin to slide on Taliesin's face as he chuckled. He jogged Thibaut's shoulders, trying to encourage him not to look so irritated, but it was clear that Odette's features and their astonishing match to her mother, was only making Thibaut more concerned. Odette could understand, things were hectic, so she stepped forward and wrapped her arms around Thibaut as he gripped her tightly and she sighed. "I'm going to miss you... of course I'll miss you all... but I'll be safe here unlike France."

"I understand, I wish it was not the case, besides, I don't want any of you dragged into a situation I'm fighting along with others. At least here, none of them can come looking for you, there are no real nobles to be threatening and... and I can trust our uncle will help you." Thibaut stated, releasing her as Taliesin beamed that he still had access to the English Veil and would do his best to keep gargoyles on hold just for Odette. The words made Thibaut sigh gently in relief but he could not help but bring his hands to stroke Odette's cheeks, his face mangling with the concern there as Odette just pouted at him and he let go. "Don't make that face... I'm giving you this chance... but when it is over I will be bringing you home."

"Will you? Well... I suppose as long as I don't make myself at home here..." Odette stated in the kind of sarcastic manner of their mother and Thibaut gave a grunt. He then hugged her again, allowing Taliesin to do the same as they then returned to their carriage, ignorant to the fact most people used cars now. Odette and Young Richard waved them off, watching and waiting until they were completely gone from view and the gargoyles were settled. When that was done, Odette looked up at Richard thoughtfully. "You made sure I'm sharing the dorm?"

"Of course... two bunks per room, no exceptions. You'll be staying with my wife's cousin Christine... she's already helped the gargoyles take things into your room and she'll help you out. Both of you are trained although she's more specialised in midwifery, you know she'll keep you safe." Richard stated firmly, smiling at Odette who gave him a more content smile in return before gently barging his shoulder with her own in thanks. He then stretched his hand out to the door and thankfully, Christine had just appeared at the door, a vibrant red head with shining emerald green eyes and a tall figure with broad shoulders that said she could take on anyone. She was quick to reach over and hug the short Odette, gripping her lovingly and then turning to her cousin.

"Room's all sorted… come on now, we'll get you settled in. But you'd better leave Richard, no men allowed in the building… off you pop, chop-chop…" Christine stated, her voice haughty and jovial as she batted Odette carefully into the building and swatted her hand towards Richard. He gave a soft snort before bobbing his head gently and then turned to leave for his car as Christine hurried in. She grasped Odette by the hand, her pale face lit up with a brilliant smile and an expression of sheer delight. "Let us look after you now sweetie, we're going to have a busy day tomorrow and we start early in the evening, the moment the sun drops."

"I'm ready for anything! I don't know the area but I know you'll teach me and I'm very excited…" Odette stated, only for Christine to give a chuckle and spin on her heel. She suddenly gripped Odette in a tight hug, rocking her gently and insisting she was a wonder, before she pulled her onwards. She was dragged into the room set out for her, her bags were on her bed but the room was large and she had a desk to herself, a set of drawers around it to use for clothes, a bed-side table and a large bookshelf ready to be used. "There's far more room here than I expected…"

"Only the best… you've got a long day ahead of you tomorrow so I suggest you go and have a good scrub, then join me to go down for dinner. We can then go and meet everyone else and you can learn the drills." Christine beamed, giving Odette a firm pat on the back before she stepped out of the room and pointed towards the shared showers that she could use. Christine then strolled out, leaving Odette to herself as she then settled down onto the bed given to her and then heaved a deep sigh of relief.

Odette had not expected her brother to agree with letting her go so quickly, especially when she'd been terrified that she'd need a proper argument. The resistance had been obvious in his golden eyes, but not in his words and clearly, he had been worrying about so much more than just her job. When the Purists had taken over the French Veil and Jacinthe's sister had married their leader's second there, it had meant that the situation between the Purists and the Vulturie were complicated. Thibaut though had opened up his islands for everyone and sneakily been rescuing who he could and now, now he'd had to send his little sister here because she would have been forced to obey Purists laws as a nurse on the mainland. Was that why he'd been less resistant? Odette was not sure but her head kept spinning as she gave a groan.

"Well, best get started, she said it would be busy." With that, Odette then began to unpack her bags and put her clothes away in the wardrobe. As she placed her long dresses and skirts, long-sleeved shirts and items that looked like they were suitable for twenty years ago if not the Victorian era, Odette grimaced slightly. Her colours were all grey, white, black or beige… she could not help but like simple colours and have a practical sense to everything she wore. She kept her long black hair up in a tight bun with a look that some might say was similar to that of a teacher's look, but as she undid her bun now and placed the hair pins in the little porcelain pot with images of sirens singing upon it, she caught herself in the mirror with her hair down and blinked.

Odette was not tall, not very curvy though she was not flat, in her neat white shirt and long grey skirt, she could not help but blush to see how much her tanned skin stood out against the colour, not to mention her silken black hair. Her hair was like her mother's, black for the most part but within the light of flame or sun, it would shimmer with brown, russet and even bronze streaks that made it unique and beautiful. She looked very much like a happier version of her mother and yet, she felt her face was not as noble and more… sweet. She felt like she had a childish look to herself and she heaved a sigh as she then gathered her gown and towel before stepping into the corridor.

She padded across to the bathroom, glad it was unoccupied and then stepping to one of the changing stalls, placing her items down and then undressing. She then strolled across to the shared tiled area and quickly turned on the first shower. The water was warm, pleasant and she was thankful as she hurried to wash before she then stepped back to her changing stall. She redressed but thought to leave her hair down as she gathered her items and then slowly marched back across to her room. She stepped in, closed the door and was about to put her items away when she spotted someone standing happily in the room and she gave a gasp.

"Why are you shocked, my dear? You knew Thibaut was not likely to just listen to what Ecclestone said and clearly he lied about a few things…" Taliesin was standing there with a pleasant expression upon his face, he had no issues with Odette at all, she kept to herself and that's what he liked. But he had to admit that right now, she shared a lot with her mother that rather unsettling him, but as she calmed he was quick to smile. "Don't worry Odette, I'll report back that everything is fine… Thibaut can be a little overprotective and to be fair, with the gargoyles around and… you being so sensible… I'm sure it will all be fine."

Odette suddenly dashed forward, wrapping her arms around him in a gentle hug that made him give a hiss of disgust. But then she snuggled into him and he could not help but cuddle her back with a grunt. She thanked him and he patted her shoulder before turning into a bat and then fluttering off, zipping past Caroline who quickly darted in to check on her. Odette insisted it was a family member double-checking and Caroline chuckled before beckoning her out as soon as she had dressed as fully as she wished. They strolled down the hall to the dining room where six other women were eagerly settling down to eat when they turned to view her.

"Oh.. you must be Mademoiselle Viper? Je ma pelle Duffy, quo ve? Oh… did I pronounce that wrong?" One of the women was a Turned Vampire who clearly had a sweet tooth, not only for the heavy amount of cake and biscuit she had on her plate, but her body was rotund and jolly looking. She had a wonderful smile and looked eager, but Odette was a little concerned as she'd been warned early on in life how vampires with a 'sweet-tooth' would mistakenly only drink the blood of humans who'd eaten high amounts of sugar or even suffered diabetes… it was an addiction but Turned vampires could thankfully eat the sweet food and could lose the weight easily by going on starvation for three weeks. "Do you speak English?"

"I do… my parents grew up in Romford. I grew up in France but its normal in the noble families to learn as many languages as possible… especially when your family's so large it gets everywhere." Odette beamed, trying to be a little jokey but not sure if she sounded like she was boasting. Instead it got a few claps of excitement from the girls as they hopped on their seats and begged to know what was happening 'across the pond'. Odette was not sure what to say, quickly turning to check with Caroline who gave a soft grunt.

"Now-now… Odette's just arrived and remember, the Purists in Europe are causing trouble there. We've all heard rumours that there might even be a dragon demon behind it, so we shouldn't badger Odette about something that might be uncomfortable." Caroline stated, beckoning Odette to settle herself down and enjoy some of the food on offer. Odette thanked her, suddenly aware how thick her French accent was and how strange it must be for them, especially when she was so used to her parents speaking both languages so easily, even switching between at times. But Caroline made sure she was sat down before she gave a clear cough. "We had an issue with the Purists too, thankfully the Covens on the island and the Sidhe courts joined together in parliament to insist that no such discriminatory measures should be passed. In fact, they were joined with by the Turned vampires and werewolves and the remaining vampire purebloods and practically kicked off the island!"

"Well, what did they expect? Their ideas and thoughts were no different to the kind of thing our grandparents suffered under with the Vilmore Clan. It was clear to see they were intending to put us back into serfdom! Besides, the Veil Agents are mainly based here these days and they weren't having it when it went against their protocols. How does the Veil Agency on the mainland deal with it?" One of the other women questioned, only to illicit a trill of laughter from Duffy as she waggled her hands about.

"No-no Tilly, they're the same all around!" Duffy snorted in amusement and then group giggled softly as Odette nodded her head in agreement. They settled down comfortably and were all starting to eat at last with just a few questions about Odette and what kind of men she liked, to which she only said she hadn't met one yet! It had caused a few giggles and insistence that she'd meet a few doctors and emergency workers that might turn her head. Then there were a few giggles that she'd be taken by Ecclestone to meet the high society to prevent that, which caused good deal of cackling even from Odette before the matron stepped in.

"Hello ladies... make sure to sleep well, there's thoughts of expecting another bombing tonight..." The matron, named Anita, was a very tired looking ghoul, she was showing how the extra life given to her kind was wearing out and finally she looked the senior being she was. Her hair was silver and falling out, though she kept it wrapped back as if she were to wear a wimple every day. Anita stepped over to Odette, her wrinkled and thin skin covered hands wrapped around Odette's smooth ones in thanks before bowing her head and then settled herself down with a groan. "You probably have not experienced it because you have been living on a small island, but Beyond the Veil, the English ground is being hit with nightly bombings by this Nazi regime on the continent. Though their war is not affecting the Veil any other way, the bombs seem to pass through the Veil and land upon our buildings…."

"I see… I have no idea what a bombing is…" Odette stated with a nervous expression upon her face that made the others grimace slightly. Though they were hopeful that Odette would not shirk at the sight of death or bodies, they were not sure how she might react to a bomb. How had any of them in the Veil really coped? For beings with intense hearing, beings that were usually immortal too… the chaos and agony caused by their bodies being ripped apart meant that the chances of reuniting their pieces quickly enough to survive was limited. The bombs killed everything close by!

"It's not something you can explain, if you've not experienced it before it will be a shock. Your ears might bleed too because it will be that loud, you will also feel like the world's falling on you with the heaviest clap of thunder and well…" Caroline tried to explain it, wishing she had a better idea. The thing was, how could you explain it unless you experienced it but terrifying? However, Duffy's face was bright as she waved her hand and Odette turned to her.

"You know when there's a storm and the dog whimpers and hides?" She stated thoughtfully and Odette nodded her head. Actually, her mind had launched right to little Vittorio and Valentino, how they reacted in a thunderstorm by hiding under the bed and whimpering for Theodosius to rescue them, followed by her brother's eye roll before he slid under the bed to snuggle with them. Odette considered how scared and upset they became and how everyone thought that was silly, but if a bomb made everyone feel just like that she could only imagine as Duffy beamed. "That makes more sense doesn't it?"

"Yes… that kind of oppressiveness… it will certainly be an experience and I am concerned about it. What are the procedures?" Odette questioned gently and she was surprised when they pulled up a leaflet written just to explain the situation. Odette held the notes gently and read it over carefully, grimacing slightly as she understood there were shelters, sirens and that one most go to them until the bombs stop or unless the wardens collect them to assist. Odette rubbed her chin, not quite sure she understood how that must work but then reading notes about hiding in closets, shelters built in back gardens and then that most of their work will be at the shelters made more sense.

"I wouldn't worry, we run the biggest underground bomb shelter where we have our surgeries that treat anyone whose injured or upset or sick during. Sometimes it's just treating shock and other times we can be in there for hours and you have insulin-dependent people as well as blood dependent to look after. We'll be going there tomorrow and you'll be having your first day getting used to the routine." Anita stated firmly as she settled herself down with a tea towel suddenly spread over her lap to help her keep clean as she started picking up the bread for toast. Odette smiled, glad to have a chance to show how useful she could be a well as glad that she had friends here already as they continued to talk onwards with smiles and happiness before the night just seemed to continue happily and even during the day, Odette slept comfortably.

The next day they gathered together with the clear goal to go out and experience the job first hand. They were all a little nervous as to how Odette would react, especially as there was always the possibility that she might overreact to the bombings. Odette was not sure what to expect from any of it, but she was ready to get along with whatever job was ahead of her as she joined them in the march in darkness down the hushed streets that were completely blackened to help prevent them being mistaken from above. The Veil's form distorted the view from above, it would not be clearly visible for someone flying above to see things like werewolves or giants bats, but the surface could not repel the machinery of human warfare… bombs dropped too close could still fall upon them. Odette understood this as they moved and she could feel the fear in the air and sense the magical protective spells that were attached to every house they passed by. But then they went down to the entrance to the underground train and Odette was surprised as soon as she stepped into the brilliant light of the well-lit tunnels.

"Black Candle Station is a hub for the London Veil Underground, most trains pass through here and it's become the marketplace during the day and night so that there's less chance of danger during either time. It will get a bit hectic around here so be careful, we always travel to and from this place together, no wandering off with others without letting me know where you are, especially when we're on duty like today. Our clinic is set up in one of the stations where the track ends and there's a carriage left on hand that has a transport point straight to the hospital if needed." Anita stated, leading them all around with a stern expression and a puffed-out chest as she seemed to barge her way through everyone that was shopping rather calmly. Odette nodded her head, but her eyes were bouncing back and forth at the different vendors with casual expressions as Caroline then cleared her throat.

"I'll take you here on our day off to look around or shop if you want to… best to follow Matron here…" Caroline grinned vividly as Odette then gave a sudden jolt of surprise, unaware that she'd been spacing out or not paying attention. She hurried to stand behind Anita so she could listen to her properly and know exactly what was happening ahead of them and around them. But Anita was ignorant to them as she came up to a very large and bulky figure that smelt strongly of werewolf and was wearing a helmet on his head and a badge over his arm that identified him as some kind of warden and Anita cleared her throat.

"This is Darren, he's the Air Raid Warden and the one you should go to if you ever get lost. He's also one of the local policemen so it's doubly important you know who he is and trust him. Darren, this is our newest member, Odette Viper… no doubt you can guess her heritage." Anita stated with a chuckle and Odette stared in surprise as Darren's face, despite being an elder man, was lit up into a happy smile as he grasped her hand, shook it firmly and then almost bowed to her as Anita swung her hand around to push the werewolf away and silence him. Her statement had already caused ears in the busy moving crowd to twitch and try to listen in, fascinated and Odette's eyes looked about in confusion before Anita gave a chuckle. "Your father became a bit of a legend around the Veil for keeping the vampire nobility here in check and improving the schools. He's practically a saint to the werewolves for what he's done for them. Darren's father trained over on the island as a child and moved over here, he was an engineer for the railroad."

"I see… I only ever tended to meet the werewolves working at the mansion, it was a long time ago since I went into the school and met people. But it's a pleasure to meet you and I will remember you." Odette stated gently and nodded her head as she then noticed the crowd moving off. She turned to look about again, mostly the room was just a huge, white-painted cave with lots of electric lights keeping it bright and colourful advertisements pasted onto the walls. There was a fruit market and a vegetable market present that was the most evident and a small little kiosk selling items that were on ration cards or restricted items that required cash as well as a ration card… things like certain meats and blood. But further down there were the busier stalls, newsagents, book stalls and second-hand items being traded or bought without the fear of ration cards. "It will be interesting to view this place in time and knowing a trustworthy fellow as yourself is on hand is reassuring."

"Uh… thank you very much, Lady Viper." Darren gulped anxiously, feeling his chest rise and his face blush, not expecting to be spoken of so kindly and he felt the desire to bow to her again. However, Anita cleared her throat and grasped hold of her arm and pulled her onwards to the little tiled archway where there were red crosses plastered about the place. Odette followed her into the room and then was smiling in relief to see the large open space that was incredibly secure and had all the services on hand to sterilise and heat equipment as well as store it. There were even beds brought in and there was an area to hold a soup kitchen too, something important if people were stuck here and Odette was eager to get to work, only to have herself pointed towards the wall near the bandages.

"Those bandages are to be washed and sterilised chop-chop… there's a fire spell around the water that will make it not only boil immediately but disinfect the items completely so it's just a case of dipping them in one by one with the tongs my girl." Anita stated, clapping her hands firmly to encourage her to start working and of course, Odette nodded her head and went over to the pile. Immediately the smells caught her by surprise… stenches of pus and rot that made the stomach coil but also the enticing scent of old blood that made her stomach relax. Her body was almost a little excited to be around blood, but Odette took in a deep breath, right down into her stomach soothing her thoughts and feelings as she pushed the concerns away and then got to work.

For the next hour she pulled up the strands, one-by-one, pinched between the tongs and down into the boiling water that was emitting a pleasant soapy smell. She held the item in for thirty seconds, pulled it up and it was gleaming white as if brand new. She took it out and lay it over an iron rack, letting it settle down and drip dry whilst the others were busy at work. The usual type of work that came in it seemed were a few mothers who hadn't been able to get to surgery hours or call a doctor out and thought it safer to come and present their children to the nurses. Mostly it was a few sore throats or infected cuts and the occasional terrifying splinter that had gone septic or into an unpleasant place! There were also a few tummy aches and even a few cases of chickenpox that meant the children were quickly bundled to a screened room and where they were sat was cleaned with spells brought by a male doctor, a warlock named Shacks… just to ensure it did not spread.

Odette was doing quite well and enjoying any kind of work offered to her as she finished the bandage pile and then was to use the same vat to clean the instruments. To be fair, Odette had been trained with an autoclave and was not sure what exactly she was to expect putting them in the same vat, but Doctor Shacks insisted with a jovial grin, that it was all certified by the Veil Medical Institute. Odette did the job and was just settling them down when there was a high-pitched wail that slapped into her ears painfully like someone thumping into the centre of her ear and suddenly she dropped onto her knees, covering her ears and giving a voiceless scream before Shacks suddenly threw a spell on her and the pain became dulled as the sound seemed bearable and she turned to them with a whimper.

"That's the air raid siren. We're likely to get inundated so we need everyone to be in tip-top shape, understand." Doctor Shacks bent down to her, grasping her shoulders calmly as she blushed heavily, looking at his charismatic smile as he pulled her up onto her feet. She thanked him, blushing still and then turning to apologise to everyone before they just laughed it off as the norm. She was grateful that they were so relaxed about it and not unkind to her, until they all heard a sound in the distance and then Shacks bundle Odette over to the others and up against the wall.

It was a sound to their keen ears like a screeching firework, only the sound was almost backwards, hinting that it was falling down before there was the strange thud and then the great vibration of the blast rattling in the air and on the ground. No matter how far away it was their keener hearing could hear the great thwump as the bomb blasted outwards before the sounds of crashing and smashing followed with belated screaming and then the sounds of more as they just remained frozen to the wall, listening as the tunnel outside was being flooded by people hurrying in as Caroline gave a growl.

"It's Boxcutter Street... ugh, most likely they got the Post Office... thankfully the second blast hit the duck pond, but the rest went outside the Veil. Gosh golly... the sirens were late on that lot!" Caroline scoffed and Shacks let go of Odette as he stepped back and looked towards Darren who was beckoning people in and then on along to the platforms unless sick or injured. From the sounds of it, Odette had learnt that tonight had been a surprise for the Veil, but she pondered how the humans beyond it must be coping.

Very quickly, there was the sound of people in pain and Darren was ushering in a few old people and nervous looking adults who were battered and bruised, maybe even concussed but thankfully not severely wounded. Caroline, Anita and the others all heaved sighs of relief to see that this was their first lot to deal with, insisting that the ambulance service would probably be better suited to work that street. Odette helped people come in and sat them down, offering tea to help soothe their shaking hands as she looked at the dirt, grime, and soot that covered them but the relief upon their faces as one of them dared to tell them what had happened.

"That blast took out the whole of the Post Office and half our house next door. Thank God that the postmaster on site was a warden and came out in time to start ushering us all out… when it hit we were thrown across the road but I don't think anyone was killed. That Strix quickly turned into his bird form and started gathering anyone he thought looked like they couldn't get to the street and on the way down here. It's bloody ridiculous… can't they keep their damn war to themselves?" One of the gentleman, an elder fellow with a curious scent about him like he was possibly part elf, shook his head and wagged his finger in disbelief to think that such a thing had happened to his house. Odette brought him over some tea before noticing his scuffed-up hands and then insisting she would disinfect and bind them for him. Immediately as he saw her, he seemed to swallow his tongue and blush as he then turned towards Shacks. "Hey Doc… surely this one's too much a lady to be left to tend to me? Surely she should be in one of them fancy hospitals…"

"That's funny Mister Henley, this is Lady Odette Viper, she's fully trained and wanted to help us out here… I dare say everyone in the English Veil has heard about the Viper Clan." Doctor Shacks chuckled in amusement but it only seemed to make the old man and his wife beside him blush more heavily as his wife insisted on thanking her greatly for the tea, asking if she should bow but Odette just laughed. She then released her French accent to enchant them all completely as she thanked them all for being so kind on her first day but that she was completely at their service. Odette was not sure how it went down with Anita, the older figure seemed almost irritated, but Caroline and the others were grinning as Shacks then snorted. "You'll only enjoy tonight Miss Viper… I guarantee you'll hate them all by the end of the week!"

"Shacks don't be rude!" Caroline barked at him, only for Anita to clear her throat so that Caroline addressed him under the correct title of doctor. He gave a cackle of delight and Odette shook her head gently, at least he was lively, but she was not sure his more cynical humour was to her liking. All the same, she continued to work and help people out and even had the honour of meeting Malcolm, the Strix Postmaster who insisted to her in private that his Parliament were allied to the Vipers and whatever had happened with Thibaut, was not of his concern. It had been a little worrying to hear at first, but she'd been grateful and insisting on helping him with his singed wings and his bumpy head soothe as she carried on happily.

The wardens came in to send everyone back home after four hours, the fire was put out and the bomb in the pond had been detonated and everyone was safe. They had beckoned everyone to go home and Odette was pleased to hear that the worst part was over and it had not been as harrowing an experience as she'd feared. She was utterly exhausted however and as the newbie, she was beckoned to clean the entire room up whilst the others finished off the tea, although Shacks insisted she had a brew with them as well. Odette was confused by the terminology at first, before understanding the nature of tea and then accepting... after she cleaned up. When they returned to the building she was quick to pass out after a wash, only to find she had to be awake at noon to clean the household and step into the next day.

The next night was rather more loud, they returned to the same place to find it was market day and the entire underground was crowded, busy, loud and there was always someone popping in to look at her or ask if they could try and sell her something. Thankfully, Odette was used to this kind of attitude in her childhood when walking around Paris and she knew who genuinely wanted to gain her attention and those who had much more obvious ulterior motives. Odette too could sense certain moods thanks to her mother's blood, she could tell when someone was selling honestly and who was trying to outdo someone else... intentions over money were clear to her and so she refused all things offered just for the sake of fairness.

Caroline and the others chuckled over it, insisting they wouldn't think a vampire of her stature to have such humility and yet Odette would just smile back and insist she was quite content with the basics. As she continued on with work it became one of those rare nights when there was no bombing and everyone that came in just came for a check-up. There seemed lots of childhood diseases running around because the kids were all pushed into the same areas to hide and chicken pox was something everyone in the Veil experienced... her poor father had caught it when the twins had as babies, though vampires got through it very quickly!

Odette enjoyed being welcomed and welcoming others, there was satisfaction in getting the work done and she was always eager to make as many smiles as she could replace frowns. The day was busy but she found herself often in the company of Shacks, who was very eager to chat with her about everything and learn about France. Odette was glad of his company, but she could sense from the others that they were jealous about the relationship and she was more than a little concerned over herself. In particular, she was very concerned that Caroline would be the most uncomfortable about it and yet she did not wish to bring the subject up in case it soured everything.

The first week carried on this way, but Odette steered away from Shacks as much as she could, focusing on her work and reading when she had a chance, which eased the tension around them all. She began to show a little more subservience to Caroline too, asking her more for help and asking the others to guide her around, making them feel more important to her and a little superior. She knew it was the best way to ensure that there was no ill feelings between any of them and thankfully things began to calm down and focus on work more and more.

It was a month into the experience that a major air raid occurred, this time there had been some kind of confusion of the Veil's defences, something many attributed to whatever chemicals were being given to the pilots that came over, but Black Candle was bombed badly! The group had been split up, Anita had grabbed Odette and in telling the others to continue work as usual, she'd pulled Odette up to help her guide the ambulance men... for right above the underground station, a bomb had taken out the nearby row of shops and tonnes of people had been in need of first aid and to be located against the sounds of screams.

Odette scrabbled around the ruins and rubble as she helped guide three men over to a patch that had finally started to smoulder. It was secure to step into and she guided the men around to her side, one of them coming to help clear rubble away from a shelter that was hidden beneath the smashed earth. Odette could hear the fearful family within, glad they were safe but likely battered about as she used her own vampire strength along with the three men to move the rubble away carefully enough they could get the roof of the shelter open and then pulled out four terrified beings from within. Odette carried one child, the ambulance carried the old granny on the stretcher and the third fellow guided out the two other adults from the room.

Once they were taken into the underground, she was out with the next group to check the other buildings. It was dark but that did not bother her, instead the scent of cooked flesh and blood made her teeth ache and her spine rattle with discomfort. The slightly chemical and metallic scents of the explosive devices and the wrecked housing were hard to sort through, but she worked hard and help identify the living and the dead with those that followed after her. Seeing pieces of a person that were charred or just seemingly alone somewhere they did not belong made her stomach knot and her mind spin. There was something so unnatural and hard to accept about this kind of damage that when she was finally beckoned back inside, Odette was not sure what to do.

She was given something to drink and then left to sit with the others she'd been working with for a while. Shacks stepped over to check on her, asking if she was alright, but pretty quickly the next group of ambulance relief came to replace those that were worn out and saddened. Amongst them was a Turned vampire, he hopped into the room bright and bold with his hair in curious curls and the kind of black that disappeared against the night sky, his eyes were a brown that turned a sort of honey golden when he looked towards the lights, his features were strong and powerful and his skin was dark and attractive. He stole the air for the moment as he stepped to Caroline who greeted him with ease and then stepped out with him and the next lot to go out hunting for trouble.

Shacks ignored him and so Odette guessed it was best to just assume this was the usual way of things, but she had sensed the slight discomfort some of the people in the building felt to see that Turned vampire. He'd not noticed, he'd been eager to work and get people out of danger, but it was something new for Odette to sense... colour usually meant nothing in the Veil... but somehow she could guess that this strange island might be a little different. All the same, Shacks patted her shoulder and pulled her over to where they were cleaning burns and bashed heads where debris had knocked people out. There was the general wail of upset people, terrified people and those still trying to regain their hearing, but Odette was quick to absorb herself into the work and forget what she had seen out there... the sight of a foot in sock and shoe just sitting precariously on a piece of rubble hauntingly as if someone had or was standing there.

Eventually the swell died down and the sudden relaxation of the warning sirens urged the uninjured out to witness the devastation. Those to lose something remained in the shelter until friends or neighbours more fortunate invited them in. Now that the scariest part was over, the hardest part of the clean-up was due and yet there were still many people to bandage and move into the hospital if they looked to have taken a turn. It was as the mood calmed and Odette was busy back to sterilising that she suddenly felt the presence of the Turned vampire beside her, a soft expression on his face and his voice lit with a Caribbean accent that made her skin tingle in excitement as he spoke.

"So… what do the French mademoiselles do for a good time? If you were human I'd suggest a little corner in town where we can eat some of the chocolate I've kept from my rations and just enjoy the evening… but as you're of my own persuasion… perhaps you'd care to join me at one of the local 'drinking establishments'?" The gentleman, Mister Pierson, was suddenly at Odette's side, looking handsome and charming as he had when aiding in rescuing people and Odette turned to him with a soft snort of amusement. She shook her head at him, they were both on duty until the end of the night helping people out, but she had the feeling that he was asking for that time and not right here and now. It confused Odette just a little, back home she was the one that hid in the library and never had the men looking at her, all of them locked on happy Selene or elegant but snappy Elaine. She was not sure what to say on the matter and thankfully Pierson pondered if it was a communication error and he gave a soft chuckle as he stretched his hand out to her. "I'm Sharp Pierson, I'm Turned yes so I guess I'm completely out of your league… but offering a bit of friendly socialisation seemed appropriate. It's Viper isn't it? Odette Viper? I uh… I saw you signing up in the council offices when you first arrived and… well, I apologise but I think you're incredibly beautiful and just now, I could see you had a very warm heart for those in need."

"You speak your mind far too quickly Mister Pierson, it's very sweet of you to say these things and I apologise, but I am under a strict watch whilst I am here. My Uncle would not appreciate me being anywhere out of sight of his gargoyles when I am on or off duty." Odette began, trying to focus on washing the equipment that had been used as Sharp continued to hover beside her. She felt very nervous; he was clearly a very attractive man and many of the other women were watching them both with a jealous expression that Odette could even feel floating in the air… though not as strong as the earlier jealousy over Shacks. She was not a girl to go out on the town, not a girl to go and run off with some stranger… she was sensible and everything seemed to warn that this Turned Vampire would not be a sensible choice. Perhaps it was her arrogant snobbery coming through, but when he made a point he would ask permission if he knew whom to ask, Odette gave a sudden snort. "Please Monsieur, there are a dozen other girls more beautiful that are worthy of your time and can spare you the time. If it is position or wealth you seek, then you must look elsewhere, my brother inherited everything and my financing comes from him and my uncle's kindness. My own dowry is worthless as I am the eighth of nine children. I am not worth your time."

"I did not say anything about your family position or indeed wealth, Miss Viper. I merely requested time to get to know you and then perhaps attempt to court you. What you are worth to the rest of the world means nothing to me… I'm not looking for fame, glory, or honour, merely a companion. If I fail to impress you when I try to get to know you, I will not continue to pursue you… I'm not seeking what you think I may seek… though I have the distinct feeling that I'll find it in you regardless." Sharp spoke sweetly, candidly and Odette found herself staring at him anxiously for a little while as she waited for the items to sterilise in the metal bowls. She was unsure suddenly about her opinions of him, unsure if it really was a warning to stay away from him or if she had just been warning herself out of the duty she still felt she owed her family. Her mind trailed back to the stories of her parents' courtship and how it had been the honesty that had really spoken to Adelia above all things and Odette gave a sigh, just what could she do?

"Are you being honest? I do value honesty above all things and… and if you mean what you say then I might consider passing you that information." Odette felt a blush forming on her face, she felt suddenly as if she were the only person in the room apart from Sharp, her general safety in being the hidden form in the corner completely lost and her body suddenly feeling vulnerable. She was trembling slightly and yet this man was just staring at her with such an affectionate eye, such a gentle eye as if he wanted nothing more than to just take her hand and share the heat of such an embrace with her on this cold night. It made her feel so awkwardly feminine, so embarrassed to even find herself so overcome by this strange figure with such warm honey-coloured eyes and such a comforting smile. When he nodded his head and brought his hand to his heart, Odette was still trapped, the only person in his view even when she could hear and sense the others moving around her.

"Honest to God; my words probably were a little too poetic – straightforwardly, I'm intrigued by you Miss Viper and I want to know about you so that I can decide whether the sensation I feel in the pit of my stomach and the bottom of my heart have any merit to them." Sharp stated with a soft smile as he looked to her and Odette almost felt as if he were holding her hand to kiss it already like a gentleman courting her in her parents' time might have. She was quick to pull her hands towards work as the world returned to normal, trying to overcome the excitement and anxiety building about within her. But the moment she removed the sterilised equipment, he stepped as close to her as he dared and whispered very softly to her. "I'm afraid you see that I might have fallen in love with you at first sight, hence my desire to find out."

"I see… that is indeed something one should not make a mistake with… but I must have time to consider and to discuss with my guardian… I'm not someone who can act in such haste." Odette stated, it was the best she could manage to not only stall for time but to give him some kind of answer that was not a no. For some reason she did not want to turn him down, she did not want him to run away from her because she was cold or fickle… yet something told her that would not be the case at all. But her words caused a sudden brighter almost childish wonder to appear on Sharp's face and he looked as if he might snatch her hand and shake it furiously as he gave a sudden bleat and then found himself getting called over by his companions.

"Thank you – you will not regret the chance, I swear!" Odette watched him leave with a firm blush upon her face and a shake of her head. How had she just managed to find someone like that in her first month in this strange country?

That weekend she received a 'summons' from Uncle Taliesin to come to the household of Young Richard and meet with him. Caroline had decided to deal with the transport by seeking out Doctor Shacks and requesting use of his motorcar. It was his evening off, but sadly not Caroline's and she was rather uncomfortable with Odette and the doctor travelling together, but Anita had no qualms and they were all more rather eager to gossip about the "exotic" gentleman to have approached her. That term made Odette's hide ripple in distaste; she'd heard the term used for Turned vampires before but on this occasion it was most definitely because he was Black.

The confusion caused by their casual racism and strange attitude towards the idea of them going out rather startled Odette. It bit into her too because this was the same country wherein her human grandfather had married a Filipino woman and that meant her mother was half Asian and Sharp had told her he was technically half too, but graciously had taken all of the best looks from both.

She'd not understood why he'd thought that need to tell her about it, but now she wondered just how many questioned his heritage and she wondered about her own too. Would she encounter a sudden level of avoidance and ignorance if they learnt her blood was not fully... blue?

"I saw you and Sharp talking, he doesn't normally bother talking with anyone there much because they're all so rude to him. I was happy you spoke with him, but I get the feeling you're not used to the colour disparity of the country yet..." Shacks stated calmly and Odette looked up to him in surprise as he drove calmly out of Black Candle and on towards the great parks and houses opened for public viewing to make money but still very much vampire territory. Odette gave a sigh and insisted she'd never remembered such attitudes back home but Shacks gave a shrug. "Here is the country all those Purists could preach and find eager ears to agree but not to follow. In the Veil or Beyond it, there is a great level of hatred here for everyone that is not a white male and it's always going to be that way because everyone in that group holds power and view this strange kind of pride in being a unique island without vampire authority and not really even listening to the Veil Agents, if you understand that."

"That is truly horrible... is it a choice to be so ignorant?" Odette scoffed and Shacks nodded his head but mused that more people willing to accept and ignore the scalding looks of others and live the way they should, would be much better. It was curious but it reassured Odette that Shacks at least was not thinking the same way as others were. It concerned Odette all the same though that there was such an attitude around the whole thing and yet... Sharp was intriguing and made her feel oddly... tingly. Whenever she thought of him saying her name or saying French words, it made her blush heavily and Shacks chuckled as he noticed.

"I've not known Sharp to come up to anyone before and ask them, normally the girls do the asking with him and he always loses interest when they start mentioning their 'differences'... he was Turned Beyond the Veil, rescuing a woman bleeding to death when she changed him. He kept working hard, got blood in little bits, but then he was caught eating a patient when it got too bad... his Godmother rescued him, then she brought him to us. Vampires of all sorts are supposed to hold value and rank, but she dumped him here, sends him money but never brought him into society." Shacks stated gently as they pulled up to the big mansion and Odette looked to him in surprise. He guessed she hadn't expected it, that a vampire godparent would ignore their godchild. He could see she only knew of that role as being as important and special, as sacred a duty as it was possible to be! It saddened her as Shacks gave a soft snort. "To them, he's as common as muck and worse for showing a heritage the non-vampire still treat separately here. Will you be kind to him, knowing that the world you grew up in is not his world?"

"The world I grew up in… by rights… I would not have grown up in had my father not worked to get recognition. He was quite prepared after he and my mother escaped to just do whatever jobs they could to survive, even going to use his law studies to help him work as a clerk or postman. My mother was willing to teach… my father's earliest days were spent sleeping on a bed with his own mother in squalid slums whilst she worked hard to just feed him, hated because she was not married and had him. I was very lucky because of my uncle and my parents' determination…" Odette stated firmly, making sure that Shacks was aware that she did not see herself as elite or stuck up as perhaps they might assume her to be. In fact, upon coming here Odette had found herself considering that the work she did and the places she was seeing getting burnt and blasted… may well have been the places she might have grown up and they might have been her family members being pulled out of blasted shelters. "I'm aware of my luck, but I'm also aware that people make do and that is a wholly different experience from what I have known. But I will learn."

"You also aren't the same level of ignorance as others, then again even the Ecclestone family here try… I guess it counts for something." Shacks sighed as he pulled up and hit the handbrake. He then insisted he'd sit back and wait for her as she thanked him then stepped across the crunching stones under twilight to the door. When she reached it, she pressed the bell and stepped back, waiting as the door opened and Young Richard greeted her. He then beckoned her in and up the stairs once he took her coat, informing her that Taliesin awaited up top. Calmly, she stepped to the hall and the house seemed to gurn and contort, twisting as a door was brought to her feet and opened. She stepped through to see her uncle on a sofa, enjoying some brandy and pushing a tray of chocolate towards her.

Odette bobbed her head and sat on the ottoman beside the sofa like an obedient child before swiftly snatching an orange cream from the offered assortment. It got a chuckle from Taliesin as he slouched back and asked how she was. Odette told him of her experiences and he listened obediently himself, hissing in interest at the revelation that bombs worked on their kindred. Odette tried not to focus on that as she explained the racism she saw but this did not seem to move her uncle, until she mentioned Sharp's name.

"Dear me, that poor boy... good to hear he's making use of himself though, some godchildren go crazy and try any way to kill themselves when abandoned. You could not imagine how lonely that existence is without others of your kind, especially when rejected for something as foolish and vapid a reason as race. At the end of it, we're all just flesh..." Taliesin groaned, it wasn't quite what Odette had hoped to hear, but she was grateful he was a little nuance. Then Odette asked what he knew and Taliesin gave a luxurious sip of the brandy, face grim as he shrugged firmly. "He was turned by one of my well... I suppose it's best to call a spade a spade... one of my favoured whores. I guess what I pay she splits with him... she's from a broken house taken down by the Veil Agents for... what was the word, soliciting with intention to steal organs. Used to be the worst little bitch in the kennel, yapping away and throwing her weight around to keep attention. I started pitying her fall and revelling in the depravity she'll commit for simple things..."

He'd stepped into his own fantasies again, it quite sickened Odette to hear but she knew since his expulsion, his life was all about revenge. Helping and watching Theo's children kept him sane, for the most part, but now Odette understood why Sharp had been so abandoned. In their society though, the action was akin to leaving a baby on a doorstep! As Taliesin drank more then sat up in his purple dressing gown with what were essentially pyjamas of black satin beneath, Odette realised she was not in London at all but one of the rooms of that old theatre on that wretched smog-bathed island.

"Uncle... are you using fairy dust to speak to me? Has it truly become that unsafe to travel now?" Odette's mind now considered the situation at home again and whom she'd left behind. Her uncle just nodded but stretched his long fingers down to grace her head with a soft pat as he took a dark chocolate from the little tray.

"No one can cross the channel at all, the French elite are on house arrest as with the Czech, Belgium and I think well, only the eastern and the Italian families are fighting... and the Swiss. Home is the only place able to move and connect people but the Crimson Veil of that Russian Dragon has started trying to absorb Ukrainian territory... if they go we could all go. But there's resistance coming, Richard, your brother and I have been arming others and we hope to remove the Purists in one great cleansing wave." Taliesin beamed, but Odette was still uncomfortable with the talk until she then thought of what she needed to ask.

"Back to more hopeful news, and... I wish to socialise with Sharp Pierson on the hope to date and perhaps marry him. Will you give me your approval?" Odette bobbed her head, trying to be dutiful but Taliesin's response was sharp and amusing perhaps....

"My dear, you are such a sensible and capable girl that no such permission is needed from me." He almost seemed disinterested, but Odette smiled and knew it was better this way until he gave her a sideways glance and a deliciously wicked grin. "But of course, should Thibaut ask I'll take the blame for letting you free...enjoy yourself."

Sharp was rather surprised when he received a letter stating that his application to court Miss Viper had been looked over and approved by her guardian... T V... which he assumed must be one of the Viper Clan but certainly not the Count. He'd not expected Odette to have actually meant it about seeing her guardian, but he was very pleased to produce the letter the next air raid that brought them together. On that night they were able to arrange a date to a 'posh place' for dinner, something Odette had yet to try here and should be an easy get to know you session.

When the date arrived, Caroline had berated Odette over the simple grey-beige skirt and jacket combo when she needed a skirt that looked fun or at least had some colour to it. Odette found herself accosted by the rest of the women into wearing a bright buttercup yellow dress that felt more suitable for a parish picnic than indoors. What's more they insisted upon doing her hair into rolls of varying types, trying to pick which was best and leaving it at 'victory rolls' that made her hair seem folded into itself without an edge and rather thick. It made her neat jawline more pronounced and her handsome neckline evident... to which she insisted upon wearing a lace choker so that none in her family would worry.

Odette was embarrassed when she looked at herself in the mirror, until Duffy had pulled out a creamy satin ribbon, gently bowed it around her neck instead of the choker and suddenly she looked more... flowery. There were a few teasing words from other girls in the dorm that worked different shifts and felt she should have a photograph taken to send home, but Odette's face went rosy as she'd insisted that her brother might flip his lid! Still, she was ready and they were all excited to see what would happen when she met with Sharp, but only Anita was permitted to escort her that far.

"It's a simple restaurant, a little fancy but nothing like you'd be used to. There's often a bit of dancing there and I should warn you that it would not be appropriate for you to dance on your first outing with him. But should anything happen, the building has an underground passage that goes into a troll's den that's working as an emergency air raid… the trolls work the underground stations around that region of Black Candle." Anita was looking like a governess, proud and stern as they walked out together, glad the night air was warm and pleasant as they strolled up the road, Odette glad to be wearing durable shoes and not something painful as they walked a good fifteen minutes before taking a sharp turn to the left and into a bustlingly bright and active high street. "This is Calder Road… this entire High Street was built for the vampire nobility to enjoy about thirty years ago and now its frequented by more than just vampires. You'll be safe here… no one would upset you."

"Thank you madam… I appreciate your concern and your assistance thus far…" Odette stated, not too sure she was quite comfortable with the way Anita was speaking to her, but what could she say when she lacked authority or knowledge here? However, the sudden whistle of greeting and the wave of a hand drew their attention to where the brilliantly decorated streetlamps were illuminating the gentleman in a neat jacket, waistcoat, white shirt and freshly pressed trousers. He was waving a neat black hat towards her, a small collection of beautiful chrysanthemum flowers stuffed under his arm as he beckoned her over. Odette had to smile sweetly, as she lifted her hand very delicately to let him know she spotted him as Anita grunted that the white shade of the flowers was bad luck, but Odette raised a hand to correct her. "Actually, the chrysanthemum has many meanings depending on the country, it can even be given to ward off evil spirits and bad luck…"

"More likely he had no clear idea what he was going to get and bought the flowers to take his fancy. I will leave you though, ensure he escorts you back to the building, does not leave you alone and that he will not come into the building with you but wait at the step until you've locked the door behind you. Understand?" Anita stated, scowling towards Sharp as he approached and Odette nodded her head gently, but her eyes were drawn to him and she found herself feeling an odd fluttering within her stomach. As Anita left she found herself oddly alone in the universe, the world around fading away in place of the handsome vampire approaching her with flowers extended and that handsome smile upon his face as Odette beamed and opened her arms out. She received the flowers and brought them to her chest, stroking the yellow and red ones gently, smelling them softly and then smiling up at him sweetly as Sharp grinned.

"I noticed Anita giving you a talking to, don't worry Pidgeon, I'll make sure no one causes you trouble and we obey the rules. To be fair, the letter I received was enough to slap me in the face… I didn't really think you could really be… well…" Sharp stated, not wanting to say he hadn't thought she was a noble, but rather that she was just too nice and sweet to talk to. He was startled because she was being so amiable and she was here, with him… he was really shocked but so happy about it too. But he was quick to notice the look of confusion upon her face and he guessed what it was from. "Pidgeon… Pidge… it's a way to refer to you, a pet name."

"A pigeon?" She questioned, but he grinned, making a point to add a d before the g, that it was a nickname, a name too… talking about how Margaret had the nickname of Peggy and yet Odette found herself unable to respond. She was not sure she could quite comprehend his meaning, but when he gave a chuckle and then took her hand gently in his, those beautiful eyes glittered under the lamplight and made her stomach flutter with butterflies. He asked her simply if such a thing would offend her but Odette found the blush returning to her face as she felt the gentle warmth of his hand and her body was tingling gently. "No… I don't think it's a bad nickname… better than calling me a little cabbage perhaps."

"Ah… is that what they say in France? Heh… I suppose we've all got some odd little pet names haven't we… but I'm glad you don't hate it, Pidgeon." Sharp stated with a pleasant expression upon his face as he brought his hand up to his mouth and planted a gentle kiss to make her chuckle. He then looped her arm out and she wrapped herself within it, smiling happily as he led her down the road together towards a very fancy looking restaurant in the middle of the path. The hint of blood or at least fresh meat tickled her nose from the warmth of the building and she could feel her body getting excited, but Sharp was more surprised when the gargoyles that covered the doorway of the seemingly Gothic structure, dropped their heads down to look at them. "Friends of yours?"

"Oh… non… but they all talk together and share information… have a nice night gentlemen." Odette called up to the creatures that looked akin to griffon only with the muzzles of some wretched hound, something not uncommon for gargoyles. The pair stepped into the foyer where the red carpet was shining ahead of them and the maître de was standing by his little podium with the collection of reservations, tutting and grinning to prove he was a vampire too. Odette looked to Sharp with a curious gaze, the servers and the chefs in this building were all vampires… pedigree not Turned and she wondered if that would make him uncomfortable, but Sharp pulled up to the podium, informed them of the reservation and a waiter was summoned.

The waiter was a bit slow, his hand shaking a little and showing age… proof he was a vampire undergoing starvation in order to end their life and Odette greeted him with a bob of her head. His voice was a little croaky and his skin was starting to show the speckles and liver spots of age as he beckoned them to follow with a slightly hunched back and Sharp could not help but feel uncertain. He could feel eyes looking at them, with a harshness as if neither of them were welcome coupled with the fact there were no vampires of a darker hue only made him feel more uncomfortable. But he'd chosen this placed against the smaller café across the road that Anita had no doubt assumed he'd have chosen, because Odette deserved something interesting and then they received a surprise.

"Ah… Lady Odette Viper… I was unaware you were in London, how are you and how is my aunt Jacinthe? I haven't heard from them since the ghastly business of the Purists started." Odette's heart heaved a sigh of relief and Sharp felt the same kind as they came face to face with Gilen Vulturie, one of the sons of Jacinthe's many older brothers but a baby about the same time Odette herself had been one. He'd been a friend to Beauregard when he'd finally entered academy and some had often remarked that he'd been a potential waste for being another late bloomer, but he'd married well… the daughter of Hungarian Count Agyar no doubt… a beauty few could compare to. No one spoke badly of Gilen anymore and with his beautiful wife with her hair the colour of caramel drawn into more extravagant rolls than her own, Odette was pleased that they had stood up to greet her and the room had gone quiet.

"I hear she is doing well, as is my young nephew although he is as temperamental as his father. I came to devote my nursing skills to this country as the situation back home meant that any noble women stepping outside the household unescorted was a potential criminal. Its ghastly…" Odette stated, she did not actually know if that last fact was true but there had been concerns when Selene had gone out on her own in Paris and been aggressively questioned as to her purpose in town. Thibaut had offered to send Selene with Odette then but Selene had put her foot down on being bullied by anyone and actually been working on doing something more useful. Still, Sharp was looking relieved as Gilen turned to him with a smile.

"Ah… you're the first man I've ever seen Odette choose to stand beside… you're either incredibly lucky or you have an exceptional charm, sir." Gilen chuckled, stretching out his gloved hands to hold onto Sharp's and give him a good shake of approval. The words seemed to startle him, he'd always assumed that many men would have courted Odette before, but he just thanked Gilen as his wife stood up to hug Odette. She then slipped her a letter, Gilen did not seem to notice, and then the pair were slowly escorted up the stairs to a table that was practically hidden in curtains and more like a booth at the opera.

"I think they got a shock down there when they realised who you were. To be greeted by a French noble too... he's your brother's nephew then? Yikes large old families are complicated!" Sharp chuckled as Odette delicately sat in the chair he steered out before pushing back in. He took his place opposite her with a broad smile upon his face before giving a deep sigh and then settling to order with her. As they watched the old figure make the slow march to the stairs, Sharp recalled spotting something and tapped his nose gently. "What's that all about?"

"Oh it's nothing... just a love letter to my brother Beauregard... the lady killer. He actually had his first experience with her beastly and very overweight mother when she was desperate to get his attention. He's never once even looked the daughter's way and he enjoys having that hold over women... it's heinous." Odette stated firmly as she lay a napkin gently over her lap as Sharp gave a knowing smile.

"Your brother may have tastes you can't always understand and it's the same with some ladies too. Her mother probably felt inferior to her own daughter and that might have pulled him in. Maybe your brother has a desire to rescue people too... just more selfishly." Sharp chuckled gently and Odette found herself unable to respond to that thought. She'd always just assumed her brother was only interested in sex and left it at that. She couldn't quite care if he was helping people, she did not understand his desires, but maybe Sharp had hit on something and she was not sure about her judgement anymore.

After a good twenty minutes, their starters arrived along with a second waiter who brought with him an expensive bottle of blood wine from Italy that was impossible to get anywhere. They had not ordered it, but it was offered with compliments to the lady and Sharp almost rolled off his chair in laughter. The second waiter had looked abashed but poured their drinks, set the bottle in the ice bucket and then insisted he would help deliver their meal. The pair then enjoyed their tiny starters, musing that this was probably the norm before rationing anyway with such a place, before settling to their main course that arrived rather fast.

"So what do you think of England then? Got a good impression and thinking of heading home when it's all said and done?" Sharp questioned gently as he cut into his steak, enjoying the scent of the meat as each stab seemed to open a pocket of aroma. Having been unable to get beef in so long, his mouth would not stop watering, his fangs were probing out and yet he was more focused on Odette's delicate manners as she sliced with ease and lifted only the smallest portions on her fork as if it were too much for her wrists.

"I haven't quite decided yet, this place is busy and loud and the scent in the air more choking, but then some days in Paris, all you can smell are the sewers! I'm weighing my options up, pondering carefully and letting it have its chance to ensnare me." Odette stated with a sweet chuckle that made her eyes light up as Sharp gave a grin. By luck that night there were no air raids or chaos to throw them from their meal and their conversation. They were relaxed as they spoke to one another about everything the other should know about themselves and their families. Sharp was impressed by her hobby of knitting and she was impressed at his own pleasure in reading about dogs... something he'd not had the chance to own but enjoyed, though he did not tell her what breed as if it might be embarrassing.

When they walked back to the dorms he rang the bell then stood at the bottom of the steps. Anita had been waiting about like an impatient spider, stomping her foot to the ground and opened the door fast. There was hardly a moment to say goodbye before Odette was yanked inside. They all questioned her about the date but she said nothing in return, only that she met a friend whilst out as well. Once left to settle in her room, Odette found herself feeling giddy and excited about when she would next see him and what they might talk about next. She enjoyed his company and knowing they could talk about anything was reassuring... yes, she liked him.

Within a week they had met in the shelters again and arranged a visit to the cinema to watch a film that seemed to be the latest thing. It was one talking about events beyond the Veil and when they watched it, they found it hard to believe such chaos was happening. Still it had been a good subject to discuss and sharing a box of sweets together had been exciting when fingers had touched aiming for the same colour. Touching Sharp was so easy and so comforting, there was that air of confidence but calm about him that said he could never take offense to anything and that sort of happiness was addictive. The warmth of his skin was as addictive and after a third date to a library for a discussion on books both had read and enjoyed, they'd held hands as they'd walked together and Odette had not wanted to let go.

They'd then spent the next month on as many dates as both could manage within their schedule, which was not often easy as their shift rotas altered regularly. They instead made sure to send letters regularly and as time went by these became rather obvious love letters. Odette could hardly believe how extraordinarily easy it was to start stating she missed someone, or their smile or hoped they thought of her. She found herself regularly swooning at the thought of being held gently in his arms, nothing obscene but just being held. It was embarrassing, but the other girls could see it for what it was and warned that she was falling in love.

Whether it would work out, they seemed to hold mixed opinions but Odette felt it would go as far as they were willing to take it.

One night, the pair had gathered up a picnic in the fading summer heat and marched to the park on the hill that overlooked the main part of the city. Usually there would be fireworks at this time of year to enjoy, but the risk of bombing had meant such things were too sensitive for people to really enjoy. The raids over the week had been harsh and brutal with more corpses being recovered than living beings. The mood had been unsettled throughout Black Candle and so Sharp had felt this was the best time to step away from the city. Lounging alongside one another on a blanket, they'd found themselves lost staring into each other's eyes for a good while before they realised that the food might get cold.

It was only rations but it was amusing all the same, they were eager to eat a little bit and they chatted a little about other things before they then found themselves sighing and staring at each other again. Sharp then surprised her, passing her a gift that was a tiny box but she was smiling all the same in excitement to be given it. She sat up with a pleasant smile, taking the object and then asking if she could open it before he nodded his head. Odette was embarrassed, she knew she owed him a gift and she made that point though he beckoned for her to open the box already. She grinned and then did so, giving a sudden gasp as she pulled it out.

"It's so beautiful…" Odette gasped, pulling out a small scarf of thin fabric, not silk but trying to look similar to it and a brilliant bright yellow. She blushed over the thought of having such a kind gift but also thinking of the yellow she wore before. He was grinning at her in amusement, beckoning to wrap it about her neck and Odette blushed even more in embarrassment before nodding her head anxiously. He grinned and gently wrapped it about her neck, knowing that touching her neck would be extremely flirtatious and right now, he would be careful not to in case she thought it was too much as Odette blushed and then held his hand lovingly. "Thank you so much…"

"You're welcome… Pidgeon." Sharp grinned in amusement, taking her hand and squeezing it lovingly before they leant forward. Their foreheads pressed together, it was the closest to a kiss and their eyes fluttered as they looked at one another lovingly. Their hands felt so warm and lovely together, they were content as they continued to eat but also they just seemed to enjoy the company in the beautiful cool air and the gorgeous darkness as they felt their bodies tingling with a growing desire for more.

The siren sounded as they were just finishing up and with a snort Sharp stood up and pulled her to her feet. It had been a nice night-time picnic in the Veil, Sharp had saved his rations to make them a pie and well, this English food was an experience. But as they packed up the nearest bunker was in the cycle archway boarder of the Veil and a harrowing place if the planes were going to drop bombs.

"Ah… shelter for two alone it seems… you alright Pidgeon?" Sharp questioned as he pulled the door open to the little seated room within the concrete structure that looked almost like it was an underground station platform with some beds and seats and a few supplies. The pair stepped inside and when Odette settled down on one of the beds with the food and a sigh, Sharp gently closed the door behind them and padded to her side. There was always the chance that they might be joined by others, but no matter what was to happen up above or in here, for now they would show abhorrence to despair and just continue their picnic. With a chuckle Odette lay it all out with a soft chuckle to be called 'Pidgeon' again, it seemed almost a vulgar term but for the one calling her such. She stretched her hand out to hold Sharp's and he smiled lovingly towards her. "Hmm... I'd love to say this sandwich meat was something substantial... or identifiable... but it's surprisingly good at repressing the desire to eat."

"Don't be so silly, we can't help the rationing, all the predators get the same amount of meat squashed into tins no matter what's in it and a pint of blood for the vampires a week. I thought I'd bring mine for us both to share, my blood isn't completely vampire so like you I can save it a little more for a nice occasion like this." Odette chuckled, her sweet French accent teasing his ears as Sharp chuckled in response and then gripped her hand lovingly, staring at her with soft eyes as she found herself blushing gently. It had taken a few weeks to get used to holding hands, Odette was exceptionally old fashioned in the romantic fashion, but she was glad that Sharp was willing to be slow with her, but he found no reason to want to be fast... every moment with Odette was just wonderful. As their hands caressed gently, they felt their bodies quivering and they wanted to come closer, they wanted to get very close in fact, but it scared them too. Just as he shuffled an inch on the bunk, there was a sudden rumble not far away as some houses were struck and they sat bolt upright.

"It's alright Odette... it's not hit the Veil and though I don't like the thought of the people beyond just dying... the rules are we aren't to interfere. Relax, we'll be fine here and everyone will be safe too." Sharp stated gently, stretching his hand out to hers again but this time lifting it to sit upon her shoulder. She jumped slightly, the thought of the ordinary humans suffering and not being allowed to help them and thereby take sides... it made Odette burn with fury. She did not think that aiding the wounded was anything but an act of charity, but Veil law was strict on the matter. Odette grasped his hand gently in thanks, turning to look at him lovingly for a moment as he rubbed her shoulder softly with a gentle flutter of her lashes as he sighed. "Let's just enjoy this moment Pidge, I don't often get you all to myself in a neat little bunker... I might want to do terrible things to you..."

"What? Like finish my crosswords before I've even started it again? You know... a woman could murder a man for such interference..." Odette teased playfully, then to her surprise his hand shot out to grab hers. He brought it to his face and then without a second thought, he kissed it and she blushed bright red. He gave a soft snort of amusement, she certainly had the cutest little blush and then, rather suddenly he straightened himself up and Odette began to quiver. As he stepped around behind her, placing his hand upon her shoulder, she could feel a sudden shortness of breath overcoming her body and she was scared that she was about to faint upon him as he bent his head to hers. His nose gently brushed hers and she gave a sudden snatch for air before he bent further and then whispered softly over her lips.

"If it means I get to see you clench your little fists, puff your cheeks and pout like some adorable little morsel... I might just do it, Pidgeon." He sighed lovingly, his lips inches from hers as his eyes fluttered softly. Odette was not sure if she was going to vomit from stress or faint, it all felt like too much and then his lips brushed gently to hers. She clapped them back in a soft little kiss and Sharp pulled back a little, leaning his head to hers as she looked at him as if she'd been slapped, too dumbstruck to really know what to do. He'd then pouted to press his lips to hers again and though she didn't move, he kissed the edge of them and an electric tingle shot down her body. It was followed by a violent shuddering of her body as she opened her mouth with a soft sound of confused pleasure that made Sharp's eyes flash. "Dear God... that was one exciting noise..."

"HELLO!" There was a sudden yanking of the door into the room and Sharp and Odette were suddenly sitting up straight as if nothing had happened, though their faces were red. The local air raid warden, a gargoyle friend of theirs called Thompson, came strolling in with his funny tin-plate hat. He was looking content to shuffle in and when he noticed the picnic basket, he plunked himself down beside them, grinning and insisting that he was famished. They couldn't deny him the food, but they were stuck frozen for a while, suddenly realising that air raid shelters were perhaps not the safest place to kiss....

But their skin was tingling and there was no doubt in either of their minds that this moment had sealed their fate. Sharp could feel it, he would never want anyone else but Odette in his life from this point on and Odette was quite sure she'd felt that moment of clarity over her own heart too!

"My name is Sharp Pierson, I am here to see one of the guests... a T.V." Sharp felt a little awkward as he stood in the Superior Hotel in the heart of the richest part of the London Veil. This area was near the old academy where he'd learnt that Odette's father had gone for university studies that he'd never fully completed and where a lot of exciting moments in their family history had happened. It seemed fitting to come to the hotel that was built opposite it, dressed out with the same kind of semi-ancient architecture to make it seem just like some sophisticated and imperial kind of place with columns out the front. He had realised the receptionist and bellboy had been looking at him with faces that insisted he was not welcome and yet when he mentioned the initials the receptionist actually seemed to take pity on him.

He was passed the room number and given instructions on how to reach it and Sharp gave an anxious gulp as he turned around onto the red carpet and then slowly began to make his way up the path towards the elevator where the door was about to close. He was able to get in there just before, glad that it was empty and that it was going up to the right floor, though his skin was prickling in anxiety as he felt as though something was staring down at him within the elevator door. Sharp gulped anxiously, not sure what to do or how to react upon meeting the brother that he would have to impress. What could he do if he made the wrong sort of impression out of anxiety?

The door pinged and the elevator jolted slightly before the door opened and a startled woman stepped aside to let Sharp out. He thanked her for the patience and then slowly walked out down to the suite at the end of this floor. He passed several rooms that had an ominous feel to them and occasionally he'd spot a human stepping to a door with a plaster on their neck… shivered and tried to ignore it. It was supposed to be something the Nobles did, paid for the pleasure of taking blood from someone's neck and enjoying that primitive sensation of the predator, but it was something frowned upon by the Turned and it made Sharp very uncomfortable as he reached the black door at the end with the white numbers carved onto it.

A sensation of dread seemed to stuff Sharp's feet into the floor, he did not want to raise his hand and knock on the door and yet he knew there was no choice. He pulled his arm up, feeling a terrible weight making his knees buckle and his arm want to lower itself, it felt like he was stuck in treacle and he could barely pull in enough air to breathe as he brought his knuckle to the door. The moment he had let his knuckle just push against the door, it seemed to open with a hideous creak and yet with it, the cloud of oppression disappeared. Sharp took in a deep and uncomfortable gulp of breath as he watched the door open and inside was a dark room lit only by a lone candelabra upon a black covered table, illuminating the neat black moccasins of the figure with thin legs in a neat pair of black trousers and wearing sock garters Sharp was sure. But within the darkness, golden eyes shined out against him and Sharp gave a gulp.

"Good evening sir, my name is Sharp Pierson… I have an appointment with you." Sharp stated, able to keep his composure and step into the door. He bent his back slightly in a bow before pulling the door shut behind him and stepping forward. Within a flash, something moved near the seated figure and the candles were out, the room drenched in darkness. For a moment Sharp held his eyes tightly shut before he slowly opened them out and let the abilities of the vampire take hold of him, the black of the room fading to shades of grey before colour was recognised thanks to the light of those golden eyes. Then, Sharp's breath caught in his throat to see neat slick-backed black hair, a red tie against a white shirt with no jacket and a glass of wine hanging between the long, lean fingers of the pallid being who looked weak and yet somewhat feminine as he grinned up at the figure. "You're… you're Taliesin Vilmore…"

"Sharp… aren't you? Get it? Not clever I know but I thought to break the tension with a little… tease." Taliesin beamed, his face brought into a viciously toothy smile that showed off how nasty and blade-like all of his teeth appeared. It was an odd quality not seen in other vampires and fed into some of the rumours that Taliesin had actually transformed to the next predator up the food chain, something forbidden to speak or think of and Sharp was trembling. He had been warned by the woman to have made him a vampire that Taliesin was the worst of the worst for every possible reason and yet, to disrespect him when he could make or break a being's entire existence, was not a good idea. "So… do you know why I might be here? You know why you're here I hope?"

"I'm here because I came to request the hand of Odette Viper from her guardian. The initials were T.V. on the letter, I foolishly assumed Thibaut or perhaps even her brother Theodosius… but now I see they stand for yourself… sir. I'm not exactly sure how it works but, if you are Odette's guardian, then the rumours of a distant relation to the Viper Clan is true." Sharp was not sure what the exact situation was between the two families, but he'd gained a little more understanding of the situation… enough to know he was being tested. Indeed, he was being tested to see just how much he was interested in Odette and how easily he scared. He had not doubted any less and now he had heard Taliesin speak and ask him a question, Sharp was less scared of this being then he would be of Thibaut. "Whether you have the permission to speak on behalf of her family or not means nothing in the end, if Odette will say yes to me, I will marry her… I'm just trying to be courteous."

"Ooooh… that's almost an exciting prospect when Odette is so… proper." Taliesin beamed, hissing out the sound of pleasure as if he'd just tasted the bravado in the air. He then brought his drink to his mouth, taking a laborious sip with a slow flutter of his long lashes and a soft sigh as if bored. Sharp was then pointed to a nearby chair and carefully, Sharp sat himself down and looked towards the older and noble vampire with a little respect, but aware he might have to fight.

"I think she'd accept it, but I know if it were to upset her family, she would never be truly happy and feel as if she had wronged them. As you said, Odette is proper but she and I are in love. There is no one else I would care to spend my life with, no matter how long or short, then Odette." Sharp stated, watching the way the golden eyes were looking him up and down like it was taking in potential food. Sharp also had to note that there was a slightly sensual manner to the way Taliesin then seemed to lounge in his chair, stretching his legs apart and making a soft moaning sound of seeming pleasure and Sharp felt a cold sweat form around his shoulders.

"What a curiously polite and rather cute thought too… yes, Odette would feel that sort of concern and yet, she is independent and very much like her mother. Adelia and I do not always get along but… I swore to Theo, her father, that I would always take care of his children in any way I could. Ecclestone and Shacks have both checked you out and informed me that you are a good sort, and your godmother is one of my toys so I know she chose you for a very noble reason… or you wouldn't be turned…" Taliesin sighed gently and Sharp was curious, he wondered if he'd be able to ask Odette about her thoughts on this fellow and whether she even liked him, but he had a feeling that Taliesin's affection was honest. He noticed the way a saddened edge fell into the golden eyes before he then gave a heavy sigh of frustration. "I will approve you… but I'm just the first step… are you free in a week and wiling to be thrown off a cliff if you fail the final test?"

"I get the feeling you're still trying to push me away, but I am willing to go to Hell and back for Odette… being with her… I feel like I finally have a reason for being in this world… a reason that is my own and not just because of a career." Sharp stated, a smile forming on his face to think about it and it made Taliesin give a rather bemused chuckle before he then heaved a sigh and slapped his face in dismay.

"You're a fool…. Thibaut's not the sort to let ANYONE take one of his sisters… but he'll make the last decision. Though, if he does say no… get Ecclestone to tell me and I'll pay for your wedding here and your permanent care… Thibaut can stick it up his nose." Taliesin stated, grinning in amusement and cackling in delight as he looked towards the young man as Sharp stood up and then stretched his hand forward to Taliesin in thanks. It was more than a surprise for him to be offered such thanks, no one tended to thank him that was not blood and he had to cackle as he shook hands with Sharp and then sighed. "Your godmother chose well, I'll make sure she and you are certainly kept comfortable…"

"Thank you… but for Odette and myself, we will look after ourselves… we do not need others." Sharp stated gently, making Taliesin cackle even more as Sharp then bowed his head and stepped to the door. Taliesin was grinning, he knew very well that if Sharp intended not to keep Odette comfortable, he might find himself on the wrong side of Thibaut. But he had to chuckle as he watched the young man leave and then turned towards the blackness of the room that Sharp had not noticed and to his amusement, a golden eye and a silver eye opened, hinting that there had been someone else observing them all as Taliesin then giggled in amusement.

"What do you think then? She's your darling little sister… your rock, I dare say… well Beau? What do you think of him?" Taliesin beamed in delight, looking over to his youngest nephew whose eyes were hypnotising and terrifying all at once. It amused Taliesin when the eyes slowly closed and the handsome young man gave a soft sound of fascination before then giving a soft sigh of thought. Taliesin was surprised however that he had said nothing yet and he gave a clear cough. "Come on now… I must hear your opinion!"

"It's clear he loves her… who the hell would come here expecting to see Thibaut if they really weren't sure of themselves? Plus… he's got a face that said he would love Odette more than anyone else." Beauregard stated with a soft chuckle of utter amusement as he stood himself up in the shadow and stepped to his uncle's side, making Taliesin's lashes flutter at the handsome young man before Beau ruffled the black hair and made his uncle give a swear of fury for it. "I do believe they'll be a great pair and I'll tell Thibaut my thoughts…"

Within a week, Thibaut had managed to arrange a way to visit, arriving at a nice little house in Black Candle that he requested his sister to attend as well as to bring her 'Sharp fellow'. It was quite a surprise to them to be lured to an area that was quite out of the way of the areas getting hit by bombs and was affluent but not too troubling. In fact, the area was comfortable, the place doctors and lawyers could afford to live in but was not something an ordinary person could walk in rather calmly. Here, Sharp and Odette arrived together and to their surprise, were met outside the household by Mhulder, who curled his lip at the sight of Sharp immediately. Even Odette jolted in surprise to see him, as she had never much appreciated him in the household or the information he always seemed to know and yet he bowed towards Odette with a chuckle.

"You're looking beautiful Lady Odette… your brother awaits you inside, just you… Mister Pierson should wait out here with me." Mhulder stated, standing calmly in his little suit and grinning happily towards the pair of them. Sharp looked to Odette cautiously, she was glaring towards the being and she stretched her hand back to grasp Sharp's, holding him tightly as she glared towards the figure with a sneer as he smiled at her thoughtfully. "I won't hurt him… or Beauregard will cut my tail…"

"Cut your tail? Then you will be safe Sharp… just don't talk to him." Odette stated firmly, turning about to give Sharp a kiss to the cheek before stepping to the staircase. She climbed up the staircase carefully, to the door, taking the latch and then feeling it unlock, turning to check that Sharp was still fine about being left before she pulled the door open. She stepped inside carefully, not sure what to expect before closing the door behind her and then looking at a staircase. To the side of the staircase was another room, the living room and she stepped inside to see an empty room leading around to a small kitchen, a chimneyed fireplace between and standing beside it, her brother. "Oh Tibbs, I've missed you!"

"My dearest little Wallflower, how good it is to see you after what feels like an age… yet in such time you've found yourself a man that even Beauregard has warned me is far better for you than I might assume. Not to mention, Taliesin said he'd pay for your wedding and what not whether I approved or not." Thibaut chuckled in amusement, sighing happily as he opened up his arms and Odette hurried to lounge in his arms. They cuddled each other gently, his arms holding about her rather more tightly than she would have expected as he sighed heavily and she had the feeling that he'd already come to agree with the others. With a soft sigh, he released her, kissed her forehead and then held her hands gently together. "Dearest Odette… mother has informed me straight up that you are a sensible woman and would choose a sensible man and so I have to admit I have given up on judging who you choose or what you wished to do in your life… so, beckon him in."

"Thank you." Odette chuckled sweetly and then pushed forward, kissing her brother's cheek in thanks before stepping back to the door and then opening it. Mhulder and Sharp had been remaining with their eyes locked together and glaring at each other, trying to battle one another with stares if they could and then she whistled out to him. Odette smiled towards Sharp as he hurried over but Mhulder gave a grunt of frustration, turning his head aside as Sharp hurried up to Odette's side. She grasped him by the hand and pulled him into the household where he met Thibaut for the first time and seemed to almost faint, but for Odette giving a squeak. "Don't faint darling!"

"Ah… sorry Pidgeon, but I was not expecting to see your brother in the face and his… well… I've seen pictures of the old Vilmore bloodline within the museum and… it's like seeing pictures of them, now I see the rumours of the Viper link to them. It's a bit of a shock." Sharp stated, not sure what to say on the matter save just speaking his mind and looking at the sudden way those golden eyes narrowed and seemed to burn before Odette gave a soft chuckle. She then kissed Sharp's cheek, making him jolt in surprise before Thibaut gave a soft chuckle of acceptance and then looked at the building for a moment.

"Its two rooms above and a nice bathroom… I thought this little house would be the best wedding gift, as I hear someone does not wish me to lend my purse to keep you both happy. Would this be acceptable for you to furnish as you will and of course, deal with your own bills?" Thibaut questioned softly, a smile upon his face that made Odette sigh and Sharp give a soft cackle. So it was that Odette and Sharp were permitted not only to become engaged, but when the war in the human world was over and the Purists dealt with in 1945, the pair were married in Paris as was expected, but using a portal, Uncle Taliesin took them back to their new home that had now been filled with the furniture from Sharp's flat and of their own choice… the pair happy to start their life as a married couple.

The clock struck four am and the pair lifted their heads to look at the cuckooing features of the Alpine clock before Odette blushed heavily for how awful an ornament it was, but Vittorio had chosen it for his aunt's wedding gift. Now they were back in their own little house in Black Candle and the chaos of the war was over as well as the joy of their wedding at the estate on the island, Odette heaved a sigh. This was her first time going to bed as a married woman, to go up and lay in a bed with her husband and feel the embrace they had been building up to for years. But as Sharp gave a yawn and stopped trying to read up on the latest changes for those within the field of emergency care, Odette continued to knit and trembled slightly for what she knew was to be expected as Sharp then stretched up and rubbed at his back with a grunt.

"Right… bedtime I think, Pidgeon… or did you want to have a bath, there's enough hot water and I'll put the kettle on now… take a bottle to the bed to warm it up for us." Sharp grunted, stepping over to the collection of hot water bottles that Uncle Taliesin had gifted, along with money and more appropriate things, insisting that English weather was terrible and beds hard to keep warm. He took it out to the kitchen, flicked on the kettle and then gently Sharp began to undress down to his vest and underwear, yanking off his socks and then stuffing them into the basket to be washed in the day. Odette remained sitting there on the chair, trembling as she lowered her needles and looked towards herself with a gormless expression of seeming dread. Sharp stepped to her side, kissing her ear to make her jump before he knelt down beside her. "We can wait till we have a honeymoon you know, we don't have to deal with the 'expectations' straightaway."

"I want to do things properly, Sharp… that does mean that my wedding night has a firm meaning and I have a responsibility but… it's awkward. I think I'm the only one in my household aside from Thibaut who actually was a virgin upon marriage. I suppose Beauregard isn't married so doesn't count, Theodora's too young to be included and Theodosius doesn't really count because he can't get married… and I suppose Selene was technically married in a way and Elaine was not really…" Odette began, breaking everything down in her mind and then realising her argument seemed pointless and more that she was jealous of the others. But Sharp kissed the edge of her lip to quiet her, before he held onto her hand and smirked up at her. He knew she was nervous and that was fine, there was nothing to be scared about with it and well, he knew what to do. But as he whispered so, Odette's eyes suddenly widened and a scowl came upon her face. "What do you mean by that? Sharp… you haven't… have you?"

"Uh… what? I told you before I've had girlfriends in the past, I thought you'd understand that meant… oh no Odette don't look like that." Sharp was panicked, Odette was getting anxious as she looked at him with wide eyes and all her eyes could tell him was terror. She was petrified that her lack of understanding on the actual initiation of the process, or indeed what to do throughout was empty. She was sitting there trembling as she closed her eyes and whispered faintly that she was worried she wouldn't be any good. In truth, she understood the woman's role was basically to sit back with her legs open and Sharp paused as he chuckled then kissed her cheek. "Don't worry darling… it's like riding a bicycle."

"If I'm supposed to rotate my legs with you stuck in the middle… I don't see how that's supposed to be pleasurable." Odette grunted softly and then suddenly, Sharp dropped right down onto the floor in laughter and Odette's face soured. She didn't think it was funny, she genuinely was not sure what she had to do in this whole scenario, and then Sharp gave a chuckle as he straightened up and pulled her up and then led her up the stairs towards their bedroom. She followed with a heavy blush, wishing she hadn't said something so stupid and as she went into the door of the room, his arms looped around her waist, he picked her up and then swung her around to make her giggle. He pulled her into his arms and then lay her onto the bed, making her snigger at how much of a monster he was as he kissed at her neck and made her chuckle. Then his hands were gliding gently over her body, making her sigh lovingly as their lips came together in gentle kisses before his hands slid to the bottom of her nightdress and hitched it up. He felt her trembling beneath him and tenderly he kissed her lips as she blushed. "You will… you will be very gentle, yes?"

"Of course Pidgeon, I wouldn't hurt you and that's why we're going to start with something else… it should make sure the whole thing doesn't hurt… but you've got to trust me." Sharp grinned softly in amusement, kissing her lovingly once more before he was suddenly slipping his hand up under her nightdress again. She trembled but she still kissed and nuzzled at him, her arms gripping about him tightly and snuggling slightly against him as she felt his hand sit on her more private place. Then he lounged back, pulling her with him and then his fingers began to slide up and down and tease at her. She quaked and jolted beneath him, making strange strained and startled sounds of concern as he rubbed at her tenderly. He kissed her, nuzzled her ear and whispered softly that it was going to get wet and that was a good thing, though she blushed heavily as they kissed again. His hand continued to stroke, tease and make her body tremble for the strange pings of pleasure that were shooting into her body. The strange warmth and the curiously pleasant sensation caused when she quivered and knew that sound her body was making, was only a good thing. "Don't be embarrassed darling…"

"Easy for you to say, you don't feel like you're going to wet yourself!" Odette blushed heavily as she felt his hand gently luring out the strange feelings of pleasure, the wet sounds in the air and then she was aware of the way he was looking at her suddenly. It was strange, as his hand stroked her most protected place, his eyelids lowered and his face seemed determined, stern, but beautiful with a glitter to his eyes and something just so handsomely intense that made her heart hammer away in utter fury. She could hardly believe that he could look so gorgeous and passionate just for touching her and his lips then came to hers. Automatically she locked lips, her eyes steeling shut as she moaned and sighed at the sensation burning into her body and urging her hips to quiver. As he kissed her, she felt drunk with his other arm wrapped about her and Odette gave a low moan of utter joy. "I think… I think I can take it now…"

"Alright…" His voice was hoarse, his breath heavy as it fell upon her skin and Odette blushed brighter to think that he was so very eager for this experience, that he was ready. She was not sure if her body was ready for it, but her skin was on fire and the noise was hard to accept, neither was the way her hips jiggled the more he brushed the sensitive bead below. Gently, Sharp leant her back into the bed, shifting his hand to his pants to ease the buttons apart to let his swollen and hard form out into the air. Odette stretched her hand out to the lamp to flick it off, too embarrassed to see that intense face anymore, but Sharp kissed her neck gently and then he opened his mouth, hissing and Odette froze in anticipation as she felt something burning hot and strangely exciting stroking against her body below. But then she was utterly frozen as she felt the fangs probing out, the Turned being's sharp little needles almost vibrating around her jugular and Odette knew what was to come.

As his fangs slid into her throat, she gave a sharp gasp and then her body flushed with a wave of ecstasy that was followed by the penetration below, pressure coming into her form, stretching her but the pain unable to be read against the fangs in her neck. She moaned lovingly, her hands wrapped around Sharp's body, feeling him rock his body back and forth as his tongue grew barbs and lashed against her skin like sandpaper. Each touch only increased the drowning pleasure that made her eyes shut and fill with water, her whole-body prickling and tingling with that strange height of sensation that could only be called pleasurable. She knew her mate was marking her, not only was he claiming her first experience as was right for a husband, but he was claiming her his mate forever, giving her the mark of her master that only a rival male would detect and meant she could never hide her marriage.

The rocking into her body seemed to stir up more fire in her stomach, making her body pinch around him, tingling and pinging as if she were laying her hand upon something that was vibrating so fast it made her lips buzz. She could not explain the sensation that was overwhelming her, but some pressure was forming in her spine, feeling like a bubble that needed to be pinched open and the more it grew the more it made her pant. There was an increase in speed in Sharp's motion and her ears became aware that he was only breathing out in slow snorts… she had to keep breathing in air, he was taking the oxygen from her blood to fuel him as he marked her and loved her and her heart hammered even more.

Some greater euphoria, brought by the thought that she was breathing for them both, he was living because of her… they were so connected and that he could only exist because of her flooded her mind! It made an ear-splitting moan of utter joy erupt from her throat as the bubble was punctured, the dam it had formed burst from let a wave of damp delicious joy drown her as Sharp removed his fangs to hiss out into a scream of ownership, blood on his lips but the job done.

They were truly mated, truly paired… truly married.

Time went by, nearly five years after the world had stopped fighting, the world was healing itself, busying itself and thankfully many exciting things were happening for the Viper Clan to focus on. Though no luck had come from Gaston and Lynette's pairing, the pair were happy and though Lynette was now an old woman, there was only joy to be had between them both. Thibaut and Jacinthe had two children, two great surprises and news from across the pond informed them all that Elaine had produced her fourth child and though there were rumblings in Mexico due to Selene's eldest son, there was only hope there for the future. Vittorio's son was a shock to everyone, the seeming Vampire King of legend but adorable, running around the household and Odette it seemed was due to give birth soon too.

Adelia was thinking it over carefully one night near the light of dawn when she was disturbed from her sleep by a curious thought. She'd found herself having a curious dream, a dream where dearest Theo had come to her and told her how proud of their family he was. It made her wake up with a start, looking for him for that brief moment he'd seemed so clear and vivid in front of her before she'd then pulled back and found herself sighing heavily. With a soft groan she'd settled back and then found it impossible to sleep for that moment, needing to ground herself and so she'd stepped out of the bedroom and walked out to the hallway, stepping to the picture of her mate and sighing gently before then the thought of everything that was happening now came to her at last.

Was it so unusual to feel tired for once? Adelia could not quite comprehend the last time she'd ever felt exhausted enough that sleep sounded like a good prospect. Perhaps it was because now, things seemed to have been settled and her family was secure. She was not sure though as she strolled around the hallway of the third floor, stepping patiently over to her room before pausing. She heard the sound from below of her two remaining single children scuttling in from a night out of doing something… Beauregard and Theodora. She found herself rather amused to think that the two babies of the household were the only ones left. Adelia watched them sneak into the library, hoping to use the stairs there to get into the back rooms and avoid waking her up… they were past curfew after-all.

Somehow, they were not adults coming into the household but children, little Theodora being chased by her elder brother as she screamed and hollered out about how many ponies she had or was promised. Beauregard had been so eager to protect his sisters that for a moment it was not even Theodora running ahead, but Odette insisting she'd identify the bird species first. Adelia sighed heavily, she'd never have thought her shy and hidden away daughter would ever have left the island, or even France to be a nurse in England… let alone to have met such a boisterous man as Sharp. It actually made her want to laugh and she just hoped that the same kind of luck in surprisingly well-matched partners would come to the other two.

With another sigh she turned her head to the library, expecting to see Selene step out with young Tlaloc beside her carrying a mountain of books only for young Malvolio to appear from nowhere to jump on him and demand to help whilst little Acelin had skipped behind for some attention. It was so hard to comprehend that Selene had not only paired with such a hulk as Xiuhcoatl, but somehow they'd produced two beautiful sons together, though she was saddened that one was no longer with them here in France. It was amusing to think that the girl that had never stopped smiling was not going to appear out of nowhere to suddenly wrap herself around her squealing uncle as Taliesin begged her to leave him alone! It made Adelia laugh even more to think of how much Theo would have been shocked to meet his great-grandson Malvolio and learn that he was not only the Vampire King but an absolute nightmare! But certainly, if Theo had been around then Acelin might have gotten a bit more affection from someone who could be a father figure as Thibaut did ignore him.

That, though, only made Adelia straighten up with a heavy sigh as she looked towards the door below her towards Thibaut's room. Gaston was no doubt within talking to his brother about business and Noel would likely be doing the same. The three elder brothers had seemed to fix the system all upon their own to work for every area they were involved, though it was hard to believe that Noel was winning with five children of his own now when he'd been the one that had clambered on the rooftops and swung through trees intent on being a primate as a child. Elaine had four children and rivalled him, but the idea of her even falling for someone enough to marry him made Adelia shake her head that her eldest daughter would have made her father faint with that choice!

Then there was Theodosius, Adelia was quite sure that even Theo would not have been able to predict that his sacrifice for their son and Valentino had resulted in them not only raising a son together but that they were in fact the grandfathers of the first Vampire King in centuries! That made her wonder too, once she had heard Taliesin and Theo talking together about why their father had gone on a strange obsession to have hybrid children... why Theo himself had been born a Dhampir and there had been the mention of the Vampire King. Adelia was not sure if, on reflection, that Count Vilmore would have tried to kill Theo if he'd known the future....

...or maybe that was why he'd tried all along.

The End

Look Out for Volume Six: *"The Crooked Serpent"*

Having weathered through having a son, Theodosius Viper and Valentino Pipistrello have been enjoying life with Vittorio growing up faster than they can guess. But something is wrong in the world Beyond the Veil and within it too there are growing concerns. A group of unhappy beings calling themselves the 'Purists' have set up a political movement that's gaining rise with the strength of the dragon in the Russian Veil. The Purists want many things but they do not want certain groups of beings within their Veil... these include the Wastes, half-breeds, Cursed werewolves and a curious group of vampiric beings referred to as the 'Sparklers'.

In the scenic Italian Alpine Veil, Vittorio is happy enough with life preparing for his vampire abilities to come through and enter academy but enjoying his friendship with Bruno, Ruprecht and Emmeline... the latter two being Sparklers. Though he fights constantly to ensure no one treats them with disrespect, the word around him is becoming more and more hostile and then, Ruprecht and his family disappear on a trip to Austria. The Purists are gaining power and when one amongst them shows themselves up to be out to remove the Viper in the Alps, Vittorio will step up and do anything to save his friends....

...most importantly to save Emmeline, whom he loves more and more every day as her family move in with his and he may have to make great changes to be with her.

But the Purists aren't just affecting Vittorio, they're affecting the entire world and the danger that the Tatzelwurm Sturm proves that this is a problem for the WHOLE Veil.

Book Six of the Viper Clan "The Crooked Serpent", look out for it in December 2022 or check out my Patreon for uploads – patreon.com/ClareSMKeating or look for echosdusk on YouTube!

Thank you so much for reading!